Praise for
The Unspoken Name

'A fun, fresh new take on the traditional fantasy quest and an adventure I couldn't put down!' **S. A. Chakraborty**

'Crisp, witty and entertaining' **Genevieve Cogman**

'From its flawless first page to its bittersweet last, *The Unspoken Name* is unlike anything I've read before' **Nicholas Eames**

'Takes all the tropes of fantasy – orcs and epic quests, dead gods and undead souls, daring rescues and last-second escapes – and spins them into something wild and new' **Alix E. Harrow**

'What a glorious book! Richly detailed, enthralling and extra-ordinary, with brilliant nods to such luminaries as Ursula K. Le Guin and Diana Wynne Jones' **Jenn Lyons**

'The action is fast-paced and emotionally compelling; the magic is dangerous, beautiful and utterly compromising. I love this book so much' **Arkady Martine**

'Stylish, classy and timeless . . . I cannot recommend it enough' **Tamsyn Muir**

'A wonderful, rich fantasy with fantastic queer characters I fell in love with' **Django Wexler**

The
Unspoken
Name

A. K. Larkwood studied English at St John's College,
Cambridge. Since then, she has worked in higher
education and media relations, and is now studying law.
She lives in Oxford with her wife and a cat.

By A. K. Larkwood

The Serpent Gates
The Unspoken Name
The Thousand Eyes

The
Unspoken
Name

A. K. Larkwood

TOR

First published 2020 by Tom Doherty Associates, LLC

First published in the UK 2020 by Tor

This paperback edition first published 2021 by Tor
an imprint of Pan Macmillan
The Smithson, 6 Briset Street, London EC1M 5NR
Associated companies throughout the world
www.panmacmillan.com

ISBN 978-1-5290-3276-5

1 3 5 7 9 8 6 4 2

A CIP catalogue record for this book is available from the British Library.

Map artwork © Tim Paul 2019

Printed and bound by CPI Group (UK) Ltd, Croydon, CR0 4YY

To Maz

O, what is longer than the way?

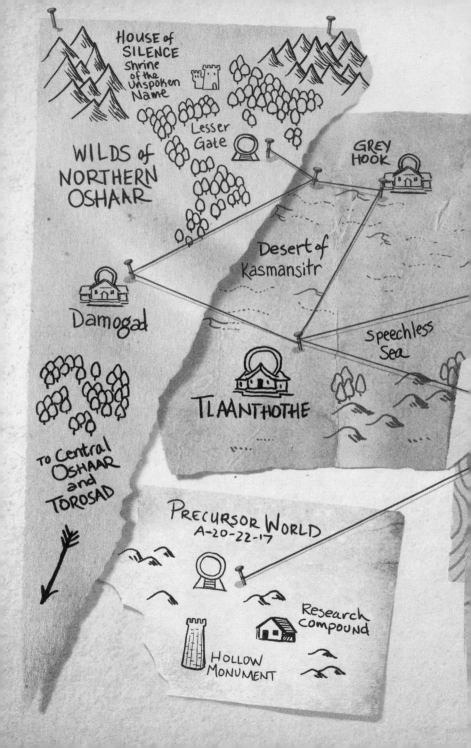

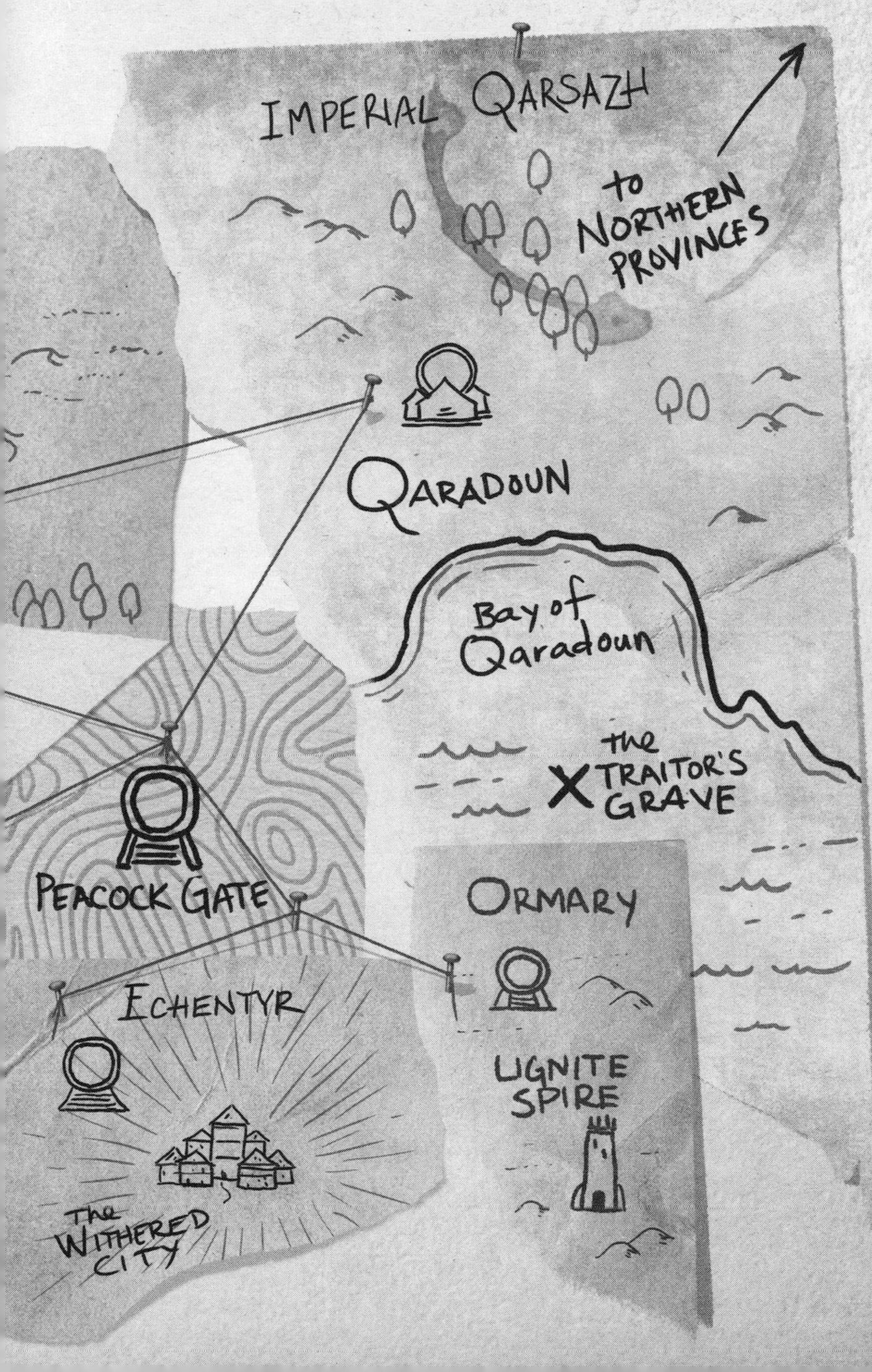
IMPERIAL QARSAZH
to NORTHERN PROVINCES
QARADOUN
Bay of Qaradoun
the TRAITOR'S GRAVE
PEACOCK GATE
ORMARY
ECHENTYR
LIGNITE SPIRE
The WITHERED CITY

Those Persons Involved

At the House of Silence

CSORWE, Chosen Bride of the Unspoken
SANGRAI, the Prioress
ORANNA, a librarian
ANGWENNAD, a lay-sister
CWEREN, Sangrai's successor
USHMAI, an acolyte
TSURAI, a novice

In Grey Hook and Tlaanthothe

BELTHANDROS SETHENNAI, a wizard
PARZA, a tutor in languages
TAYMIRI, a kitchen maid
TALASSERES CHAROSSA, an unhappy young man
GENERAL PSAMAG, a mercenary
BIG MORGA, Psamag's second-in-command
TENOCWE, an officer in Psamag's company
SHADRAN, another officer
ATHARAISSE, a serpent
OLTHAAROS, an old enemy of Belthandros
NIRANTHE, Olthaaros' sister
AKARO, one of Olthaaros' agents

Citizens of Imperial Qarsazh

DARYOU MALKHAYA, a Warden
DR. LAGRI ARITSA, a priest and scholar
QANWA SHUTHMILI, an Adept
QANWA ZHIYOURI, a High Inquisitor
TSALDU GRICHALYA, aide to High Inquisitor Qanwa

Imperial Quincuriate

VIGIL, a Quincury seconded to the Inquisitorate
SPINEL, a higher research Quincury
SABRE, a middle-ranked military Quincury

Divinities

THE UNSPOKEN ONE, of Oshaar
IRISKAVAAL THE THOUSAND-EYED, of Ormary and Echentyr
ZINANDOUR, the Dragon of Qarsazh
THE SIREN of the Speechless Sea

Pronunciation Guide

th is always soft as in "thin."
ai rhymes with "cry."
ay rhymes with "hay."

Oshaarun

OSHAAR: *oh-**shar**.*

OSHAARU: *oh-**shah**-rue.*

OSHAARUN: *oh-**shah**-rune.*

CSORWE: ***ksor**-way;* rhymes with "doorway"; *ks* as in "books."

SANGRAI: ***sang**-grai.*

ORANNA: *o-**ran**-uh.*

ANGWENNAD: ***ang**-gwen-ad.*

CWEREN: ***kweh**-ren.*

USHMAI: ***ush**-mai; ush* rhymes with "push."

TSURAI: ***tsu**-rai; ts* as in "cats."

PSAMAG: *psuh-**mag**; ps* as in "lapse."

MORGA: ***mor**-guh.*

TENOCWE: *ten-**ock**-way.*

SHADRAN: ***shad**-ran.*

Tlaanthothei

TLAANTHOTHE: ***tlaan**-thoth-eh; tlaan* rhymes with "khan"; *thoth* rhymes with "broth"; *tl* as in "atlas."

TLAANTHOTHEI: *tlaan-thoth-**ay***.

SETHENNAI: *seth-**en**-ai*.

BELTHANDROS: *bel-**than**-dross*.

CHAROSSA: *chuh-**ross**-uh*.

TALASSERES: *tal-uh-**seh**-rez;* *tal* rhymes with "pal."

OLTHAAROS: *ol-**thah**-ross*.

NIRANTHE: *near-**an**-thee*.

AKARO: *ack-**ar**-oh*.

Qarsazhi

Qarsazhi has some interesting consonants:

dh is like the first sound in "them."

kh is like the final sound in "loch."

ts is as in "cats."

zh is like the middle sound in "vision."

QARSAZH: ***kar**-sazh;* both *a* sounds are long, as in "father."

QARSAZHI: *kar-**sazh**-ee*.

QARADOUN: *kar-uh-**doon***.

QANWA: ***kan**-wuh*.

SHUTHMILI: *shuth-**mee**-lee; shuth* rhymes with "push" more than "tooth."

ZHIYOURI: *zhee-**you**-ree*.

ADHARA: *a-**dhah**-ruh*.

DARYOU: ***dah**-ryou*.

MALKHAYA: *mal-**khay**-uh*.

MAYA: "May" like the month.

LAGRI: ***lah**-gree*.

ARITSA: *ah-**ree**-tsuh*.

TSALDU: *tsal-du.*

GRICHALYA: *gree-**chal**-yuh.*

TAYMIRI: *tay-**mee**-ree.*

PARZA: ***par**-zuh.*

ZINANDOUR: *zin-**an**-dor.*

LINARYA ATQALINDRI: *lin-**ar**-yuh at-kuh-**lin**-dree.*

Echentyri

ECHENTYR: *eh-**chen**-teer.*

ECHENTYRI: *eh-chen-**teer**-ee.*

IRISKAVAAL: *ih-riss-kuh-**vaal**; vaal* has a long *a* as in "father."

ATHARAISSE: *ah-thuh-**rai**-seh.*

PENTRAVESSE: *pen-truh-**vess**-eh.*

ISJESSE: *iz-**jess**-eh; j* as in "judge."

Others

ORMARY: ***or**-muh-ree.*

KASMANSITR: *kaz-man-**seetr**;* final *r* as in French "théâtre."

TARASEN: ***tah**-ruh-sen.*

I

The Chosen Bride

By the touch of thy hand shall the black lotus bloom
Thus shall we know thee, handmaid of desolation
By the corruption of the seas
By the fading of all things
Thy name shall be forsaken and thou shalt be my bride
Thus spake the Nameless One upon the plains of dust.

from *The Book of Unmaking*

1

The House of Silence

IN THE DEEP WILDS of the north, there is a Shrine cut into the mountainside. The forest covers these hills like a shroud. This is a quiet country, but the Shrine of the Unspoken One is quieter still. Birds and insects keep away from the place.

In the valley below the Shrine is a temple known as the House of Silence. Its acolytes leave offerings at the foot of the steps that lead up to the Shrine, but they do not come any closer.

Every fourteen years, in spring, when the streams in the hills begin to thaw, a procession leaves the House of Silence. The Prioress rides in a palanquin with six bearers. Despite the cold these bearers are naked from the waist up. Every other day of every other year they are farmers and woodsmen, but on this day they have an ancient purpose to serve. They walk the road of white stones that leads into the hills.

Going before them all is a girl of fourteen, wreathed with flowers and veiled in white. At her side she leads a spotless bull calf on a gilded chain.

The procession halts at the foot of the steps to the Shrine. Here is a stone altar, in which a channel is carved. Here is a vessel set at the lowest point of the channel. Here is a bright, sharp knife.

The girl leads the calf to the altar and they cut its throat. The blood runs black in the dim spring light. It splashes on the frozen stone and flows into the vessel.

She takes the bowl of blood. She climbs the steps to the Shrine. She is never seen again.

One month before the day of Csorwe's death, a stranger came to the House of Silence. Csorwe did not see him arrive. She was down in the crypt, listening to the dead.

In the underbelly of the House there were many cellars, hollowed out in the grey strata of the sacred mountain. Deepest of all were the crypts, where the eminent dead among the Followers of the Unspoken Name were sealed to strive for rest. Rest was not something that came easily here, so close to the Shrine of the god. The dead scratched at the walls and cooed in sad imitation of living song.

Csorwe was sitting in the antechamber trying to pick out the words, as she did from time to time, when she heard someone coming down the passage. She drew her feet up into the alcove, hoping she might not be noticed. A bubble of candlelight approached and opened. It was Angwennad, one of the lay-sisters.

"Csorwe, dear, come out from there, you're wanted upstairs," said Angwennad. The other lay-sisters called Csorwe *miss* or, unbearably, *ma'am*, but Angwennad had been Csorwe's nurse, and there were certain liberties permitted to her.

Csorwe slipped down from her perch. She didn't think she was late for afternoon prayers, but it was easy to lose your place in time—even, as she knew, when you only had so much time to lose.

"There's a pilgrim here for you," said Angwennad. "Very foreign. Shabby looking, although I can't say I'm surprised about that. They're saying he came through the hills on foot."

Pilgrims visited the House of Silence every now and then. Most of them wanted nothing more from Csorwe than a blessing, but Angwennad was looking at her with a soft anxiety that suggested this visitor needed something more demanding.

Upstairs, Angwennad took her place at the back of the hall. The priestesses were already kneeling in rows down either side. Prioress Sangrai took Csorwe aside and explained that the pilgrim required a prophecy, as was his right.

The acolytes set out lacquered trays and tapers, and the Keeper of Black Lotus went from tray to tray, tipping out dried leaves and stems of lotus from her censer.

When it was time, Csorwe set off alone down the centre of the hall, toward the dais at the far end. The hall was lit only by candles, and by the dim glow of the lotus as it began to smoulder. The faces of the others were like pale thumbprints in the haze.

At the dais, the Prioress and the librarian stood to one side with the stranger. Csorwe got a brief look at him as she approached, but she kept her eyes down and her pace stately. On the dais was a high-backed chair. Csorwe took her place here, holding her head high, looking straight ahead. The rows of priestesses and acolytes, the Prioress, the librarian, and the stranger, all blurred and faded at the periphery of her vision. All she could see was the darkness and the empty air occupying the great vault of the hall.

The fumes of the lotus rose among the pillars, sweet and elusive. Once the Keeper of Black Lotus had completed her round, she came to Csorwe with a porcelain cup, in which the seeds and petals of lotus gleamed in resin. It gave off a fine, black, coiling smoke.

The Followers of the Unspoken Name bowed their heads all at once, repeating in one murmuring voice:

"Unspoken and Unspeakable One, Knight of Abyss, Overseer of the Eaten Worlds, praise and reverence unto your Chosen Bride. May she intercede for us."

Csorwe raised the cup and took a breath. Cedar, pepper, incense, and underneath it all the irresistible perfume of the lotus. Her sight darkened, and a pleasant ache crept up her limbs, followed by a numbness. The lights in the hall were very far away, and they shimmered as though underwater. With each breath, they dimmed a little more.

In waking life, Csorwe had walked every one of the crypts and cellars beneath the House of Silence. She knew them by sight and by experience, by touch and by heart. Under the sway of the lotus, she felt the shape of them as though she had them in her mouth. The whole mountain was riddled with hollows, and at the heart of the mountain was the greater void.

She plummeted through the dark, and felt the eyes of the void upon her.

The presence of the Unspoken One crept in slowly at first, like the first reaching wavelets of the tide, rising gently, prying into the burrows of sand-creeping things. And then all at once it was impossible to ignore: a vast invisible pressure, a single focused curiosity that weighed her with impersonal hunger.

Then, a voice, and a face. Back in the hall of the House of Silence, the stranger was kneeling before her, making the salute of sealed lips in respect. His face rippled and gleamed, swimming as though reflected on the surface of a pool. Although he must have been at least forty years old, he had no tusks at all. He was the only foreigner Csorwe had ever seen, and she wished she could see him more clearly.

"Chosen Bride, I most humbly ask a boon of the Unspoken One," said the stranger. He spoke Oshaaru with a curious accent.

"What is it that you desire?" It was Csorwe's own voice, but, of course, she did not feel her lips move. The Unspoken One held her in its grip.

"Knowledge," said the stranger.

"Knowledge of that which has passed away, or that which is to come?" said the Unspoken One. Its attention flickered over Csorwe's thoughts, testing. It found no resistance. She had been schooled for this. She was a clean vessel for the voice of the god.

"Knowledge of that which lives in the present moment," said the stranger.

This was unorthodox. Disrespectful, even. Csorwe braced herself for the anger of the Unspoken One. It seemed to notice her attention, and she felt a kind of reassuring caress, like the chill that rises from an open tomb.

"Speak, then," it said, still using Csorwe's voice.

"Unspoken and Unspeakable One, where is the Reliquary of Pentravesse?"

Csorwe had the same familiar feeling of plunging uncontrollably through nothingness. Bright objects flickered and passed out of sight. And then she felt the touch of the Unspoken One again, turning her attention.

She saw a rosewood box. It was eight-sided, inlaid with gold, about the size of a man's clenched fist. It seemed close enough to touch, but this wasn't Csorwe's first time prophesying and even through the fog of lotus she knew it was only a vision.

A close, thick darkness gathered around the box, like a velvet bag drawn tight, and then the box itself disappeared from view. The vision ended, as though deliberately snatched away. She reached for it again, fumbling into the dark, but couldn't reach it.

"It is hidden from my sight," said the Unspoken One.

Disgust and disbelief were emotions unbecoming of a god, but the Unspoken was certainly capable of displeasure.

"But it does still exist?" said the stranger. He did his best to keep his voice level. Csorwe did not miss the note of satisfaction.

"It is intact," said the Unspoken One. That was as much as the stranger was going to get, it seemed. The Unspoken One drew back from her, like a wave falling back down the shore, leaving only a sheen of brightness where it had touched, and then nothing.

She was herself again, on the dais, in the House of Silence, with the bitter aftertaste of lotus in her mouth. Her head swam, the cup fell from her fingers, and she fainted.

Csorwe slept through afternoon prayers, woke in her own cell, and stumbled down to the refectory for dinner. The black lotus was not known for its gentleness after the fact. Her head felt both thick and fragile, like a hard-boiled egg, and her throat burnt as though she had been screaming.

A group of novices—Csorwe's agemates—were clustered around a single table. Some of them looked round when she entered, but most paid no attention.

Until Csorwe's thirteenth birthday she had lived and studied with the novices. Still, she had no friends among them. The Chosen Bride of the Unspoken One was set apart by protocol, but also by pragmatism. There was no point cultivating the friendship of a Chosen Bride. Most of the novices came from farming families; they understood that it was no good getting fond of the pig before the season of butchery.

Csorwe took a bowl of cabbage soup and sat at another table. The others were all talking about the stranger. He was a wizard, it seemed, from a far-off city that none of them could pronounce. They got quieter and quieter until the whole group was gathered around Ushmai, who was whispering that she thought the stranger-wizard was good-looking.

Csorwe sat and ate her soup, thinking it through. In thirty days it would be the time. That meant twenty-nine more dinners after this. She tried to pay more attention to the soup, to take her time with each bite and savour it properly, but the lotus made everything taste like rust.

Her thoughts kept wandering back to the stranger. If he was a wizard, why was he so shabby? Where were his servants? What was it he wanted so badly that he had come all this way alone? The box she had seen in her vision must be very valuable, or very sacred, or both.

The novices fell silent in unison, and Csorwe looked round to see what had startled them. The stranger was standing in the door to the refectory. He had to stoop to enter.

Csorwe peeped up at him, pretending to eat her soup. He had dark brown skin, a huge amount of hair bound up in a clasp, long pointed ears, and a full beard. She had never seen anyone like this before. Oshaaru such as Csorwe were grey-skinned and golden-eyed, and the few men she had ever seen were clean-shaven.

He wore a long, ragged, outlandish coat, patched all over so that it was impossible to tell what the original cloth had been. There were traces of embroidery in among the patches, threads of gold and silver that glittered when he moved. It was possible he had been a rich man many years ago, but only if he had been a beggar since then.

Still, he didn't look like a poor man, at least not like the poor country men who lived near the House of Silence. Stooping was not a habit for him.

He looked around the refectory for a while, and then, to Csorwe's horror, he sat down opposite her.

"My name is Belthandros Sethennai," he said. "I believe we've met, though I didn't have a chance to introduce myself at the time."

She said nothing, looking down at the half-eaten bowl of soup.

"There's no need to worry. I did check with the Prioress. She finds it theologically permissible for you to speak to me."

It wasn't the theology that had been bothering her so much as the watching eyes of the novices, but she looked up at him. It was very odd to see an adult without visible tusks. His face looked so innocent and unguarded without them that it was difficult to gauge his expressions.

"I wanted to thank you for your indulgence of my curiosity, earlier on," he said.

Csorwe stared at him. It was both absurd and improper to accept thanks for prophecy. She imagined him pouring a glass of wine and thanking the bottle.

"I hope the experience was not too draining for you," he said. She shook her head. "I wish I could express how much the information means. I spent so many years investigating the history of the Reliquary without even beginning to imagine it might still exist in fragments, let alone intact—but I won't bore you with ancient history. I always manage to believe people are interested in my research, despite all evidence to the contrary." He smiled. "If you can spare me a little more of your time, the Prioress tells me you might take me to visit the library?"

In the library of the House of Silence, there was a book bound in the skin of a murdered king, or so it was said. There were books in cipher, books in obsidian, books in whale hide. There were atlases of ruined cities and blighted worlds. There were useless maps to every treasure ever lost to time, and lexicons of every forgotten language. The library of the House of Silence was a monument to entropy.

It was also beautifully warm, because the librarian had bullied Angwennad into bringing her twice the usual allotment of firewood.

The librarian was sitting at her desk when Csorwe came in with Belthandros Sethennai. Her name was Oranna. She was young enough that Csorwe remembered her initiation from acolyte to priestess. Her eyes were the colour of beeswax, and she wore silver caps on her tusks. She didn't look up as they came in, but knew exactly who was there; she had perfected this trick as an acolyte and it served her well as librarian.

"So," said Oranna. "The Reliquary of Pentravesse. If you'd asked me yesterday, I would have said you'd come to the right place."

"But today . . . ?" said Sethennai.

"Today, it transpires, though contrary to all logic, that the Reliquary still exists. That which lives in the present has no place here. Here you will find the truth only about those who are dead, and that which is dust."

"That's a pity," said Sethennai, wandering down a row of shelves. His hands were stuffed in the pockets of his awful coat, as if he had to restrain them from touching the books. "Still, I'd like to see what you have on the Reliquary. Even if it's nothing but lies."

Oranna's brow twisted with suppressed aggravation. "Csorwe," she said. "Stop hovering by the door, will you, and come and sit by the fire."

Csorwe did as she was told, and settled down to watch a phalanx of sparks creep up the side of a log. When Csorwe was little, Angwennad had told her about imps who lived in the hearth and warred over the ashes. It was painful to remember that now. She should have put those things behind her.

She sat and half listened to Oranna and Sethennai. The librarian was never eager to take down one of the books, and her distaste for the stranger was palpable, but she had opened a heavy folio and was looking for her place.

"The Reliquary of Pentravesse is said to mark its passage through the world, in the sense that a scythe marks its passage through the grass," she read. "Seek patiently. Listen for strange accidents, disastrous coincidences, events that slip their reins. You may chart the progress of Pentravesse's final work through an unsuspecting world. This is the nature of the curse upon the Reliquary."

"Greed and ambition pursue it," said Sethennai, as if he too were reading aloud. "Bad luck, ill judgment, and unintended consequences follow in its wake." He smiled at her. "But the idea is irresistible."

Csorwe happened to look up just as Oranna did, and saw the look that passed between the librarian and the wizard. Imagine two spies who pass in the street and recognise one another, before each disappears into a different crowd. Ordinary wariness is replaced with shock, delight, terror—and then the moment passes.

Csorwe saw Belthandros Sethennai only once more in the House of Silence. He stayed in the guest wing, visited the library from time to time, and troubled nobody, as far as Csorwe knew. Her time was taken up with preparations for the day that was to come. There was no ceremonial name for it. Csorwe thought of it as *THAT DAY*. She prayed and meditated for hours each day. She studied *The Book of Unmaking* and *The Dream of Fly Agaric* with the Prioress. She fasted and burnt lotus as the books required.

These preparations were tiring. At first, she slept each night as though she were already dead. Then she began to wake in the small hours, and lie awake, in the grip of a sickly fear, as though just realising what was going to happen to her. As though she hadn't known since she was old enough to understand it. On her fourteenth birthday she would go up to the Shrine of the Unspoken One and that would be the end of her.

The summer would come. There would be another Chosen Bride. The novices would get their adult tusks and make their vows as acolytes. The world would continue, but she would be gone.

One night she got up from her cot, unable to stand it any longer, and let herself out into the corridor. *Here I am,* she thought. *This is me, in two weeks' time. Here I am, walking up to the Shrine. This is the end. This is how it will feel at the end. Thy name shall be forsaken and thou shalt be my bride.*

The flagstones were ice cold underfoot. There was no light,

but she knew the House of Silence too well to trip. She climbed the stairs to the library, at first thinking only of the steps in the mountainside. Then she saw the line of golden light under the double doors of the library, and thought of the warmth of the fire and the comforting smell of pine smoke, the truth about those who are dead and about that which is dust.

She went into the library as quietly as she could, avoiding the door that creaked. Somehow, she hadn't thought there would be anyone inside. She had imagined the fire wasting all that heat and light in solitude.

She knew at once that she had made a mistake. The librarian and the wizard were there. Sethennai sat by the hearth, as though bathing in the glow of the fire. His ragged coat hung on the back of his chair. Oranna was taking a book down from a high shelf, and froze as Csorwe came in, like a cat surprised in the act of stealing scraps. Csorwe stepped back, let the door swing shut, and scuttled back into the dark.

She knew at once that she had seen something she should not. Whatever the meeting in the library had meant, it was not for her eyes, and the punishments for idle curiosity were severe.

Hasty footsteps followed after her. Incoherent flashes and shadows fluttered over the walls: the light of a lantern carried by someone in a hurry. Oranna caught up to her without much difficulty.

"What are you doing, Csorwe?" she said, in a low voice, careful not to wake anyone else. Csorwe was beginning to realise that she wasn't the only one here who had broken the rules. "It's the middle of the night."

Csorwe couldn't explain. She shrank back into the darkness. A moment later, Sethennai appeared at Oranna's shoulder.

"Couldn't you sleep?" said Oranna, and then her face cleared, as though she understood, and was somehow relieved. "You're afraid."

Csorwe nodded. At that moment she couldn't have said whether she was more afraid of Oranna or the Shrine.

"Ah. The Chosen Bride," said Sethennai. He hung back behind Oranna, in the dark, and Csorwe couldn't tell from his tone of voice whether he was suspicious or just curious. "Having doubts?"

Oranna ignored him, still looking down at Csorwe. "Fear is no fault," she said, quoting the Book. "It is right to fear the Unspoken One. The only fault is to seek out consolation in falsities."

Csorwe nodded, staring down at her bare feet.

"I knew the Chosen Bride who came before you," said Oranna. Csorwe startled. This topic was not forbidden, but it was almost unthinkable. Csorwe thought she was the only one who had ever wondered about it. "We were novices together. She was afraid at first, but when the day came she was quite calm. You will find the same peace, I'm certain. Remember your meditations."

Csorwe assented, and Oranna led her back to her cell. The librarian was not known for such considerate gestures. Csorwe wondered whether Oranna meant it in honour of the Bride she had known. She wished Oranna had said more about her. What was her name? What had she said and done? Perhaps Oranna was the only one who remembered.

By the time she got to sleep, she had almost forgotten about Sethennai.

*

Another sleepless hour suspended between midnight and dawn, one week before the day of sacrifice. Csorwe wrapped herself in a blanket and went down to the crypts. Her slippers scalloped the dust as she wandered.

The dead were never quiet in their cells, but they were loudest by night, singing their tuneless, wordless song and battering at the doors. Csorwe went on past the smaller cells, toward the grand central chamber where the Prioresses of ages past were buried, sealed behind a great iron door.

Some of the old Prioresses had been so virtuous they had sewn up their mouths; they died from thirst rather than utter a blasphemous word. The door was marked with the sign of sealed lips, and Csorwe made the salute automatically: three fingers pressed to her lips, between her tusks.

The iron bolt was so cold it ached to touch, as though it drew the living warmth from Csorwe's bones. Metal shrieked on stone as she drew it back and lifted the latch. At the noise of the door opening, the dead fell silent.

She saw the revenants at the edge of the circle of candle-light, standing among their biers like dinner guests waiting to be seated. Slowly, as though they were shy, they began to approach her. There were dozens of them, wrapped in their shrouds, reaching and watching. She stepped toward them, shutting the door behind her, and walked out into the gathering crowd of the dead. Their bony fingertips ran through her hair and brushed against her bare skin with a kind of desperate gentleness.

Csorwe sat down on the edge of a bier and they gathered around, as though she had brought news from the living world. The Prioresses had lived and died here in the House of Silence, and though the presence of the Unspoken had revived their bodies, their souls had returned to the earth. Their eyes were empty sockets. There was nothing they could tell her.

That day arrived. Csorwe moved like a mannequin from one place to another, not really noting where she was or what was happening. They dressed her in white silk and lace, and crowned her with white dog roses. Angwennad told her that she was a brave girl, that the years had passed so quickly, that she had never really believed the day would come.

She was anointed with resin. The scent of lotus mingled with the animal smell of the sacrificial calf. Everything was set in motion. This was the end. It was almost over.

The procession reached the altar at the foot of the steps. The priestesses came forward to kill the calf, their yellow habits blazing against the mossy stone of the hill. Csorwe stared directly ahead, and saw the knife as a flash of light in her periphery.

The blood of the calf filled the bowl to the brim and spilled over. They held out the bowl to her and she took it, clasping the slippery metal in both hands with difficulty.

Then they drew off to each side, and all—the priestesses, the acolytes, the Prioress and the bearers of her palanquin—bowed, once. The librarian watched as Csorwe turned to face the steps.

The way rose steeply. If she had looked back she would have seen the tops of the priestesses' heads, and the House of Silence below them, and beyond that the forests, rising and falling like black waves, far into the distance. Perhaps as far as the village where she was born. She did not look back. She looked down at her reflection, as it rippled in the bowl of blood.

She reached the top of the steps. The wind plucked at the hem of her dress, raising goose pimples on her calves. Her shoulders ached. Weeds blew in the wind where they grew between the slabs of stone. There were mosses, and small grasses, and flowers that had survived the frosts.

Nobody had walked here for hundreds of years but those who were chosen as she was chosen.

She tried not to think about the flowers. They were scentless. She had seen them so many times. She had seen as many flowers as she needed to see. She had eaten enough cabbage soup. She had listened to the dead scratching at the walls for long enough. It was time. If she faltered now, she would never go on.

She turned her eyes to the doorway. It yawned in the side of the mountain, raw, open, and lightless. Neither moss nor grass grew close to the rock face. No living thing was permitted to pass through this way but she who had been chosen. She walked toward the door, and stepped through.

She came into a round chamber, whose walls were hollowed with passages that led deeper into the mountain. In the middle of the chamber was a shallow pit, faintly delineated by the light from the doorway.

At the edge of the pit was a notch of smooth stone, wide enough for her to kneel comfortably. It was impossible to tell whether the place had been smoothed as a kindness or simply worn down by centuries of use.

She thought of the girls who had come here before her, and brought with them the offering of blood for the Unspoken One. If they were so chosen, so perfectly selected for this honour, perhaps they had known the same uncertainty, here in the silence of the halls under the hill. Perhaps they had spent the last minutes of their lives like this, lost in apprehension in the dark. But perhaps it had been easy for them. Perhaps they had done what had to be done, and gone straight on into the deeper places, to find what waited for them.

She knelt down by the edge and tipped up the bowl; the blood ran into the pit, gleaming in the darkness. At once the interest of the Unspoken One closed on the room, and again she felt the full force of its regard pressing in on her. It knew her. It recognised her. The room was empty; nothing breathed here but Csorwe herself. The Unspoken One waited farther on, deeper down in the mountain.

Soon she began to feel self-conscious. Her knees and shoulders ached from long kneeling in one position. The pit had been sucked dry of blood. The Unspoken One was there, but it offered no guidance. The chamber was still dark; the passages beyond were even darker.

"This isn't supposed to happen," she said, out loud. "Where am I supposed to go?"

"An excellent question."

There was a man in one of the passages. She jumped to her feet, and the empty bowl clattered on the rock with a blasphemous jangle.

"Where do you think you are supposed to go?" said the intruder. It was a voice that suggested power and confidence, but it was not the voice of a god. Her fear gave way swiftly to outrage.

"It's you—I know you," she said, bracing her hands on her hips. "You can't come here. Come out of there. You'll die."

Belthandros Sethennai stepped out into the chamber, smiling mildly. He held a lantern in one hand, and he watched her almost as intently as the Unspoken One did.

"So you can speak," he said. "I did wonder."

"If you don't leave here it will kill you," said Csorwe. The Unspoken One was in the room all around them, in the very weight of the air. "This is blasphemy. You can't be here. Nothing alive is allowed to leave this place."

There were laughter lines bracketing the man's mouth, and they deepened as she spoke.

Csorwe crossed her arms and dug her nails into the soft flesh of her inner elbow. "Don't laugh at me. How dare you. This is my death. It was marked out for me."

"Yes, I know," he said. He strode across the room to get a better look at her, stepping lightly over the pit and raising the lantern. She saw that the sleeves of his coat were rolled up and he was wearing a pair of heavy leather gauntlets. "Death awaits us all, O Handmaid of Desolation. But I don't have to die here, and nor do you."

She had hardly dared to dream that something like this might happen, that someone might decide there had been a mistake. It was blasphemous even to imagine it.

"I'm not coming with you," said Csorwe. "This is a false consolation. You can't make me leave."

Sethennai leant back against the wall nearby. "I won't make you do anything," he said. "If you want to go down into the cave and see what the Unspoken One makes of its offerings, please yourself." He took a breath, steadying himself against the wall as though concentrating. "It's unfair of me, I know, to spoil the crowning purpose of your young life by turning up and making cruel remarks. If you're certain that this is what you want, I'll make myself scarce, and leave you to your transcendent experience."

Csorwe knew when she was being made fun of, and clenched her hands in her skirts. "This was my honour," she said. Tears of anger prickled in her eyes. "I was chosen for this."

"Well," said Sethennai. "Now you have been chosen for another occupation, unless you prefer to die in the dark rather than work for me. Do you imagine you are the first Chosen Bride to doubt the fate assigned to her? Plenty of your predecessors ran away rather than face the Unspoken in its lair. Most of them froze to death in the woods, and their remains still lie where they fell."

Csorwe turned her back on him. This was a mistake: now she was facing the way back out onto the hillside, back to the weak sunlight and the frozen grasses. The Shrine was too high for her to see even the roof of the House of Silence, but she saw the distant shimmer of mountains, the forest, the hills, the white arcs of birds rising on the wind.

"I can't," she said. "Where could I go? I would freeze to death too."

"It's very difficult to run alone," said Sethennai. "You would not be alone. You would be with me." The laughter was gone from his face; his brows drawn together in concentration. His gauntleted hands were clenched tight at his sides. Deep in the mountain, the Unspoken One was beginning to notice him.

"The Prioress—" said Csorwe.

"She will never know you're gone," said Sethennai. "Make your choice, Csorwe. Stay here, or come with me. We are running out of time."

"But the Unspoken One will know," said Csorwe. She could feel the beginnings of its outrage already, building and crackling under the earth.

"Yes," said Sethennai. "It will. The secret of greatness is to know when you should risk the wrath of god."

He took off his gauntlets and held out a hand, and she took it. His hand was smooth, long-fingered, bearing a gold signet; hers small, blunt, and stained to the wrist with calf's blood.

"Come along, Csorwe," he said, "and let the Unspoken One cry for you in the pit."

2

The Maze of Echoes

C SORWE HAD BEEN SENT to die before breakfast. By the evening of that day, she and Sethennai were far from the Shrine, aboard a riverboat. This was a new experience among new experiences. For the first night and day she lay on a coil of rope in the bilges, wishing she was dead, as she deserved.

On the second day, something worse than guilt occurred to her. There was a chapter that Csorwe had always enjoyed in *The Book of Unmaking*, detailing the proper punishment of a traitor. *By the shore of the corrupted sea, in the shadow of the coal-black tower, she forsook the Nameless One. May the abyss consume the breaker of promises! May the maggots eat the flesh of her vessel! May her name be forgotten utterly!*

"What would you do," she said, picking her words with caution, "if the Prioress found out, and came to get me back?"

"How would she ever find out?" said Sethennai. "You went up the mountain and you did not return. If the Prioress was so keen to ensure that you were devoured by the god instead of, for instance, going on the run with a strange man, perhaps she should have kept a closer eye on you."

"She might notice *you're* gone," said Csorwe, and added, very daring, "The librarian might notice."

Sethennai laughed. "Oranna might notice long enough to be glad to see the back of me."

"But what would you do if she came after me?"

"I suppose I'd have to kill her," said Sethennai. He was very cheerful, sitting up at the prow and watching the murky banks as they passed. "Csorwe, even if it occurs to her that you are alive—even if she makes a spectacular leap of logic and realises you are with me—even then—how would she ever find us? We are *long gone*."

They left the river, and at last they came to one of the Lesser Gates of Oshaar, green as a cat's eye, sunk into a cliff face at the bottom of an overgrown valley.

Csorwe had seen Gates drawn and described before, but never in person. They had seemed easy to picture—a circle of green fire, burning in a frame of stone, large enough for someone to pass through—but the reality was both more solid and more strange than she had imagined.

The Lesser Gate was twice as wide as Sethennai was tall, and the flickering light that it cast turned the earth and the undergrowth greener than grass ever was. Bands and fronds of liquid light swarmed across its surface, swirling like leaves in the wind.

It hummed, like a glass bell, struck once and left to reverberate in eternity.

Csorwe had an uneasy feeling that perhaps it was forbidden for her to leave Oshaar, but dismissed it. Like Sethennai said, they were long gone.

"You just go through?" she said. "Does it burn you?"

Sethennai held out a hand, shimmering in the light of the Gate, and she took it. They stepped through as one, and then they were falling, like two twigs in a waterfall. Csorwe tumbled weightless into nothingness.

When they landed, the first thing she heard was the sound of wind. Her other hand, the one which was not still clenched like a claw in Sethennai's, opened and closed against the current. For a while she was aware of nothing but the edge of the air against her palm.

"This place is called the Maze of Echoes," said Sethennai.

Gradually her sight returned, and she gazed out at the Maze, as if by gazing she could make sense of it. They stood on a ledge above the place where a steep valley dropped away, down and down, out of reach of light. Pillars and arches of rock massed in the darkness, like misshapen brides, veiled and wreathed with mist. Fragments of sky like pieces of eggshell were visible in places, though not the places one usually saw the sky.

Sethennai pointed to a track that wound along a cliff face. "This way," he said. "It's not so far, really. The Maze is only an interstice. A great celestial entrepôt."

Csorwe nodded as though she understood a word of this, and followed him. You heard of someone travelling by Maze, as they might travel on horseback or in a wagon. She knew you had to go through the Maze to reach other worlds, alien countries, dangerous places utterly unlike Oshaar—but she hadn't imagined it anything like this.

As they travelled, Csorwe wondered what Sethennai meant by *not so far*. The journey soon became the longest she had ever taken. They passed through valleys, under arches, and through narrow passages in the rock. They trailed along the bottom of a gorge, in whose walls maze-gates like great emeralds glittered, high up and far out of reach. The sound of them, singing one to another across the deep, was like a choir far away. Shivers prickled at the back of Csorwe's neck.

At times they stopped, and Csorwe slept. Once they saw a far-off mazeship passing through: the hull of polished maze-oak, and the sail canopies belling above the hull like a growth of mushrooms. Up close, it would have been the grandest and brightest thing Csorwe had ever seen, but the mists of the Maze dulled its pennants, and it passed in oblivious silence.

All these wonders meant that it took her a long time to realise that she missed the House of Silence. She missed her cell. She missed the shape of the day: the prayers at every interval, the making of offerings, meals in the refectory, and all the rest. She could never have gone back to that. Even if she had stayed, those days were over. If Sethennai hadn't come for her she would be dead by now.

These facts drifted along behind her, like huge tethered clouds, though she did her best not to look at them directly. She had betrayed her people. She had betrayed her purpose. She had betrayed her god.

She missed her home. They would have killed her if she had stayed. But still she missed it.

Well, she said to herself, she was away, now, and Sethennai had some other purpose for her.

After a while they left the Maze, coming out through another Gate into another world. Csorwe was tense with anticipation, struggling not to betray to Sethennai the fact that this was entirely new to her and almost entirely terrifying. In her old life, Csorwe had accompanied the Prioress on her annual procession to visit the faithful in their villages, but this had never taken them farther than a few days' travel from the House of Silence.

She couldn't conceive how far they had come. Not just far from the House of Silence but far from Oshaar, from the whole realm of the Unspoken.

They had emerged from the Maze onto the edge of a still lake. A flight of white birds rose like a scattering of petals on the dark foliage.

"What kind of world is this?" said Csorwe, because it seemed childish to say, *Where are we?* The birds were the first living things they had seen for days.

"An old and quiet one," said Sethennai. "I'm afraid to say I don't know its name."

"Do people live here?" she said.

"No," he said. "For the moment, I think it's best that we avoid company." His eyes were sombre, but when he saw Csorwe was watching he smiled again. "In the colleges of Tlaanthothe, there are dozens of scholars who catalogue the worlds and give an accounting of their peoples. I'm afraid I tend to leave them to it. But when we get there, if you still want to know, we can ask them."

"Is that your home?" Csorwe didn't want to try pronouncing *Tlaanthothe*. With her tusks, she worried it would come out as more spit than word. "Are we going back there?"

"Of course," said Sethennai. "In good time. Tlaanthothe is the jewel of all cities. You'll love it."

He stalked along the lakeshore, inspecting stones. Once or twice he picked up a flat one and skimmed it across the water.

"What's it like?" said Csorwe, running to catch up to him. In the House of Silence, it was unseemly to ask many questions, but Sethennai seemed to enjoy explaining things.

"Tlaanthothe is a university town," he said, then frowned,

realising the word wasn't familiar to her. "A place of learning. Or at least, it was. I don't know what my enemies have done to it." He grinned at her. "I owe you a confession, Handmaid of Desolation. You've put your trust in a vagrant. Tlaanthothe is a long way off, and I am as much an exile as you are. The ways are closed to me. My enemy stole my city and banished me."

Csorwe watched the ripples spreading in the water and tried to make sense of this. "Is your enemy a wizard, too?"

"Not a particularly skilful one," said Sethennai.

"So you *are* a wizard," said Csorwe, feeling cunning. "Everyone said you were, but I never saw you do any magic."

Sethennai laughed at that. "I am too far from my patron," he said. He tilted his head to consider her for a moment. "Magicians among your people call on the Unspoken One. They draw their power from the Shrine. But my goddess is very far away. She might not hear me if I call, and I don't want to exhaust myself by calling without success."

"Am I—I mean, are you—do you want me to learn magic?" she said. A twinge of anxiety gripped her. She did not want to call on the Unspoken One for any reason.

"No," he said. "Magic is not like other trades. It runs in the blood. Of course, a practitioner must study and hone his skills like anybody else with a gift, but the gift itself is something that cannot be earned. Nor can it ever be cast off. I was born into the regard of my goddess and I will never be free of it. The Unspoken One has no such hold on you. It spoke through you, but you never used its power for your own ends."

He tried another stone, which bounced only once before dropping gracelessly into the lake.

"In some ways it is a mercy for you," he said. "The use of magic levies a heavy tax on the body."

"Even for you?" said Csorwe.

He smiled. "The thing with taxes is that one can be clever about when and how one pays. But I do not use magic without need."

He bent to select another stone from the shore.

"My enemy thinks that if I can't get into Tlaanthothe, I will be cut off from my patron altogether. He has thrown every possible obstacle in my path. But he underestimates me."

This stone skipped three times before sinking, and he turned to Csorwe, exultant. "And I very much doubt that he will ever see *you* coming."

At the far end of the lake they found their next Gate and travelled back into the Maze. Csorwe soon got used to this. They passed through many maze-gates, across greying deserts and bare hillsides, into other worlds and back again into farther reaches of the Maze, skipping from one to another like a needle looping thread from one side of the cloth to another. Occasionally they saw birds and trees, but never other people. This made sense to Csorwe now that she knew that Sethennai was avoiding some powerful enemy.

And then they came out of the Maze of Echoes, and into the first city Csorwe had ever seen.

Her first impressions of the city were grubby and confused. Dull, punishing heat. The smell of dung and sweat and sawdust. Dust in the air, choking her nose and mouth. Worst of all, everywhere was a senseless jangle of noises and voices, all interrupting and cutting across each other.

Csorwe covered her ears with her hands and buried her face in her clothes. They waited in some kind of stable yard while Sethennai negotiated for a wagon. Once the wagon materialised, Csorwe curled up in the back and subsided into misery.

The boardinghouse was somehow worse. You could hear every cough, every grunt, and every burst of ugly, angry laughter in every room. Night brought no relief. Surrounded by voices, Csorwe couldn't help feeling she was being watched.

Sethennai woke her the next morning. It was easy to tell when he was excited: his pointed ears fluttered, his eyes twinkled, and every fibre in his body became springy. Arriving in the city had restored something to him. Csorwe pulled the blanket over her head.

"We're going to the market," he said.

The market was dirtier and louder and more chaotic than she could have imagined. A many-headed crowd surged around them, shouting, staring, grabbing. Csorwe clenched her fists at her sides. She had heard from the priestesses how terrifying and corrupt the cities were, and she saw now that they were right. She didn't see how anyone could live in such a place without going mad.

Csorwe prayed for the Unspoken One to open up the earth and devour the city, and tried to keep her balance.

"You do get used to it," said Sethennai.

She doubted it. The crowds reminded her of the presence of the Unspoken, only more aggressive. It ate mindlessly at her, threatening to sweep her away.

She refused to reach for Sethennai's hand. If he realised how helpless she was then he would certainly regret saving her from the Shrine.

The crowd swelled and surged and Csorwe tripped over a

stranger's foot. She fell flat on her back and at once the sky was blotted out by the swarm—cages of chickens, three dogs on a chain, a gang of children almost completely naked—but before she could be trampled to death Sethennai was there. He buffeted the chicken-seller out of the way and lifted Csorwe to her feet.

"Keep hold of my arm," he said. "You'll learn to find your way. Once you know how it works, it will be easier."

He cut a path through the crowd for them, leading her toward a flight of steps that wound up the side of a building. She stopped at the bottom of the steps, shaking her head.

"Come on," he said. "Trust me."

She followed him, hanging on his arm, and they came to a roof garden, thick with ferns and strange bulbous flowers. There was nobody here, and Csorwe's panic began to abate. In the centre of the garden, an old bell tower reached toward the sky. Sethennai beckoned her up the steps.

From the top of the bell tower they could see the whole extent of the city. It rose in a haphazard way from the grey hills, sprouting and tumbling over its ancient walls like a patch of lichen growing on a stone. It was monstrous, but at least now she could see the beginning and end of it.

"Are you afraid?" said Sethennai.

She swallowed. She couldn't bring herself to nod.

"Nothing in this world has earned the power to frighten you, Csorwe," he said. "You have looked your foretold death in the face and turned from it in defiance. Nothing in this world or any other deserves your fear."

"Yes, sir," she said. At that moment she was too sick and stunned to really hear the words, although she returned to them later, many times.

"Do you see the Gate?" said Sethennai.

It hovered above the docks in the far distance. The haze dimmed its colour, turning it yellowish, like a sickly moon swimming among the fumes.

"We won't be here forever," he said. "We'll be safe from my enemies for a time, so we can rest and you can learn without having to look over your shoulder. But this isn't home. Tlaan-thothe lies through the Gate, and it's waiting for us."

The city was called Grey Hook. Sethennai explained early on that he had chosen it for their shelter because its people spoke Csorwe's mother tongue as a lingua franca, and because they were very nice, discreet minders of their own business.

Sethennai never explained to her exactly how life was going to work from now on. He seemed to trust that she would figure it out, and for the most part she did.

He still talked to her as though she interested him. She accompanied him on many of his errands around the city, and they ate their meals together. Most of these were lentil curries from the vendor in the square below the boardinghouse, because he couldn't cook.

It turned out that Sethennai seriously intended to pay her a wage. For what services, she wasn't sure, and the idea of asking was distantly frightening. What if she asked him why he'd brought her here, and he admitted he'd made a mistake?

After deductions for room and board the wage wasn't very much, Sethennai said, but it was still *money*, something Csorwe had hardly seen before, and never owned.

She hated the money, in fact, because it seemed to have been got for nothing. The little stack of copper coins, all for her pains in sitting around in the boardinghouse, terrified of the outside world and everything in it. It could not go on. Sooner or later Sethennai would realise he was paying her to be afraid. By that time she would have to get her act together.

The first time she steeled herself to leave the boardinghouse on her own was to resolve the serious matter of breakfast. Sethennai didn't like getting up in the morning, and there was nothing to eat in the boardinghouse. It would be so good to get breakfast ready before he woke up. She knew where to buy food. The market in the square started trading at dawn. It really couldn't be so difficult. They spoke her language here, so she could make herself understood. She was fourteen years old. Most people her age were already working for a living.

Nothing in this world or any other deserved her fear. That was all very well, but there was a great difference between climbing the steps to the Shrine of the Unspoken and going out to buy groceries. Csorwe had spent a lifetime readying herself to die, not to talk to strangers.

The market was full of gorgeous things Csorwe had never eaten and hardly knew the words for—tomatoes, hot peppers, baskets of fruit like huge, soft gems—but eggs, bread, and onions were cheap and easy to recognise.

"Six eggs, please," she said, stopping at the chicken-man's stall. She couldn't face asking how much the eggs cost, so she just held out a fistful of coins and hoped he wouldn't cheat her.

The chicken-man was Oshaaru, which could have helped a bit, but at the sound of Csorwe's accent—purest, deepest old country— he squinted down at her, as though she might be mocking him. Then he decided that, no, in fact, he was mocking her.

"*How* many eggs, milady?"

She repeated herself. The anger bubbled up faster than she expected, taking her by surprise. If he knew what she really was he wouldn't talk like that.

She suppressed her rage. She wasn't what she really was, not anymore. She wasn't the Chosen Bride. Nobody was going to come to her for prophecy. She was just another anonymous customer and the chicken-man would have forgotten all about her by the end of the day. And that was good.

The chicken-man seemed faintly disappointed that she didn't want to play along, but he didn't mind taking her money.

"Here without your boss today?" he said, handing over a box of eggs.

"That's right," said Csorwe, with an unbidden swell of pride. "I'm picking up breakfast."

Back at the boardinghouse, she fried the onions in a pan over the fire, and scrambled the eggs in with them. The result was not perfectly beautiful but perfectly delicious: creamy eggs jewelled with golden onion. She ate her portion from the pan. Sethennai appeared as she was mopping up the scraps with a crust.

"I didn't know you could cook," he said. He was still in his nightshirt, with a silk scarf wrapped around his head.

"You ought to eat yours or it won't be good," she said, holding out his plate.

He blinked at it and rubbed sleep out of one eye, as if unable to comprehend the form the morning had taken.

Csorwe was pleased that he didn't ask questions. She didn't want to explain that she had done kitchen duties in the House of Silence. She would rather Sethennai think this was just a natural talent. He ate all of it, anyway, and seemed to like it.

After breakfast, he was much revived, and asked Csorwe all about her conversation with the chicken-man.

"Oshaarun will serve you well here in town," he said. "But of course when we get home it will be necessary for you to speak the language of my city as a native. I happen to think Tlaanthothei is a beautiful language, so I was thinking I would teach it to you myself. Have you ever learned any other language?"

"Oranna the librarian tried to teach me," she said, uncertainly. "So I could read the old books."

"Ah," said Sethennai. His eyes narrowed in private amusement. Until that moment, Csorwe had all but forgotten that he too had met Oranna, that she'd spied them working on some scheme in the library after hours.

She watched him carefully, wondering whether he'd say anything more. With each day that passed in Grey Hook, the House of Silence felt less substantial, as if the first fourteen years of her life had been a lotus hallucination. She didn't know how it might feel to talk to Sethennai about everyone she had left behind, whether it would make them real in her head again, whether that might be a good or a bad thing.

"The Unspoken One has been worshipped in many tongues over the centuries," Sethennai went on. "Although it prefers to see them plucked out. Ironic, really. Did you make progress with your lessons?"

Oranna had not had much patience with her as a pupil. It wasn't that Csorwe hadn't tried, but the warmth of the library had made her sleepy, and her mind had wandered.

"I can do verbs in the present tense," she said. If Sethennai thought it was worth trying to teach her something, she wasn't about to admit how useless she had been. *"The queen sleeps in the castle, the servants bring the message to the master."*

"Oh, good," said Sethennai. "If you've learned to put up with that kind of nonsense, the battle is almost won. Well, come and sit by me. We'll begin with the Tlaanthothei alphabet and go from there."

After a time, a letter arrived for Sethennai, written in cipher and containing a note of credit.

"So I do still have friends in the world," he said, and winked at Csorwe.

They left the boardinghouse and rented rooms above a wineshop. Ciphered letters arrived for Sethennai once or twice a month, as his friends in Tlaanthothe kept him informed of the activities of his enemy.

Csorwe discovered that the enemy's name was Olthaaros Charossa, though Sethennai almost never spoke it out loud, and even then in a low voice, all six syllables infused with distaste. This was the usurper wizard who had brought about Sethennai's exile.

While Sethennai schemed, Csorwe studied. Three days a week they spoke nothing but Tlaanthothei at home, and it came to her more easily than she had expected. It was good to be able to speak Sethennai's own language to him, although she still didn't understand his jokes.

At Sethennai's prompting she spent some of her saved wages on clothes. Her existing wardrobe was a pile of mismatched tunics and leggings, acquired secondhand and threadbare from the Grey Hook market. The dress she had worn up the stairs to the Shrine was folded neatly away in a drawer that she never opened.

Sethennai had offered no guidance, so she had to guess. All Sethennai's clothes were brightly patterned, though ancient and much mended. Csorwe considered dressing to match, and rejected the idea. She would look like a housecat trailing after a tiger.

She had never chosen her own clothes, and didn't want to make a spectacle of herself. It had been so much easier to be the Chosen Bride and just have Angwennad bring her the right habit for every day of the calendar. In the end, to escape from the tailor's shop, she chose some plain tunics and a lamb-leather coat.

Sethennai was in a good mood when she got back to the apartment. "I've bought myself a present, too," he said, beckoning her inside. "Come and admire yourself."

The present turned out to be a mirror of real silvered glass, hanging on the wall of their sitting room. Csorwe had never seen such a thing. The Prioress of the House of Silence had strong views about personal vanity, so the novices and acolytes had been confined to small mirrors of polished copper.

She tried not to appear too fascinated by the new mirror, or by the weird spectre of her own clear, true-colour reflection. Grey skin, grey freckles, and yolk-yellow eyes were obscured by an overgrown mop of black hair. It turned out that her nose was slightly hooked, which she liked. The points of her milk-tusks poked out at the corners of her mouth.

With a jolt she realised that she might now live long enough to get her adult tusks. They didn't come in until you were fifteen or sixteen, so she had never imagined what they might look like. She stared at herself for another second, then folded up the feeling and put it away, like the dress, in a safe place where she didn't have to look at it.

She had chosen the new clothes well. She looked smart, but more to the point she looked like anyone you might see going about their business in the streets of Grey Hook, any one of a thousand couriers and apprentices. There was no way anyone could detect that she had ever been over the threshold of the House of Silence.

"Well?" said Sethennai. She realised she had been staring, and stepped back, shoving her hands into the pockets of her new coat.

"Think I need a haircut," she said.

On her fifteenth birthday, to mark the end of the first stolen year, Sethennai gave her a dictionary called *The Various Tongues of the Echo Maze, for the Traveller.*

Around this time she lost her milk-tusks and gained a Qarsazhi tutor named Parza. He was an exile, full of sorrow for his homeland and even more irritable with Csorwe than Oranna had ever been.

"The Qarsazhi are difficult people," said Sethennai. Csorwe had grasped this much. Qarsazh was an empire spread across many worlds, ancient and rich and huge enough that they had heard of it even in the House of Silence.

"Parza is particularly difficult," Sethennai went on. "But don't worry about him. You need to learn their ways but you don't need him to like you."

Csorwe had only ever heard of Qarsazh as a place of cruelty

and corruption, but Parza was a sleek, small, affected person, with copper-brown skin, a neatly pointed beard, and very smooth grey hair, which he wore in a single coiled braid. His other traits were coffee drinking, homesickness, a delicate stomach, and religious devotion, although it was hard to tell which of these were the ways of Qarsazh and which the ways of Parza.

Csorwe made slow progress with Qarsazhi. The words were difficult—half-jagged and half-elusive—and Parza was openly disdainful of her clumsy pronunciation. But Sethennai needed her to learn, and she owed him her best efforts.

Alongside Parza there came a whole programme of study, and a whole succession of tutors—most of them eccentric, some certainly criminals. Csorwe had more than languages to learn. She learned to navigate the city. She learned to cook eggs the proper Grey Hook way, with hot pepper and pickled cucumber. She learned to fly a cutter, and to fight: first unarmed, then with knives, and finally with the sword.

Grey Hook was a strange place. One day she saw two people kissing on the Bridge of Flies, in public, where anyone might see them. One afternoon she fell asleep in the courtyard and got a sunburn the colour of basalt. She learned to understand the city at night, its voices, its cries, its distant music. She learned how to eat mealworms, how to speak her mother tongue with the Grey Hook accent, how to run and climb and creep through the battered streets, and how to wrap her hands for a fistfight.

From the old crooks and soldiers who were her tutors, she learned about the hungers that live in the heart of every city, and she was educated in the threat, the promise, and the scientific accomplishment of violence.

*

There were a few other expatriate Tlaanthothei in Grey Hook, mostly tall and dark as Sethennai was, all with long tapered ears. But their neighbourhood was on the other side of the city, and Sethennai was not interested in associating with his countrymen.

Instead, he had adopted the pseudonym "Dr. Pelthari," and taken a job as a medic with the Blue Boars, a mercenary company whose barracks were just across the square from the apartment.

Csorwe wondered at times whether he missed Tlaanthothei food and habits, the way she occasionally missed cabbage soup and plainchant, but if he did he never showed any sign of it. He hadn't explained much to Csorwe, but she understood that he had been thrown out of Tlaanthothe, that his enemies had lied and conspired and whipped up public feeling against him. He still had his friends, who sent him their coded letters from time to time, but any Tlaanthothei stranger could be an informant for Olthaaros Charossa.

When Csorwe turned sixteen, Sethennai gave her a sword of folded Torosadni steel, and requested that she be allowed to join the Blue Boars' newest recruits for sparring practice.

She had dreaded this. It had been so long since she'd had to deal with a class of her peers. She imagined the Blue Boars would all know each other. They would have their own team jokes and they would not be happy to meet an interloper.

To begin with it was actually worse than this. She wasn't the only Oshaaru or the only girl, but she was the youngest and smallest, and it was irresistible to the Blue Boars to treat her as a kind of mascot. But they soon learned that she was also the fastest and least merciful, and that she had been training for longer than most. Once she tripped the enormous Corporal Valmine on his face during training, they started to take her more seriously.

The Blue Boars all wore their hair long on one side, and shaven on the other. After a few months they took Csorwe to the company barber to get hers done to match.

She got home that evening to find Sethennai absorbed in one of his ciphered letters. Only when she brought him a glass of wine did he look up at her and notice the change.

"Joining up with the Boars permanently?" he said, after a second. There was an odd expression on his face, veiled as usual by ironic amusement. Csorwe stared back at him, and realised with horror that he might be upset with her—that it might be possible for something she did to wound him.

"No!" she said. "No—they were all getting theirs done—didn't think you'd mind—"

"Why on earth should I mind?" he said, shifting effortlessly into cheerful bemusement. Csorwe couldn't tell whether she was imagining a bitter undercurrent. Surely he didn't think she might leave him to become a mercenary?

Occasionally, yes, she thought it was a shame they couldn't just stay forever in Grey Hook. It was a shame she couldn't spend the rest of her life exploring the rooftops and making new omelettes and memorising verb forms with Parza.

Still, she knew they were leaving sooner or later, and she was used to living with a deadline on the horizon. She liked Valmine and the others, but it was only thanks to Sethennai that she had these years at all.

"The Boars are a very respectable company," he added. "And I suppose if you prefer to run with them—"

"I don't," she said, with vehemence, almost angry that he could think her so ungrateful. "I'm not joining up with them. They treat me like a baby anyway."

This was true, Csorwe reminded herself, recalling now with shame that she had let Valmine carry her around on his shoulders after they'd got their haircuts.

"Well, if the soldiering life calls to you, far be it from me to stop you, although I must warn you it's quite likely you'll lose a limb," he said. "But you do know we aren't going to be here forever."

"I know," she said. There was no future for them in Grey Hook, and it was no good getting settled here. "Tlaanthothe."

He smiled at last. It was an immediate relief. The tension went out of Csorwe's body like tea leaves uncurling in water.

Beyond the Gate of Grey Hook, far away across the Maze, Sethennai's city still waited for him—and for her. This was the purpose for which she had been chosen and trained. One day, maybe soon, they were going home to defeat Olthaaros Charossa.

3

The Curse-Ward

A LETTER ARRIVED ONE day when Sethennai was travelling with the Boars, and Csorwe was suffering once again from the pluperfect subjunctive.

"Must you be so slow?" snapped Parza. "You cannot travel to Qarsazh and talk like this, unless you want them to think you are a barbarian and laugh in your face. Again. We covered this last week. *If-only-I-had-travelled-to-the-town*," he chanted, tapping the cover of his lexicon in time with the words. The point of his beard bobbed up and down like a bird pecking at a worm.

"If only you had stayed at home," she muttered, baring her tusks at him behind his back. Her adult tusks had come in over the last year. Nearly full grown, they still ached at the roots sometimes, and Parza's lessons seemed to make them worse. She ignored Parza's hiss of displeasure as one of the maids from the wineshop knocked at the door with the post.

The letter was bulkier than usual, a heavy packet of waxed paper, tied with several loops of string and sealed with a lump of unstamped beeswax. The name *Belthandros Sethennai* was neatly inscribed on the front.

Csorwe spent as long as she could tipping and thanking the maid. Parza was supposed to leave in a quarter of an hour and she was prepared to scrape every minute of freedom that she could.

"Stop wasting time," said Parza, from the sitting room. "I will not leave until you can recite it perfectly. I have all day."

"Wonder why they kicked you out of Qarsazh," said Csorwe under her breath, and stalked back into the room with the letter in her hands. "I have to deal with this," she said. "Might be important."

This wasn't exactly a lie. She often helped Sethennai with his correspondence. It was good practice in languages for her. If this one was ciphered then she couldn't actually read it, but opening the packet and filing the contents in Sethennai's cabinet might save her from Parza's example sentences for another thirty seconds.

Parza huffed and shuffled his papers, but he wasn't about to interfere in Sethennai's business. Csorwe sat down at the desk with the packet and began snipping through the strings.

As she cut the final strand, she realised what she had missed. Sethennai's letters were always addressed to *Pelthari*. Nobody here ought to know his real name.

"Oh, shit," she said.

"Such language," said Parza, clicking his tongue. "But I suppose if Dr. Pelthari will encourage you to associate with street persons—"

Csorwe barely heard him. Her pulse began to race, beating out a rhythm of dread against her breastbone. She shoved the packet hastily away as the beeswax seal began to peel of its own accord, flaking off in shards and turning to dust.

Behind the wax seal, there was a sigil worked on the paper in some red-brown pigment, a spiral of interlocking curves that squirmed on the page. Looking at it was like biting into a peach and finding several worms wriggling inside.

"What are you—" said Parza, coming up behind her. "*Sorcery*," he said, in a low harsh voice she had never heard from him before. "Mother of Cities, this is a house of corruption—"

"It came in the post, Parza," she said. She shoved back the chair and stood up, not taking her eyes off the packet. She controlled her breathing as she had been taught, making a physical effort to damp down the panic that rose in her. Was the packet going to explode? She knew so little about magic—what should she do?

Parza was praying in Qarsazhi, stumbling over the couch toward the door. She ignored him.

The letter was unwrapping itself. The leaves of paper unfolded with a dry, leathery sound, like scales on sand. There was a strong smell: hot metal, scorched hair, and—something else, something Csorwe hadn't encountered for years. A whisper of incense, a shadow of lotus.

"By the gods—" said Parza, now flat against the front door of the apartment and wrestling with the handle. "Run, you blind fool, don't just stare at it—"

Csorwe did not want to see what was inside the packet. But how could she explain herself to Sethennai if she let the apartment burn or explode or whatever was about to happen?

With a calm that startled her, she returned to the table where they'd been studying, and sized up Parza's lexicon: a slab of leather and parchment as thick and heavy as a paving stone.

The letter was still unleafing itself. Csorwe lifted the book over her head and dropped it on the packet. There was a crunch, and silence.

She fell back into the chair, winded with delayed terror, and sat there for a moment or two, watching. Just in case. Once she was as certain as she could be that the packet wasn't going to come back to life, she crept out onto the landing and found Parza.

"I dealt with it," she said.

"You cannot *deal with* magic," he said, glaring at her. Parza often glared at her, but this was a different quality of anger. He was still terrified.

"Suppose I should just have run away like you did," said Csorwe.

"Yes," said Parza. "If you had been educated in a civilised country you would know that. Run away and inform the Inquisitorate—not that such a thing exists in this godsforsaken world—"

"Well, I dropped the lexicon on it," she said, knowing he would shriek about it.

"My lexicon!" said Parza. "How—" He broke off. She followed his gaze to see that something was seeping out from under the door to the apartment. Curls of some dark substance, like liquid smoke, were branching and creeping across the floorboards toward them.

"Mother of Cities," said Parza. "You dealt with it, did you?"

"I—" The smoke was already a few feet from the door, moving much faster than it should. The stuff was billowing up from the floor, rising in puffs and then narrowing into thready black tendrils. It seemed to be reaching out for her. She wished she hadn't left her sword inside, useless as it was likely to be.

For a second she was frozen with guilt and terror, staring at the escaping smoke as Parza pushed past her to get away from it.

"Magic is an abomination to the gods," he said. "May the Nine forgive us for—"

She ought to warn them downstairs. This was the wineshop's busiest time of day. There would be dozens of people in the taproom, innocent of what was going on up here.

Sethennai had done everything he could to keep a low profile. He never used magic here. But they would have no choice but to leave Grey Hook now. Parza had already seen too much, and if dozens of patrons were thrown out of a wineshop—well. This would be the end of their comfortable life.

She'd known it had to end sooner or later, but the idea of cutting it short through her own thoughtless actions was more than she could bear. Why had she accepted the letter? She had ruined everything because she was frustrated with Parza, of all things.

Parza was still gibbering. She opened the door of the nearby linen cupboard and pushed him inside. She'd figure out how to deal with him later, or Sethennai would.

"Stay here," she said, ignoring his protests. "I *will* deal with it."

She shut the door on him and strode back toward the apartment, squaring her shoulders and snapping her tusks, as if faking bravado might help somehow.

She realised now that she should have destroyed the sigil on the envelope. She didn't know much about magic, but Sethennai had warned her about this kind of device. If you could break the control sigil, the rest of the working was supposed to come apart like a wagon with a busted axle. If she could get to the desk and tear up the paper . . . well, she had no idea what would happen, but it was the only plan she had.

She opened the door to the apartment and stepped inside. It was as dark as night. The smoke blotted out any light that filtered through the shutters. The air smelled thickly of grave dirt, and mingled with it—again—the scent of burning lotus. Breathing it in, Csorwe felt a familiar sensation—the numbness of body, the dimming of sight, the taste of rust—and for a moment she thought she would drown in it. The rush of unwelcome memories threatened to close over her head and carry her away: the hall of the House of Silence, the insinuating presence of the Unspoken One, the weight of the bowl of blood in her hand.

She clenched her fists and willed the memory away. If she breathed in any more lotus she was going to fall down and start gibbering before she could do anything about the sigil. She held her breath as she struggled toward the desk. It was like fighting through syrup. It took a terrible, infuriating effort to move her legs, as though these three years of training had abandoned her all at once and left her weaker than before. She was less than halfway to the desk when she tripped over a footstool. Her knees gave out altogether and despite her efforts she gasped, sucking in huge gulps of the poisoned air. Her vision clouded and she felt herself falling again, as though the floor had opened up and revealed an abyss.

The crypts beneath the House of Silence never ended, she saw, as her thoughts scattered in panic. She was never going to be free. They were underneath her wherever she went and now they were claiming her.

No. The boards under her hands and knees were real. She was real. She was still here, in Sethennai's apartment. She was no longer the girl who had climbed to the Shrine, with no idea that there was any world beyond. That was behind her.

Her body was numb, and moving each muscle was an effort. But she managed to get to her knees, and to drag herself from chair to table and up to the desk, where Parza's lexicon still sat on top of the crushed letter. The smoke was spiralling out from under the book. The smell in the air was much thicker here, and she felt the crushing, obliterating pressure of the lotus on her sight and reason.

She swatted at the book with hands that felt like empty gloves, but she couldn't muster the strength to lift it. At last she managed to grip the edge of the packet and drag it out some way from under the book. The clouds of lotus-smoke seethed around her, pulling her down into a vision.

It would be so much easier if she would just let herself go. If she would just drink in the fumes, and sleep and dream and float in the darkness and the deep.

No–no! she thought, as her knees slackened again and she slid back to the floor. She hauled on the paper, furious with her weak body and sluggish mind.

It was too late. The years had made her body strong, but they had sapped her tolerance for the lotus. As she blacked out, she heard the sound of paper tearing, but she was too far gone to wonder what it might mean.

Someone lifted and carried her, and she struggled feebly.

"Csorwe," said a voice. "Be calm." It was Sethennai.

He put her down on what she now realised was the couch in their apartment. The lotus fog was gone. A brief flash of relief gave way to trepidation. Sethennai did not look happy. He was dressed in his Blue Boars uniform. He must have returned from his assignment to find the apartment trashed and Csorwe half dead. He must be furious.

"What happened?" he said, in a flat voice that she had never heard before.

She was both cold and sweaty, as though she had just run through the rain. She unclenched her clammy fingers, revealing a ripped sheet of waxed paper that had been crushed in her fist.

He took it from her and unfolded it, flattening it out against his knee—and revealing half the sigil, roughly torn across. Like a beetle pierced with a pin, it was no longer wriggling.

Sethennai startled, drawing his hands back from the dead sigil as if it might still bite. "This was part of a curse-ward," he said. "What made you think you could handle this?"

"I didn't want to ruin your cover," she said. "I'm sorry."

He closed his eyes and breathed out slowly, visibly controlling himself. "I think you're going to have to explain exactly what happened."

She did, her face hot with shame. Sethennai relaxed a little when he learned that only Parza had been there to witness it.

"He's not a chatterer," said Sethennai. "Perhaps I'll raise his salary." He still looked grim enough to worry her. A dull sickness had settled in her belly, rivalling the lotus headache that thundered behind her eyes.

"There was lotus in it," she said. "You know, from the—you know."

"I do," said Sethennai.

"I'm sorry," she said again, averting her eyes.

He sighed again. "It was an error of judgment," he said. "I expect better from you. But there is no harm done. I am very glad of that."

"Do we have to leave the city?" she said. "Was it Olthaaros?"

He went to the desk to retrieve the other half of the paper, unfolded it, and held it up to match the two halves of the control sigil.

"No, I don't think it was," said Sethennai. To Csorwe's immense relief, he sounded intrigued. He never stayed angry when something piqued his interest. "If Olthaaros knew where we were, he would have come for us himself."

He looked back at the paper. The broken sigil had the quality of an old bloodstain, inert but vivid.

"And I very much doubt that Olthaaros would have primed his curse with ashes of lotus. No. This was a different friend. One who possibly likes me even less." He smiled to himself. "Still so bitter."

"I don't understand," said Csorwe. She wouldn't have admitted it if she hadn't been so exhausted. Her head felt like it was full of slime and pins. With the arrival of relief, all the fight had gone out of her, and she wanted to go to bed. "Are we in danger?"

He was still smiling. It seemed that Csorwe had faded from his list of immediate concerns. "Not imminently. This wasn't a serious attempt on my life. You were never supposed to open the packet."

"I know, I shouldn't have—" she said.

He shook his head. "It was meant for me. You could understand it as part of a game. A little bubble of poison, now lanced. Oranna may want many things, but she doesn't want me dead."

"Oranna—you mean *that* Oranna? The librarian?" said Csorwe.

"She hasn't ever forgiven me for leaving her in the House of Silence," he said.

Csorwe still remembered Oranna's first meeting with Sethennai in the Library, and the look that had passed between them. With a sharp jolt she realised what such a look might have meant.

"You mean—" she started, and couldn't think how she could possibly phrase it.

It was surprisingly hard to come to terms with the idea of Sethennai having a—having any kind of—well, he wasn't that old—but maybe she was making a crude assumption and that wasn't what he'd meant at all?

"Were you . . . in love?" she said, not meeting his eye. She'd picked the wrong word. Too small and ordinary.

"In love?" said Sethennai. He sounded charmed, as if Csorwe was a parrot that had unexpectedly learned a new word. She shrivelled further into the couch. "Not really, I don't think," he said, sounding like he'd never considered it.

She had learned from the Blue Boars about what people might get up to on their own time, and all kinds of words to describe their activities, but even trying to think of Sethennai in the same sentence made a heavy door slam shut in her brain.

She had begun to feel so clever and knowledgeable lately, getting good at swordplay and conjugations, but she had managed to miss this completely. She buried her face in one of the couch cushions to hide her blush. Sethennai, however, had been distracted again by the letter. The matter was evidently closed.

The surface of the desk, around Parza's lexicon, was grubby with lotus-dust, settled into spirals around the book.

"Hmm," said Sethennai, poking the book with the end of a pen. "Safety first."

He retrieved his gauntlets from inside his coat and pulled

them on. Csorwe almost never saw him wear them: only when he meant to use magic, it seemed. The gauntlets were made of soft dark leather, and like everything Sethennai owned, they had once been etched with some kind of decoration, now faded with long use and wear.

He removed the lexicon and inspected it, raising his eyebrow. The back cover was scorched and cratered in a deep whorl, and a good chunk of pages were burnt through.

"I'll have to pay Parza for this," he said.

"Sorry," said Csorwe. "It was the nearest thing."

Sethennai grinned at her. His good mood seemed to be restored, as though Oranna's letter really had been a fond message from an old friend. "Quick thinking, though. And if you're going to destroy a book, I'd much rather it be Parza's than one of mine."

He returned to the desk. Where the lexicon had been, there was a similar hole burnt into the surface of the desk. Csorwe cringed a little to see it, because the desk had been expensive, but Sethennai was so cheerful that he hardly seemed to notice.

"Now look at *this*," he said, scooping up a handful of slender objects from the ruined desk. Csorwe craned her neck to see. Cupped in the palm of his hand was a collection of little bones, most no bigger than a matchstick. They had been imperfectly cleaned, and some were still linked by shreds of dry skin and cartilage. "Oh, we're lucky that you didn't completely destroy them. I can use this."

Csorwe slid farther down on the couch, half listening. She needed a drink of water to wash out the taste of rust, but she couldn't coax herself into getting up just yet. This news about

Oranna had jarred her, and she couldn't work out why. It wasn't as though she really thought the House of Silence and all its denizens had ceased to exist the moment she left. But it was not pleasant to learn they were really still so close.

"How did Oranna know our address?" she said, still half buried in the couch.

"I'm afraid that's because I took the risk of writing to her," said Sethennai. "She and I spoke long ago about collaborating on our research. I wanted to know whether she was still interested. I suppose this is her answer."

He was back at his desk, arranging the collection of bones in some kind of order, thimble-sized skull and tiny serrated jawbone and all.

"Guess she said no," said Csorwe, hoping she was right.

"Hmm," said Sethennai. "I'm not sure. You see, this is the skeleton of a small bat."

He sounded bewilderingly pleased. Csorwe muffled a groan in a cushion.

"No such animal is native to northern Oshaar. They like warm places. Oranna has left the House of Silence on her own initiative. This isn't a denial—it's an invitation. She must have a lead on the Reliquary."

Sethennai left the apartment that night after Csorwe finally went to bed, and took the bat skeleton with him. It wasn't unusual for him to disappear overnight. He was usually back by morning, but Csorwe found herself wishing he had stayed behind. She didn't think Oranna was about to turn up at the wineshop and demand that Csorwe go back to the Shrine, or anything like that—but the apartment felt less secure, like a still-usable cup with a single crack.

She couldn't help thinking about Sethennai and Oranna, as little as she wanted to. It was unsettling that she'd missed some huge aspect of his character, and hadn't even known there was anything to miss. It made her wonder what he was like when he was away.

She was woken by a knock on the door. It was still the middle of the night, and Sethennai was back. He tossed her a date pastry and told her to pack a bag.

"The mailship leaves in an hour," he said, as if surprised she didn't already know the plan.

"I'm coming with you?" she said, still surfacing from sleep. "Where are we going?" She knew from long experience that it was no use trying to tell him that she was supposed to have sparring practice that morning and lessons that afternoon.

"Echentyr. The Withered City," he said. This obviously meant nothing to her. "Bring your sword and something warm to wear."

"I always do," she said, already out of bed and searching in her drawer of winter clothes. "How long will we be gone?" she said, but Sethennai had left the room.

Although it was the middle of the night, the dockside was crammed with people. The mailship loomed up ahead, a huge, heavy-laden vessel, listing slightly in its mooring cradle. Csorwe and Sethennai ducked around a woman who was arguing with a crewman about shipping a tank of live eels, and past a team of dockers loading barrels of arrack, and then they were up the gangplank and aboard.

Sethennai paid for a private cabin. Csorwe threw her bag onto the top bunk and peered out of the porthole. The ship had already unmoored and was beginning its ascent to the Gate of Grey Hook.

"Where's Echentyr?" said Csorwe. "I was listening to the others when we got on board. Everyone else seems to think we're going to Torosad."

Torosad was the largest city in Oshaar. It was a long, long way from the House of Silence, but it was still closer than Csorwe ever wanted to go.

"They are going to Torosad," said Sethennai. Perhaps he spotted her scowl, and relented. "Echentyr is in a dead zone. Nobody in their right mind will take us there. When the ship stops to refuel we'll hire a cutter and take ourselves."

They were getting close to the Gate by now. Green light came in through the portholes, swirling and flickering as though thousands of wings beat within it. Csorwe peered out and saw the frame of the Gate itself, big enough to swallow a dozen mailships.

This was the first time Csorwe had Gate-travelled since their arrival in the city. It turned out that the experience wasn't as unpleasant on board a ship as it was on foot. You still had the feeling of dropping out of reality, but at least the solid timbers of the ship didn't change. This was some comfort: Csorwe felt as though she had dropped out of reality when she opened the cursed letter, and was falling still.

"You think Oranna's in Echentyr," she said, picking her words carefully. Sethennai did get annoyed if you asked him too many questions, or if they were foolish. "Because of the bat."

"Quite right," he said. "That bat lived many centuries ago,

when the jungles of Echentyr were still green and growing. But if you look closely at the deep structure of its bones, you see that it's been degraded at every level by magic. There's the original cataclysm that killed everything in Echentyr, of course—hence the dead zone—and then there's another layer of post-mortem damage. I think she probably reanimated the poor little beast."

Normally, Csorwe would just nod and look attentive, but she was still struggling for her footing, trying to work out how to place Oranna in the constellation of Sethennai's concerns.

"And you think she's got the Reliquary," she said. "Or she knows where it is. Or something."

"Hmm," said Sethennai, settling back on the lower bunk. "I don't know about that. I'd be surprised if she's got it outright. I imagine she's persuaded herself she has a lead."

Seeing that Sethennai was planning to rest, Csorwe scrambled up into the top bunk and laid her head on her backpack.

"But I do want to see what's made her think that," he said. "I've been looking for the Reliquary since before you were born. Unless she found something in the library of the House of Silence after all . . ."

Even after all these years, Csorwe knew little more about the Reliquary of Pentravesse than what she had seen in her original vision. It was an eight-sided rosewood box. It was as ancient as it was valuable. And she thought Pentravesse was a person rather than a place, but that was just a hunch.

Csorwe had never been naturally curious, and the House of Silence had always been pretty clear about what you deserved if you poked your nose into things you didn't understand. But she couldn't help wondering what it was he wanted badly enough to swallow his pride and go running after Oranna. Even if he liked her, or had liked her, or at any rate if something close to liking had once existed between them, he wasn't someone you could summon at will.

She gazed up at the crisscrossed timbers of the cabin ceiling, trying to think up a sidelong way to get round to it. "Who was he, sir?" she said, eventually. "Pentravesse, I mean."

"Ah," said Sethennai. She couldn't see him, but he sounded reassuringly warm and drowsy. He had the knack for making himself comfortable almost immediately, even if he had been running and scheming all night. "Pentravesse. The Master of Devices. Yes."

Csorwe should have known what she was getting into. She pulled the blanket over herself and listened.

"Pentravesse was born over three thousand years ago, in Ormary, a country which no longer exists. His origins are not recorded. But he went on to become the greatest magician—the greatest inventor—perhaps the greatest genius who has ever lived.

"Before Pentravesse, you understand, magic was nothing more than prayer. Magicians were prophets, bound to their divinities, mad and sick with their power. They could heal and harm and call down visions, channelling the power directly through their own flesh and bone, but they were limited by the strength of their own bodies and minds.

"Pentravesse was the first to learn how to drain off the power of a patron divinity into the physical realm, to ground and trap it in mundane matter, to order one's workings with control sigils. The development of the mazeship, the alchemical engine, half of modern medicine—all rest on his discoveries. His patron was a goddess of the old order, demanding tribute, fealty, and sacrifice. But I think she too must have had an eye to the future.

"Pentravesse was just like any other mage in one respect, of course. Mortal flesh can only bear so much. Divine power is a wonderful thing, but it is also a poison. When Pentravesse realised he was dying, it's said, he devised a plan. All his knowledge, his unfinished work, his plans, schemes, predictions, secrets, inspirations—all were preserved and contained within the Reliquary.

"Nobody knows exactly what it contains. Most of the scholarship is rather unimaginative. Blueprints for apocalyptic weapons, the formula for eternal life. I like to think he might have been more thoughtful than that. Whoever discovers it will solve one of the greatest puzzles of history. But more than that. Pentravesse changed his world, and all worlds, forever. Whoever claims the Reliquary will inherit that legacy. Imagine, Csorwe, what I could do with that knowledge."

Csorwe had to admit to herself that she had always assumed Sethennai knew everything about magic already. A sleepy vision came to her of Sethennai dressed all in gold, accepting back his crown as Chancellor of all the world. If she had been wide awake she would have rejected this as childish and embarrassing, but in her current state, she could luxuriate in it. In this vision, Oranna and Olthaaros Charossa were long defeated, and Sethennai had the Reliquary in his hands. Csorwe was beside him, watching over him, his most reliable agent. He was Pentravesse's heir, and she was the one person in the world whom he truly trusted.

In time, the soft rumble of Sethennai's voice mingled with the creaking of the timbers, the muted sound of the wind, the distant chime of Gate-song, and lulled her into a half-sleep.

Despite being woken in the middle of the night, despite her lingering lotus hangover, despite the fact that Sethennai was at his most mysterious—she was beginning to feel contented. Sethennai had forgiven her mistake with the letter. He thought that she was worth bringing along, that she would actually be useful.

She tried to forget that Oranna might be waiting for them at the end of the journey. She might, or she might not. And either way, whatever Oranna meant by all this, Sethennai would be there to take Csorwe's side. It was ridiculous to worry that Oranna would somehow drag her back to the House of Silence. Sethennai would never let that happen.

4

The Withered City

C SORWE DOZED THROUGH THE rest of the journey, and stumbled through the refuelling station after Sethennai, still half asleep. The next time she really felt awake, she was sitting in the hired cutter, picking at a steamed bun Sethennai had bought her in the station canteen. Sethennai was at the wheel of the cutter, concentrating on navigation. At first they joined the traffic leaving the station, a great river of ships that split and split and thinned out as vessels moved off toward the Gates that would take them closer to Oshaar, Kasmansitr, Qarsazh, Tarasen. Sethennai broke away as soon as he could do so discreetly, wheeling off in a wide arc, down and around beneath the station. They passed through a narrow and flickering Gate, which spat them out in a part of the Maze that was all jagged needle-spires, stabbing upward in unforgiving ridges. There were no other ships to be seen. Csorwe wriggled down in the cutter, drawing her arms up into the sleeves of her winter tunic.

It was impossible to tell the time in the Maze. When fragments of the sky were visible, they shifted constantly from golden false-dawn to blue false-noon to violet false-dusk, and sometimes to shades of crimson or sea-green never seen in the sky of a living world. By Csorwe's estimation, they travelled for a day and a half, pausing occasionally to eat more steamed buns, which were increasingly unappetising the colder they became.

They were already far from the usual routes. They passed through several Gates, but never saw another ship or another living soul.

By now Csorwe could usually gauge Sethennai's mood from his posture. As they approached their journey's end, he started to sit up straighter, not tense but focused.

Csorwe was almost used to Gate-travel by now, but passing from the Maze into Echentyr was more of a shock than usual: from grey jumbled stone and cold clear wind into a dry stillness. It was just warm enough to be uncomfortable, and the air tasted grimy. Below them the landscape stretched away, flat and yellow-grey, blurred and buried in haze. In the distance were structures that could have been towers, wrapped up in clouds of dust.

Something was wrong with the sky. One moment there was a clear expanse of faded grey—the next it bloomed with fresh spikes and promontories of stone. Pillars the size of mountains speared suddenly through the heavens, then flickered away. All this happened in silence, as if they were nothing more than clouds coming and going.

"This is why they call it a dead zone," said Sethennai, taking the little ship hastily down toward a plateau just below the Gate. "It's not safe to be in the air. We'll be all right on the ground if we keep moving."

They landed and Csorwe hopped out of the cutter, swinging her backpack onto her shoulders. This was the first time Sethennai had ever taken her out on one of his expeditions, and she was determined that he wouldn't regret it. If they found Oranna, she was going to be completely professional.

They climbed down from the plateau. From horizon to horizon, the plain seemed to be littered with fallen columns or pillars. The dust in the air made it difficult to make out detail, so they were close to the ground before Csorwe realised what she was actually seeing. Not columns, but the corpses of colossal trees. Thousands of them, fallen in ranks as though flicked down by a single blow, fanning out from a point of impact far ahead.

Csorwe feared it would be slow going, clambering over the dead trees, but as they reached the ground she saw how big they really were. Each trunk was wider than she was tall, and the spaces between them were like city streets. The trees and the gaps alike were thick with dust, the colour of old paper. Csorwe reached out to touch the nearest tree and found her hand sinking to the wrist in dust. Their footprints were equally deep.

They moved out from the plateau. At first, Csorwe jumped every time a shadow fell suddenly across her path, but it was only the strange formations moving and disappearing in the sky.

"It looks like the Maze up there," she said. The newest formation was a vast spiral complex, like an ammonite seen in a broken mirror.

"It is," he said. "The living world decays and the bones of the Maze come through. The Maze grows out of dead worlds the way mushrooms grow out of tree stumps. In a thousand years or so this place will be entirely eaten up."

They used to talk about the eaten worlds back at the House of Silence. She hadn't entirely understood what that had meant. The eaten worlds and the decline of all things . . . she strode on ahead, shaking her head as if she could physically dislodge the thought.

Up ahead, crossing her path as it wound between two colossal trunks, was a single trail of footsteps, and a row of wheel ruts. Csorwe nudged Sethennai's arm and pointed.

"Look! Do you think it's Oranna? Could she have come this way?"

Sethennai nodded, looking down at her with something very much like pride.

"She must be heading towards the city," he said. "It's not as though there's anywhere else to go."

Csorwe followed Sethennai along the trail, still gloating over his pride like a hot drink on a cold day. She was so busy nursing the feeling that she almost walked straight into the first skeleton.

You might have taken it for another fallen tree. Like them, it was massive, thickly coated in grey-brown dust, lying inert as if discarded where it fell. But then you saw the individual ribs, curving up in an unbroken palisade. You saw the whole helix, looped over and under the wreckage of the forest: the dry bones of a gigantic snake.

Csorwe shrank back against the nearest tree trunk, stricken by the sight of the huge fleshless head. She could have comfortably curled up inside one of its eye sockets. Each one of its teeth was several times larger than her sword.

"Don't worry," said Sethennai. "They can't hurt you."

"Are there more of them?" said Csorwe.

"Many more," he said. "All dead." He sounded almost sorry about it, which was such a rarity that Csorwe forgot her fear immediately. "This won't be the last one you see. But they've been dead for centuries. They're no harm to you."

Sethennai was already moving on. Csorwe couldn't help looking back as they passed the enormous skull, wondering how this creature had looked in life, how it had moved, what kind of prey it must have eaten.

Soon after that they came to a wall. Dust was heaped up against the smooth flanks of the masonry, but above the level of the dust the wall was carved in every direction with friezes: trees and serpents and rivers, wound together as though the stone itself had melted and flowed into shape.

"The city of Echentyr proper," said Sethennai.

There was a huge round opening in the wall, which must once have held a door. Beyond it, and above the wall, Csorwe spotted the same towers she had seen from the air. They were unlike any building she had seen before. They had a strange undulating quality, tapering in and out, branching like corals. It was eerie to stand before a city as silent as this. There was no sign that anybody had ever entered or left, except for the single trail of Oranna's footprints winding in through the empty doorway.

"I suspected as much," said Sethennai, striding into the city.

Beyond the walls, the streets were as wide and deep as river gorges, and they were crisscrossed everywhere Csorwe looked by the bones of serpents. They must have died here in their thousands.

"There were snakes even in the city?" said Csorwe. She had been imagining that the wall existed to keep the serpents out.

"This *was* their city," said Sethennai. "They weren't monsters, Csorwe. The serpents of Echentyr were scholars, philosophers, scientists, poets. In its heyday their city was a beacon."

He led Csorwe on through the streets. At times, the bones were piled so thickly that they had to climb in between the ribs. Csorwe had once seen a frigate being built in the shipyard of

Grey Hook, and some of these ribs were not much smaller than the ship's timbers.

Eventually the footsteps crossed a sort of round open plaza, heaped with skeletons. They were lucky to have Oranna's trail or it would have been difficult to chart a course through the labyrinth of ribs.

This must have been a busy part of the city, Csorwe thought. A market square, maybe. All the philosophers and scientists must have sent their servants out for food occasionally. And then they had all died. Had it been slow? Had they known what was coming?

"What happened to them all?" she said. She remembered something he had said about a magical cataclysm, but she had no idea what that might mean. "Who killed them?"

"A goddess," said Sethennai. He looked pensive, distracted perhaps by the prospect of an encounter with Oranna, but after a moment he gestured to a dais in the middle of the plaza. Csorwe had been focused on finding their way, and hadn't spotted it. On the dais stood a colossal statue of a hooded snake. The sculptor had picked out every one of its scales, like individual petals. It didn't look like any snake Csorwe had seen in life. It had three pairs of eyes set into its head like a row of jewels, and another four pairs worked into the hood, and all down the great ornate body were more eyes. Huge dead stone eyes, staring unblinking at nothing for centuries . . .

"This was how they imagined their goddess to look," said Sethennai. "Iriskavaal the Thousand-Eyed."

"They were killed by their own goddess," said Csorwe. It wasn't so hard to believe. The Unspoken One chose its own sacrifices, after all.

"Yes," said Sethennai, "the serpents were loyal to her for many centuries. By all accounts they loved her. They fought and died for her and their mages drew on her power for their workings." He paused beside a smaller skeleton. The skull only came up to Csorwe's shoulder.

"Iriskavaal had made enemies, as the powerful always do. In the end some of the Echentyri lost faith, and they betrayed her."

Csorwe shivered. It seemed like a mistake to talk about these things in front of the statue. It was too easy to imagine those eyes moving.

"Iriskavaal's throne was shattered into shards," said Sethennai. "Her earthly mansion was laid waste. Her shrines were desecrated. The gods do not die as we die, Csorwe, but they can be reduced, and they can suffer."

Looking up at the statue he made a kind of half gesture, raising his hand toward his face. Csorwe did this occasionally when she began to make the Sign of Sealed Lips, forgetting that she no longer owed the Unspoken One any kind of salute.

"Iriskavaal's suffering was such that she turned from the world," said Sethennai. "Her last act was to curse Echentyr in its entirety. She destroyed all life in this world with a single word. All their temples. All their universities. All that knowledge gone for nothing."

He ran a hand over the lower jaw of the small serpent's skull, brushing away the dust to expose an expanse of bone.

"They paid for their treachery in full," he said.

Csorwe had never seen him melancholy before. She wasn't sure whether he was sorry for the Echentyri or their goddess, or just for the universities. The air was thicker and dustier and warmer inside the city, but she began to feel cold.

"Come on, sir," she said, taking an unspeakable liberty by touching his sleeve. "The trail."

If there was one thing Csorwe had learned it was that you could eventually get used to anything. After a couple of hours in the ruined city, she was no longer surprised by the dust or the bones or the gigantic scale of the place. Even the statues of Iriskavaal lost their power to shock. Even the growth and decay of mountains in the sky no longer bothered her.

They followed the trail up a spiral walkway toward the doors of an enormous round building. Even through the dust, Csorwe could see that its walls had been decorated with more friezes: serpents in crowns and headdresses, serpents pulling trestles, a ceremonial skin-shedding, battles and triumphs. This world had contained a whole history. She began to understand why Sethennai had been so quiet.

"Some people never change," he said, leading Csorwe through another empty circular doorway. "Of course she's here. This was the Royal Library of Echentyr."

Inside, dozens of crescent galleries rose in tiers over a central concourse that could have swallowed an entire neighbourhood in Grey Hook. The Royal Library was as grand and dead as the rest of the city. There seemed to be no books left on the shelves, and Csorwe assumed they had gone to ash along with everything else in Echentyr.

They crossed the concourse. Occasionally a light rain of dust cascaded from the ceiling, making Csorwe jump. She felt like a mouse crossing a field, always aware that a hawk might be somewhere overhead.

"We'll be all right," said Sethennai. To Csorwe's surprise, he made no effort to keep his voice down, and it echoed in the vaults above. Maybe he wasn't interested in taking Oranna unawares. "This place has stood long enough."

They reached the shelves on the far side of the concourse. She saw now that they weren't all empty: most were crammed with narrow clay cylinders, mounted on spindles. They were closely inscribed with a script she didn't recognise, so different from Oshaarun or Tlaanthothei or Qarsazhi that she wouldn't have guessed it was writing if she hadn't been told this was a library.

The cylinders were nearly as tall as Csorwe herself, and when she reached out to touch them they turned on their spindles as though the mechanism had been lately oiled. The clay was rough and cold, snatching warmth from her fingertips.

"Imagine how it must have been," said Sethennai. There was a note of longing in his voice, which faded as he went on. "But I don't know what she's playing at. I've been here already. I combed this place years ago for record of Pentravesse, and I'm certain I didn't miss anything."

"Have you never been wrong, Belthandros?" said a voice from a balcony high above.

Csorwe had hoped she would have time to compose herself before this encounter. She hadn't imagined Oranna would take *them* by surprise.

The librarian leant on the balustrade, looking down at them. She was wearing the yellow habit of the House of Silence, with the hood down and the sleeves rolled up to the elbow.

She looked exactly as Csorwe remembered her, except that now Csorwe had seen enough people to know how to place her. She had soft features and a rounded figure, and in repose she would have had a floating, unearthly prettiness, like a swan seen from a distance. Up close, when you could see her eyes and the sardonic twist of her mouth, you remembered that a swan could break your arm.

Sethennai, of course, betrayed no sign of shock. He laughed. "I don't admit to my mistakes any more than you do. Shall we come up to you, or will you come down to us?"

"I'm occupied," she said. "Come up, if you must."

"I should have remembered how you feel about sinking to my level," he said, steering Csorwe toward another walkway that sloped up to the next floor.

Up in the gallery, Oranna had set out her books and papers on a canvas sheet under one of the shelves. To judge from the volume of notes and sketches, she must have been here for some time.

Oranna looked Csorwe up and down. Csorwe was newly grateful for her clothes and her sword and even her embarrassing Blue Boars haircut. There was not even a trace of recognition on Oranna's face.

"My assistant," said Sethennai, as if that resolved the matter. "I'm surprised the Prioress let you go," he went on, leaning against the balustrade. Oranna made no answer. She had returned to the nearest cylinder, and seemed to be reading it by tracing her index finger over the characters. "Unless you're here without leave," he added. "A devotress of the Unspoken in the stronghold of its ancient enemy."

"Sangrai will forgive me when I bring back the Reliquary," said Oranna without looking up. "And this world is no longer anybody's stronghold." She pursed her lips between her tusks and turned the cylinder back as if she'd missed something.

"Risking the wrath of the Unspoken for a myth?" said Sethennai. He knelt over the canvas to inspect her drawings.

"You know as well as I do that it's real," she said. "Intact and extant, if you remember."

"Well, it's not here," said Sethennai.

"Because you couldn't find it?" said Oranna. She was still looking at the cylinder, but Csorwe could tell she had stopped turning it. "I see."

"You wouldn't have written to me if you weren't interested in what I had to say about it," he said.

Csorwe was suspended between relief that Oranna didn't really seem to have noticed she was there, and embarrassment that she had to witness whatever was going on here. She had never heard Sethennai talk to anyone like this, or anyone dare to respond in kind.

After a long pause Oranna spoke again. "Why shouldn't it be here? Iriskavaal was Pentravesse's patron, was she not? It's known that he visited Echentyr before its destruction. Some of my sources suggest the Reliquary was created here."

"Even so," said Sethennai. "The Reliquary has been stolen and moved and hidden a dozen times in a dozen worlds since its creation."

"So we've heard," said Oranna. "But what if we were wrong? *I'm* not too proud to admit it's possible."

"That's absurd. It couldn't have survived the cataclysm."

"I don't see why not," said Oranna. "It would have been within Iriskavaal's power to spare it."

"It was within her power to spare the Echentyri, too," said Sethennai.

"The Echentyri defied her," said Oranna. "Pentravesse was loyal to his death. In any case, hear me out. The account of the first appropriation of the Reliquary is over twelve centuries old, and it has always been taken for truth. But I have a new, contemporaneous source which suggests it was an invention."

"Do you really?" said Sethennai. Behind a thin veil of irony, Csorwe could tell he was interested. His ears twitched like a cat's.

"In *The Record of Isjesse*," she said.

Sethennai frowned. "*Isjesse* is incomplete. I've read the fragments and there's nothing about—"

"You've read some of the fragments," she said. From the pocket of her habit she withdrew a slim leather case, opened the catch, and held it out to Sethennai, although she wouldn't actually hand it over to him.

"Oranna . . ." he said.

Csorwe had been keeping her distance, reckoning that she probably wasn't needed here, but she heard the warning note in Sethennai's voice. His frown deepened, and his ears were drawn up tight against his skull.

Inside the case was a rag of wrinkled papyrus, about the size of Csorwe's palm, covered in minute, pale handwriting.

"I've seen this," he said. "I never translated it, but someone tried to sell it to me, years ago. It's a trick."

The caution in his voice made the hairs on the back of Csorwe's neck prickle. She couldn't understand how, but they were in danger. She slipped away from them, glancing down toward the concourse below. How many other entrances were there? They were connected to the higher galleries by other walkways and bridges, but the only access to their gallery from below was the way they had come.

"More fool you," said Oranna. "I *have* translated it. And I have consulted with the Unspoken. It is genuine."

"I don't doubt it's genuine," said Sethennai. "But it's a trick. It's from Olthaaros Charossa's personal library in Tlaanthothe. I could never work out why he released it. But it's clear now that he intended to lure me here."

Oranna's eyes narrowed momentarily with anger. "Of course it's about you," she said.

"Yes," said Sethennai. "And I can see that's very irritating for you. Believe me, I'm extremely irritated with myself for paying any attention to your letter in the first place. But there isn't anything we can do about it now. Olthaaros must have a watch on the Gate. We are not safe here. We may have very little time to prepare ourselves."

Csorwe couldn't see any sign of intruders on the other galleries. They hadn't seen any other footsteps, or heard voices as they entered, but then they hadn't imagined they would be followed.

She peered over the balustrade. There, at the main entrance of the Royal Library, a cloud of dust was forming, like the mist at the foot of a waterfall.

"Sir," she said. "Look!"

"Ah. Very little time at all," said Sethennai. "Olthaaros is here. Or one of his henchmen."

"May the Unspoken eat your heart while you still live, Belthandros," said Oranna, sweeping her books and papers into a bag. "Who is Olthaaros?"

"An old friend of mine," said Sethennai.

"Well," she said, hoisting the bag onto her shoulders. "Since you've thoroughly ruined my work here, I think I'll leave the two of you to your reunion."

"I take it you no longer want to collaborate," said Sethennai.

Oranna laughed, bitterly. "You don't know the meaning of the word," she said, and stalked away. Despite everything, Csorwe felt a small measure of relief to see that Oranna was leaving. Whatever her claim on Sethennai had or hadn't been, it was over.

Oranna leapt with surprising nimbleness onto a higher walkway, and from there to one of the arc-bridges, which crossed the concourse from above. There must be a way out higher up. So it wasn't too late to escape if they had to.

"Should we go after her?" said Csorwe, as Oranna's footsteps died away and the hem of her yellow robe vanished in the upper stories. She didn't say *Should we run?* because she knew Sethennai would not.

"No," said Sethennai. "I want to see this. I want to see who this is, and what they have to say." It wasn't often that he was so direct about his intentions. He was already pulling on his gauntlets.

Below, in the concourse, the dust cloud rolled toward them, swelling outward and upward. They began to hear the noise of it, a sandpapery hiss. The dust roiled like a mass of leeches around some central moving point, a dark speck at the heart of the storm.

"Csorwe, get down," he muttered, stretching and clawing his hands.

She crouched obediently, peeping between the balusters. Sethennai knelt beside her.

The dust subsided. At its heart was a man in a black wide-brimmed hat. He walked out to the centre of the concourse, and stopped. He looked around. Csorwe imagined him sniffing the air.

Underneath his hat, he wore a metal visor, and he was dressed all in black, black petals of hide and tarred metal from neck to ankle. They flapped and clinked as he walked.

Csorwe kept low, watching hungrily, as though by seeing she could keep the situation under control. The truth was that she had no idea what might happen. Olthaaros was the only person Sethennai ever admitted had beaten him. She clung to the balustrade, digging her nails into the stone.

"I can help," she said, pushing away her fear. It was no use to her now. She couldn't be afraid. "I have my sword." Never mind that she had only ever used it for practice.

"I know," said Sethennai. "But you must run, if it comes to it."

"It won't come to it," she said, staring up at him. Knowing that something might happen to him was one thing. Hearing him admit it was another.

"Olthaaros is not a merciful man—"

"I don't care," she said. "I won't run. You know I won't."

"Belthandros!" called the man in black, before Sethennai could answer. He was looking up at the gallery. He knew exactly where they were.

Under his breath, Sethennai gave a soft bark of laughter, and seemed to relax.

"Couldn't even be bothered to turn up yourself," he muttered. Then he stood up and leant his folded arms on the balustrade.

"Akaro," he called. "How nice to see you. Are you taking my side at last?"

"Taking *your* side?" said Akaro. He sounded younger than Sethennai. Perhaps much younger. He scanned the pattern of galleries and seemed to spot the walkway. "Come down and face me."

"How tiresome," said Sethennai, loudly, before turning back

to Csorwe. "I can handle this one. He's an idealist. Stay here. He won't hurt you."

Sethennai unfolded himself languidly and went down to meet him.

"I suppose Olthaaros has sent you," said Sethennai, standing at the bottom of the walkway.

Akaro looked away. "Olthaaros is the Chancellor of Tlaanthothe, the leader of my city, my mentor, and my friend. Yes. He sent me to find you."

"Olthaaros was *my* friend," said Sethennai. "My friend, my student, and my colleague. Just like you. He wanted Tlaanthothe, so he betrayed me and sent me into exile. And now he has sent you to murder me. That seems a little vindictive, don't you think? I am doing my best to live a quiet life. Olthaaros already has what he wants."

"He knows you're still looking for the Reliquary," said Akaro, miserably. "Sethennai, he only let you *live* because you said you'd given it up."

"If he believed that then he's much stupider than I thought he was."

"It's dangerous," said Akaro. "Look where it's led you. Look what Iriskavaal did to her own people! Echentyr is dust, and Ormary is *gone*. That knowledge is better lost. She was a monster, and Pentravesse was nothing but her puppet."

Sethennai laughed. "Wise words from Olthaaros' most devoted mannequin."

"Don't do this. Come with me," said Akaro. "If I tell him you came quietly, and—"

Sethennai laughed again, and Akaro looked more miserable still. "You do know that Olthaaros sent you because he knew it would hurt you?" said Sethennai. "He could have sent any one of his attack dogs. He could have tried sending *Psamag*, and wouldn't that have been entertaining. But he knows you were loyal to me. He's testing you. He wants to know just how low you'll sink for him."

Akaro's shoulders slumped, but Csorwe wasn't fooled. He was already falling into a fighting stance. He had no weapon she could see, but a wizard didn't need one. She prayed Sethennai had spotted what he was doing.

"You must know how deeply I regret this," said Akaro.

"No more deeply than I regret your stubbornness," said Sethennai. "It's a shame. I thought you were cleverer than the rest of Olthaaros' circle."

"I hope I can prove equal to any in courage, at least," said Akaro thickly, as if on the verge of tears, and he took a step toward Sethennai, and raised his hands. A wave of force threw Sethennai back, but he caught himself in time and landed on his feet, hitting the ground with a twist that threw a wall of dust up in Akaro's face.

This was nothing like the fights Csorwe had witnessed in Grey Hook. It was the kind of thing she had once imagined: two wizards from the ancient world, meeting in a ruin to fight out their grudges. It should have been a wonderful thing to see. But she found herself frozen in place, with the sweat running down the back of her neck.

They fought in silence, with the occasional hiss or grunt of impact, driving invisible waves and blades of force at one another. They moved like duellists without blades, lunging and parrying, but without once touching each other. Black petals and green brocade flashed as they dodged and struck. From the way they mirrored one another it could be a dance, except that the force of each impact rattled the cylinders on their spindles, yards away.

At first the two seemed evenly matched, but she knew Sethennai hadn't been expecting this and hadn't had time to prepare himself for the fight. He seemed to be slowing. She remembered everything Sethennai had ever told her about how magic weakened the body and wearied the mind. She didn't know how long he could last.

If something happened to him—no. She forced herself to confront it. If he *died here,* there would be nothing for her, even if Akaro spared her life. She would be nobody—worse than nobody—someone who had betrayed her god and failed her master. Who would have her? What would she do?

Unspoken One, she thought. *Give him strength. Let him live, I beg you.* She was no mage, but she could still pray. She pushed aside her guilt for calling to the god she had abandoned. For Sethennai, it was worth it.

Sethennai struck as though throwing a punch at Akaro, striking sparks where his feet touched the ground. Akaro parried, and lunged back, and just for a second seemed to throw Sethennai off-balance.

And everything became very clear in Csorwe's mind. There was nothing in the world that mattered but this. She didn't need the Unspoken One. She had her own sword, and Akaro didn't know she was there.

Sethennai had told her to stay where she was, and that Akaro wouldn't hurt her. But Csorwe didn't deserve to live if she abandoned him now. This was what it came down to. If Sethennai died here she would avenge him or die with him. This was what she had been shaped for. This was the point of her existence.

She drew her sword, rose silently, and crept down the walk-way, staying out of sight.

She saw what happened next as slowly and clearly as if it was a story someone was reading to her. Sethennai drew back, clearly mustering power for an all-out attack. Akaro feinted toward him, gliding past at an angle, and Sethennai fell for it. He struck too soon, and Akaro jabbed him in the chest, summoning a shock wave that shook the galleries and brought another hail of dust from the ceiling.

Sethennai's foot slipped on a loose stone and he tripped. Akaro did not miss his opportunity. He kicked Sethennai's feet from under him, bringing him to his knees.

"Surrender," said Akaro, breathing hard. "Home—I will tell them at home—I will tell them you cooperated."

Sethennai gazed up at him, and said nothing. Csorwe crept forward. Her heart raced. Every grain of dust seemed to thunder beneath her feet. The hilt of the sword was warm to the touch. She braced it in both hands.

"Sethennai!" she called, and as she did so she struck, plunging the sword into Akaro's back, at the place where one petal of armour met another. There was a terrible noise. Akaro gave a broken cry and fell, his limbs shaking and twitching in the dust. Csorwe pulled out her sword and stabbed him again, pinning him down until he stopped wriggling.

He was dead. It was strange that it had been easy. As easy as her exercises. She pulled out the sword and wiped the blade clean. Tlaanthothei had bright red blood, but she noticed distantly that where Akaro's was pooling on the floor of the library it looked as dull and dark as her own.

Sethennai rose to his feet, straining for breath. He looked at Csorwe and laughed with delight.

"Brilliant child!" he said. "My god. Excellent Csorwe. It's a shame, of course. What a shame. Akaro was never so stupid when he was my pupil."

Csorwe didn't say anything. She wasn't sure what she should say. Normally she would have wrapped Sethennai's praise around herself like a fur-lined cloak, but she barely heard what he said. She was vaguely surprised that he was laughing, but perhaps he was glad to be alive.

She had grown up among the dead but she had never killed anyone before. It was hard to make sense of it, to see that this man who had been fighting and talking only a minute before was now nothing more than the skeletal priestesses under the House of Silence. Less, in fact, because he would not rise again.

Csorwe helped Sethennai arrange the dead man on the ground, laying him out on his back as if he were asleep. He was heavy. It must have required such power to move so lightly. Once it was done, she realised she was shivering, and sheathed her sword so she didn't drop it.

When this was done Sethennai knelt at Akaro's head and unfastened the visor of his helmet. It came away easily and he laid it on the ground, a bowl of dull metal.

"Foolish boy," said Sethennai again. Akaro *had* been young, or young as the Tlaanthothei reckoned it. His eyes had rolled back in his head, and streams of blood ran from his nose and mouth, marring the delicate features. "Idiot boy. Perhaps Olthaaros thought—well. Well. There was no persuading him."

And now there's no undoing it, thought Csorwe. *I can't take it back.* Akaro was dead. There had been no other way to protect

Sethennai. So this was just another thing she was going to have to learn how to manage.

Sethennai folded Akaro's hands on his chest and covered him with a cloak, and they left him in the library of Echentyr.

For a week or two, Csorwe and Sethennai drifted from one backwater to another. Sethennai picked an obscure route through the Maze, following some design of his own. This was done carelessly, as though it was his personal whim and a great joke to continually double back on themselves and spend a long time laying false trails.

Csorwe was happy to be on the road again. Navigating new places, staying vigilant for new threats, tiring herself out by walking and carrying the bags, all meant she could keep her mind off the subject of Akaro's death, although he appeared in her dreams sometimes, drenched in blood and still walking.

One night, they took shelter in a ruined chapel, in a lonely world on the borders of Qarsazh. Sethennai was tending the fire. Csorwe lay in her bedroll, looking up at the shattered icons of the Qarsazhi pantheon and thinking distantly of Parza. He had never found out what happened to his lexicon.

"Will we ever go back to Grey Hook?" she said. The Blue Boars would be back from their assignment by now, and she wanted to ask them how it had gone. If they went home, back to their routine, she was sure she would feel normal again.

After a while Sethennai spoke, still prodding at the fire.

"I'm not convinced it's safe for us to go back," he said. "Would you be very sorry to leave it behind?"

"I miss my own bed, I guess," she said. She didn't want to

admit to missing the Boars. It was enough for Sethennai to have doubted her loyalty once. "And all our stuff is there." She knew even as she spoke that it wasn't going to happen. If Sethennai had meant them to go back, they would have gone back. "But I don't mind," she added hastily.

However much she had hoped to stay, it was time to put it aside. Grey Hook was in the past, and her future was with Sethennai.

"I've made up my mind," he said. "Now that Olthaaros has found me once, he'll find me again, and I don't wish to repeat that ugly scene with Akaro. And you've proven you're ready. As much as I've been enjoying this little holiday, it's really about time that we returned to Tlaanthothe."

5

Two Completely Predictable Things

T HE DESERT CALLED THE Speechless Sea was of black
sand, scattered with shards of volcanic glass that sparkled
like the stars. A chain of hills emerged from this desert, as
though the night sky was punctured by a row of vertebrae. Built
on the largest of these was the city of Tlaanthothe.

The city's perimeter was a hexagonal wall of gleaming black
rock, colossal in every dimension and monotonously ugly. Its outer
faces were striated with useless columns of lava, frozen in place like
an array of icicles. At every corner of the hexagon was a watchtower,
and set into the south face, like a carbuncle in a ring, was a fortress
of the same blasted stone. Outside the city, near the fortress, a small
town had scattered itself across the foothills, looking as though a
convoy had crashed and spontaneously generated houses.

Before continuing to the city proper and its Gate, the
mailship descended into this flotsam town, and Sethennai
disembarked. He had kept the forged paperwork identifying
him as Dr. Pelthari, but was now dressed in the cap and gown
of a Tlaanthothei lawyer. Csorwe was dressed as his valet, in a
formal suit with a stiff collar. She scratched the back of her neck.
Sethennai took a harmless, childlike delight in disguises, but her
tolerance for the suit was wearing thin.

An official stamped their papers and welcomed Dr. Pelthari to town. Another official looked through their things, but found nothing amiss. They were travelling light, since almost all their possessions were still in Grey Hook.

They took rooms in a shabby boardinghouse across the road, as if this was another ordinary stay in another ordinary town. All shabby boardinghouses had their own unique smell. This one was mostly onions, with a hint of drains. Csorwe cleaned her sword to calm her nerves.

Tlaanthothe and the wall were visible from the windows of the boardinghouse, as present and as inaccessible as a thundercloud.

"So how do we get in?" said Csorwe, peering up at the city. She had to assume there was a plan. Sethennai always gave the impression of having a plan.

Sethennai sat at the table under the window, lacing his fingers across his stomach.

"Well, don't get any ideas about shinning up the wall itself," he said. "Plenty have made the attempt and died. There's only one way into Tlaanthothe, and that's through the fortress in the wall."

If it was that easy, Sethennai could have gone home long ago, but he was obviously working up to something.

"I guess Olthaaros has guards there," said Csorwe.

"More than that, I'm afraid," said Sethennai. "The fortress is currently occupied by an entire battalion of mercenaries. Olthaaros brought them in to help throw me out of Tlaanthothe in the first place. Nobody enters or leaves the city, through the fortress or the Gate, without passing through their security." Sethennai leant back in his chair, gazing up at the ceiling, and put his feet up on the table. "All this for me. It's been years. Olthaaros really must have hated me."

"Because of the Reliquary," said Csorwe.

"Among other things," said Sethennai. "I hope you didn't listen too hard to everything Akaro said. Olthaaros doesn't care about whether the Reliquary's dangerous. He doesn't want to use it. He just doesn't want me to find it because he can't bear the idea of someone else getting something he doesn't have." He rolled his eyes. "That's why he took the city from me. He's from an old noble family, and he couldn't stand the idea of someone like me getting the Chancellorship. The Reliquary would just add insult to injury."

"Someone like you, sir?" said Csorwe. She had never really asked him about his past. Something had always warned her off, a sense that this was a bruise that Sethennai did not want prodded—and after all, he never bothered her about her life before he'd met her.

"Oh, I'm nobody," said Sethennai with immense satisfaction. "Or at least I was. Sadly, becoming somebody has its downsides. I'd never make it past security into the city."

"You really think they'd recognise you?" said Csorwe.

"Well, I'm fairly recognisable," he said. True: he was tall even for a Tlaanthothei, and twice as broad as the average. He could shave his hair and beard if he had to, but it would be hard to hide his stature. "And Olthaaros has sensible reasons for wanting to keep me out, even now."

He sat up straighter, leaning on the table to get a better view of the city. "I have been gone from Tlaanthothe for longer than I care to think about," he said. "And I dearly love my city. But it is not just homesickness that calls me back. My patron goddess has her earthly mansion within the city. I have been out of the Siren's presence for too long. My powers run low, like a stream after long drought. Even little Akaro nearly defeated me, as you saw. But once I get back into the city . . . Olthaaros knows he cannot face me at full strength. To throw me out in the first place he needed a whole swarm of allies he has since alienated. All I need is to get through the fortress, and then he's mine."

"They'll know we're coming," said Csorwe. She gave the blade of her sword one last wipe with the oiled cloth. "Since I—since Akaro won't have come back. The soldiers will be looking out for you."

"Quite," said Sethennai.

"I could do it," said Csorwe. She hadn't realised until that moment what Sethennai was getting at. She replaced her sword in its scabbard, trying not to let the sparks of apprehension and excitement show in her face.

"Even if they know you have an assistant," she said, "I could be anyone. People don't notice me. I could do it." She worried at times that Sethennai might think she'd forgotten what she owed him. He never mentioned it, but she owed him her life, and the obligation gnawed on her like a worm in an apple. This was something she could do for him on her own.

Sethennai smiled. "Yes. You could."

But first, there were preparations to make. Sethennai spent a few days away from the boardinghouse, secretly writing to his contacts and meeting with their agents. Getting into the city was the hardest part, but there would still be barriers to cross once they were inside, and for that he needed more allies than Csorwe.

While he was gone, Csorwe studied climbing and creeping

around the boardinghouse, until she could crawl quietly across the ceiling beams and navigate the creaking hallway without making a sound. She also practiced with the sword, for the first time since she had killed Akaro. It felt good to have it properly back in her hands, as though she were a knife that had finally been sharpened after lying dull for weeks.

Sethennai came home to find her rehearsing the forms before the speckled mirror.

"Ah," he said. "I'm afraid you won't be taking that into the fortress."

Csorwe lowered the blade, catching her breath. "—what? Why, sir?"

"Because you're going to pose as a servant looking for work at the fortress, and they might be a bit surprised if you turn up with a deadly weapon."

"Oh," said Csorwe. Her shoulders dropped. "I was thinking I would go as a mercenary recruit." She had worked hard on her training with the Blue Boars, and she wanted to prove that her time with the mercenary company had made her more useful to him, not less. She still squirmed with guilt whenever she recalled that Sethennai had once suggested she might leave him for the Boars.

"And if they were ordinary mercenaries, I'd be tempted to let you," he said. "But they are not. They are led by General Psamag." He glanced at her, possibly expecting a reaction. "Ha! I forget how young you are. Psamag is, or was, a famous Oshaaru warlord. Infamous. Notorious. Long before you were born he commanded armies for the clan-liege of Torosad."

Csorwe wondered whether it was strange how little she knew about her homeland. She had never visited Torosad or any of the other great cities of Oshaar. Nor did she want to, but it was odd that her tusks marked her to the whole world as Oshaaru, when in fact she had seen less of the country than Sethennai had.

Well, Torosad with its warlords and clan-lieges had never been her place. The area around the House of Silence was nothing more than a coin-sized patch of mountain and forest in the far corner of any proper map of Oshaar, and even that was long behind her.

"Psamag had a lurid reputation," said Sethennai. "Killing prisoners, massacring civilians, burning villages, heads on stakes—everything rumour can devise, and most of it true— although I do *not* think it was true that he had an elite force of undead soldiers as his personal bodyguard. Eventually the clan-liege of Torosad found him to be a liability. So he was banished, and finding, as one does, that he had a set of skills for which people were prepared to pay him, he became a mercenary. If you were rich, Psamag became the man you needed for the nasty jobs, the things you didn't want to admit to your civilised friends. So, of course, he was the man Olthaaros needed to help get rid of me."

"Still don't see why I couldn't pretend to work for him."

"Because he's smart," said Sethennai. "He's wilier than Olthaaros. And if he caught you it wouldn't be a clean death."

"But I'm still going to be sneaking into his fortress," said Csorwe.

"As a servant you'll probably never run into him. Everyone will think you're harmless, and you can explore the fortress as much as you like if you pretend you're running errands."

Csorwe sighed. He was right, of course, as much as she would have liked to bring her sword. "Can I take a knife?"

"If you must," he said. "But do not underestimate Psamag. The only reason he's still here is that he feels Olthaaros owes him more money. I have to admit it does bring me some joy to know that Olthaaros has found it impossible to get rid of him. Psamag describes it as *safeguarding his investment*. He's dangerous, and he has a long memory. The best thing you can do is to stay out of his way as much as you possibly can."

Three days later, Csorwe made the trek across the Speechless Sea to the walls of Tlaanthothe. When it got dark she slept under the stars in a rock crevice, like a scorpion.

The fortress in the wall was constructed around an enormous door, as heavy, ugly, and impenetrable as the wall itself, though perforated at the base with several doors of more reasonable size. The doors were staffed at all hours by armed guards, who checked the passports and permits of those who hoped to pass through, in wagons or on foot.

The traffic approaching the city was constant and slow. The queue of wagons, carriages, cattle, and small mazeships tailed back into the desert for nearly a mile, and the roadside was dotted with stalls selling ironwort tea and hot skewers to the travellers.

Close up, the fortress itself was a jagged mass of stone protruding from the desert. It looked older, as though the earth had coughed up a clot of crenellated rock that had stuck in its throat. On top was the Great Gate of Tlaanthothe, like an emerald on top of an incredibly ugly jewel box, where the big ships came in.

Csorwe unfolded herself from her crevice and dropped lightly from ledge to slope to the surface of the road. It was early morning, still half dark. She slipped into the queue close to the door, behind a large covered wagon bearing the brandmark of a Qarsazhi weaving company.

She watched as the wagoners exchanged paperwork with the fortress guards. Then there came a painful groan as one of the smaller doors creaked open. The wagon passed inside and the gates slammed shut.

Csorwe greeted the fortress guards with false brightness. It was the first time she had spoken Tlaanthothei to anyone but Sethennai and she was self-conscious about her pronunciation.

They spent a worryingly long time inspecting her passport and letter of reference, but Sethennai had put some effort into forging these, and they must have been convincing enough to pass, because they handed them back to her.

"You need to take your coat off," said one of the guards.

"What?" said Csorwe, instantly on guard. "Why?"

Under the lamb-leather coat she was wearing a plain knee-length tunic and sandals, suitable for her disguise as a servant. But underneath that she had a very serious knife strapped to her leg.

"We're searching everyone who comes into the fortress," he said. At least he didn't sound sleazy about it. Maybe it was too early in the morning.

She took off the coat obediently and handed it over, stony-faced. One of them shook it and turned out the pockets, finding nothing. It was a good thing she had left all her travelling gear hidden up in the hills. Unless they'd find it suspicious that she didn't have anything on her? How thoroughly were they going to search? Sethennai had been right. It had been a mistake to bring any kind of weapon. What should she say? Could she claim she'd been frightened of bandits on her journey?

She was so glazed that it took her a second to realise the guard was handing her coat back to her.

"You can go," he said.

They waved her on through the smallest door. Beyond was an enormous wagonyard, full of people, pack animals, and vehicles. Nobody paid any attention to a servant girl. Csorwe's nerves were frayed from her encounter with the guards, so she was glad not to be bothered.

She kept her head down and her eyes on the ground as she made for the kitchens. This was her own idea, and she was pleased with it. Any place as big as the fortress needed somebody to cook and wash up, and Csorwe had always been good at kitchen chores.

The kitchens were loud and very crowded. Csorwe made herself useful—fetching water or chopping garlic or taking a turn at the roasting spit. It was several hours before anyone realised she was not meant to be there.

"I'm new, sir," she said, staring up into the folds of a pristine apron, and the thick moustache that loomed above it between a pair of narrow tusks.

The cook raised one eyebrow.

"New today," she said. "I might have come to the wrong place."

"Hm," said the cook. "Maybe."

"Please, sir," she said, making her voice soft and plaintive. "They told me I'd find a job here." She held out her false passport and a letter of recommendation from the alleged Dr. Pelthari.

The cook glanced at the melon that Csorwe had been seeding and slicing. She was handy with a knife, so this was neat work. Each slice was so fine that the flesh of the melon was translucent, like a wafer of ice. He looked around the kitchen, one side of his moustache twisting up as he chewed his lip.

"Well, heaven knows we could use another pair of hands. Fine." He took her papers away and handed them off to someone, and that was the last she heard of them.

She sliced melons for the rest of the day, and when the sun set, she followed a group of the other girls to their bunkroom.

"New, are you?" one of them said, resigned but not unkind. Most of the kitchen staff here were Tlaanthothei or Oshaaru, but this was a Qarsazhi-looking girl, slight and pretty, with coppery skin and very straight black hair in a long braid. "I'm Taymiri. Guess I'd better show you where to get sheets and things."

Taymiri showed her to a spare bunk. Csorwe didn't say much, suddenly fearful. Her plan was flimsy at best. It was only a matter of time before somebody realised she wasn't who she said she was, and that she wasn't meant to be there.

"You're quiet, aren't you?" said Taymiri. "Homesick, I expect. It's not so bad here once you get used to it. I'll show you 'round tomorrow."

Csorwe lay awake in her bunk. She had got used to the sound of Grey Hook at night. The fortress was different: footsteps, echoes, chains, and the rumblings of great mechanisms.

There were no windows in the bunkroom, and the doors were shut at night. Only a flickering band of torchlight came in at the threshold.

All she needed to do was find a way to get Sethennai past the fortress without being noticed by the soldiers. They had been right to assume there was no use trying a direct approach. There must be another way. The fortress was older than the city itself, Sethennai had told her, and there were strange things under the earth: secret ways, secret rooms, and caves that reached deep beneath the desert.

She would need to use every moment she could to explore the fortress, to learn its ways and routines. There would be some way to sneak Sethennai through. She would do what she always did: she would work, and watch, and listen, and wait.

Once everyone else was asleep she unstrapped the knife from her leg and hid it under her mattress in the bunkroom. Just in case.

By the end of the first week everyone seemed to have accepted Csorwe's presence. After three years travelling with Sethennai, Csorwe thought she might have forgotten how to deal with girls her own age, but it was just like being back in the House of Silence. She was used to living like this, elbow to elbow. It had its constants. Aggravation, thwarted hope, and gossip: each fed the other like the three-headed snake that had been advertised in Grey Hook's Market of Curiosities. Most of the others were from poor families out in the sticks. They weren't very interested in Csorwe, but they were grateful to her for taking on the duties they disliked, mostly carrying barrels up and down the stairs. Even better, they were busy enough not to notice that Csorwe was the first to take on any task that involved visiting restricted or inaccessible parts of the fortress.

Taymiri was the leader of the bunkroom, it turned out, because she had been there longest, and was both calm and ruthless. She liked Csorwe, or at least she liked Csorwe's efficiency. She had ambitions beyond the kitchen, and saw Csorwe as a useful cat's paw, or even an ally.

Csorwe learned that Taymiri's mother had been cut off by house and Church in Qarsazh for conceiving Taymiri while still unmarried. Taymiri's ambition was to become rich enough that she could find her grandparents in Qarsazh and throw them out in the streets.

One afternoon, Csorwe was napping in the bunkroom, enjoying her allotted half hour's rest before preparations for dinner. Taymiri came to Csorwe's bunk and shook her briskly awake.

"Shh!" said Taymiri. "Come with me. I don't want the others in on this."

Csorwe dressed hurriedly and followed Taymiri out of the bunkroom to the winding darkness of the corridor. All the passages were close and narrow and uncomfortably warm. Csorwe wished too late that she had brought her knife, just in case, but there would have been no way to hide it from Taymiri.

"What's happening?" she said, once they were clear of the bunkroom.

"Some of the General's table staff are sick," said Taymiri. "There's a big dinner on and they need two from the kitchens to fetch and carry plates."

Csorwe nodded, suppressing her excitement and alarm. Sethennai had told her to stay out of General Psamag's way. But then . . . she had never seen the General's quarters, and she needed more information if she was going to make progress. She had explored the fortress as thoroughly as she could, from the cellars up, but she knew there were regions that were closed to her. There were undercellars, and caves beneath the undercellars, and hollow passages in the walls that seemed to have no openings. It might be risky to cross paths with the General, but it would be idiotic to miss this opportunity to cover new territory. As a waitress she would be virtually invisible, and perfectly safe.

Taymiri was as agitated as Csorwe had ever seen her.

"And I'm not *that* type of girl, of course, but if I'm going to catch anyone's eye I don't see why it shouldn't be one of the General's officers," said Taymiri as they hurried toward the stairs to the upper levels.

"Right," said Csorwe. Stranger things had certainly happened.

"Maybe we can even find one for you, Soru," said Taymiri, becoming magnanimous. This was what they all called her, an amendment of her real name, which suited the Tlaanthothei accent. It meant "sparrow." "What kind would you prefer?"

Csorwe did not know what to say. She considered what Taymiri wanted in a man. "Rich?"

Taymiri slapped a hand over her mouth to stop the sound of her laughter ringing out in the hall. "Obviously. But apart from that!"

"I don't know," said Csorwe. After a pause: "Tall?"

For a while, back in Grey Hook, Csorwe had thought it was possible she was interested in one of her tutors, a broad-shouldered ex-mercenary with a pleasant smile. However, after careful observation she concluded that *he* was interested only in young men from the Pretty Birds Gentleman's House of Entertainment.

"They'll all be *tall*," said Taymiri, and seemed to give up.

In a back pantry, Csorwe and Taymiri were met by an official, hardly any older than they were, who gave them a change of uniform.

The official was Tlaanthothei, like Sethennai, with dark brown skin, pointed leaf-shaped ears, and close-cropped curly hair. He had the basic shape of a wrought-iron railing and a look of focused, furious anxiety. His ears twitched every half a minute or so.

"General Psamag has certain requirements of his waiting staff," he said, sounding like he had a cold, and glaring at Csorwe and Taymiri, plainly doubting their ability to meet those requirements. There followed a lecture on the placement of cutlery, delivered in a monotone. "There will be drinks, the General is going to make a speech, and then there will be three courses, like I explained. Any questions?"

"Think you'll have any luck marrying him, Taymiri?" said Csorwe, once he had gone.

"*That* was Talasseres Charossa," said Taymiri. "He is a puckered arsehole. Or, I guess, he's our liaison from Chancellor Olthaaros. He's here to try and tell the General what to do, even though everyone knows if General Psamag wanted to, he could throw Olthaaros out on his face, like they did with the old Chancellor."

It was lucky for Csorwe that she was good at keeping a straight face.

"Did you say Charossa?" she said, after a decent interval. "Isn't that the Chancellor's name?"

"Oh, yes," said Taymiri. "He's his *nephew*. Probably why he got the job."

Csorwe tucked that little piece of knowledge away for later consideration. Maybe it meant she ought to avoid Talasseres Charossa. Or maybe she ought to stay close and try to find out whom he spoke to, in case he gave anything away? Without Sethennai's guidance she felt adrift. There were endless choices to make, hundreds of possible directions.

She reminded herself that she did have a plan. Tonight she was going to stay in the background and get a sense of the main players at the fortress, their loyalties and alliances. That was a useful place to start, and it would keep her safe and inconspicuous. Sethennai couldn't object to that.

The upper levels of the fortress were surprisingly beautiful. Here the floors were of polished hardwood, the walls were hung with fine tapestries, and the dust sparkled in beams of sunlight from above. From somewhere close by, Csorwe could hear the sound of a woman singing. It was not at all how she had imagined the General's personal quarters. It was almost disappointing.

The walls of the dining hall were crammed with hunting trophies. Boars, stags, the frail antelope of the Speechless Sea, lions and tigers, elephant heads and mammoth heads, side by side, philosophical in death: all stared down glassily from a dark expanse of hardwood panelling. The walls bloomed with horns and spines and crests, unfurling themselves across the panels like an exuberant moss of bone. Psamag had skimmed the riches of many worlds, and brought back their heads to be stuffed.

"Stop dawdling!" said Taymiri, who had already memorised everything she might need to know in this situation. She seized Csorwe's arm and towed her down to the vast dining table, where the others were adjusting place settings. The other waiting staff were not pleased by the appearance of Csorwe and Taymiri, but they had no choice in the matter.

Beyond the table, at the far end of the hall, the floor dropped away into a pit. There was no rail to warn the unwary, just shining boards and then a sheer drop. From the dining table, Csorwe could not see what was in the pit. The others moved around the table with choreographed precision, paying it no mind. Csorwe kept quiet, as usual, and listened.

It seemed that this dinner was given in honour of Captain Tenocwe, the favourite of General Psamag, who had won some kind of victory on Psamag's behalf out in the desert. If rumour was to be believed, Tenocwe was as handsome as he was fearsome, and he served in all things as the warlord's right hand.

"Assuming he uses his left hand to . . . you know," said one of the servants, and laughed.

"Oh, I don't know," said another. "Tenocwe is *very* devoted."

Csorwe blushed. Obviously she had heard plenty of this kind of thing with the Blue Boars but she never knew how to respond to it.

None of them mentioned the pit in the floor. None of them even looked at it. Csorwe was kept too busy to go and inspect it, but it tugged at the edge of her attention. Before she had a chance to look any closer, they were instructed to file to the back of the hall and wait for the guests to arrive.

"Remember, I get first pick," Taymiri whispered, bobbing on her toes. Csorwe nodded.

The officers filed in. All of them were Oshaaru, mostly huge and visibly scarred, their tusks chipped and cracked. One was missing a tusk altogether, making his face look oddly lopsided, half formed. Csorwe felt a twinge of sympathy, trying not to imagine how it must have felt to lose one.

Psamag had brought them all with him when he had come to work for Olthaaros. Tenocwe, that evening's guest of honour, was younger than most, but just as battered. At the end of the line was the only civilian and the only Tlaanthothei among them: Talasseres Charossa, his clothes exquisitely pressed. In this company, he looked younger, unhappier, and more tightly wound than ever. He hadn't got the ear twitch under control. Csorwe wondered what was bothering him so badly. He had seemed uptight when they'd met him earlier, but he now appeared to be an actual nervous wreck.

Two singers serenaded the guests as they took their seats. Csorwe recognised the voices from earlier, though she had assumed they were women. These appeared to be young men— both Qarsazhi, both ethereally lovely—but their voices were high, sweet, and piping.

"They've had their bits cut off so they sing better," Taymiri hissed. "They do that in Qarsazh, sometimes," she added, with a hint of national pride.

They waited for almost an hour, and the music gave Csorwe a headache. At last the grand doors opened, admitting, first, a pair of Oshaaru soldiers. They were identical, bald, gigantically muscular, and naked but for their sandals and their beaded loin-cloths. Their tusks were capped with shining hooks of brass, and they were clearly quite dead. Their flesh was pallid, except where it was veined black, and a smell of embalming fluid wafted along with them as they marched down toward the table. They were followed by two more, just as identical and just as dead, with little clouded eyes staring directly ahead of them.

Csorwe blinked. Of all the rumours about General Psamag, Sethennai had dismissed the revenant bodyguard the most quickly, yet here they were. Their clammy feet slapped on the parquet. Taymiri's mouth fell open.

Csorwe felt like a spinning top wheeling off course. She hadn't seen revenants since the House of Silence. This was necromancy out of the old country.

She had taken to thinking of Oshaar as *the old country* rather than *home,* though she had been gone for only three years, because she never intended to go back. But sometimes, it seemed, the old country could come to you.

The bodyguards took their positions, exact as automata, and General Psamag entered the room. Despite all the rumours, and all she'd learned, Csorwe was not prepared for the first impression of Psamag. He was white as a ghost, one-eyed, and handsome in the style of a shark. He was dressed in blackened chain mail, and wore his sword strapped to his back. His only ornament was a lump of jet on a chain around his neck. His tusks were sharpened to dagger points and his eye gleamed like cut diamond.

All this was not enough to convey the sheer force of his presence. This man held their lives in the palm of his hand. Taymiri released a barely audible gasp. Csorwe's fingers tightened nervously on the cords of her apron as she tried to recover her focus.

The officers saluted, and Psamag strode to his place. Discreetly, four more dead bodyguards filed into the room behind Psamag and took their places.

"Well, my friends," said Psamag. "Here we are. Let's drink!"

There was a roar of approval from the officers, rattling the cups that Csorwe and the others had set out so neatly. For a while, Csorwe was kept busy going back and forth, filling and refilling drinks. The officers were hard drinkers, especially Tenocwe, who was making the most of his position as guest of honour. Csorwe couldn't help noticing that Psamag drank no more than one cup, and his eye never lost its chilly gleam. Something was not quite right.

The older officers sitting closest to Psamag also seemed to sense that something was amiss. They laughed and boasted, but there was something hollow about it, something tense with expectation. Csorwe darted from seat to seat refilling glasses, watching them all as if this were a puzzle she could solve before things began to go wrong. As if she had any power at all to affect the course of events in this room.

Psamag's second-in-command, an enormous old woman with a shaven head, didn't laugh at all, and nor did Talasseres Charossa. Gradually, apprehension began to settle around the table, like falling ashes, and they all fell silent. Csorwe realised she was holding her breath.

"So," said Psamag, without raising his voice. Csorwe watched Tenocwe hushing his friends on either side. "You all know why we're here, but in case some of you are already too drunk to remember—Charossa, would you care to remind us?"

Psamag drew out the syllables of the Tlaanthothei name with open disdain. Talasseres Charossa winced.

"The victory of Captain Tenocwe, sir," he said, seeming to know as he said it that it wasn't going to be the right answer.

Psamag smiled, baring a row of sharp teeth between the mighty tusks. Talasseres relaxed for a moment, then jumped almost out of his seat as Psamag slammed one enormous fist into the table. The jet pendant around his neck bounced. "Incorrect! Guess again. Big Morga, you want a turn?"

Big Morga was the second-in-command. She watched the scene from under heavy eyelids, with a kind of world-weary amusement.

"We're here because you put us here, sir," she said.

"Now, Morga here has been with me since before most of you

lot were tusked. You know why? Any takers? Surely one of you quick lads has got a smart answer for me?"

Silence.

"Morga's got a firm head on her shoulders. She knows who put her here. She knows who holds this place. She knows who owns her loyalty. And she's lived long enough to see fifty. You think maybe there's what you'd call a correlation there, friends? I suggest you think on it."

There was a pause, and the table staff came in to refill the cups, Csorwe among them. There had been no need for Sethennai to warn her away from Psamag. He was like a sharp cliff edge. He fixed your attention even as you wanted to back away. And he was not yet finished with his speech.

"Still, Charossa's got a point, hasn't he?" he said. "Where's my man Tenocwe? Stand up, there, son, let the others see the hero of the hour." Psamag was clearly enjoying himself by now, and that worried Csorwe more than anything.

Don't panic, she told herself. *He doesn't see you.*

All his attention, in fact, was fixed on Tenocwe, who rose somewhat unsteadily to his feet. He gave an equally unsteady salute and grinned at his mates.

"We've all heard the tale, so I won't bore you all with it now," Psamag went on. "Tenocwe and his squad destroyed a whole pack of raiders in the Ramskulls, and raided their stockpiles for good measure. They won't vex us again soon." He paused, and looked around the table. "Come on! Let's have a cheer for the man! My right hand, Tenocwe, everyone!"

The cheer rose rather ragged than enthusiastic. By now everyone knew something was wrong. Csorwe bit her lip, inadvertently driving her new adult tusks into her cheeks, hard enough to bruise the skin, and winced.

"They don't sound too proud of you, Teno," said the warlord, with terrible conciliation. "Funny, that. I wonder why?"

Tenocwe said nothing. Nobody said anything. In the horrible silence, there was nothing to be heard but a dry slithering sound in the pit. The high colour drained from Tenocwe's face, and his eyes widened. The game, one way or another, was up.

The nearest servant, a few feet from Csorwe, was watching the scene with a fixed expression of wide-eyed terror. Csorwe's pulse skittered like a bug trapped under a glass. Every instinct told her to run, or at least to close her eyes before she could see whatever terrible thing was certainly about to happen, but she could hardly move.

There was a shriek of wood on stone as Psamag pushed his chair back and rose to his feet. He strode down the dining table, and Csorwe had a vision of what it must be like to face this man in battle, rising like a dust storm. He stood over Tenocwe, dwarfing the younger man.

"My friends, you want to hear a cautionary tale?" said Psamag, resting a hand on Tenocwe's shoulder, in a way that might have looked friendly, if Tenocwe had not been shaking like a reed in the wind by now. "Look at this. A promising young man, a fine soldier, a trusted officer, just ready for all the fruits of this world to tumble into his lap. We ought to be celebrating his victory tonight. This ought to be a proud moment for me. You want to know what's put me out of the celebrating mood? Imagine my disappointment. My right hand, a man I've known since he was a boy: scheming against me with the Chancellor's men."

This had exactly the effect Psamag was going for. The room

reeled, then exploded with disbelieving cries. Tenocwe could hardly speak, shaking his head and mouthing frantic denials. Some of them pushed back their chairs to distance themselves from the traitor. Morga did not look surprised at all. Talasseres Charossa seemed to have been expecting it too. His shoulders were drawn up tight and his face was a mask.

It took Csorwe a few seconds to understand what it all meant. She had half convinced herself that Tenocwe was one of Sethennai's contacts, that she might be next to be discovered, but it was hard to feel any kind of relief at this revelation.

Psamag produced a sheaf of papers and held them up in his fist, before letting them float one by one to the table. "Letters, to our good friend Captain Tenocwe from *the friends of Olthaaros*. It's all here. You can look for yourselves, if you choose." Psamag's heavy head swung from side to side like that of a bull about to charge, and he clicked his tongue. "Oh, Teno. Why didn't you burn them? Didn't I teach you better than that?"

"Sir, no, sir, this is—" was all Tenocwe could manage. Psamag clapped another hand to his shoulder, and lifted him bodily off the ground.

"Will anyone speak in his defence?" said Psamag, casting his eyes across the assembly. None of Tenocwe's mates spoke up. None of them would meet his eyes. Again they heard the noise from the pit, softly rattling.

Many of the servants turned their eyes away, and Csorwe realised they had seen this happen before. Taymiri was frozen in place, staring at the luckless Tenocwe. Csorwe had never seen her at a loss like this. If she had been closer Csorwe might have tried to catch her eye, but they were all too far apart, isolated in their own pockets of helplessness.

Every one of Psamag's footsteps sounded on the boards like a whipcrack as he walked toward the pit. Tenocwe was struggling now, calling out to his friends for help. Many did not even look up from the table: as a show of uncaring, or because they could not face him, or because they could not bear to see what was about to happen.

"Kin betrays us," said Psamag, still walking. Tenocwe's wriggling troubled him no more than the empty struggles of a hooked fish. "Friends betray us. What can we rely on in this dark world, my smart captains? There's only two things that never change. Two completely predictable things."

Psamag's ability to hold an audience was uncanny. The officers were rapt, with horror or with admiration or both. Talasseres Charossa was swaying ever so slightly, perhaps wondering if he was next.

"First! No man can escape the death set down for him! Isn't that right, Teno?"

Tenocwe whimpered and fell still. The warlord held him almost tenderly, without showing any sign of weakening under his weight.

"The second sure thing is the first and most favoured of my wives. She is swift. She is terrible. And she is as loyal in her way as the hunger of the desert. Atharaisse! Sand-wife! Come up!"

The slithering in the pit grew louder and louder, mingled with the rattling of chains. Something was rushing toward them. Csorwe's limbs twitched with the desire to flee, just to turn and run before she could even see what was coming.

It reared up over the edge of the pit like something breaking from the surface of a pool. Swift as the flash of wings, yet somehow lazy in its unfurling, it rose coil upon coil, surveying the assembled company through eyes as red as raw flesh. Atharaisse was a serpent of monstrous size, white as bone, and appalling in the intelligence that glittered in those unblinking eyes.

The skeletons in Echentyr had been nothing to this. It was the difference between a drawing and the reality. Csorwe could only stare, transfixed. Her mouth had fallen open. You could not run from something like this. You could not hope to fight it. You could only curl up and hide and make yourself small enough to escape notice. She hadn't felt like this since the last time she had been in the presence of the Unspoken.

The wicked teardrop of Atharaisse's head was larger than Csorwe's whole body. Her mouth opened like a red cave, and the pink forked tongue that flickered out was thicker than a man's arm. Her coils hushed on the stone and she brought her head in to rest on the edge of the pit.

Psamag strode toward her without hesitation, stopping only a few feet from the tip of her snout. Still, he wasn't quite as brave as he looked. Iron hoops banded Atharaisse's neck, fixed in place by prongs hammered through her hide and into the flesh. The white scales were stained here with trails of rust. Each hoop was made fast to the wall by heavy chains.

"How do you do, Queen of Serpents?" said Psamag, mock courteous.

Atharaisse did not open her mouth to speak, but they all heard her voice resounding in the chamber, or somehow within the coils of their own ears. The voice was a low, harsh hiss that thrummed like a swarm of bees, but Csorwe could not mistake the desperate misery in it, a yearning barely disguised.

The terror still rang in Csorwe's ears like the discordant ringing of bells, but she found she could begin to ignore it. Was it possible that Atharaisse was from Echentyr? Were there other serpent kingdoms? Perhaps some of them had escaped the cataclysm. It was hard to imagine Sethennai had been wrong, but perhaps if Atharaisse's ancestors had been travelling abroad at the time . . .

"I am hungry, sir," said the serpent.

"You're hungry, too?" said Psamag. "I've been kept from my dinner. How long has it been since you've dined on the meat of traitors, sand-wife?"

"Sixty days, sir," said Atharaisse. Her eyes flicked from Psamag to Tenocwe, who had gone utterly limp, looking up at the face of his death in abject surrender. There was a wheedling note in the serpent's voice.

Csorwe remembered the Royal Library of Echentyr, all the friezes showing the serpents as statesmen and warriors. Psamag must have utterly broken Atharaisse's pride. A cold and unanticipated hatred flooded through her, for the General and for the whole company that sat and looked on. How unfair it was for someone to survive the vengeance of their god and then suffer like this at the hands of someone so mortal, so essentially *small*.

"I have a morsel here for you," said Psamag, and without apparent thought or effort he cast Tenocwe into the pit. There was a terrible succession of noises: a shriek, and a rattle of chains, and the rush of scales on stone.

"Ahhh," said Atharaisse, caressingly, and then there was another scream, swiftly curtailed.

The coils sank away out of sight, and there was silence so absolute that Csorwe could almost hear the pounding drumbeat of her heart.

Talasseres Charossa's hands were fastened to the edge of the table, as though his fingertips might bore through solid wood. Psamag turned to face him, with a still more terrible smile. It wasn't over yet. Csorwe's fists tightened involuntarily.

"Of course," said Psamag, "our respected Chancellor Olthaaros knew nothing about this incompetent treachery. I spoke to him today. He condemns it, in fact. So, I want no repercussions for our valued liaison. Do you hear?"

As he strode back up to his place at the head of the table, he murmured, in a loud stage whisper, *"Better luck next time, Talasseres."*

He stood for a moment, surveying them all. "More wine!" he said, after a moment savouring the silence. "And bring in dinner."

Csorwe was grateful to be able to leave the room, even briefly. Her legs felt shaky, as if she'd been in bed with a fever. She told herself sharply to keep it together. She'd told Sethennai she could handle this. She'd seen death before. She'd met dangerous people. She *was* a dangerous person. She willed her knees to stop wobbling, and followed the others to fetch the first course.

The first course, naturally, was rock-snakes, skinned, marinated, and simmered whole in a red wine sauce. Csorwe saw now how Psamag had ended up with his reputation. Taymiri, serving Talasseres Charossa, looked almost as sickly as he did. Psamag ate the snakes with relish, and cleaned the sauce from his plate with a crust of bread.

The rest of the meal went off as expected. The stew of rock-snakes was followed by a more innocuous roast goat, and the mood in the hall relaxed somewhat.

At last, the dishes were cleared, and Csorwe and Taymiri were released. Taymiri had latched onto one of the officers, so Csorwe had to make her way back to the bunkroom alone. She didn't mind the chance to sort through her thoughts. Really she ought to take the chance to explore the fortress, but she was still trying to make sense of all she had seen that evening and she didn't trust herself not to get lost.

Halfway back to the bunkroom, she heard a miserable gurgle of suppressed weeping from behind one of the pantry doors. She stopped still to listen. No further sobbing followed, but there was a pause, then a series of thuds and thumps, as of somebody kicking the shit out of a crate of melons.

She opened the door. Inside, Talasseres Charossa was kicking the shit out of a crate of melons. It took him a second to notice her, by which point it was too late to pretend he had been doing anything other than what she had seen.

"Get out!" he said, in a snuffly growl that was perhaps meant to be intimidating. His eyes were red and bloodshot, and his ears drooped.

"What's wrong?" she said.

"That is none of your—this is insubordinate, you know, this is pretty fucking insubordinate, did one of the others put you up to this? Go back and tell Shadran he can eat a dick, I will not be disrespected by a *waitress*—"

"What's wrong," said Csorwe, "*sir?*"

"*Nothing*," said Talasseres. "Who the hell do you think you are?"

"I'm not really a waitress," she said. For a moment she teetered on the brink of telling him everything. The idea of having an ally was very tempting. He must know the fortress, and perhaps he could help her find another way in and out. But Talasseres Charossa was Olthaaros' nephew. However much he hated his existence here, he was not someone she should trust.

"I know," he said, "you're a scullery maid or something. Do you think I'm going to lie awake at night like, oh no, I called that girl a waitress and, oh my god, *she's not a fucking waitress?*"

Csorwe remembered his lecture about place settings and struggled against laughter.

"I'm sorry about Tenocwe," she said, trying at random for an angle. If she wanted his information, she was going to have to find some kind of purchase.

"I don't give a shit about Tenocwe," said Talasseres. "Anyone that stupid deserves to be snake food. Anyone that stupid ought to cover themselves in sauce, go out into the desert, lie down on the ground, wait for snakes to come and eat them, and save the rest of us from having to sit and listen to Psamag trying to be *funny.*"

"Still," said Csorwe.

"I didn't have anything to do with Tenocwe," said Talasseres. "*I'm* not stupid. It's not my fault if my fucking uncle Olthaaros decides he's not really all that bothered about getting me killed."

"Oh," said Csorwe. She had learned, from long experience with Sethennai, that sometimes you just needed to provide punctuation until someone had finished saying what they were going to say.

"Yeah," said Talasseres. "*Tlaanthothei liaison,* fuck off. I'm a hostage here."

He kicked the box of melons again, stubbed his toe, and made a noise of long-suffering disgust that could have curdled milk.

"Maybe you should leave," she said.

He laughed very long and bitterly at this. "And how do you think I'm going to do that?" he said. "I could try the door or the Gate if I wanted a quick death, I guess, but I don't want to give Psamag the satisfaction."

"There are other ways, aren't there?" said Csorwe, hoping he was too deep in his sadness to notice she was being very mysterious for a scullery maid.

"Oh, sure, there's the way through the caves, but I'm doing my best to avoid getting eaten alive by the fucking snake," said Talasseres. He sniffed, and tried to make it sound like he was clearing his throat. "Who are you, anyway?"

Csorwe was desperate to know what he meant by *the caves*, but she didn't push her luck. "My name is Soru, sir," she said, with a little curtsy.

"Well, Soru," he said, "piss off."

At last, Csorwe returned to the bunkroom. She felt as though she had been through several rounds with the Blue Boars' finest, but she still lay awake for a long time before she could sleep. Could she use Talasseres Charossa? He couldn't possibly be an ally, but perhaps he was a weak spot that could be exploited. That was Sethennai's area of expertise rather than her own. But Talasseres knew the layout of the fortress, and he was clearly dying for someone who'd listen to his complaints. She could do worse than talk to him again. Next time she ran into him she'd be ready.

In the days that followed, everyone learned that Tenocwe had been executed for his treachery, but Csorwe and Taymiri never told the rest of their bunkroom about what they had seen.

A few nights later, Csorwe was woken by the sound of someone trying very hard to make no sound at all. She peered out from under her sheet and saw Taymiri dressing hastily by the light that came in under the door.

"What's happening?" said Csorwe. She was exhausted, but maybe there had been another summons to Psamag's hall.

Taymiri jumped, and snarled. "Go back to sleep— Oh, Soru, it's only you. Help me with my hair."

She had divided her hair into four braids, and directed Csorwe to drape these in artful loops from forehead to nape and fix them at the back with a silver pin. This was difficult to accomplish in half darkness, but Taymiri was more than usually patient with Csorwe's lack of expertise. The coils of hair were smooth and heavy as woven metal. Csorwe had the sense that she should not take any time longer than necessary to do this, that it would be taking some kind of liberty.

When it was done, Taymiri looked much older, like a grown and rather intimidating woman. This somehow disquieted Csorwe, as if she ought to have recognised sooner that her friend had another side to her.

Taymiri finished tying her shoes and hauled Csorwe out into the hall. "Don't tell the others. I'm going to meet Shadran. *Captain* Shadran."

Csorwe blinked, both startled and rather impressed.

"I mean it. Don't tell anyone. It's not a sure thing yet, and I won't have them crowing over me if it doesn't come off."

Csorwe nodded, which made Taymiri laugh for some reason.

"Of course, you never tell anyone anything," said Taymiri. "You even looked surprised there for a minute. I didn't think anything could surprise you."

A moment's pause. Taymiri smiled to herself, as though considering whether to tell something secret.

"You're sweet," said Taymiri, in Qarsazhi. It took Csorwe a

second to make sense of the words, so she managed not to give away the fact that she understood.

Then Taymiri stood up on tiptoes and kissed her on the mouth.

Csorwe had never been kissed by anyone before. Total astonishment, like a flash of bright light, dazzled her senses. Then it was over.

"Wish me luck! I'll see you tomorrow," said Taymiri, laughing again, and she ran off down the hall.

Csorwe went back inside and sat on the edge of her bunk. She couldn't have been more dazed if Taymiri had slapped her in the face. At least she would have known what to make of that. After a while she could almost believe she had imagined the whole thing, except for the cool, fading imprint of Taymiri's lips on hers, no more substantial than dust, but somehow difficult to ignore. She wiped her mouth on the back of her hand and tried to go back to sleep.

It was embarrassing, in a way, that Taymiri was having so much more success than Csorwe with her secret ambitions. Sethennai was relying on her for this, and things were moving so slowly. She needed to be bolder. She needed to find out what Talasseres Charossa had meant about the caves, and about the snake. Unfortunately, she needed to return to the General's quarters.

6

The Serpent

THERE WAS NO MOON over Tlaanthothe that night, and the clouds blotted out the stars. The fortress lanterns hung alone, a heavy baleful yellow, in otherwise unbroken darkness. It had been a week since Tenocwe's execution. Csorwe and the others had been kept hard at work, and she hadn't been able to get away as quickly as she'd hoped, especially since Taymiri was watching at all times.

Taymiri hadn't mentioned the kiss, but then, they hadn't been alone together since. It had made certain things clearer in Csorwe's mind, but on the whole she was grateful to have her secret schemes keeping her occupied so she didn't have to think too much about it.

In the end—whatever she had felt, whether or not she would have liked it to happen again—Taymiri had her own aims and her own loyalties, and Csorwe wasn't going to fool herself into thinking she was a part of them, any more than Taymiri was a part of her own plan.

Earlier that night, Taymiri had sneaked away to meet Shadran again, and Csorwe didn't think anybody else was observant enough to notice when she too slipped from the bunkroom.

By night, the stuffed heads on the walls of Psamag's dining

hall looked even more dead than before. Csorwe crept along the wall beneath them, keeping to the shadows. Despite what she was about to do, she felt almost exhilarated. For weeks she had been kept sheathed, wrapped in cloth in a dusty drawer. Now, at last, the edge would bite.

Or, just as likely, she would get bitten, and nobody would ever hear from her again. She wondered whether she was the first agent Sethennai had sent into the fortress, or whether there had been failures whose bones lay forgotten somewhere, shaken down to the bottom of the fortress like marbles in a jar. He'd certainly never mentioned any predecessors. She would just have to make sure she didn't fail.

She made her way softly to the edge of the pit. The floor dropped away to a smooth basin of sand far below, where the serpent Atharaisse lay in coils, draped with chains as though with jewels.

High above, an iron lantern hung on a chain from the ceiling. By this faint illumination Csorwe saw the marks of Atharaisse's captivity. The walls were battered, and her white scales were stained and scarred, red-brown with blood and rust.

It was no use to stand around and stare at her, anyway. Beyond Atharaisse, set into the very base of the far wall, was the mouth of a tunnel, leading away into darkness. This was the unfortunate conclusion of all Csorwe's investigation. This tunnel led down to the caves beneath the fortress. If there was any other way to reach them, she hadn't found it. The caves reached deep, a network spreading between city and desert. This was how she was going to sneak Sethennai back into Tlaanthothe. She had no other choice but the pit.

Nothing in the world has earned the power to frighten you, Sethennai had said, long ago.

"Thanks a lot, sir," she muttered, and slid down into the pit. She landed with a little puff of sand, and let out a slow breath. The back of her neck prickled. Her hands were damp with sweat.

Atharaisse's coils rose on all sides, like walls of breathing ivory. No amount of ill treatment and degradation could make her less frightening. Each of her scales was the size of Csorwe's palm, gleaming in the moonlight. Csorwe flattened herself against the wall of the pit and inched her way crabwise toward the mouth of the tunnel on the other side.

As Csorwe reached the midpoint, she heard a low, whispering sigh. She only had time to freeze as Atharaisse uncoiled like a snapped string. Her eyes met Csorwe's with terrible swiftness, keen and red.

"Quail," said the serpent, hissing like water on gravel in Csorwe's head. Her mouth opened, revealing two fangs, each as long and slender as a shinbone. "For thy doom is upon thee. We are Atharaisse, most ancient and most exalted scion of Echentyr."

Csorwe bowed, and straightened up to meet her eyes again. Despite the circumstances she couldn't help feeling a spark of satisfaction that she had been right.

"Good evening, ma'am," said Csorwe, with only the faintest tremor. As much as she had hoped Atharaisse would stay asleep, she had planned what she was going to say. "I am honoured to stand in your presence."

A fine membrane twitched over Atharaisse's eyes, and retracted.

"Our subjects here have lost their manners. They do not regard us as they ought. What manner of thing art thou?"

"I am nothing," said Csorwe. "The smallest of my master's creatures."

"If so, we find it ill mannered in him to send you," said Atharaisse. "To our grandeur is owed his foremost envoy."

"Of course," said Csorwe. "It's my fault. I wanted to meet you. Ma'am, I have seen Echentyr."

The great head moved closer, slipping over the sand until the tip of Atharaisse's snout was less than an arm's length from Csorwe. The wall was at her back. There was no getting away.

"And what hast thou seen, in the ruin of our world, that made thee so eager to look upon us? To laugh, perhaps, at our reduced estate?"

"No, ma'am," said Csorwe, with sincerity. "It was—it was—" She searched for the right word, unsure what she could say about the enormous strangeness of Echentyr that wouldn't get her eaten. "It was *impressive*. I saw the, uh, the Royal Library. I wanted to see you and learn how it had been before."

Atharaisse tasted the air with her tongue, the double point almost touching Csorwe's face.

"No," said Atharaisse in a low, furious hiss. "We recognise thee. Thou liest."

"I swear to you, ma'am," Csorwe whispered, flat against the wall of the pit. "I am telling the truth."

"Thou servest at the table of a parasite. A flea may believe that he is king, and summon other fleas to dance attendance, and bite the flesh of his betters, but he is less than dust before us! We are the last daughter of our world! We survived the ruin of Iriskavaal! And we will see the craven Psamag suffer!" Her tail thrashed in the sand, stirring up choking clouds.

"I am not Psamag's servant," said Csorwe. "My master sent me here. He desires Psamag's death as you do."

This might have been an overstatement. She was pretty sure

Sethennai wouldn't shed a tear at Psamag's funeral, but he had never specifically asked Csorwe to murder him.

"Master! What master? Do not lie to us again. Our people dealt with the Thousand-Eyed One in the morning of all worlds and were granted the true sight. We cannot be deceived."

"My master is Belthandros Sethennai," said Csorwe. "The *rightful* ruler of Tlaanthothe." This was a shot in the dark, an admission she had hoped not to make, but Atharaisse's eyes flared with recognition, bloodshot and brilliant.

"Ahaaa," she said. "That is a recollection that escapes us not. And what has become of the exquisite Belthandros?"

"He's all right," said Csorwe.

"Come away from the wall, little mouse, and let us look upon thee properly," said the snake. She withdrew her head a little way, and Csorwe had no choice but to step out into the middle of the pit, and let Atharaisse circle around her, inquisitive interest shining in every scale.

"There is a familiar smell of wizardry about thee," said Atharaisse after a while. "And thou desirest the extermination of this false warlord. Very well. Thou comprehendest not the scale of our magnanimity. We would have eaten thee. But as a mark of our favour to Belthandros we will let thee pass. Thou wishest to go down into the tunnel, no doubt, into the narrow places where we cannot go."

Csorwe had not been conscious of holding in her breath, but now she let out a gasp of relief. This indignity seemed to amuse Atharaisse, at least.

"Yes, ma'am," she said. "But . . . there's one more thing." Somehow, between the fear of imminent death and the fear of accidentally saying something insulting, she had come up with a new idea.

"Thou art truly like him," said Atharaisse, still not unamused. "A bold, presuming, insolent little delicacy. But certainly it refreshes us to be addressed in terms of proper respect by such an impertinent scrap. Ask, then."

"Ma'am . . . are your fangs poisonous?"

"Ahh," said Atharaisse. "The sacred terror. The blessing of Iriskavaal. The kind death, the cold fire, the destroying sweetness . . . they are *venomous*, little hatchling."

So it was that Csorwe found herself climbing the serpent's flank to reach the vast concavity of her open mouth. She balanced upon the scaled rim, and reached out to touch a hollow fang that could have pierced her through without difficulty.

"Ah, thou askest much, and thou darest much," said Atharaisse, her voice throbbing in Csorwe's head though her tongue and her teeth remained perfectly still. "For the hunger of ages tears at us still, and the urge to bite is very strong. Thou art audacious."

At last Csorwe leapt to the ground, holding in one hand a tightly fastened waterskin, plump with venom. She bowed again. Atharaisse purred.

"Go thy way, little crumb."

Csorwe resisted the impulse to bolt under the retreating loop of Atharaisse's tail and run full pelt toward the tunnel in the back wall. She bowed several times as she left, making her way with slow courtesy. Only once she was safely into the tunnel did she stop, and slide down the wall, and rest until her limbs had stopped shaking.

The tunnel led into a maze, which could have been devised

by some previous lord of the fortress to torment his captives. Csorwe found her way to a buried stair, curving downward, under the surface of the desert. Perhaps some other ancient lord had intended this way as an escape route in times of siege. For Csorwe, it was a long downward climb, down a channel so narrow that she could not spread her arms to either side. Then the staircase ended, and opened into darkness. She had reached the caves.

Csorwe was about to step out into the dark, but some impulse, some caution, wired deep in the animal part of her brain, made her stop. On the left-hand wall of the passage, above the bottom step, there was a red, fist-sized glob of something like wax, plastered to the rock just below head height. There was a sign stamped into the wax, a quintuple curlicue so unpleasant to look at that it could only have been magical. The whole thing looked not just dangerous but disgusting, as though the wall had sprouted a purulent boil.

Csorwe stepped back very slowly. Shock caught up with her as she realised how close she had come to blithely walking past the thing, and her heart began to race.

"It's a curse-ward," said a voice out of the darkness above her. Csorwe had her knife out before her brain could make sense of the words.

It was Talasseres Charossa. "So it's true," he said, blandly, as if people drew knives on him for breakfast, lunch, and dinner. "You really aren't a waitress."

Csorwe lowered her weapon. If Talasseres had wanted to attack her, he wouldn't have announced his presence. Probably, he would have just shoved her down the stairs.

"Why are you here?" she said.

"The same reason as you," he said, and gestured down past Csorwe to the darkness below. "Looking for another way out."

"What does it do?" said Csorwe, indicating the curse-ward. It was clearly different from the ward Oranna had sent in her letter to Sethennai. She wasn't sure whether the sign stamped into the wax was the control sigil, or whether there were more signs buried underneath. Either way, touching it would be a mistake.

Talasseres reached into his bag and pulled out the gnawed bone of an old chicken leg, holding it with some disdain. Shreds of gristle adhered in places. He threw it overhand into the stairwell, and just as it was about to pass the bottom step, the curse-ward flared, and the bone was gone, leaving—perhaps—a smear of black smoke. There was a greasy smell in the air, like burning fat.

"It's my uncle's work. He wouldn't know a light touch if it grabbed his balls. Air and rocks pass through fine," said Talasseres. "Anything that's alive, or used to be alive, goes up like that." He snapped his fingers. "But if your next question is going to be *How do I disarm it?*, you're shit out of luck."

"How many times have you been down here since we talked?" said Csorwe.

Talasseres shrugged, which she took to mean *every night*.

"You think there's a way through," said Csorwe. She wondered whether he had come past Atharaisse, or if there were other ways through the labyrinth of passages.

"If it was easy to get 'round, Olthaaros wouldn't still be Chancellor, would he?" said Talasseres.

Csorwe watched him. She was sure there was a catch coming. Talasseres seemed so blindly grateful for someone to talk to that she didn't have to push him even a little bit to keep going.

"You can't disarm it," he said. "But there's an amulet, a protective charm—" He looked at Csorwe doubtfully.

"I know what an amulet is," said Csorwe, unable to stop herself.

"Oh, do you? Well, bully for you, you're going to love this next part, because the fucking amulet belongs to General Psamag and he wears it 'round his neck, day and night."

"The jet pendant," she said. She had seen it that night in the dining hall. It had seemed then like an odd choice of jewellery for an old soldier.

"You're observant, aren't you, Soru?" He sounded less caustic, more interested, and she realised she ought to have kept her mouth shut.

She shrugged. "Just curious."

"Well," said Talasseres, his interest glazing over as he looked back at the curse-ward. "It'd be a quick way to go, anyway."

General Psamag's private quarters were in the very highest lofts of the fortress. The walls were hung with fine tapestries, oil paintings, ceremonial weapons, the rarest treasures of a dozen worlds. Here, in the deepest watches of the night, Csorwe crept from room to room, scarcely disturbing the air.

It had been a week since she had spoken to Talasseres in the cave. She had known since then what she needed to do, but knowing and doing were very different things.

You frightened of spiders, Csorwe? one of her teachers had asked her. He was a retired cat burglar, one of Sethennai's many shady old friends. *You frightened of ghosts? Whatever it is you're scared of in the dark, that's what you become.*

I'm not scared of anything, she had said, and he had laughed at her. She was scared now, but she did as Sethennai had taught her: turned the fear into fuel, burnt it to propel herself onward.

She made it past the outer guards. Two of Psamag's revenants were patrolling in the next corridor, staring ahead with milky eyes, but revenants weren't any more observant than living men, and she passed by them easily. There were two more in each successive room, and neither of them turned from the furrows they were polishing in the floorboards.

In the antechamber to Psamag's bedroom she paused to check the dagger strapped to her belt. Within the sheath, the blade was freshly sharpened, and Atharaisse's venom glistened on the steel. Just in case. This wasn't going to be an assassination unless it had to be.

The door to Psamag's bedchamber was ajar, and darkness lay beyond. Inside, someone was sleeping. She heard nothing else. No other footsteps, no breathing. The hinges made no sound as she crept inside.

A soft haze of moonlight came in at the windows, and by this weak illumination she determined the shape of a bed, and someone lying on it. She managed a single step toward it before a cold hand closed over her mouth and nose, and something like an iron bar tightened around her waist, crushing the air from her lungs. There was no use trying to cry out. She bit down, but the revenant's skin was tough as cured hide, and it made no reaction, simply holding her as she wriggled like a worm pinched from a bait-pot.

"Don't smother her, Dead Hand," said a voice, calm but perfectly alert. "We're going to have a conversation."

There was the hiss of someone striking a light—a flare of brightness in the dark—and then a lantern was lit. She saw the bed, rich with hangings, and the shape of someone asleep, deep in shadow. Dead Hand's grip clamped around her face was beginning to darken her vision. Sitting on a chest at the end of the bed, naked from the waist up, was General Psamag.

Somehow he had known. She had slipped.

"You two, disarm and restrain her," he said, rising and stretching. "No gag. Like I said, we're going to talk."

Another revenant came out of the shadows. There was nothing Csorwe could do as they hoisted her to a beam and bound her raised arms to it. They found her dagger easily enough and took it away.

This was the end, then. She calculated, as though from very far away, how soon the pain would become unbearable, stretched in this position. She had not been schooled in interrogation—*Not yet*, Sethennai had said—but she had heard her tutors talk sometimes, about how breaking people's fingers was all very well but how much easier to let their own weight do the work for you.

For such a huge man, Psamag moved with graceful economy, and when he spoke his voice was quiet and unemphatic.

"Someone sent you here to me," he said. He leant on one hand, running his thumb over the knifelike point of one tusk.

She shook her head. She would not betray Sethennai.

"Yes," he said. "Someone sent you to kill me."

Belthandros Sethennai had stolen her from the very mouth of death. She had no fear of anything, and no one could compel her. She would say nothing. Let them hurt her. Let them do what they wanted. She would not speak, even if they wrenched the life from her.

"You've been stealing away from your bunkroom by night," he said. "You've been plotting. Tell me who sent you, and who you are working with."

Csorwe said nothing.

"Silence does you no good," said Psamag. "I know what you've been up to." He turned to the table where the revenants had put down the poisoned dagger, and turned it over in his hands. Then he went to the bed, and drew back the curtains. There *was* someone lying there. She could see the top of their head on the pillow. "Wake up," he said, in slightly gentler tones.

It was Talasseres Charossa, naked but for a wrap tied around his middle, making him look skinnier than ever. He blinked hard, his ears drawn up flat and tight against his skull, as though he'd been woken by an alarm bell.

"Sorry, sir?" he said, making a visible effort to relax.

"Why don't you tell me again what you were saying about our friend Soru's irregular conduct," said Psamag.

"There isn't any more to tell," said Talasseres, in what was clearly meant to be a flirtatious tone. Then he looked up, and saw the scene set out in the bedroom, and his eyes widened. Csorwe looked back at him without expression, and after a second's naked shock, his expression hardened.

"You can't blame me," he said. "If you're stupid enough to do something like this."

Csorwe returned his gaze steadily.

"You really can't blame me," said Talasseres. Something almost like disgust flickered in his voice.

Psamag said nothing throughout this exchange. Finally he laid a hand on Talasseres' bare shoulder. "Leave, if you prefer. This won't be easy for you to watch."

Fierce pride warred with unease in Talasseres' eyes. At last he bobbed his head and scrambled from the room.

Psamag used no instruments but the revenants, utterly dispassionate in their strength and obedience. He asked no questions beyond the first two. Who was she working for? Who was she working with? Silence was answered with pain. Csorwe began to answer with nonsense, drawn from some new well of defiance. Who did she work for? The Pretty Birds Gentleman's House of Entertainment. Who was she working with? The nine old gods of Qarsazh.

Perhaps an hour passed. It was impossible to tell. Csorwe's existence stretched and narrowed, drawn into white-hot threads like molten glass.

The General grew tired of this, and sent for a pair of pliers.

"You're young," he said, reaching out to touch one of Csorwe's tusks with a sharp-nailed forefinger. "These are new. Only a coward sends a child to do his work."

"No," Csorwe mumbled, too weak even to snap at his hand. She could hardly move her head. Every breath came shallow and tearing.

Psamag laughed. "No? Defending the one who put you here? This isn't my fault, child. It's my duty to protect my interests. What's happening to you is down to the one who sent you to this place." He fit the teeth of the pliers to her tusk, cold against the feverish heat of her cheek. "You know what you have to do to end this. Just one word, little friend, just the name of the one who sent you to kill me."

"Go fuck yourself," said Csorwe, though the words came out slurred, not at all the cry of defiance she had hoped.

"As you please," said Psamag. "Dead Tooth, pull her right tusk for me. Then we'll see how much she likes her boss."

Some unreckonable span of time had passed. Psamag had dismissed the revenants. Csorwe was still hanging from the beam.

"Whoever you're working for, you've failed them," the General was saying. "There's no point holding out. I think you know that, at heart. You're being obstinate, and it's not achieving anything but more pain for you. You've tried hard, and that's admirable in its way, but you're clinging to a lost cause."

Csorwe paid him no attention. She could still hear the tusk's root breaking, like the creak of a branch as it snapped. There was a raw hollow where the tooth had been, like a bowl full of blood, and a sour taste in her mouth, mingling with the iron. Perhaps she had been sick. It was hard to tell: she drifted in and out of consciousness.

"Your boss is a powerful individual," said the General. "So it won't do any harm for you to tell me. We already have a good idea where you came from. And do you think that you really matter to them? This bit of stubbornness won't do any good, and it won't be noticed. It's a shame to sacrifice yourself for no thanks and no reward. Nobody is coming to take you away from here. What happens is in your hands."

"Kill me, then," said Csorwe thickly. She felt the blood spill from her lips. In her mind's eye there was a dark tunnel in a hillside, and a calling voice she could not name. She hoped that this was a premonition of death. She had given nothing away, but she didn't know how much longer she could resist.

On the edge of her hearing, like a gleaming of white light, came the sound of a silver bell ringing. It hurt, like salt in the wound. Psamag shook his head as though trying to rid himself of a mosquito, then started as he recognised the sound. This was no product of Csorwe's imagination. A bell was ringing.

Psamag frowned and drew back from her, then turned away entirely. The bell made such a soft sound, like a child's rattle. He muttered in disbelief under his breath, and strode out of the room.

Csorwe was alone, and the binding on her right wrist had come a little loose. Psamag would kill her when he came back, and she was too weak to escape his apartments without help. But if she could reach the knife she had brought, she could end this on her own terms. The gift of Atharaisse might come good after all. As the seconds passed in silence, she worked her arm free, slowly, slowly, inch by inch, in agony. Her left arm alone could not hold up her weight. She fell with a snap as the bone broke, and passed out before she hit the floor.

The minutes passed, and she did not die. She crawled across the floor, dragging her broken arm, and reached the table where her dagger lay, and lived through every moment of it. She struggled in humiliation to knock down the dagger, and grasp it in her good hand, and shake it loose of the sheath. Atharaisse's venom still shone on the blade, and she wondered whether Psamag had intended it for her in the end. But she was not dead.

She inched facedown across the floor, nudging the dagger after her. Minute by minute the pain caught up with her, and when it became too much she had to lie still. Every jarring breath steamed on the floorboards. She left a trail of blood, still pouring from the socket of her ruined tusk, and the old verses came back to her, out of the years behind her and *The Dream of Fly Agaric*: *From those that are chosen, blood riseth to their mouths and spilleth from their lips, as nectar from the flower.* Such a pretty way of putting it. She coughed and spat—blood and saliva and little shards of tusk enamel—and drew breath, and dragged herself upright, and hid behind the door to the room, propping herself against the wall.

When Psamag came back, he realised at once that something was wrong, and his instinct was to hang back in the doorway. Csorwe meant to spring out from behind the door and cut his throat. Instead, she fell hopelessly against his shoulders, and dragged the blade loosely across his collarbone. The horror of failure made a white-hot pit in her guts. All she could hope was that she had broken the skin, that Atharaisse's venom might at least slow him down.

If Psamag was a dead man, he hadn't realised it. He stumbled into the room, roaring, and flung Csorwe at the nearest wall. The hilt of the dagger was slippery with blood and sweat, and it slipped from her hand like a fish as she landed. She jerked out a hand, but shock and terror numbed her reflexes, and the dagger clattered on the tiles before bouncing away across the floor of the General's bedroom.

Psamag strode toward her, and turned her over with the toe of his boot. His steps seemed slower than before, unless she was imagining it. *Please,* she prayed. *Unspoken and Unspeakable One—please—*

Her eyes and mouth were full of blood, but she felt the concussion as Psamag's body slammed into the floor. By some miracle he fell backward, away from her.

For some time—hours, perhaps—Csorwe just lay there, next to the General's enormous corpse. She knew she needed to get up. Someone was going to come looking for the General, sooner or later, and then she would be dead. She heard steps and voices, far away and distorted, as the fortress began to wake up. Her mind was fogged and dizzy, and she wanted nothing more than to lie very still and wait for the pain to end or be ended.

At one point, she remembered why she had come here, and managed to get up onto her elbows to search Psamag's body for the jet pendant. There was no sign of it. She crawled under the bed, and slowly faded into unconsciousness.

When she woke, someone was searching Psamag's room, discreetly but methodically. Csorwe bit her lip to stop herself calling out for help, but one of her upper teeth sank into the socket of her missing tusk, and she made a noise like a wounded animal. The footsteps stopped.

"Well, well," said a voice, and a hand worked its way under her shoulder. Someone picked her up and set her on Psamag's bed.

It was Big Morga, the second-in-command, huge and fearsome as a warship in the closeness of the chamber. Csorwe could only groan.

"Ugly little thing, for one of the boss's. Young, too." Morga made a faintly disgusted noise. "You killed him?"

Csorwe was too dazed to process the implications of any of this. She must have made some motion that looked like nodding. Morga's eyes were bloodshot with exhaustion but she looked delighted to see Csorwe, and Csorwe did not think she had seen a more terrifying expression in her life.

"Well, you've made my life a lot easier, so I'm sorry about what I'm going to have to do to you. They'll be baying for blood downstairs." Delight gave way to a carnivorous look of satisfaction. "Jawbone, come and bring her down."

Jawbone was one of Psamag's revenants. Clearly, he recognised Morga as his new commander. Jawbone hoisted Csorwe over his shoulder, and she bit down on a scream as her broken arm bent at an awkward angle. The pain obliterated all else as the revenant carried her downstairs. When it faded she allowed herself a moment's surrender to bleak humiliation. Pinioned to the beam in Psamag's quarters, she had clung to her purpose. She had been able to fight. Now there was nothing she could do to resist.

At last she was dropped with a yelp on some hard surface. Crockery clattered around her, and another white-hot lance of pain drove up through her arm.

With difficulty, Csorwe looked up, and the glassy eyes of a hundred mounted heads stared back at her. She was lying where she had been dropped, on her back like a dying woodlouse, on the table in Psamag's dining hall. Cutlery and shattered plates all around her. The officers stood around the table looking down at her.

"The traitor, as I promised you," said Morga. She grabbed Csorwe's hair, wrenching her head up. Csorwe winced, trying to focus on the faces of the officers who surrounded her. "This is the spy. She killed the General. She's been here for weeks, and none of you noticed her."

Csorwe just lay there, looking up at them blearily, too weak to struggle.

"And who do you think was paying her?" said Morga, hauling

Csorwe half upright. She held the point of a dagger to Csorwe's forehead. Pressed it down, puncturing the skin. "Who envied our place?" She dragged the blade. Blood ran in burning streams down Csorwe's face. "Who is it that's envied Psamag since we started?" She slashed downward, cutting Csorwe's face open from cheek to chin. The carelessness was more startling than the pain. Morga looked around at the table with a mirthless grimace. "You notice who's missing from our table today. Looks like Talasseres has gone back to his uncle."

Muttering went around the table. Csorwe couldn't distinguish one looming face from another.

"We'll hunt Olthaaros down, you hear me?" said Morga. "He'll die for this. But in the meantime, what do we do with traitors?"

"The snake pit," said one of the officers, as though it was obvious. "The sand-wife." The others realised this was the right answer almost at once, and the cries of approbation turned quickly to a chant. *Sand-wife, sand-wife, sand-wife,* punctuated with the stamping of feet and the pounding of fists on the table.

Morga smiled. "This piece of shit sent our friend Tenocwe to die in her place. It's time to make it fair."

Jawbone plucked Csorwe from the table by the scruff of her neck as if she were no more than a stray dog. Vomit rose in the back of her throat and she swallowed hard, futile as it seemed to resist another humiliation among so many. Fear smothered all other suffering as Jawbone strode toward the pit. Atharaisse's ivory coils were heaped in the dust below. Csorwe had no hope that she would show mercy twice.

The great intricate head rose above the lip of the pit, and Atharaisse's voice sounded, with a hiss like the wind that scoured the plains. It was some time before the company realised she was laughing.

"This is the sweetness of our longevity," she said. "Between rust and rot, time devours all enemies. Endurance is all. But we see thou hast a morsel for us."

Morga nodded and Jawbone strode toward the pit. Csorwe's fear dissolved. Of all the monsters she had met, Atharaisse was the most honourable, and her weapon the most merciful. No slow death on the rack, no dissolution in the presence of the Unspoken One, but a venom that destroyed with swift kindness.

Jawbone held her out, like a falconer offering his glove, and Atharaisse plucked her free. And then she was raised above the company, dangling, as the glassy eyes of dead things wheeled before her.

"Have no fear, hatchling," said Atharaisse, soft in the aching interior of Csorwe's skull. "Thou hast shed the blood of the tyrant. Thy courage is worthy to be honoured, and I honour thee."

The dirt floor of the pit swooped down to meet her as Atharaisse slid back down into the pit, snapping her jaws in imitation of feeding. Morga made some more remarks, and the company returned to a kind of uneasy merriment, as Csorwe was held safe in a curl of smooth white scales.

There were shallow tunnels woven in the stone around the pit, and here Atharaisse left Csorwe to rest, slumped in the dust by a still pool of water. For days, it seemed, she slept, and drifted in dreams. In these visions she saw Echentyr alive again. Stars wheeled above the great city. All the windows were illuminated, and beneath them a parade of serpents moved, their jewel-bright

scales glinting under garlands of flowers. A gaze of understanding fell upon her. She was perceived, and she remained
whole.

When she woke she drank from the pool, and washed as best
she could, flaking crusts of dried blood from her face. Every part
of her body was in agony, as though her limbs were competing to
see which could hurt more.

Atharaisse was gone. There was only one way to go now. She
picked herself up and stumbled away into the dark.

At the bottom of the stairs, on the step above the curse-ward,
lay the amulet, as though it had been thrown up from below.
The chain was wound firmly around a roll of paper, only slightly
charred at the edges by the action of the curse-ward. Csorwe
hunkered down on the steps, unfolded it, and read in disbelief:

> *No hard feelings.*
> *Tal Charossa*

There were no more curse-wards like the first one, only a
silvery blue seal a few feet farther in. She flinched back from it,
and it emitted the soft sound of bells, exactly like the ones that
had distracted Psamag before. Talasseres Charossa must have
passed this way, and inadvertently saved her life.

The stairway opened up on a cavern. In places you could see
the cave had once been graciously paved and vaulted, a broad
underground boulevard. There were two archways, more or less
whole, and beyond the arches two passages branched off from the
cavern, pointing in opposite directions. There were waymarkers
at the mouth of each passage: *CITY* and *OUTLANDS*.

Csorwe had no idea how she made it out of the caves. She

emerged from a crack in the outland hillside half a mile from the fortress.

It was midmorning. After weeks in the dimness of the fortress, the sunlight was blinding, and she half wanted to recoil back into the darkness and hide again.

She had found her way through. She could get Sethennai back into his city. But it was hard to feel triumph when her mouth was full of her own blood. She could hardly think in a straight line long enough to tell what success meant.

Morga must have closed all the doors to the fortress, because the traffic tailed back a good two miles into the desert.

Csorwe crept nearer to the queue of wagons. Somehow, there were still people in the world talking and laughing. Somehow, people were still selling food at the stalls. The smell reminded her of the curse-ward—hot fat, burnt meat, charred bone—but she was so hungry she would've eaten her own leg if someone had put it on a skewer.

She stumbled toward one of the stalls, trying not to cower any time someone looked at her. She must have been quite a sight, caked in blood and dirt and rags. The stallholder backed away from her, holding out a fan of meat skewers to her as if to ward off the devil. She took them, turned her back on the fortress, and walked away into the desert.

7

The School of Transcendence

"Y OU SHOULD BE DEAD," said Sethennai.

"I know," she said. "I made some mistakes."

She was lying on her bed in the boardinghouse, stiff as a corpse. Her arm was in a sling. Sethennai had given her some kind of draught that numbed the pain, and she felt dull and puffy. The cold air tugged at the open wound in her face, and she observed it with detachment, as if it were a feature of the landscape. She probed the place where her left tusk had been and found the ragged socket. Nothing but a splinter of enamel remained, half-buried in the gum.

"I'm sorry," she said, although really she was too tired to be sorry for anything, too much in pain, and too surprised that she was still alive.

"If a man breaks his sword on something it was not made to cut, he can only blame himself," said Sethennai, somewhere above. He faded from her vision. "Csorwe, you are my sharpest edge. We will repair you."

She curled her hand at her side, testing whether she could make a fist. Blood was drying in uneven sediments on her palm.

"Go back to sleep," he said.

"I'm sorry," she said again, mangling the words around the gap in her gums.

"Sleep," he said, and touched the lip of the bottle to her mouth again. The drink was just as bitter as before, but this time she fell asleep at once.

When she woke again, Sethennai was still there, and he held out a mirror so that she could see herself. On the left, her one remaining tusk curved up, strong, white, and shining. On the right was its mirror image, wrought in yellow gold. Where it met her gum the flesh was still raw, and there was a tightness of stitches in her slashed lip, but she seemed more or less whole. She snapped her teeth and the golden tusk rang with a reassuring solidity.

"How?" she said.

"Gold outside. Living bone inside, apparently. I contributed a little sorcery. Don't ask me where the doctor found living bone. The gold is a little bit of showmanship. It's stable, but not very strong. Don't try to gore anybody."

"Expensive," she said. "How much?" She didn't even want to think about *sorcery*. Sethennai used his power so sparingly that she had spent her first two years in his company half-believing he called himself a wizard as a joke.

Sethennai smiled. "I told you. Sharpest edge and all that. Consider it a gift."

Csorwe nodded, and winced. She was beginning to regain sensation in her face: the stitches that curved down her cheek and through her lip looked and felt like a black centipede crawling on exposed flesh.

"I've asked the doctor what we can do about the scarring," said Sethennai. "Here, drink again and he can take a better look at it." Again he held up the bottle of sleeping draught. Csorwe tried to shake her head, and raised a hand.

"Don't need," she said.

"Exalted Sages, Csorwe, drink. I'm not letting the man sew up your face while you're awake."

"No," said Csorwe. "Leave it."

Sethennai eyed her, clearly doubting her reasoning. Whether it was the pain or the drug, she could not make her mouth move fast enough to explain properly. She had always been a plain thing. If she had earned her adult tusks she had earned this too. Some part of her, she noted with a little click of recognition, relished the idea of being marked, the way the hilt of her sword was notched for her fingers.

"Leave it," she said again, and this time Sethennai didn't argue.

Csorwe woke in the darkness, and for a few unending moments couldn't remember where she was or what had happened to her. In her dream she had been trapped somewhere, pinioned and unable to escape. Now even the sheet covering her was too heavy, but somehow she couldn't throw it off.

After a while, someone came into the room with a lamp. The light obliterated her vision, but she recognised Sethennai's silhouette and his footsteps.

"Hush," he said. She realised she must have been crying out. "What's wrong?"

She couldn't explain, couldn't really move her lips to form words.

"It's all right," he said. He sat down in the chair by her bed. "We're almost home, Csorwe. You did this for me."

She still couldn't get out from under the sheet, but she began to understand and remember where she was. The bedclothes were wrinkled and damp from thrashing around, and the room smelled of sickness. She wished someone would brush her hair and bring her a warm towel to wash her face, as Angwennad had when she was a little girl, but even half delirious she knew she couldn't ask Sethennai to do these things.

"It's all right," he said again, in a low, soft voice, as though addressing a frightened animal that threatened to bite. "You'll be well soon. In Tlaanthothe you'll have your own room in the palace, looking out over the gardens. We've spent too long out in the desert. The city is more beautiful than you can imagine, I promise."

She closed her eyes again, and tried to lie still, focusing on the voice, even if she couldn't make sense of the words.

"In the city there are flowers everywhere," he said. "Flowering vines and aloes and fruit trees. There is a fountain in every square, with clear flowing water. We'll be safe there, with the Siren watching over us. Once we're inside the walls none of our enemies can reach us. We'll be unconquerable."

When she woke the next morning she didn't remember very much of this, only a flash of light in the darkness and a fading vision of fountains.

Sethennai left the boardinghouse one night soon afterward, and came back the next day, buoyant with delight and unable to settle in any one spot.

"This is astonishing," he said. "I've had my ear to the ground and it looks as though no one suspects it was us who killed Psamag. Not even remotely. Morga thinks Olthaaros sent you, and Olthaaros thinks she's covering up the fact that she killed him herself. I had worried we'd lost the element of surprise, but instead they're all chasing each other's shadows. This means we can still pick our moment. Absolutely wonderful."

"What about Psamag's amulet?" said Csorwe, cringing inwardly because she hadn't even considered the element of surprise. However pleased Sethennai seemed, she still felt she'd failed in some respects.

"They don't seem to have noticed it's gone," said Sethennai. The amulet was hanging around his neck, and bounced whenever he gestured, which was often. "Our way should be clear. I have a few more logistical questions to resolve and then Olthaaros can find out what's coming to him. Assuming you wouldn't rather stay behind and rest?"

"I'd rather break my other arm," said Csorwe.

"I'm glad to hear it," said Sethennai. "You've done an excellent job and you deserve to see the results." He stretched, tipping his chair back, and beamed, with a sunny warmth that made Csorwe briefly forget she was in pain.

For the next few days Sethennai went out to his meetings, or sat muttering over his books. Csorwe ate soft foods and wondered what was coming next. Tlaanthothe seemed like a real prospect at last, and she was realising how little she knew about it, for all Sethennai spoke of it as home.

For one thing, there was the Siren. Csorwe hadn't thought much about that. Only now did she begin to fully consider the fact that entering the city would mean coming back into the presence of a god. She remembered how the presence of the Unspoken had felt. Csorwe had no way of knowing whether Sethennai's goddess would be anything like that.

And how was it going to be, when they finally encountered Olthaaros? She wondered whether he would back down when he realised Sethennai was back in full force. Sethennai was very confident that things would go his way, but Csorwe couldn't help remembering his fight with Akaro. She wasn't in good shape to help him if something went wrong. This was why she hated to be ill or injured. You were left too much time to speculate, rebounding from one unknown to another like a rubber ball that got faster and faster as it went.

In her most optimistic moments, she hoped Tlaanthothe might be rather like Grey Hook. Sethennai gave the impression that it was cleaner and prettier, but there would still be new territory to explore—interesting food to buy at the market—more languages to study, maybe. And she would still be useful to him, now he knew she could be trusted with a task on her own.

At last she could walk again without wincing, and it was time to leave.

Csorwe tried not to look at the fortress as they approached. Once they were down in the caves, she had plenty to distract her, starting with keeping her balance one-armed.

They reached the cavern with the curse-ward, and the stairway reaching up into the fortress. Sethennai stopped to investigate the wards. He probed at the wax with a pencil, leaning frighteningly close. He had Psamag's amulet around his neck, but Csorwe still had to clench her good hand to stop herself from dragging him away.

"Crude but effective," he muttered. "That's Olthaaros all over."

*

They emerged into Tlaanthothe on a perfect spring morning, just after dawn. A warm breeze was blowing, carrying heat from the Speechless Sea, and they came up a hidden stair into a cluster of plane trees in the middle of a formal park.

The old brocade on Sethennai's horrible coat gleamed like choppy water in the sun. He wore a ragged scarf over his hair, and he walked with a stick. He was already wearing his gauntlets, partially hidden inside his sleeves.

"Oh, my city, I missed you," he said, under his breath, as they emerged from the shadow of the trees. "Exalted Sages, how I missed you."

A change came over him, like the sun coming out, as they entered the city. He looked somehow more vital, more lively, more and more delighted with the world and everything in it, more suffused with power and self-confidence. Under his rags, his eyes were bright with joy. Perhaps this was what it meant for him to come back to his goddess.

Tlaanthothe was indeed very much quieter and very much cleaner than Grey Hook. Outside the park, the boulevards were empty, peopled only with polite rows of obelisk cypresses. Despite her apprehension, Csorwe smiled when she saw there were fountains playing in the squares, just as Sethennai had promised.

"Where is everyone?" she said. She was wrapped in an equally threadbare cloak, with the hood pulled low over her face.

"It's early," said Sethennai. "Or perhaps they know a change is on its way, and they're staying at home." He smiled again, with a glimmer of menace that made Csorwe gladder than usual to be on his side.

They picked their way down Broad Street, doing their best to look unremarkable.

At the top of Broad Street stood the School of Transcendence, a grand edifice of white marble and copper verdigris, with a pointed dome like a closed water lily. Two armed guards stood at the door, dressed in the jade-and-ivory colours of the city, and one of them stepped forward as they approached.

"Now, then," he said. "You're going to have to move along. There's no begging in Broad Street."

Sethennai came up the steps to meet him. "I am the lawful Chancellor of Tlaanthothe," said Sethennai. "The usurper Olthaaros Charossa deserves none of your loyalty. Stand aside."

The captain's eyes widened with fear and recognition. His mouth opened, shaping several different sentences before settling on *"Never!"* His hand went to his sword. "We will never—"

Whatever he had intended to say came to nothing. Sethennai gave an offhand flick of his wrist—his gauntlets hissed—and a rent opened in the air, six feet tall, distorting everything around it. The captain faltered and his sword froze in mid-swing. Something was coming out of the opening in the air, something with long-pincered jointed legs, tearing the opening wider as they came. Csorwe watched with awful clarity as they seized hold of the captain, pulling him into an embrace like a lover's. The man screamed, a brief thin sound, and the legs curled around him and dragged him into the tear, which closed as though the man and the legs and the scream had never been.

All this happened within a few seconds, and Sethennai let his arm drop to his side. His brow glittered with sweat, and his hands trembled. He didn't have to say anything else. There wasn't much you could add.

The other soldier stared at the place his captain had been, then dropped his weapon and put his hands up.

Sethennai swept past him to the great bronze door of the School of Transcendence. He knocked three times, each knock reverberating around the square with the sound of a great bell. His gauntlet sparked like a hammer striking an anvil.

Sculpted in bas-relief on the door was the shield of Tlaan-thothe: a cup borne up by two bronze horses whose hindquarters tapered into the bodies of fish. At the first knock, their fins and crests flared in alarm. At the second knock, they slithered away from the cup, sinking back into the door as though retreating into underwater caverns. At the third knock, the door's resistance broke and it opened, soundlessly, into darkness.

The inward chambers of the School of Transcendence were vast, cold, and still. Fine shafts of sunlight filtered down through apertures in the vaults above. This place was even quieter than the still city outside, and even emptier. Csorwe and Sethennai trooped down the grand entrance hall toward another set of high bronze doors. These doors were cast in the likeness of banks of thorns, impenetrable and thickly barbed, with no sign of a handle or keyhole.

Out of the shadows darted a small group of people, unarmed and frightened. All of them were Tlaanthothei, and the points of their ears were drawn up high and taut, flicking occasionally. Leading them was a woman in long pleated robes. The others seemed to be her servants. At the sight of Sethennai, most of them squeaked and fell back, but the woman drew herself up and stepped forward. She was a gentle-looking person whose face was creased with laughter lines, but she showed no sign of softness nor amusement as she approached the wizard.

"Niranthe," said the wizard, matter-of-fact.

"Sethennai," said the woman, in the same tone of voice, as

though they were meeting on a matter of business alone. Then her resolve cracked and something like desperation showed beyond it. "Safe passage," she said. "You promised safe passage for the household and a place for my son."

She gestured to the young man by her side.

It was Talasseres Charossa.

Csorwe bridled, digging the nails of her good hand into her palm. Talasseres looked past her as though they'd never met before, and up at Sethennai. It took all her restraint and a lifetime's experience of waiting quietly at the sidelines not to throw herself at him.

"So," Talasseres said. "You're here to kill my uncle."

"Is that going to cause trouble between us?" said the wizard conversationally.

Talasseres' lip curled in what was perhaps meant to be a cynical expression. Drawing back from his teeth it looked more like a snarl. "No," he said.

The wizard made no answer, only nodded his approval. "The door, Niranthe?"

She stepped forward and passed her hands over the surface of the door without touching, then pricked the palm of her hand on one of the thorns. The blood disappeared as if the interior of the thorn was a hollow needle, and certain of the vines retracted with a metallic slithering sound. The door split down the middle and stood ajar.

"Safe passage," said Niranthe urgently.

"Yes, yes, of course, and a position of favour for your son," said Sethennai. He sounded relatively calm, even entertained, though such anxious prodding usually aggravated him. "That was the agreement. I do not need to be reminded. Where is Olthaaros?"

"We've hardly seen him. He's been shut up in his study for weeks. I haven't spoken to him since Talasseres returned."

"He must know I'm here for him by now," said Sethennai.

"He knew you were coming. He went into the Inner Chapel," said Niranthe. "He's preparing his defences. He believes the Siren will take his side."

Sethennai laughed. "Perhaps I shouldn't speak ill to you of your brother, but it does amuse me that the man has spent so long refining his art, soaking up all the power that abides in Tlaanthothe, and understands so little. Less than nothing. Niranthe, please, feel free to go. You and your household are under my protection."

Niranthe and her flock moved out toward the door. Talasseres stood where he was, his fists clenched at his sides and his chin raised in defiance.

"Tal!" said Niranthe. "Quickly!"

"I want to stay," he said.

Niranthe looked from her son to Sethennai, bewildered then indignant.

"It's all right," said Sethennai. "Let him stay. If he's going to work for me then he may as well learn my methods early on."

"You won't let him come to harm?" said Niranthe.

"I suppose you'll just have to trust me," said Sethennai.

Talasseres didn't ignore Csorwe. To ignore her he would have had to notice her in the first place. His eyes slid past her, and her broken arm, and her mutilated face, as though there was nothing in the world but his mother and the wizard. Then he fell in line.

A position of favour? thought Csorwe in disbelief. But then, she hadn't told Sethennai exactly what had happened in the fortress—how Talasseres had cost Csorwe her tusk and nearly her life.

Beyond the door of thorns was a library, almost as large as the serpents' library in Echentyr. The marble floors held maps of the stars inlaid in gold. They passed globes of a hundred worlds and busts of a hundred scholars, and came to the Inner Chapel, which was sealed with another bronze door.

Though flanked on either side by graceful statues, this door was not grand. It was rather low, so that Sethennai would have to stoop to enter, and it was very, very heavy. There were grooves in the floor, making three concentric semicircles that spread outward from the door. Here Sethennai paused.

The statues on either side of the door were two old Tlaan-thothei philosophers, Csorwe supposed. A man with a high-domed forehead and a magnificent beard, and a woman whose hair fanned out above her head like the crown of an umbrella pine. They both had expressions of ferocious curiosity. Each of them held a golden chalice between their folded marble hands. Sethennai took the first chalice and poured what it contained into the outermost circle in the floor.

"Brine," he said, setting the first chalice back into place and taking the next. "And this is oil of myrrh."

The smell of the oil of myrrh spread through the antechamber as he poured it into the second circle, heavy and bittersweet. "I hope you're taking notes, Talasseres," he said. He had never explained any of his art to Csorwe before, and she felt a stab of jealousy, as instant as it was unworthy. "Salt water is the sacred substance, that which was corrupted. Oil of myrrh presents as an offering of the richness of the earth, the passing glory of that which is mortal. And last—" Sethennai fumbled in his coat pocket and withdrew a teardrop vial, sealed with wax. "The three wards are completed by that which has been long dead. Bone dust from Old Ormary, before its fall." He prised off the seal and began sprinkling the dust into the third groove.

"This opens the door, sir?" said Talasseres. Csorwe seethed, and tried to suppress her anger, fully aware that it was the wrong time for it. This was supposed to be the moment of Sethennai's triumph. She would deal with Talasseres Charossa later on.

"Oh, not at all," said the wizard. "The door is not locked. The three wards prevent what is within from escaping. The goddess at the heart of my city is not to be underestimated. If we had time I should have preferred thrice three wards—brine and blood and gold, myrrh and camphor and balsam, bone and ash and dust—but this will serve."

Csorwe followed the wizard into the Inner Chapel. The chapel was of bare stone, and it had the damp chill of a cellar. It was lit by a single suspended oil lantern, swaying on a chain. The shadows shivered as though the room was immersed in deep water.

Standing on a dais at the centre of the room was a great shard of dark crystal, twenty feet tall, smooth and jagged. It gleamed in the rippling light as if wet. It looked as though it had been splintered away from some larger whole: near the top, it was thin and sharp enough to be translucent.

It was incongruous. More than incongruous. This was something that had pierced through into the ordinary world. Around the stone, every particle of dust was stilled in its motion, floating on the air. Csorwe remembered the texts of her childhood: *The Unspoken One stands with its kin beyond the circle of the world.*

There was a god in the stone. Bound within it, as the

Unspoken Name was bound in its Shrine. Now that she knew, Csorwe thought she could sense it, as you might sense another person in the dark by their breath. It was quiet, but it watched, and it waited.

Standing before it, like a child before an indifferent adult, was Olthaaros Charossa. He was gaunt and bald and clean-shaven, dressed in an austere grey robe. More of a contrast with Sethennai would be hard to imagine. Olthaaros' ears were flat against the sides of his head, and he was concentrating so hard on the stone that he did not turn to look at them.

There were two or three bundles lying on the dais before the stone. As they drew closer, Csorwe recognised them for what they were. Talasseres gasped. They were bodies in servants' shifts. Their blood had pooled around the base of the stone, only visible as a dull sheen in the light of the lantern.

"The cooks," said Talasseres under his breath, numbly, as though he was not aware he was speaking at all. "Mother thought they'd run away . . ." He stepped toward them, and at that moment Olthaaros turned.

"Oh, Talasseres," he said, with an air of weary long-suffering. "I heard you were back. Psamag really should have done the decent thing and pushed you out of a window." He looked from Talasseres to Csorwe to Sethennai, and his eyes narrowed with anger. Csorwe pulled the door shut. If she saw Talasseres standing near a window any time soon, Olthaaros might get his wish.

Olthaaros' mouth twisted with bitter laughter. "Well, well, Belthandros. Here you are. And I suppose you've convinced them all that yours is a righteous cause."

"I didn't sacrifice my kitchen staff," said Sethennai.

"Do they know you murdered Akaro?"

"Akaro did your bidding willingly. And it really is embarrassing, you know, how little you understand." He strode across the room toward Olthaaros, stopping a few paces away. "The Siren of the Speechless Sea is a fragment of one of the world's most ancient powers. A shard from the broken throne. She does not serve unless it suits her. Unless she is courted. And you have ever been an inept suitor."

"Always obscene," said Olthaaros.

"Always accurate," said Sethennai. "I suppose you imagined that spilling a few gallons of blood in her name would obligate her to serve your ends? She will not save you. I am here to take back my city, Olthaaros. If you wish to save yourself you will beg my forgiveness."

Csorwe stayed back, pressed against the wall by the door, keeping an eye on Talasseres in case he decided to do something he would regret. At this point she became aware of a presence in her own mind. The touch of the Siren was quite unlike that of the Unspoken Name. This felt like a caress of warm water, rising slowly among smooth stones. Like the Unspoken Name she promised oblivion, but more softly. How sweet and soothing it would be to give way to her. Her voice curled around Csorwe like coils of vapour, gentle, ethereal.

Then it stopped and cold reality returned, sudden as a blast of wintry air.

You are already forsworn, said the Siren. *I have no interest in a discarded vessel.*

The presence receded sharply, and Csorwe was alone in her own body. To judge from the glazed look in Talasseres' eyes, the Siren was speaking to him. She kicked him in the shins. He came back to life with a jerk, and glared at her.

"No hard feelings," she hissed.

Olthaaros and Sethennai faced one another now, each braced to act.

"Beg your forgiveness?" said Olthaaros. "And am I expected to believe you would show me mercy? You are a monster of pride, Sethennai." From the sheath at his side he drew a hooked dagger, already dark with the blood of his servants.

"Very well," said Sethennai. His gauntlets sparked in readiness.

Csorwe had seen and committed enough violence that she no longer expected it to be impressive or exciting, but the two wizards in combat were like nothing she had ever witnessed. Each man moved like a spark, and raised dust in terrible shapes around him: waves and claws and kites of dust, great beasts of dust that warred in the upper air.

The whole room crackled, filling with the smell of hot metal. Csorwe's surviving teeth buzzed in her skull, and blood seeped from the root of the gold tusk. She dug her nails into her palms. It was all moving too quickly. The two shapes moved faster and faster in the clouds, summoning flame against shield against blade of dust.

She and Sethennai had come so far together. She couldn't bear for him to come this close to home and fail. But she could only watch, and wait, and trust.

At last there was a single convulsion—a single invisible shock wave—a single blow or strike or puncture. The dust cleared, and Olthaaros lay at Sethennai's feet.

Csorwe let out a long breath. Talasseres Charossa observed his uncle's defeat closely but coldly, without reaction.

Olthaaros was not dead. He scrabbled for purchase on the

blood-slick floor, rising to an unsteady crouch. Sethennai stood and observed, hands folded behind his back in an attitude of casual grace.

"This is ugly and foolish, Olthaaros," he said. "We are both thinking men. There was no need for this."

Olthaaros stared at the ground and muttered a curse, summoning all the dignity he could manage before falling back, his neck craning upward like that of a tortoise flipped onto its back.

"Please," he cried, breathless and rasping.

"There is no need to beg me," said Sethennai, with great satisfaction. "I know what mercy is."

"Not you," said Olthaaros, with venom, and he raised his eyes again to the obelisk. "Please—please—"

No, said the Siren.

They all heard it, not so much a word as a great resonance, a single note of negation. Olthaaros snarled in defiance, rising again, and from the cuff of his right wrist he flung a small fletched dart at Sethennai. As he moved, his elbow skidded on the bloody floor, and the dart fell far short, hitting the ground with a faint silvery noise, perfectly audible in the silence that followed the Siren's denial.

Csorwe glanced at Talasseres and saw his lip curl with some strong emotion. Disgust, she thought, or disappointment.

"How unworthy," said Sethennai, picking up the dart and turning it over. He was beginning to settle into his triumph, radiantly amused. In such a mood he was inclined to be benign, and Csorwe wondered whether he would spare his enemy. But he strode over to Olthaaros, and pressed the toe of his boot down on his neck. They listened as Olthaaros choked, convulsed, and lay still.

So Belthandros Sethennai returned to his city, and so ended Csorwe's education.

II

Buried,
But Not Deeply

For seven days and nights the Traitor Goddess lay dying in the lap of the sea. Her blood drained into the dry sand, and her curse fell upon the creatures of the earth.

May your heirs suffer as I suffer. May they drink of my poison. The inheritance of mankind was despoiled, and the corruption of the Traitor was in their veins, and in all generations her curse was known.

from the Qarsazhi prose epic *The Shaping of the World*

8

The Watchtower Bell

Five Years Later

DARYOU MALKHAYA PULLED ON his winter coat and boots, buckled on his sword, and set out into the end of the world.

It was midafternoon, and the feeble sun was already sinking, turning the sky to scarlet. This world had been a long time ending. Its name had been the first thing to go: when its people died out, they took their languages with them. Now the light drained away and the world froze slowly to death.

Cheerful stuff. The place had an official designation, assigned by Malkhaya's superiors at the Imperial Survey Office of the Church of Qarsazh. *Precursor World Alpha-Twenty-Something-Something*. When Malkhaya had first been stationed at the compound, he had assumed the researchers would have a friendly nickname for the place, *Snowball* or *East Nowhere* or something, but he was soon put right. There were only two scholars at the compound and neither of them was the frivolous type.

Qanwa Shuthmili was already out in the yard by the gate, beginning her inspection of the inner security perimeter. This was a chain of flags and lanterns, suspended from the ring of stakes surrounding the compound. The red sunset made her white Adept's robes look grisly.

"Aren't you cold?" he said. She was wearing only a light coat, and she had taken off her gloves.

Malkhaya understood that Shuthmili was a highly trained and powerful Adept, that her resemblance to a twenty-two-year-old girl was basically incidental, but he still wished she would dress for the weather.

"I'm used to it, Warden," she said, running her bare hands along the cord of the perimeter. The flags and lanterns looked to Malkhaya like a cheerless sort of festival, but the inner perimeter was their final line of defence against anything that might come up out of the dying world and try to devour them.

Well, technically, as their sole Warden, Malkhaya was the final line of defence, but the hope was that the perimeter would give him some advance warning.

He followed her around the circuit. The compound was built inside the enclosure of a ruined farmstead, on a ridge overlooking a frozen lake. The watchtower and the lodge had been constructed by the Survey Office a few years ago, and from the outside they looked as stark and unwelcoming as the landscape itself. The Nine-Petalled Rose of Qarsazh flew from the top of the tower, a flash of darker red against the bloody sky. The windows were dark: Lagri Aritsa had a bee in his bonnet about conserving oil and wouldn't light the lamps until it was full dark outside.

"Everything is in order," said Shuthmili when they reached the gate again. Her breath smoked in the air.

"Do you need to rest a minute?" said Malkhaya. He knew magic was exhausting. Part of his duty was to keep Shuthmili from crashing.

She looked at him blandly. "I do this every night, Warden," she said. Malkhaya had tried to encourage her to call him by his given name—after a few months even Aritsa had given up on calling him *Warden*—but formality seemed to come to her more naturally than familiarity.

"We could take *Prosperity* when we do the outer perimeter," he said, just in case.

They were lucky to have been assigned a cutter. Normally the Survey Office was stingy about these things, or possibly the Church as a whole felt that it was spiritually valuable for a person to have to walk around on his own two legs. Malkhaya suspected their good luck had something to do with Shuthmili's aunt. In theory an Adept had no personal ties, but it couldn't hurt to share a name with a senior Inquisitor.

"I'd like the walk," she said. "I've been inside all day."

Malkhaya supposed that if he'd been sitting at a desk with Aritsa deciphering inscriptions all day, he wouldn't mind a walk either.

They made their way to the outer perimeter, down to the shore of the frozen lake. There were ruins here, ploughing up from the shore at an odd angle.

"This was a fort, once," said Shuthmili. "The Precursors fought over this lake."

"Oh, yeah?" said Malkhaya. It was so rare for her to volunteer conversation that he felt he ought to encourage it, but he didn't know what he could add.

"They're all gone, now," she said. "The lords and their fortress-builders."

Malkhaya had been assigned to the compound for almost a year, and he still hadn't grasped what was important about this particular Precursor society. According to the Survey Office, they were among the ancestors of modern Qarsazhi civilisation, but nothing about their ruins and barrows felt familiar to Malkhaya. The Precursors had built masses of tombs and carved yards of inscriptions, and then they had died out, along with anything else that lived in this world.

His ignorance made it difficult to understand what Shuthmili and Aritsa were talking about most of the time. Malkhaya had been a Warden of the Church all his adult life, and had worked for the Survey Office for most of that time, and he had never thought much about his charges' research. His job was to keep them safe, not to get distracted by the flotsam of lost Precursor cities. But then, he usually had at least one other Warden to keep him company. Spending months with nobody but Aritsa and Shuthmili often made him feel that he was shepherding two fractious children—and sometimes that he himself was the fractious child.

The full patrol of the outer perimeter was a little more than three miles, an hour's walk in near-silence. Occasionally Shuthmili murmured something to herself as she reached up to check the flags or rekindle the lanterns, but she didn't say anything to Malkhaya.

The red sunset had faded by now, and the flags of the outer perimeter were the only bright colours to be seen in the grey dusk. Everything else in the dying world was the colour of earth, ash, or ice. The only sound was the sighing of wind among the ruined fortifications.

There was no vegetation left in this world. It would be very difficult for anyone or anything to sneak up on them. Malkhaya should have felt secure. This was a nice, safe billet. This world's greatest threat to them—as he regularly reminded Shuth-mili—was the cold.

Sometimes when a world died quickly, it began to decay, and all kinds of nasty things could happen. On previous assignments Malkhaya had seen the dead rise and mouths open in the ground. He had seen the teeth of the Maze beginning to bite through the sky. But this world was fading so slowly and quietly that they hadn't seen even a single revenant. The Precursor dead had slept peacefully for centuries.

Oddly enough, this didn't make Malkhaya like the place any better.

"Warden, look," said Shuthmili. He turned, expecting that she was pointing out yet another Nine-blessed inscription—and stopped dead.

In the sky above the far end of the lake, visible in the gap between two hills, was an unfamiliar mazeship.

"Mother of Cities," said Malkhaya under his breath.

"There's no delivery scheduled," said Shuthmili. The Survey Office sent a ship once a month to drop off fuel and supplies. It had already been and gone earlier that week.

"No," said Malkhaya. "That's not a Qarsazhi ship." He stared at it, as if he could wish it away. "The lights are all wrong."

"Then who is it?" said Shuthmili.

"I don't know," he said, tracking the ship until it passed irrecoverably behind the hills and away. "Bigger than *Prosperity*. Much smaller than a standard Imperial frigate. I don't think it's a warship, unless it's a very tiny corvette—" He realised Shuthmili was looking as bewildered as he did when she talked about inscriptions, and tried to take a more reassuring tone. "It's not ours. But that doesn't necessarily mean we need to be afraid. It was moving away from us."

"There shouldn't be anyone here," said Shuthmili. She sounded less frosty than usual, more like her actual age. "Nobody else comes here. That's part of the reason I was assigned this placement. My Quincuriate assessment is in two months, and—"

"No, I know," said Malkhaya, keeping his voice level. Shuthmili did not need to know how much the ship worried him. "We'll go back up and tell Aritsa. See what he thinks." They had almost completed the full circuit of their patrol. It wasn't far to get back up to the compound.

He glanced back, watching for a moment longer, but there was no more sign of the ship. It might just be looters. They would soon discover there was no treasure in this world worth taking, and leave again without doing any harm.

He knew exactly how vulnerable they were here. Their isolation was their first defence, but it also meant they couldn't easily call for help. The nearest Qarsazhi world was many Gates away.

"Should we go and investigate?" said Shuthmili, sounding calmer. The perimeter lanterns lent her eyes an inquisitive gleam. Malkhaya would have preferred her to stay at least a little bit alarmed.

"We'll see what Aritsa thinks," said Malkhaya again.

Shuthmili lifted her chin as though about to object.

"We can't do anything now," he said. "It's dark and we've lost sight of the ship. And like you said, you've got your assessment coming up. You need to stay quiet."

After a second's reluctance, Shuthmili nodded.

"What about the rest of the patrol?" she said.

"Don't worry about it now. We need to get you back up to the compound."

Malkhaya truly hoped it was looters, and that they were the usual kind of ill-informed chancers, without any information about the Qarsazhi compound or its personnel. There was no treasure in the Precursor ruins, but that didn't mean there was nothing valuable here that could be stolen. Their research work for the Survey Office was real enough, but it wasn't the only reason they'd been stashed away in this distant and forgotten world. Malkhaya just had to hope that, whoever was on board that ship, they didn't know about Shuthmili.

The watchtower bell rang once as Malkhaya and Shuthmili crossed the inner perimeter into the compound.

Dr. Lagri Aritsa was waiting for them at the door of the lodge. He had lit the lamps at last, and the slit windows cast golden reflections that flickered on the frozen earth. Above the watchtower, the sky was starless black, marked in places by large pale shapes, like cat's eyes in darkness.

"You two were gone far too long," he said, rubbing his thin hands together to keep warm. Everything about him was thin, from his lips to his greying hair. Malkhaya suspected he had only come out because he was concerned about them, and wished he had stayed inside in the warmth.

"Shuthmili, you are freezing," Aritsa went on. "Come inside. And we must get you fed."

"Please don't worry about me, your reverence," said Shuthmili, following him in.

The lodge was invitingly warm after being outside, smelling of incense and pine logs and freshly made coffee. Malkhaya draped a blanket over Shuthmili, who sat down before the fire without complaint. Aritsa brought her a bowl of rice and beans before fetching the coffee for himself and Malkhaya.

Malkhaya drank gratefully, helping himself to two biscuits despite Aritsa's disapproval. He was glad to have the chance to fortify himself before breaking the news about the ship they had seen.

Aritsa took it better than he'd expected. He paced a little before the fire and muttered a prayer to the Mother of Cities, and then seemed to compose himself.

"Robbers and raiders are vile, but inevitable, and easily handled," said Aritsa, with surprising firmness. "You're certain it wasn't a Qarsazhi vessel? The delivery ship might have got into difficulties and returned."

"As certain as I can be," said Malkhaya. "It was pretty dark."

"We haven't been troubled by looters before," said Aritsa. "I wonder what they think they're here to take."

"Yeah, me too," said Malkhaya. He glanced discreetly at Shuthmili and hoped Aritsa would get the message.

"This is a grave world," said Shuthmili. She had finished her food and was curled up in her blanket, watching the fire. "The dead lie underground in their thousands. They are buried, but not deeply. That could be an attraction, for some."

"Always a ray of sunshine, Shuthmili," said Malkhaya, trying to smile.

"Warden—your reverence—" said Shuthmili, turning to face them. "We don't have to wait to find out what they want. We could go looking for them first. I could help. Magic can be used for things other than maintaining the perimeter, you know."

Aritsa pinched the bridge of his nose. "I know you want to

help, Shuthmili," he said. "But consider what you were taught. *Personal glory is one step from pride . . .*"

"*And pride is the downfall of all Adepts,*" she said, sitting up very straight. "Yes. But I'm not looking for personal glory, I only—"

"You want prove yourself worthy of the trust that has been placed in you. It's natural. But you must understand that it is too easy to compromise yourself like this. The Traitor is insidious. She plays on both base and noble impulses. And with your assessment for the Quincuriate so soon, we cannot risk even a whisper of corruption."

At the mention of the assessment, Shuthmili subsided back into her chair and nodded. Aritsa knew as well as they all did how much the Quincuriate meant to her. Malkhaya had once seen her folding up paper packaging from their supply drop to use for her notes.

"Your duty is to shed light, Shuthmili," said Aritsa. "As is mine." He touched the Nine-Petalled Rose embroidered across the breast of his priest's vestments. "Once you are joined with your Quincury you will shed such light."

"Yes, your reverence," she said. "I hope so."

"I have no doubt of it," said Aritsa. "We in the Survey Office consider ourselves fortunate to have you for a short time, but the Quincuriate is your future. Do not allow yourself to be distracted." He gave her an uncertain smile; Aritsa was not a smiling man, so this made him look like someone trying to pronounce a foreign language for the first time.

Malkhaya had never seen Shuthmili smile either, but she bowed her head in respect. "I will be careful," she said.

The two men ate the rest of the rice and beans, and Malkhaya finished his usual chores. After evening prayers Shuthmili retired, claiming she was going to sleep, although Malkhaya suspected she would be studying for her assessment into the small hours.

"The timing of this ship's arrival concerns me," said Aritsa. He steepled his hands on the table and propped his face against them.

Malkhaya sat opposite Aritsa and poured himself a glass of whisky. An Oshaarun single malt was his main luxury these days. He would have offered it to Aritsa, but he knew how the priest felt about alcohol: it would only elicit a lecture about how strong drink was a poison to flesh and spirit.

"What about the timing in particular?" said Malkhaya, sipping his whisky.

Aritsa tapped his fingertips thoughtfully. "I didn't mention this before for fear of upsetting Shuthmili. The most recent delivery brought a letter from Inquisitor Qanwa."

High Inquisitor Qanwa Zhiyouri was the head of the house of Qanwa, a leading light of the Inquisitorate, and one of the richest women in Qarsazh. She was also Shuthmili's aunt.

"What does she want this time?" said Malkhaya.

Inquisitor Qanwa had taken a much more pointed interest in the activities of the Survey Office since her niece had begun her assignment. Malkhaya found this surprising. Most houses had nothing to do with their mage offspring once they had been safely taken up by the Church. This was one reason Malkhaya had felt obliged to look out for Shuthmili, cut off as she was from the supportive network of house loyalties and duties. It wasn't something you really wanted known, that your own blood had become a vessel of the Traitor. But it seemed that Qanwa Zhiyouri was a particularly fond aunt, or a particularly liberal-minded Inquisitor. Malkhaya slightly resented her for it, but it was her prerogative. Loyalty to house and hearth was what distinguished Qarsazhi from barbarians.

"We are honoured that the High Inquisitor has such an enthusiasm for our work," said Aritsa, afflictedly. He took a deep breath and settled his hands on the table. "She has given the Chancellor of Tlaanthothe permission to send a party of scholars to join us here and conduct some excavations."

Malkhaya tried not to laugh. Only Aritsa could think this was on a par with the imminent threat of raiders.

"How many scholars are we talking?" he said, sipping his whisky.

"Two!" said Aritsa.

Now Malkhaya did laugh. "Aritsa, we can deal with two Tlaanthothei. There's plenty of space here for them, although I can't promise they won't bang their heads on the ceilings. And they won't stay long, surely?"

"Inquisitor Qanwa said nothing about that," said Aritsa, bristling.

"They won't," said Malkhaya. "They won't like the cold any more than we do."

"Well, they are arriving next week, so we will find out soon enough, I fear," said Aritsa. "As I said, I do not like the timing."

"Coincidences do happen," said Malkhaya. "It's my job to be paranoid, but based on what you've said I don't think this is anything."

Aritsa sniffed. "Two sets of strangers in less than a month, when we have been left in peace for so long?"

"It is odd," said Malkhaya. "But we don't have time to write back to Inquisitor Qanwa now. So unless you want to turn these Tlaanthothei back at the Gate, we may have no choice but to see what they're like."

Malkhaya took *Prosperity* out to meet the Tlaanthothei visitors at the Gate. Over the past week they had seen no more of the strange mazeship. Maybe it was already gone, slunk back to the Gate overnight. They had decided it was best not to tell the Tlaanthothei anything about it—no use putting them on edge over a threat they could do nothing about and which might never materialise.

From above, the dying world was almost beautiful: the air was cold and clear and before the sun began to set the sky was a delicate pearl-blue. The Gate was mounted in a cliff, gleaming like a gigantic oracle-pool. Malkhaya approached at the appointed time and landed *Prosperity* to wait for the visitors.

They came through the Gate on foot, and Malkhaya got a good look at the two of them long before they saw him. He tried to gauge how difficult they might be to deal with, and how much of a fuss Aritsa was going to make.

The first was a young man who looked just as Malkhaya had imagined a Tlaanthothei student would—tall, dark, thin, fashionable cheekbones, very pretty in an inaccessible way. Twenty years ago Malkhaya could have made a real fool of himself for a face like that.

The other gave him pause. She was Oshaaru, stocky and grey-skinned, her hair cropped short like the boy's. She would have been unremarkable, if not for the horrific scar that curved all the way down one side of her face, from forehead to chin, cutting through eyebrow and lip on the way. And one of her tusks seemed to be a prosthetic! Malkhaya had his own share of scars, but none so big or so obvious. The poor girl was hardly any older than Shuthmili, but the scar looked to be long healed. She must have been through some kind of violence in her home country. You did hear about all kinds of Oshaarun clan warfare, after all. He made a mental note not to stare at her.

They were both carrying swords, which gave Malkhaya a twinge of unease. If they'd been travelling on foot through remote parts of the Maze, it was only sensible to go armed, but he hadn't been expecting to have to sort the guests directly into his personal index of threats.

Well, nothing to be done about that now. He got out of the cutter and waved them aboard.

"On behalf of the Imperial Survey Office of Qarsazh, welcome to Precursor World Alpha-Twenty-uh-well."

"Talasseres Charossa," said the Tlaanthothei, in lightly accented Qarsazhi, as he scrambled up into the cutter. "You can call me Tal." He grinned down at Malkhaya. "And this is my valued colleague Csorwe."

The girl with the appalling scar nodded to Malkhaya and followed Tal into the cutter.

"Sor-weh?" said Malkhaya, giving it his best shot.

"Close enough," said Tal, beaming at his valued colleague.

Csorwe just shrugged. Malkhaya hoped he hadn't offended her. Maybe she didn't speak Qarsazhi well, or she was one of those scholars who didn't do small talk.

"Well, I'm Daryou Malkhaya. I'm the Warden here," he said,

swinging himself back up into the cutter after them. "We've been looking forward to visitors all week," he said. "Aritsa has put on his *company* vestments. How was your journey?"

Daryou Malkhaya was a squarish, clean-shaven man in his forties, who looked like a neatly made cabinet. In other words, he was exactly the kind of big handsome idiot that Talasseres found irresistible. It didn't do Csorwe any good to know this, but once realised it was impossible to deny.

She huddled down on her bench as the cutter swooped over the frozen hills, and tried not to pay attention as Tal put on his most languid drawl to flirt. He sounded as though the Charossa family as a whole had been bored for the last eight hundred years.

"So you're here to see the Hollow Monument, eh?" said Daryou, either oblivious or just polite. "You must be pretty keen on ancient history, unless you've come all this way to enjoy Aritsa's cooking."

Tal did his modest expression. "Oh, well . . . the life of a scholar has its own rewards."

That was one way of putting it. Talasseres generally only looked at a book if he thought Sethennai was watching.

"I was never much of a scholar, I'm afraid," said Daryou, grinning at him. "I mean, I *can* read, but Aritsa sometimes has to explain the big words."

"Oh, is that why you became a Warden?" said Tal, returning his smile.

"That's the natural assumption, isn't it?" said Daryou, not unamused.

The wind was bitingly cold. At least it was a brief flight back to the Qarsazhi compound. Csorwe told herself firmly that they weren't going to spend more than a week here. That was more than enough time to follow up this tenuous lead, given that she was going to be stuck the whole time with Talasseres, the worst person alive.

"Huh," she said, as they approached the lodge. "Two security perimeters."

"Cleverly observed," muttered Tal under his breath.

"True what they say about our good old Qarsazhi paranoia," said Daryou. "Not that I think there's anything wrong with taking security seriously."

The lodge was sparsely decorated inside, just whitewashed walls, wool hangings, and stone. In a niche above the fireplace was a high-relief icon of one of the Qarsazhi gods: a young man with sword and shield trampling on a dragon. He had an intensely distant expression, as though conjugating verbs in his head.

"Take a seat wherever you like," said Daryou. "I have to carry out my evening patrol, but Aritsa will be with you shortly."

They duly sat and waited.

"Enjoying yourself, Sor-weh?" said Tal, once it was clear Daryou had left.

No point correcting him on this. She'd tried, early on (*It's like* doorway—), but Tal only found it funnier if you struggled.

"We're supposed to be scholars," she said in an undertone. "Don't fuck this up."

"I love working with you," he said. "You're always so *fun*."

"Yeah, feeling's mutual," said Csorwe. "I'm serious. You think Sethennai's going to thank us if they throw us out before we can get the Reliquary?"

"Oh, come on, you don't even really think the Reliquary's here," said Tal.

Before she could answer, there were footsteps from the next room, and another Qarsazhi appeared—an elderly priest, carrying a heavy-laden tray of coffee cups before him as if to ward off the guests from approaching.

"Good evening," he said. "I am Dr. Lagri Aritsa, the director of research here."

On closer examination, he wasn't actually much older than Daryou. He must have swabbed up old age, like a sponge, by touching too many old books. He set down the coffee tray and inclined his head to them. It was possible that in Qarsazh this was a deadly insult. Parza hadn't ever managed to convey much Qarsazhi social nuance to Csorwe. She had left his lessons feeling universally uncouth.

Talasseres introduced them both, perhaps hoping he could coax someone else into mispronouncing her name, but Dr. Lagri didn't fall for it. He poured coffee and told them that he had prepared a traditional Qarsazhi rice broth for their dinner. All in all, it didn't start as badly as Csorwe had feared.

"So, the two of you are here to visit the Hollow Monument," said Dr. Lagri.

"That's right," said Tal. "We're Sethennai's doctoral students," he added, with what Csorwe felt was undue haste. She bet Tal would *love* to be Sethennai's doctoral student.

"An intriguing choice," said Dr. Lagri. "But then, this world is absolutely riddled with intrigue. Thousands of sites, almost all buried. Thousands of years of history. We've barely made a start here. We couldn't catalogue it all if we had a hundred lifetimes." He sighed in evident pleasure. "May I ask what it is about the

Monument that specifically caught your interest? I know it was one of the few sites that was partially documented before we arrived . . ." He clasped his hands nervously, trying to suppress some kind of enthusiasm. "Or perhaps you read my paper?"

Of course neither of them had, but Tal nodded enthusiastically.

"Oh, yes," he said. "Remarkable findings. Chancellor Sethennai recommended it to me." This might even be true. Sethennai had read Lagri's paper, and then he had shut himself up in the inner library of the School of Transcendence for three days to consider the implications.

Lagri looked as though he needed to shut himself away for three days to deal with these implications. "My word," he said. "Well, it's only a descriptive piece—there is still much work to do—"

Over the past five years, the search for the Reliquary of Pentravesse had stalled as the newly reinstated Chancellor Sethennai consolidated power in Tlaanthothe. He had deals to strike. He had paid off Morga and the rest of the mercenaries, circulated the news that Olthaaros had been sacrificing his own house staff, and settled back into government as if it were a beloved and comfortable armchair. Csorwe and Tal had been kept busy applying bribery and threats as the occasion demanded. Sethennai had not found much time for treasure hunting, and there had been no new leads.

That is, not until Dr. Lagri Aritsa published his paper, "Preliminary Observations of the Hollow Monument of Precursor World A-20–22–17." This had been enough for Sethennai to come up with a new theory, apparently a wild reversal of accepted historical fact. Csorwe didn't know much about that, but Sethennai was clearly convinced. He'd almost packed his bags and come away from Tlaanthothe himself. If it wouldn't have meant leaving the Siren's protective sanctuary, and abandoning the Chancellor's business, he would have done so. As it was, he'd ordered Csorwe and Tal to drop everything and head out to meet the Qarsazhi in their dying world.

Tal kept Dr. Lagri talking, managing to head off any awkward questions about the actual contents of the paper. Csorwe hated to acknowledge it, but Tal was doing a decent job of pretending to be a scholar, better at any rate than her own uneasy silence. Chatting over coffee always made her feel like she was trying to cut a cake with a hammer. At least it gave her time to listen and observe.

It was soon full night outside. Over the crackle of the fire, Csorwe heard the wind whipping round the watchtower, and wondered what Daryou was up to, out there in the dark.

Something chimed far overhead, a single clear note. Tal startled, and Csorwe smirked at him.

"Ah!" said Lagri Aritsa. "Nothing to fear. The watchtower bell rings whenever the perimeter is crossed. That will be the others returning."

A few minutes later the door opened, admitting a blast of chilly air and Daryou Malkhaya, looking tense. If Csorwe hadn't already known he was here for security, it would have been obvious from his gait and the way he positioned himself in the space that this was a fighting man.

Following after him, with one gloved hand resting in the crook of his arm, was a young woman. She was dressed all in white, from her gloves to the high collar of her surcoat to the fur lining of her boots, making her olive-brown complexion look vivid by contrast. Two fine plaits of dark hair rippled over her shoulders beneath a white hood. She surveyed the room dispassionately, unblinking, like an ermine in its winter coat. Csorwe realised she was staring back, and averted her eyes.

"Ah, yes, the Tlaanthothei delegation," said Daryou, who had clearly forgotten that Tal and Csorwe were going to be there. Csorwe wondered what had happened. "Excuse me—it has been a tiring day—Aritsa?"

"Yes, of course," said the priest. He returned to the kitchen and brought a large bowl of rice broth. As he did so, Daryou steered the girl in white to the far end of the table.

She ate as though ravenous, with a single-minded focus that was oddly unsettling, as though she had opened a second mouth, full of jagged teeth.

"Hope you've been enjoying Aritsa's hospitality," said Daryou, taking a seat closer to Csorwe and Tal. "Have you had the lecture about wasting firewood yet?" He gave them both a brittle smile. Tal grinned back. Csorwe was still watching the girl in white.

"This is our Adept, Qanwa Shuthmili," said Malkhaya, gesturing toward the girl. "Shuthmili, you know, you *can* say hello."

Qanwa Shuthmili looked up at them now, as though she had only just noticed that they had visitors. The carnivorous look had faded, replaced with a haughty detachment that said, *I really have more important things to think about than you.* Csorwe didn't know what an Adept was, but she had seen the look a hundred times on the faces of desiccated collegiate scholars back in Tlaanthothe. It was strange to recognise it on someone her own age.

"Good evening," said Shuthmili, and held Csorwe's gaze for a moment, as though trying to identify an unusual moss.

Lagri Aritsa brought food for the rest of them and conducted an elaborate blessing over the table, thanking a whole panoply of gods for their providence, as if to make up for his rudeness in feeding Shuthmili first. When he took his place at the table, Shuthmili's interest passed at once to him, becoming almost eager. "Your reverence, we saw it again—"

"I see. I'm not sure this is the moment to bother our guests with our internal business," said Aritsa. "We'll discuss it later."

Shuthmili said nothing but "Certainly, your reverence," and returned to her bowl of broth.

Tal appeared to be too busy with Daryou Malkhaya to notice this obviously suspicious behaviour. Csorwe wondered what he thought he was doing.

The rest of the meal went smoothly. Shuthmili hardly spoke again, and didn't mention whatever it was she'd seen. Eventually Lagri Aritsa showed Tal and Csorwe to their quarters, which were just as austere as the rest of the lodge. This room was appointed with another ceramic icon of the dragon-slaying god, his eyes bulbed like fish eggs.

Tal had to tuck his knees up to his chest to fit into the narrow cot bed. Over the last five years he had put on muscle, but he still looked as though someone had deliberately stretched and rolled him out into this knotted shoelace of a man.

Bunched up in her own cot, Csorwe tried to think how many times she had shared a room with Tal. It was exhausting just trying to calculate it.

If Sethennai knew how much they despised each other, it didn't stop him sending them out together. A little healthy competition was good for them, apparently. And—though she hated it—she saw the logic of sending Tal with her on this assignment. He was better at dealing with people than she was. Still, she wished Sethennai had trusted her to do this alone.

In theory, it didn't matter who brought back the Reliquary.

Belthandros Sethennai's happiness was like the sunlight, there for anyone to enjoy. However, for his own sordid reasons, Tal wanted to be the one to hand it over, and Csorwe was personally opposed to Tal ever getting what he wanted.

"There's something they aren't telling us," said Tal, once they'd put out the light.

"No shit," said Csorwe. "You would've noticed if you hadn't spent so much time batting your lashes at *Malkhaya*."

"Keep your beak out of it," said Tal. "I noticed. And I was getting somewhere with him."

"You're not going to get anywhere with a Qarsazhi," said Csorwe. "They're too religious."

Tal snickered into his pillow. "Shows what you know."

"Just don't be an idiot," said Csorwe.

"Oh, come *on*, Csorwe. I only ever want information. I'm just better at getting it than you. If you weren't such a virgin you might not have such a gruesome suspicious mind."

"Information," said Csorwe. "That's what you want from Sethennai, is it?"

She expected Tal to swipe back at her immediately. Instead there was a chilly silence, which thickened and expanded to fill the little room and suffocate the conversation. Tal's loyalty to Belthandros Sethennai had curdled long ago into this awful unspoken thing. She didn't think Sethennai realised, but Csorwe had known for years. They had plenty more important reasons to hate each other, starting in Psamag's fortress and unspooling from there, a whole history of spite and malice, but this one particularly festered, because—no matter how Tal tried—Csorwe was the one Sethennai had chosen for himself, and Tal was the one he'd taken on as a favour.

She lay back on her bunk, regretting what she'd said. Tal had a good way of tricking you into taking the cheapest possible shot, then looking wounded. They were supposed to be working together, god help them both.

At last Tal's breathing slowed until she was fairly certain he was not feigning sleep. He had fallen asleep with his pack under the blankets with him, and curled up around it like a clenched fist. Possibly he suspected she might go through his things in the night.

Csorwe lay awake. Sometimes it felt like sleep was on the other side of a wall, and she could only get there if she beat the wall down with her own head. Eventually she got out of bed and dressed again. Failing sleep, it was time to do what she did best: sidle around at night and eavesdrop. If the Qarsazhi were hiding something, they might stay up and talk about it after the visitors had gone to bed.

She crept out into the corridor. The door to the central room of the lodge was closed, and no sound came from within.

She opened the door a crack and peered round into the central room. The Qarsazhi girl, Shuthmili, was still sitting at the table, leaning over a large open book, surrounded by pages of notes.

As Csorwe loitered, Shuthmili turned a page and made a note on one of her papers. In her right hand she held a brush-pen, of the kind Parza had owned, which Csorwe had not been allowed to touch. From time to time she chewed the end of it, or twirled it in the air. Her hand was as delicately tapered as the brush itself and moved like water.

Csorwe blinked away *that* observation and scanned the rest of the room as best she could from behind the door. Was Shuthmili alone? If so, Csorwe wanted to ask what she'd been talking about at dinner, but she didn't know how to phrase it without making it obvious that she was here with an ulterior motive.

"You can come in," said Shuthmili without looking up from her work.

Csorwe cursed herself for blundering, but drawing back now would look even stranger. She sidled into the room and over to the fireplace as though what she'd intended all along was to get a better look at the painted icon over the hearth. The god was made in the likeness of a barefoot Qarsazhi boy, with a long braid swirling around his body. The dragon had the head and torso of a woman. Her scaled body coiled around a pile of bones.

"Linarya Atqalindri destroys Zinandour," said Shuthmili, making Csorwe jump again. Her voice was cold, deep, and distant as an ice well. She hadn't moved from her position at the table, and was still holding the brush in her hand.

"Sorry?" said Csorwe.

"Light destroys darkness. Wisdom destroys chaos and corruption. The hero of mankind destroys the Traitor," she said, smiling. The smile looked hollow, wispy, as though it might blow away in a light breeze, and was accompanied by a dark and unsettling stare. "Haven't you seen it before?"

Csorwe couldn't work out whether this was meant to be condescending or genuinely curious. Either way, a direct question was more than she expected.

"Well, there's one in our room," said Csorwe. "But I don't recognise it." She remembered that the Qarsazhi had nine different gods, and that the worship of these gods ordered every part of life for them. Csorwe knew about that from the House of Silence, but nine gods still seemed like a lot to keep straight, and she couldn't remember many of their names.

"Oh. That's unusual," said Shuthmili. She looked down at her papers as if composing her thoughts. It was a relief to have some respite from the intensity of her gaze, but Csorwe was oddly unhappy not to have met her expectations. For the first time in a while she wished she'd paid more attention to Parza's lessons.

"I don't know much about your religion," she said.

"I think you may be the first person I've ever met who doesn't," said Shuthmili. "But I don't have many unusual experiences, so it isn't unwelcome." She dipped her brush in water, dried it, and put it away, clearly deciding that Csorwe was worth talking to.

"So what religion do they follow in Tlaanthothe?" said Shuthmili. Csorwe didn't think she was being teased; sometimes Tal would feign fascination to take the piss, but Shuthmili's interest seemed sincere, if unnerving. Csorwe remembered how she had behaved at dinner: head bowed, eyes low, rarely speaking. This was quite a transformation.

"Erm," said Csorwe. "Well, none, really—" Tlaanthothe was apparently organised on the principles of a philosophical treatise composed in ages past by the Exalted Sages. Csorwe hadn't bothered to learn about them. Sethennai didn't seem very interested in them, and she didn't think they'd approve of her.

"And you?" said Shuthmili, "You don't worship any Oshaarun god?"

"No," said Csorwe, preventing herself with a physical effort from adding *not anymore*. She hated that this still had the ability to take her by surprise. It had been eight whole years. It should have been long behind her.

Shuthmili didn't seem to notice anything amiss, or else she was too curious to let it stop her. "And what about Belthandros Sethennai?" she said. She uttered the name with a kind of relish.

"We don't really talk about it," said Csorwe. "I think . . . if Sethennai ever encounters a higher power, I'll wait and see who blinks first."

"But surely he worships his patron?"

Sethennai regarded the Siren as a powerful older woman capable of being charmed. Women of a certain age loved Sethennai, even when they were giant snakes or evil rocks. "Not really," said Csorwe, deciding this wasn't appropriate for Shuthmili's ears. "He gets his power from her. She gets . . . something out of the arrangement, probably."

Shuthmili laughed, almost silently, covering her mouth with her hand.

"Hmm," she said. "Yes. I suppose that's broadly how it works."

"You're a mage?" said Csorwe.

"I'm an Adept," said Shuthmili. Csorwe hadn't heard the Qarsazhi word before; it sounded clinical. "A Church-trained practitioner."

"Didn't know that was a thing," said Csorwe, remembering how Parza had reacted to magic. *An abomination to the gods*, he had said. Csorwe was just tactful enough not to repeat it.

"I suppose the Church thinks it's better to train us than not," said Shuthmili.

It was generally a mistake to get too curious about the people you met on this kind of mission, and yet. Knowing that Shuthmili was a mage explained something about why she was here, but it didn't explain anything about why Daryou and Lagri treated her with such attentive care, as though she might explode at any moment.

"Do you have a patron?" said Csorwe, now utterly distracted from asking Shuthmili about whatever it was she had seen on her patrol. "Where do you get your, uh, stuff?"

"You really *don't* know anything," said Shuthmili. This seemed to be a compliment. She waved at the icon again. "Eight of the nine gods of Qarsazh take no mortal supplicants. It is a corruption of the mortal estate to partake in divine power."

Csorwe had not known this either. She wasn't sure she understood it now. Most likely Sethennai would call it all so much Qarsazhi nonsense.

"All magic is a corruption," said Shuthmili. "To use magic is to violate the ordered structure of the cosmos, to step outside one's allotted place . . . but some are born into it, and corruption has its uses. Even to the Church. My patron—patron of all Qarsazhi mages—is ninth of the Nine. The dead goddess." She bit her lip, perhaps in case this sounded too impressive. "Well, that's theologically debatable."

"What, that she's really dead?" said Csorwe.

"Or that she's a true goddess," said Shuthmili, with another wan smile. "Or that she is truly mine. Zinandour. The Dragon of Qarsazh. The Traitor. You truly don't know?"

"No," said Csorwe. "Tell me."

"Zinandour was a goddess of chaos and corruption. She turned against the other gods, and was cast out, and she gives us her power because she is trying to find her way back to the mortal worlds. So you see, we walk on a knife's edge. To make use of that power without opening yourself to corruption is . . . tiring." Shuthmili looked up at Csorwe with an expression halfway between curiosity and melancholy. "She is why we are feared. Why I am feared. I could be the gate through which she returns."

The fire had burnt low, turning everything in the room into a glimmering reddish silhouette. There was no sound but the shifting of the embers and the far-off senseless howling of the wind.

Into this stillness, like a rock dropped into a pond, broke the sound of the watchtower bell.

One chime, then another, and then a constant, insistent jangle. Footsteps pounded on the staircase as Lagri and Daryou rushed down from the floor above, and Qanwa Shuthmili rose unsteadily from her chair.

When Csorwe was ten, one of the priestesses had run lotus-mad, and they had found her in the woods, drinking blood from the neck of a deer. When they brought her back to the House of Silence, she was bloody from chin to navel, shaking with dreadful ecstasies and cursing death upon anyone who touched her. At last they brought Csorwe to see her, strapped to her bed in the infirmary. The wretched woman looked up at the Chosen Bride, took a shuddering breath, and died. The expression on her face had been indescribable.

Now Csorwe saw it again in the person of Qanwa Shuthmili.

"They're here," she said.

Csorwe's body reacted faster than her brain. There was a threat and she had to deal with it. She dashed back to the bedroom to grab her sword and followed Daryou to the door. Tal followed moments later, instantly alert.

"What's happening?" said Csorwe.

"Intruders! Intruders at the perimeter!" said Lagri.

"Raiders!" called Daryou, already heading out, with his weapon in one hand and a torch in the other. Csorwe ran after him, out into the night.

Daryou ran down the ridge, a moving point of flame. The intruders were coming up from below, illuminated by the perimeter lanterns. There were four or five of them, ragged, shambling, but purposeful.

As Csorwe followed, realisation hit her like nausea; like a cold hand clawing in her guts.

These were not raiders. They were revenants. No living person moved like that, stumbling at speed over the jagged ground, always on the point of falling, shedding mummified skin.

Their faces were bare and withered. The dry skin clung to the bones. The eyelids were like knots in a tree trunk. The lips had shrunk away, revealing teeth that stood up in sharp yellow ranks.

All of them were armed with great jagged broadswords. As Csorwe and the others approached, they drew them in unison.

Csorwe closed with the nearest of them. Tal and Malkhaya were somewhere nearby, and she had to trust they could take care of themselves. Cut, thrust, block. Back and forth across the ridge, never advancing nor retreating. The revenant was slow, but relentless. In a fight, her awareness narrowed and clarified, like lensed light, to only this, only the blade, only the terrain, only the position and the intentions of the enemy. Under other circumstances she might have enjoyed this. Now, between the darkness, the unfamiliar ground, and the impassive skeleton grin of her opponent, she wanted to end it as soon as possible.

She felt something give way as her sword severed the dry sinews in the revenant's neck, and it went down. Whatever force held its bones together failed all at once, and its limbs disintegrated as it hit the ground. Csorwe was already looking for the next one.

Tal made short work of his corpse, and between them they dealt with a third. There were more of them coming up from the valley. Two—three—and there could be others, but

Csorwe had plenty to handle in the present without worrying about the future.

There was a muffled cry and the skid of a body falling hard on loose rock. Csorwe caught her breath and looked in the direction of the cry. A revenant wearing a long veil had Malkhaya on the ground. It made a rattling sound and slashed his face with the point of its blade.

From behind her, Csorwe heard a scream. There was a blur of white robes at the edge of her vision as Shuthmili scrambled up a row of rocks.

These revenants did not show emotion. They had no body language. Their empty eye sockets never gave away their next move. And yet, at the sight of Shuthmili, Csorwe's adversary startled.

Csorwe used the opportunity to slip within its guard, driving her blade up and under its exposed ribs, cutting into the shrivelled remnant flesh within. The revenant stumbled back. The gristle of its joints was already sundering. Csorwe tripped it on its face and turned to the next, struggling to see what was happening to Daryou Malkhaya.

Malkhaya was on the ground, alive but winded. The veiled corpse stood over him, facing Shuthmili. She had been a woman, this revenant. Her fleshless mask was haloed by a dry braid of hair and a coronet of metal flowers.

"Will you save him, Adept?" said the revenant princess. Her voice was breathy, leathery, like a bellows. Malkhaya wriggled, trying to inch away from her, but the revenant had her blade at his throat. "Will you?"

Shuthmili ignored her. She looked at Malkhaya, twisting and writhing on the ground. There was an unmistakable question in this look. She did not need to speak the words *May I?*

"Do it," said Malkhaya, choking for breath.

Shuthmili pulled off her gloves, raised a hand, and closed it, slowly, digging her fingernails into the heel of her palm. Her expression was dispassionate, unseeing, illuminated from within by an appalling brightness. The revenant princess hissed as though burnt, and her sword fell from her hand. Shuthmili watched with blank and burning focus as the revenant stumbled back from Malkhaya and dropped to her knees.

"Stand down, Shuthmili," said Malkhaya, struggling up onto his elbows. "I'm fine."

Shuthmili didn't seem to hear him. Her fist was clenched, a single tight punctuation mark of fury. The revenant princess writhed, noises of unformed agony escaping from her throat.

"Shuthmili!" said Malkhaya. "Stop!"

There was a moment of suspended motion, hung by a brittle thread. Csorwe had not been afraid for a long time, but she tasted a drop of the real dark crawling vintage just then. *I could be the gate through which she returns . . .*

The other revenants fell, as though their legs had been kicked out from under them, and shuddered. They shouldn't have been able to feel pain. The dead were beyond suffering. And yet the veiled princess thrashed like a beetle caught in a web, and Shuthmili watched.

"They're dead, Shuthmili. Let them go." Malkhaya's free hand fell on Shuthmili's shoulder, although Csorwe had the irrational conviction that she would burn to touch, and he shook her gently. At last, like the turning of the seasons, she looked up at him, and her hands fell loose at her sides.

There was a sound like an exhaled breath, a smell of bone

dust, and the revenants on the ground disintegrated. The four of them were alone on the hillside.

Tal straightened up, and Shuthmili started like a hound sighting a hare.

"What was *that*?" said Tal. He turned on them, keeping the higher ground. Malkhaya had his arms round Shuthmili, and his hands were shaking slightly. Shuthmili's eyes were open and staring, and her lips were parted, baring small pearly teeth. There was no expression on her face but blind, vacant hunger, as though the illumination had burnt her away and left a void.

"Think it through," said Malkhaya, through clenched teeth. He wasn't angry, Csorwe judged, but frightened.

Malkhaya held Shuthmili's bare hands in his own. Either a brave or a reckless man, and as far as Csorwe was concerned they were more or less the same thing. "Go up to the lodge," he said, shaking slightly. "Get Aritsa. He has a sedative—"

At the lodge, Aritsa was already shoving bottles into a bag. He followed them back to the field of bones, to find Malkhaya cradling Shuthmili in his lap. She was shuddering, as though trying to shed her skin.

"What does she need?" said Aritsa, opening up his bag. His white vestments fluttered around him, making him look like a ghost.

"Give her a full dose," said Malkhaya. "She's overstrained herself." He waved at the layer of corpse debris dusted across the hillside, and laughed weakly.

Aritsa knelt over them, dripping the contents of a vial into Shuthmili's mouth. At last she stopped twitching and lay still. Malkhaya rose to his feet, lifting her easily, and without a word began trudging uphill toward the lodge.

Csorwe and Tal followed him. All around them, the barrens of the dead world echoed.

Back at the lodge, Aritsa and Malkhaya lit the lanterns and banked up the fire, laying Shuthmili out on a pallet in the central room. Aritsa prayed out loud. Malkhaya prayed silently and paced.

Eventually Malkhaya broke away and came to speak to Tal and Csorwe, as though shielding the priest. "You're not the only one with questions," he said. "We'll talk in the morning."

9

The Hollow Monument

ARITSA AND MALKHAYA WERE sitting at the table when Csorwe and Tal emerged the next morning. The Qarsazhi looked very solemn, as if they had prepared notes for this encounter.

"Shuthmili is resting," said Aritsa, almost before they could take their seats, and Malkhaya poured them coffee.

"What the hell is she?" said Tal. "And why don't you keep her on a leash?"

Tal was used to Tlaanthothei magic. Sethennai's magic. Clean, economical, controlled. Whatever they had seen last night, it had been none of those things.

Lagri Aritsa frowned, and Malkhaya winced.

"Shuthmili is a valued Church Adept," said Aritsa eventually. "Our Adepts are not beasts of battle. They are treasured national assets."

"I saw your treasured national asset melt nine skeletons to death," said Tal. "How do we know you've got her under control?"

"Shuthmili was raised and trained at the School of Aptitude in Qaradoun. She was an exemplary student for more than ten years," said Aritsa. "She is shortly to be considered for tether to the Imperial Quincuriate—"

Tal's expression betrayed how much he knew about whatever this was.

"Has she hurt you?" said Malkhaya. He didn't seem at all friendly this morning. Clearly Tal had fluttered his eyelashes in vain.

"No," said Tal, reluctantly.

Csorwe finished her coffee and set down the cup. "Look," she said. "We have a bigger problem, don't we?" Aritsa and Malkhaya watched her, impassive. "There's someone else here. The dead don't rise of their own accord, not like that. Not with that kind of purpose."

"This is a dying world," said Aritsa. "The phenomenon of revenance is well documented, and—"

"No, Csorwe's right," said Tal, for the first time in history. "Last night, one of the revenants *spoke*. You know how unlikely that is? They have a whole proverb about how many tales dead men tell. If you need reminding, it's *no tales*. Someone was pulling on its strings, or I'm a fucking turnip."

Malkhaya rested his big square chin on his big square hand. "It's true," he said. "It spoke to Shuthmili. It provoked her deliberately."

"So," said Csorwe. "If I've got this right, we're dealing with a necromancer who can afford to raise nine revenants from the dead and control them remotely."

Even back at the House of Silence, nobody would have raised a revenant just for the sake of it. They rose naturally in the crypts if you left them long enough. It would be like planting in midwinter—a pointless waste of energy to interfere with a natural process.

"Yeah, and I'm pretty sure you two knew about this, didn't you?" said Tal. She almost snapped back at him, before she realised he was backing her up. "If you didn't know it was a bloody necromancer, you knew there was *something* out there. Any reason you decided not to tell us?"

"Well, you haven't been one hundred percent straight with us, either, have you?" said Malkhaya.

"Haven't we?" said Csorwe, sitting back in her chair.

"Sethennai said he was sending two scholars. If you two are scholars, I'm the Emperor's beard-trimmer. Scholars—sorry, Aritsa—don't run towards the fight, and if they get in one, they don't fight like *that*."

"We're his agents," said Csorwe. "We can defend ourselves."

"And you're lucky we can," said Tal, "or you'd be smeared halfway across the landscape."

Malkhaya dropped his hands on the tabletop with a thud, exhaling sharply. Tal often had this effect on people.

"Malkhaya, calm down," said Aritsa, after a long, unpleasant pause. He looked very weary. "We have had our suspicions, yes. We did not choose to share them. Perhaps that was an error. It is done, now. However . . . prudence suggests we should pool information. There are few capable of dealing with the dead. And of those capable, fewer still are willing."

Aritsa explained about the unfamiliar ship the Qarsazhi had seen, first a week ago and then on the night Tal and Csorwe had arrived. Csorwe listened with mounting apprehension.

There was a nursery rhyme they sang in the House of Silence: *This is the road the dead walk. This is the road of bones.* Despite herself, Csorwe remembered all the old songs. A sickly suspicion sprouted within her, uncurling pallid roots. If she was honest with herself, it had been growing since last night, since their encounter with the revenants.

Sethennai couldn't have been the only person who read Lagri Aritsa's paper. There were others out there who wanted the Reliquary.

"The question is what we do now," said Malkhaya. "We're clearly no longer safe here. If you ask me all five of us ought to take *Prosperity* and head to the Gate. But, uh, Aritsa—what do you think?"

The priest rubbed his eyes and blinked at them. "I am loath to abandon this world," he said, with unexpected resolve. "There is still so much work to do. The Survey is not the most lively office of the Church, but we have a long history of perseverance."

"Right," said Malkhaya, clearly torn between affection and exasperation.

"We're not leaving either," said Tal, in his worst and loudest drawl. "We have a date with the Hollow Monument. We've dealt with worse than revenants—"

Csorwe kicked him under the table, although maybe it was too late to bother keeping up the pretence that they were real scholars.

"Perhaps one of us could go and call for help?" said Aritsa.

"I could," said Malkhaya. "But it would be several days' journey to the Atalqaya nexus. I'd be happy to go, but I don't like the idea of leaving you and Shuthmili unprotected."

Or in company with these hooligans, I bet, thought Csorwe.

"It's never a good idea to split up," she said. She rose from the table and went to peer out of the window. Outside, the morning sun turned the dying world a washed-out grey.

"Agreed," said Malkhaya.

"But there's no immediate sign of danger," said Aritsa.

"You're lucky if you get a warning," said Malkhaya. "We've had ours."

"Sounds like you've had *several*," said Tal, who never knew when to leave well enough alone. Before Malkhaya could jab back at him, there was a sound from the staircase. They all startled. Shuthmili was leaning on the banisters. Csorwe wondered how long she had been listening.

"Ah," said Shuthmili. "Good morning."

There was a flurry of activity as Aritsa and Malkhaya rose to offer their assistance. One of them actually helped her down the stairs.

Shuthmili looked soft and newly washed in fresh white robes, and she had the same look of pristine detachment Csorwe had noticed last night, like a veil separating her from the world. Now Csorwe looked more carefully, it was much closer to weariness than haughtiness. There were deep, purplish shadows under her eyes, and she rubbed her hands together as if they were cold.

"Warden, your reverence, I couldn't help overhearing—" she started.

"Shuthmili," said Aritsa, looking pained. "Please don't concern yourself. All will be well."

"I ought to repair the outer perimeter," she said. "It was breached last night."

"Not immediately," said Aritsa. "We have discussed this. It is not safe for you to make use of your powers so soon after your exertions last night."

"I am much recovered," she said.

"You may feel that," said Aritsa, "but we now know what we are dealing with, and—"

"Exactly," said Shuthmili. For a moment her eyes brightened, as if she'd only woken up in that moment. The effect was startling, like coming up into the sun from out of a cold cellar. "I heard. There's a dangerous necromancer somewhere out there and we need to defend ourselves. Without the perimeter we'd have *no* warning of—"

"Our first responsibility is to keep you safe, Shuthmili," said Malkhaya.

Shuthmili lowered her eyes, and went on, without raising her voice or looking up at the two men. "No. Your first responsibility is to keep other people safe from me. I am a calculated risk, and there is no point in keeping me here if I can't be of use. If I can't do anything, I am *nothing* but a risk." Her hands were twisted tightly together, the tension visible even from here.

"We shouldn't just wait here," she went on. "We waited before, and it didn't prevent them from attacking us. We need to find out what they're doing and stop them."

"Whoever it is, they're here for you," said Malkhaya. Aritsa twitched. "I know. But we have to be straight with her. Shuthmili—there are people out there who, uh, who might—"

"Yes, I know," she said. "There are people out there who would like to kidnap and enslave me. I know I'm valuable. But the Church believes I'm also useful in the field, or I would still be cloistered in the School of Aptitude, in perfect safety. I am an asset. So *use* me."

Discontent and uncertainty moved like shadows across Malkhaya's face. Lagri Aritsa looked unmoved.

"Nobody knows better than I do how much you have trained or how hard you have worked," said Aritsa.

Shuthmili sagged back into her chair, her lashes falling again. Csorwe felt a moment of terrible pity for her. She remembered how it had felt to be attended to at every moment. Even as a child Csorwe had found it smothering. Shuthmili was a grown woman, and didn't have a crypt to escape into.

"The Traitor will lie to you," Aritsa went on. "She will try to assure you at every turn that you are doing the right thing, that your superiors are blind and misguided, that the stable order of your life is a cage rather than a sanctuary. You cannot let yourself be won over."

Tal rolled his eyes. Csorwe knew what he would suggest: let the Qarsazhi deal with their own problems and go hunting for the Hollow Monument by themselves. The trouble with that, as far as she could tell, was that all their problems were the same problem.

"Look," she said. "You were right. We haven't been straight with you."

"*Csorwe, what the fuck are you doing,*" said Tal under his breath.

"Sethennai sent us to this world to look for an artefact in the Hollow Monument," she said, ignoring him. "Maybe the necromancer wants Shuthmili, but it's just as likely they want our thing, too."

Lagri Aritsa blinked disbelievingly. "This is a Qarsazhi Precursor world," he said. "Any artefact here would belong to—"

"Put it aside a minute, Aritsa," said Malkhaya. "Go on."

"Shuthmili's right," said Csorwe. "We have to go on the attack before this person can find what they're looking for. If we leave it too late, we won't stand a chance." This was just a guess. She didn't know what kind of time or effort it would take to get the Reliquary open, but she needed to get them moving. The Qarsazhi knew the Hollow Monument's layout and location. Without them, Tal and Csorwe would be searching at random. If the Reliquary was here in this world then they couldn't let someone else get to it first.

Tal finally seemed to get it. "Yeah," he said. "They'll be able to saunter up here and pull your perimeter apart whenever they feel like it. If you want to stay in this world, you've got to do something about them now. And we can help."

Shuthmili looked up at Malkhaya, not quite daring to hope.

Malkhaya squared his shoulders. "It isn't safe. I still think we should leave."

"That might indeed be wise," said Aritsa. "Still—"

"Your reverence," said Shuthmili, perhaps sensing that the priest was an easier mark. Csorwe was cautiously impressed. "This world is a part of our history. Isn't it worth risking something of ourselves to protect it?"

This struck home. Aritsa nodded, slowly, looking something like a snail peering out of its shell.

"Perhaps I could go," he said. "You could stay here with Malkhaya."

Shuthmili let out a single sigh, then seemed to collect herself, betraying no further sign of disappointment. It was almost painful to watch. Csorwe wondered how dull her life had been that she was so desperate to run into danger.

"Aritsa, you know I can't possibly let you go alone," said Malkhaya.

Csorwe let them talk it out and went to get her things ready. Eventually, Malkhaya would realise that his choice was between leaving Shuthmili alone at the lodge and letting Aritsa travel into the Monument with only Tal and Csorwe's doubtful protection. They were all going to have to go together.

Manipulating the Qarsazhi left a sour taste in her mouth, but she was sick of this cold world and sick of spending time with

Tal—and worse, she had her own suspicions about whom they might find in the Monument.

In the years since Echentyr, they hadn't seen or heard from Oranna, but Csorwe hadn't forgotten. Bats, and books, and parcels tied with string, all sometimes gave her pause. Every recollection came with a little twist of fear, an accompanying ache of curiosity. Remembering that life went on at the House of Silence, that people came and went, was like looking at a fallen log and imagining all the woodlice wriggling underneath. It was better to put it out of your head, but part of you wanted to know, even when you'd hate the knowing.

She felt much the same about trying to work out how things now stood between Oranna and Sethennai. Sethennai rarely spoke of her, and never with fondness. Csorwe had to assume that things between them had ended in Echentyr, if not long before.

She swept these thoughts aside. It wasn't complicated. If Oranna was here, and meant to steal the Reliquary, then she was Csorwe's enemy, and by now Csorwe was well used to dealing with those.

Prosperity was no bigger than a fishing boat, with two red canopies and a quiet alchemical engine. The lodge and the watchtower sank away beneath the ship as it unhitched from its moorings and floated into the sky. The grey land receded. The lake, the hills, the ridges were like a drawing in charcoal, loosely sketched. The only flashes of colour were the flags of the security perimeter, and soon even they were invisible.

Aritsa and Malkhaya were occupied handling the ship. Tal, at the end of his tolerance for company, had gone to lean over the side. Csorwe and Shuthmili were the only ones left in the cabin.

Shuthmili was curled up on a cushioned bench, withdrawn into herself. Csorwe wondered if she was travel-sick. Under ordinary circumstances Csorwe would have appreciated the silence, but she still didn't know what to make of Shuthmili. She had been surprised at the way the Adept had held her ground in front of the two men. She was certain there was more to learn.

"You've been to the Monument before," Csorwe said after a long pause. She knew lots of people who were experts at winkling out secrets, but she wasn't one of them. All she knew was that you had to start small and work from there.

"Yes," said Shuthmili. "The three of us went a few months ago. But I'm afraid we didn't get very far. Just a survey of the grounds and the top level of the structure. Dr. Lagri wanted to write up the findings before we returned. I've been working on translation for him. I did some of the work for his paper, actually—I heard you might have read it . . . ?"

"Er," said Csorwe. "Not so much."

Shuthmili gave her another thin smile. "I knew it," she said. "If you were a real student you would have fallen over yourself to tell me about all the inscriptions *you've* translated."

Csorwe blinked, taken aback. "You're right," she said. "Sethennai sometimes needs a blunt instrument. That's what I am."

"Aren't we all," said Shuthmili mildly. "And he's sent you to steal some valuable Qarsazhi cultural heritage, apparently."

"Ah," said Csorwe. "Yes. Well."

"Don't worry," said Shuthmili. "This world died long before Qarsazh existed. It's hardly ours."

"So didn't you mean what you said?" said Csorwe. "About protecting part of your history and all that?"

"Of course I did!" said Shuthmili, then seemed to recall who she was speaking to, and looked down ruefully. "Mostly. I just don't want to leave. I know Warden Daryou wants to take me home. He's probably right, really, but . . . I just need a little more time."

"For your translation." Csorwe recalled her days labouring over Parza's texts and wondered how anyone could be so eager, but Shuthmili was clearly an unusual specimen.

"Yes," said Shuthmili. "I've worked hard on it. It matters. We do have a responsibility to the past—and to the future—to save what we can before it falls away." She looked hard at Csorwe as if she thought she might be laughed at, then lowered her eyes. "And I want to make it *good*, since it's probably the last thing I'll do under my own name—"

"How's that?" said Csorwe.

"Well, this is just a holding assignment for me, until my Quincuriate assessment," said Shuthmili, then noted Csorwe's expression. "Oh, you don't know—"

"Sorry," said Csorwe, biting back a smile at Shuthmili's obvious eagerness to explain.

"The Quincuriate are the strongest Adepts in Qarsazh. I've been training since I was a child. I always wanted to join Spinel Quincury and research new magic—build new devices—but I wouldn't mind any Quincury really, even Cedar—that's civil engineering—" She paused, looking more enthused than Csorwe had ever seen her. "I'm sorry. I'm going too fast. I'm just not used to talking to someone who doesn't already know all about it."

"It's all right," said Csorwe. Shuthmili almost sounded like an ordinary person when she was excited. No, in fact, not an ordinary person, because Csorwe didn't know anyone else who got this excited about magic besides Sethennai, and he was less ordinary than most. "Go on," she said.

"There are only ever a set number of Adepts in the Quincuriate," said Shuthmili, needing no more encouragement than this. "They work in teams of five. There won't be a place for me until one of them dies, so they sent me out here until then to keep my skills sharp."

"Sounds like they're pretty certain you'll pass the test," said Csorwe. "You seem smart."

"Well, I can't get complacent," said Shuthmili, though obviously pleased. "I mean, I think I'll pass. Probably. But you know—this is the one thing I do—this is my one path—I want to do it as well as I can. The work here is important, but it's just one Precursor world. It's not really that much in the grand scheme of things, I know. Once I'm joined to the Quincury there will be bigger things—projects that can affect all of Qarsazh. But this was the one thing that was given to me to do, for now, just as myself. I really wanted to do my best here."

"Yeah," said Csorwe. "That makes sense." They were all here to do their best, after all. The plan had always been to arrive, search, and leave, and there was no real reason to change that. Quick and clean, like a knife going in. But she did find herself hoping they wouldn't do too much damage to the Qarsazhi in the process.

The Hollow Monument was a windowless bulk of black stone, not high but very broad, crouching at the bottom of a bowl-shaped valley. From the air, it looked organic rather than architectural, as though it had been held and hollowed out by the elements alone.

A wall of dry stones encircled the valley. They landed *Prosperity* on a ridge outside this enclosure. The five of them disembarked and set off toward the wall. There was no sign that anyone else had been here recently, no sign of the enemy's maze-ship. Csorwe wondered whether she could have been wrong. Even so, they couldn't afford to let their guard down.

Past the opening in the wall, the air was still. A thin mist settled on the glassy earth, and on the other tombs: plain barrows and low monoliths, flocking like seabirds on a misty shore, around the great island of the Hollow Monument.

They picked their way between the tombs toward the wide, slot-like entrance to the Monument, and Malkhaya and Shuthmili examined the interior face of the doorway for curse-wards.

"We didn't find anything last time we were here, but better safe than sorry," he said. "If Aritsa's to be believed, our Precursors liked a security perimeter almost as much as we do."

"Not the Precursors that bother me so much as the necromancer," said Csorwe, standing over them. The ancient dead couldn't do much to harm them without the help of the living.

"You and me both," said Malkhaya. Once he'd realised this expedition was inevitable, he had backed down with a good grace. Out here, Shuthmili and Aritsa paid real attention to his advice. Perhaps that was all he'd really needed.

He straightened up, satisfied the doorway was safe. The Monument yawned before them. The door was missing, but it was difficult to see what lay more than a few feet from the opening: the faint impression of stairs descending, and then only darkness.

They lit their lanterns and took their first steps into the Hollow

Monument. The steps sank swiftly into a damp, claustrophobic chill. The light from the doorway quickly faded, leaving them with only five bobbing lanterns and the sound of their own footsteps. Csorwe realised Malkhaya was humming to himself under his breath to keep his nerve.

Csorwe traced the surface of the walls with her fingertips, feeling the cold of them even through her gloves. They were carved in places with interlocking lines, by turns sinuous and geometric.

"It's writing," said Shuthmili, drifting up beside her like a pale jellyfish.

"This is one of the ritual inscription forms of Precursor writing," Aritsa added, close behind.

"What does it say?" asked Csorwe.

"It's a lament or tribute to the dead buried here," said Aritsa. "We are welcomed to pay our respects."

At the bottom of the steps, they came to a series of bare, narrow chambers. Sometimes the Qarsazhi ordered them to keep to single file, or to edge one after another round the edges of the chamber. Even Tal knew better than to challenge them on this.

"This place is a nightmare," he muttered, catching up to Csorwe as the Qarsazhi paused to examine a wall carving. "How long before we can drop them?"

"We're sticking with them," said Csorwe. "Safety in numbers."

"If the priest tells me to watch my step again I'm going to push him down the stairs," said Tal, which was as much acquiescence as she was going to get.

They came into a larger chamber, entirely carved with the indecipherable script. In the light of their lanterns, the carvings seemed to pulse and flow. Half a dozen grand corridors branched off from this chamber, and in the walls of these corridors were hundreds of little doorways, now entirely empty of doors.

"Ah, the main atrium," said Aritsa, quite happily. He seemed to have forgotten they were looking for an enemy. "We believe this structure would have served as a royal mausoleum of sorts. Less important cadet branches would be buried on higher levels. As we descend, we will meet with the more distinguished dead."

Each empty doorway led into a cell, and in each cell was a plain stone sarcophagus.

"We tend to find these burials in multiples of twelve," said Aritsa. "It seems to have been a sacred number to them. I wouldn't be surprised if there are at least twelve thousand here!"

The lay-sisters had kept a beehive in the gardens of the House of Silence. Once Angwennad had showed Csorwe the little hexagons, neatly capped to keep the larvae safe inside. She thought of it now. She imagined the Precursors shutting corpses away in their coffins, still fat and wriggling, ready to pupate into something grand and strange.

Beyond the rows of little tombs, they came into a confusing honeycomb of chambers and passages, which must have served some purpose long ago. All ways looked the same. The corridors overlapped and interlocked, and soon it became clear they were going in circles. If Csorwe thought about it too hard, she started to feel travel-sick.

"There's too much *space* in here," said Tal. His jaw was set, and his hands clenched at his hips. He always found this kind of thing difficult to deal with. Ordinarily Csorwe would have taken the chance to get one over on him, but she was equally on edge.

"Oh, yes, this is always fun," said Malkhaya bleakly. "It happens in a lot of old places, when you get too far in. This is about where we had to turn back last time," he added, half hopefully.

"It's a function of the death of this world," said Aritsa. "Theologically we would refer to it as *lenition*. The world becomes softer."

"Time and space relinquish their shackles," said Shuthmili. This must have been a quotation from something, because none of the Qarsazhi looked as alarmed by it as they should.

"It isn't dangerous in itself," said Malkhaya.

"Well!" said Tal. "Good to know!"

"This is as far as our knowledge takes us," said Aritsa. "Beyond this we don't know what we'll find."

They took another set of stairs down. The floor below contained more tombs, arrayed around a central hall. Here, one wall was occupied entirely by a mirror-polished sheet of obsidian. Before it was a stone pedestal, and a basin, full to the brim with black water.

"Oh, and this is remarkable," said Aritsa, pausing before the obsidian mirror. The light of his lantern flashed and winked on the surface. "How curious! It truly *does* look like the precursor to a Qarsazhi temple! The offering—dish—the oracle pool—*remarkable*."

Here they paused, so Aritsa could take notes, and the rest of them could eat.

"If I pissed in the corner," muttered Tal, "do you think all twelve thousand ghosts would haunt my dick forever?"

"Yes," said Csorwe. "Hold it in."

He made a disgusted noise and stalked off, perhaps to find somewhere less haunted to relieve himself.

Shuthmili wafted past the mirror behind Aritsa. She caught sight of her reflection, and paused, as though waiting to see what it would do. Her reflection looked levelly back at her. Its eyes were pools of darkness, its gloves bone-white. Csorwe remembered how Shuthmili had looked during the revenants' attack on the lodge, and shivered.

The only noises within the monument were their footsteps, their breathing, the faint metallic clinking of the hot lanterns, the scratch of Aritsa's pencil. There was no wind. No creak of hinges. Wood and metal had rotted and rusted long ago. Only the rock remained.

There was a scream from one of the far doors.

Csorwe grabbed her sword and pelted toward the noise, immediately angry with herself for letting Talasseres out of her sight.

It wasn't long before she found him. He wasn't under attack. He wasn't even hurt. He was in one of the sarcophagus cells, standing over a fresh corpse.

It was a young Oshaaru man, very beautiful and evidently dead. He had been laid out carefully on the sarcophagus. He was crowned with white dog roses, and he was quite naked. His skin was of a grey so pale he might have been carved from ice, except where the clean wounds of the sacrifice were still dark and freshly washed. He wore an expression of great tranquillity, and there was no other mark of violence on him, but at his mouth, which was sewn shut, in a line of twelve neat stitches from tusk to tusk. The sign of sealed lips.

"It's them," said Tal, in a low voice, on the edge of panic. "It's them, isn't it? It's your death cult. Your people. I should have known."

Her first instinct was to deny it. Tal knew far too much about her past, and he could never resist the chance to salt that particular wound, but there was no mockery in his voice this time. He was right.

At least this boy was too young for Csorwe ever to have known him. She didn't even have the heart to laugh at Tal for crying out.

Csorwe remembered her lessons. The Unspoken One was deeply rooted in its Shrine, in its earthly mansion within the sacred mountain. To draw on its power when far from home, you needed to make a pathway. There was no surer way than this, the ritual of oblation.

Tal straightened up, and quickly managed a little cynical bark of laughter.

"They do take it seriously, don't they?" said Tal. "These people really believe. What do they think a god of death is going to do for them anyway?"

Csorwe didn't answer. Giving Tal a reasonable explanation was like giving a ball of wool to a cat.

"No, tell me," said Tal, quirking an artificial smile that looked like he was having a spasm. "I'm interested. What is the advantage, anyway? Pray to the Unspoken One long enough and in the next life you'll have all the babies you can eat?"

Before she could answer, Malkhaya rushed in, followed by Aritsa.

"By the Mother of Cities," said Aritsa, and dropped to his knees beside the dead boy. She thought he might be weeping, then realised he was praying, his hands clasped tightly in his lap.

"Oh, bloody fuck," said Malkhaya, in a hollow voice. "Look

at this. What kind of—" He swallowed and straightened up. "We'll have to burn him. We can do that for him, at least."

"We don't burn our dead," said Csorwe, without thinking. He should be taken home and interred in the crypts beneath the House of Silence, as all such oblations were. It made no sense to feel strongly about this. She hadn't known him. "Oshaaru don't, I mean," she added. Poor boy, to have only strangers and traitors to attend to his corpse.

Csorwe had read about the ritual of oblation, but she had never heard of anyone actually performing it. It bothered her, for reasons other than the obvious. There were not so many pious young virgins in the remote forests of Oshaar that anyone could afford to exsanguinate them at will. Their enemy—the necromancer—must very badly need to rely on the power of the Unspoken. Which made sense. You would, if you intended to raise a troop of revenants and attack a Qarsazhi outpost.

Could it really be Oranna? She had to admit it was possible—even likely. But she couldn't imagine Prioress Sangrai authorising such an expedition, or giving Oranna permission to sacrifice a lay-brother. But perhaps things had changed since those days. Csorwe hadn't been old enough to pay much attention to politics at the House of Silence. It was hard to imagine the librarian sewing up the lips of a corpse, but it wasn't *that* hard.

Lagri Aritsa straightened up and sighed. "Needless," he muttered. "A pointless desecration." He looked down at the corpse, and sighed again. "You were right, then," he said. "Our enemy is here." He sounded more disappointed than anything.

"Csorwe," said Tal. She ignored him. "No, listen," he said. He reached out as though to catch her elbow, then thought better of it.

"Don't care, Tal. Save up all your great jokes and try them out on Sethennai when we get home."

She stepped out of reach, still looking at the corpse, with the sensation that she had missed something. That they had failed to spot some obvious trap. She looked over the sacrificial wounds again, wondering if there was some kind of message encoded there.

"Would you *listen*, you big moron," he said, in a whisper.

"Shut up, Tal," she said. Her nerves were screaming, loud as the watchtower bell. Something was wrong. Something out there was terribly wrong. "I think this is a diversion. They want to keep us busy."

"That's what I'm trying to tell you!" he said. "Where the hell is that girl?"

The atrium was empty. The corridors were silent. Shuthmili was gone.

10

The Divinity Underground

DARYOU MALKHAYA WOULD HAVE searched all twelve thousand cells for Shuthmili. He seemed ready to look inside every sarcophagus, and if Tal hadn't been present, Csorwe might have offered to help him. At last Lagri Aritsa took him by the arm and steadied him.

"Malkhaya," he said. "Stop."

"What do you mean? We have to find her!" said Malkhaya. He was still struggling, but couldn't bring himself to throw the old man off. Instead he kept moving down the passage, dragging Aritsa after him. "The necromancer must have taken her," he said. "She wouldn't just wander off."

"Shouting and slamming doors will not convince them to bring her back," said Aritsa.

"She could be—"

"If that's so, there is nothing that either of us can do to help her," said Aritsa, marching Malkhaya back to the atrium. "If she is dead, she is at peace. If she is corrupted, then haste will do us no good. If she is alive, then we must use our heads."

Tal and Csorwe followed at a distance, and he pulled her aside, into a corner of the atrium. He was obviously shaken, his ears quivering like a frightened rabbit's.

"She could've got lost," he said, glancing back over his shoulder. "If I lived with these creeps I'd get lost as soon as I could."

Only a few hours ago Shuthmili had been with Csorwe in the cutter, eager to do her best. Csorwe imagined where she might be now, perhaps afraid, perhaps in pain . . . but she pushed the thought aside. Fretting wasn't going to help anyone.

Tal shifted restlessly from one foot to another. "I say we ditch them all," he said. "They're no use to us anymore. We're here for the Reliquary, not to get bogged down looking for some—"

"Calm down. Just because *you've* started screaming at the sight of a corpse—"

"Oh, get fucked," said Tal, making a futile effort to sound calm.

"—doesn't mean *I'm* losing my touch."

Tal looked as if he might scream. She'd better dial it back.

"Think for a second," she said. "It's obvious that whoever has Shuthmili wants the Reliquary too—and—look." She took a breath. Time to take a risk. "Did you ever hear Sethennai mention Oranna? You know—one of his *old friends*—"

Another time, she might have goaded Tal a little more about this, prodding him for a reaction to Oranna as a competitor for Sethennai's interest. Probably for the best they didn't have time for that.

"I guess," said Tal, recovering some of his composure. "Vaguely. Shit, you think it's her?"

"Could be," said Csorwe. "I've met her. She means business."

"You really think she killed that boy? I thought she was a librarian."

"She's from the House of Silence," said Csorwe, wondering grimly why she'd ever thought it was a good idea to share her suspicions with Tal. "We're—*they're* into sacrifice."

"Woooow," said Tal, spreading on layers of scorn that didn't do anything to hide the tremor in his voice. "*Ye olde House of Silence*. You must be looking forward to seeing her. This place must be a real home away from home for you two." He gestured to the rows and rows of tombs around them. "You can have a good old-time corpse-fondling party down here." He fell silent as Aritsa approached.

"I will wait here," said Aritsa. He looked older and wearier than before. "In case Shuthmili is simply lost, and returns to us." He didn't sound hopeful. "One cannot overestimate her value to the Church and to the state of Qarsazh. I can assure you of our gratitude and the Church's generosity, if you will accompany Malkhaya down to the lower levels to search for her."

The air in the Hollow Monument was very still. This place had been sealed for uncounted ages, and nothing had moved. Everything perishable was gone, the people were rag and bone in their tombs, but the monument was still standing.

Something had preserved it.

Something that had collected like dew in crevices of the rock, as the Unspoken One had come to rest in the bowels of the sacred mountain. Some ancient power, biding and gathering itself in darkness.

Csorwe and the others felt it at about the same time. It was like hearing voices in the wind.

"There's something here, isn't there," said Malkhaya.

They nodded. Csorwe and Tal had spent enough time with the Siren to recognise the feeling. Something grand and alien was beginning to notice them. Somewhere deep beneath, it waited and listened. Latent, potential, vigilant.

"The lenition," said Malkhaya. "Damn it, damn it, damn it. I thought it was too much. It happens when worlds die, but this is something else."

"A god," said Csorwe. No point dancing around it.

"Yeah," said Malkhaya. "When something like that settles down somewhere, decides to make its earthly mansion, it distorts the place. Hollows it out from inside, like a tapeworm. It's like what they do to—"

He stalled. Csorwe felt no inclination to complete the thought. She knew as well as anyone what the gods did to people.

"We'll deal with it when we get to it," she said, stalking on down the corridor, past doorways and more doorways and passageways that looped in endlessly on themselves.

After a few minutes, Malkhaya stopped again, blinking like a man waking from a dead sleep. "Do you smell smoke?"

The scent was sweet, funereal, and familiar. Csorwe's stomach twisted. It was not woodsmoke, but burning lotus. Recollection took her with such violence that it blinded her. Falling through darkness—the gathered faces in the halls of the House—the litany of the Unspoken—

"Slow down, Csorwe, you idiot," hissed Tal, and she realised she was walking toward the source of the scent.

They followed the smoke out onto a long gallery that crawled along a sheer wall. There was a larger chamber below, but it was too dark to make out any detail. The scent of lotus was wafting up from the lower level.

The gallery had no guardrail. If they fell it would be a drop straight onto the stone floor far below. They inched their way along, flat against the wall. Then, with almost blinding brilliance, a pair of lights appeared in the lower chamber, illuminating two figures in a doorway more than thirty feet below. There was nowhere for Csorwe, Tal, and Malkhaya to go. They shrank into a crouch, pressed against the wall. It was no good: if these figures looked up, they would be seen.

The two strangers started across the room. The first was an Oshaaru woman, not tall but stately. Her long hair was loose, falling down her back in a shining mass. Her tusks were capped with chased silver that gleamed in the lantern light, and she moved with unmistakeable purpose and certainty. She lifted the lantern, and Csorwe saw her face clearly.

It was the librarian of the House of Silence. It was Oranna.

Csorwe felt no satisfaction at having been right. Instead, some inner alarm began to ring frantically. She felt her pulse beat harder in her throat.

Another woman followed, like a cygnet after a swan, dressed in the familiar yellow habit. She was carrying a torch of lotus-straw.

Not just Oranna, then, but a whole expedition from the House of Silence. And Csorwe was here to face them alone.

"I think she may be beginning to wake," said the acolyte. Csorwe recognised her, but found she couldn't remember her name.

"Oh? Has she spoken?" Oranna's voice was as sweet and as chilly as Csorwe remembered it. Csorwe took a deep breath, digging her nails into her palms under her cloak, telling herself it was good that her suspicions were confirmed, that it gave her more information to work with.

"Only muttering," said Oranna's subordinate. "Shall I order them to burn more lotus?"

"No," said Oranna. "I want to speak to her. Bring her down to the theatre to join me."

So Shuthmili was being held somewhere, most likely drugged and unable to fight for herself. Csorwe forced the image away. Tal wasn't wrong: they really weren't here to get distracted. Malkhaya could handle it. The Adept was not her responsibility.

Oranna and the acolyte moved out of sight, their lanterns blinking out one by one as they disappeared into darkness.

Csorwe rose, and turned to see that Tal had Daryou Malkhaya in a headlock, with his hand clamped over the Warden's mouth. Malkhaya's fists were clenched on the edge of the gallery, as though he had been on the point of leaping down to the floor below.

"Shut *up*," said Tal, in a harsh whisper. "Are you *insane*? Are you *fully fucking deranged*?"

Malkhaya threw him off. "They've got Shuthmili," he said, remarkably controlled for someone who had been in such close proximity to Talasseres' armpit.

"Yeah, I got that. *She* is the big scary necromancer you've all been pissing yourselves over," said Tal. "What were you going to do, fall on her head like a fucking anvil? It's a sheer drop! Shit on my life, you people are stupid."

Tal's favourite thing to do was pick a noisy, pointless fight at the worst possible moment. Csorwe thanked the Unspoken that Malkhaya seemed to be used to doing as he was told, and didn't rise to it.

"All right," said Malkhaya. "Then what?"

Csorwe was already moving on down the gallery. There was another door. "Further down," she said to Tal. "Come on."

*

Oranna went down to the theatre to wait for her prisoner. This was the deepest part of the Hollow Monument, a natural cavern that had been hollowed out and tiered for hundreds of spectators. At its centre was a hollow basin, stepped down by degrees to the surface of an offering-pool. This pool never froze or stirred. It was a still, black mirror.

Oranna paused to look down at her reflection, a golden shadow on the surface of the water. Yes, even after thirty-six years drawing on the power of the Unspoken, beating back the tide that eroded her flesh and bone, she looked well. A little underfed, but well. This was not vanity, she told herself, unless vanity was satisfaction with a hard-earned achievement.

Beyond the offering-pool was a colossal pillar, of ice or translucent stone. It was jagged at its peak, as though it had been snapped off from some larger structure. Though eyeless, it seemed to survey the theatre with the blank gaze of a statue. Motionless, inhuman, but alive. This was the heart of the monument, the seat where the god rested and sang.

This was its song, endlessly repeated, like a single note echoed into infinity:

> *Beyond your sight, beyond your sense, beyond the ecliptic*
> *of your understanding: here am I.*
> *Come to me and rest.*
> *Lie down in darkness.*
> *Set aside the cares that burden you.*
> *Sleep as you so greatly desire.*

"Do shut up," said Oranna. She had heard quite enough of this since their arrival at the Hollow Monument a week ago. If she had wanted to rest she would have stayed at the House of Silence and drifted into oblivion with the rest of them.

At the base of the pillar was a statue of a kneeling man, or so Oranna had first assumed: an enormous naked warrior or athlete, both muscle-bound and literally bound to the pillar by dozens of iron chains that stained the ice with rust.

Oranna was not often wrong, but she had soon discovered her error. This was no statue. It had been a living person. It was now something between a corpse and a revenant, blue-grey and stiff with frost. Every inch of its skin was encrusted with ice crystals.

Some of the acolytes in Oranna's retinue had been quite scandalised by the sight of it, but Oranna's own view was that once you had encountered Belthandros Sethennai there wasn't much left that could impress you as far as men were concerned, even if this one was about eight feet tall.

His frozen hands were clasped. Just above them, bound to his chest by innumerable narrower chains, was a small, octangular box.

Oranna stepped toward the man in the ice, and reached out with one uncurling hand. Before her fingertips could touch the Reliquary, she stepped back, laughing. "I'm not *quite* so foolish," she said. Her attempts to retrieve the Reliquary from the statue had already cost two acolytes, not to mention the young lay-brother she had sacrificed for the ritual of oblation.

She was getting closer, though, and was nowhere near the end of her resources. It was wonderful to know that she had found it first. Perhaps Belthandros had given up. Perhaps he was content with a mortal life. Perhaps over the last five years he had got comfortable in his palace, surrounded by barrels of resin-wine and flexible Tlaanthothei consorts. That was his own concern.

In any case, Belthandros had never fully grasped the possibilities that the Reliquary offered, never understood the true relationship that Pentravesse had shared with the Lady of the Thousand Eyes.

The urge to touch the Reliquary was surprisingly strong. Oranna lowered her hand deliberately. She would hold it soon enough. In the meantime there were other things to attend to.

As if prompted by the thought, one of Oranna's acolytes came down the steps into the theatre, followed by a cluster of revenants, carrying the prisoner between them.

"Where should we put her, librarian?" said the acolyte, Ushmai.

Oranna gestured toward the stone chair that stood between the pool and the pillar, and sent them all away.

She stood watching as the girl in the chair stirred, then sat up, gripping the arms in a panic. She waited as Shuthmili got her bearings. She had been given enough lotus to keep her groggy, but not enough to be utterly disoriented.

"Qanwa Shuthmili," said Oranna. "That's your name, isn't it?"

"You know that it is," said Shuthmili quietly. Unconscious, she had been nothing to look at—a small face with a thin mouth and an unremarkably pointed nose—but now she was awake, her eyes were as wide and dark as the offering-pool.

"The finest Adept in three generations," said Oranna. "A match for any in history. Earmarked from childhood for the Imperial Quincuriate, yes?"

Oranna hadn't set out to learn about Qarsazh's secret weapon, but in the course of research into the Reliquary you could end up hearing about all kinds of interesting things. There had been whispers about Shuthmili across many worlds. Many of the whisperers had an acquisitive gleam in their eyes. Some of them had come right out and said it: *Imagine what we could do if we had something like that.* It had been a delightful coincidence to discover that Shuthmili could be found in the same world as the Reliquary of Pentravesse, but, after all, there was no coincidence where the Reliquary was concerned.

"Personal glory is one step from pride," said Shuthmili. She met Oranna's eyes with a steady stare.

"What a shame, for that to be so," said Oranna. "What a cruel shame for you, to have been born with such a gift, into a society which regards it as a mutilation."

On her travels Oranna had met a few Qarsazhi mages— runaways from the School of Aptitude or from their assignments—and every one of them had been a furtive, sleepless, guilt-racked disaster. They never lasted long on the outside. By comparison, Shuthmili seemed remarkably composed.

"My aptitude is neither a blessing nor a curse. It is a duty. My duty is to shed light," said Shuthmili, clearly parroting from doctrine.

"In a sane country you could have been whatever you wished," said Oranna. It was Qarsazh's wastefulness that truly irritated her. "A leader, if you chose. Zinandour is a remarkable divinity. It is a shame that her power is reviled."

"I know where my future lies," said Shuthmili, with the same steady composure.

"In the Quincuriate?" said Oranna. "You must know what that will entail for you." Knowing how the Quincuriate worked made it hard to understand how anyone thought of the Unspoken One as a cruel god. The Qarsazhi had devised something far worse, and they were only mortals.

"Of course," said Shuthmili. "I have no fear of the tether."

"And why should you, I suppose?" said Oranna. "Your handlers have no more use for your ingenuity and ambition than the Quincuriate will. I am sorry to have brought you here like this, but I'm sure you see that I could never have approached Dr. Lagri Aritsa directly. The truth is that I need your help."

Shuthmili began to say something, as Oranna had expected. Oranna ignored her, and so did the god in the pillar, still singing its unchanging song. *Come to me and rest lie down in darkness set aside the cares that burden you.*

"You will have perceived that there is an entity abiding in this place," said Oranna. Shuthmili gave the slightest nod. "You Qarsazhi have little interest in gods other than your own. But perhaps you've heard of Iriskavaal the Thousand-Eyed, and her dying wrath."

"Of course," said Shuthmili. "Iriskavaal was a petty tyrant. Her followers rose up in defiance."

Oranna was surprised they told it like that in the School of Aptitude. In her experience the Qarsazhi did not like to think too closely about either tyranny or rebellion. "Iriskavaal's throne was reduced to splinters. She perished more truly than your own goddess, for instance. Zinandour was banished from the mortal realm. Iriskavaal was *broken*. It is a more terrible death than any of us will suffer. An unknowable and immortal mind broken into hundreds of fragments. Each one limited, confused, suffering, comparatively powerless."

"That does sound difficult," said Shuthmili. There was no alteration in her tone of voice or expression—both were perfectly flat—but Oranna knew when she was being mocked.

"If you think your confusion and suffering is something to

boast about, imagine struggling on for thousands of years, alone," she said, sharply. "Most of the fragments have somehow been lost. Until recently I knew of only one surviving piece, the poor hapless creature they call the Siren of Tlaanthothe. It was enslaved by mortal mages, bound into the service of Belthandros Sethennai and others like him. But now—"

"The divinity in the pillar," said Shuthmili. Oranna felt a warming glow of triumph. It was always so easy with the clever ones. Despite Shuthmili's efforts, Oranna could tell she was beginning to be interested.

"Quite," said Oranna. "We've taken to calling it the Sleeper. After the shattering of the throne, this fragment somehow came to rest here—diminished, but not without power. The people of this world must have worshipped it before their decline, but it has been trapped alone in this place too long. It has lost its mind. I came here hoping to win it to my cause. That has yet to happen, but I have some resources left at my disposal."

"I don't see how this adds up to you needing my help," said Shuthmili. "If you mean to make a tribute of me—"

"Good heavens, no," said Oranna, rather shocked. "There is no value in an unwilling sacrifice. Even your people recognise that. No." She wandered back toward the pillar. The frozen face of the dead man stared down at her, impassive. "Have you ever heard of the Reliquary of Pentravesse?"

To Oranna's surprise, Shuthmili nodded. For the Qarsazhi, the very nature of the Reliquary made it something heretical. Shuthmili must have read something she shouldn't.

"The Reliquary is here," said Oranna. She gestured back toward the pillar, toward the box chained in the dead man's hands. Best to give Shuthmili a moment to take in the whole strange tableau. If Shuthmili was shocked by the sight of it, she showed no sign. "It was stolen. Perhaps the thief panicked, or was pursued, or simply intended to hide it until they could use it safely . . . they sealed it here, in this moribund world, with this unfortunate gentleman bound to the pillar to serve as lock and guard all at once. As a piece of magic it's sickeningly good. The same curse, powered by this man's torture and slow death, binds the Sleeper and the Reliquary together."

"A gigantic curse-ward," murmured Shuthmili.

Oranna smiled. She was certain that curse-wards did not form part of the curriculum at the School of Aptitude. Shuthmili had *definitely* read something she shouldn't.

"Yes. I'm sure you can see how badly things would go for someone who tried to take the Reliquary without removing the binding." Those in Oranna's retinue who had made the attempt had died screaming.

"I really don't understand how I'm supposed to help you," said Shuthmili.

"I am a necromancer," said Oranna. "A skilled and well-read necromancer, but this kind of close spell-logic is not my forte, nor that of my patron. The Unspoken One is not much of a lockpick. I need a Qarsazhi-trained mage, with all that sinister algebra and fetish for mechanism. I need an Adept. I need you."

"I can't do this," said Shuthmili.

"Don't doubt yourself," said Oranna. "They keep you hooded and tethered like a hawk. There is so much you could accomplish if you could only extend your hand."

"I know," said Shuthmili. "Who has the right to stop me? Wouldn't I like to use my powers for something more magnificent? Don't I deserve to use the gifts I've been given? I know."

"Well," said Oranna. "Don't you?"

"Ma'am . . ." Shuthmili blinked slowly. "Do you think . . ."

Oranna did not smile. She watched Shuthmili with unbroken focus.

"Do you think they would ever let me out of the School of Aptitude if I was *really* so gullible? They train us for this kind of thing, you know."

Oranna laughed. "Well, perhaps not." Really, it would have been a shame if Shuthmili had agreed too readily. Oranna was always pleased to meet someone with backbone. "But you understand the position you're in. And you know what it is that I need from you."

She left Shuthmili to consider it, watched by two of the revenants, and returned to Ushmai.

"Do you need anything, Librarian?" said Ushmai, rubbing her thumb nervously over one of her tusks.

"How many intruders are inside the Monument now?" she said.

"We think four or five," said Ushmai. The Sleeper had softened the inner architecture of the Monument so thoroughly that it was difficult to keep track of unwelcome guests; but at least it also kept them slow and disoriented. "Some of them are armed," Ushmai added.

"Don't worry about that," said Oranna. "That's why we have the revenants." Oranna's undead followers outnumbered the living, even considering the ones Shuthmili had already destroyed. The ritual of oblation had provided the power, and the Monument itself had provided the corpses. "Take some of them and bring me back another Qarsazhi. You'll probably need to split them off from the group first."

Ushmai nodded. If not the brightest of the acolytes, she was at least the most reliable. Oranna could be reasonably sure she would pull this off.

"Oh," said Oranna. "On your way out can you begin sending the others down to the theatre? It's nearly time to begin."

Time to find out exactly how much blood the Sleeper needed to drink before it would listen.

"Will I be needed, Librarian?" said Ushmai.

"No, not this time," said Oranna. "Thank you."

Csorwe should have noticed sooner that Daryou Malkhaya had disappeared. There were only three of them. She had been at the front of the group, with Tal in the middle and Malkhaya bringing up the rear. She should have been on alert the second she lost track of his footsteps. But something about the Hollow Monument killed your senses and dulled your awareness. They only realised he was missing when they paused in an alcove to get their bearings.

"Shit," said Tal. "How long has he been gone?"

"I don't know," said Csorwe, too unsettled to worry about admitting her failure to Tal.

The Hollow Monument stretched out around them, an unreadable web of passages like the echoing veins of a giant. Malkhaya had been a trained soldier. It shouldn't have been so easy for anyone to take him, without even a scuffle.

"Maybe he got lost," said Tal. He sounded as rattled as Csorwe felt, glancing up and down the passage every minute or two, rocking on the balls of his feet as if readying himself to run. "Could've gone off to look for the girl." He didn't even wait for

Csorwe's response. "Yeah, and maybe we'll get the Reliquary no problem and Sethennai will give us a fucking trophy. I know."

"Look, we have to stay together," she said.

"Wow, gross," said Tal.

"I mean it. We shouldn't lose sight of each other."

"Oh, yeah, imagine if you got dragged off into some kind of skeleton murder hole, I'd *hate* that," said Tal, sounding fractionally calmer.

There was no need to discuss looking for Malkhaya. It was just the two of them now, and they knew what they were here for.

For the first time, she could believe that the Reliquary might actually be within her grasp. She couldn't imagine how it would feel even to see it. She would never have met Sethennai if not for this one thing. If he hadn't wanted it so badly she would be dead, bones among bones in the Shrine of the Unspoken One. She knew exactly how much she owed. Returning it to him would be the proof that he had chosen correctly, that all Csorwe's training and practice and dedication had made her truly worthy.

She was sure Tal was thinking something similar. Well, they had to get the thing before they could fight about it.

Another passage, another atrium, another row of sarcophagus chambers, another stone staircase—and then they saw lights up ahead.

They came out onto one of the upper tiers of the theatre, and for the first time heard the unearthly song that rippled through the chamber.

"Come to me and rest," muttered Tal. "Yeah, great, really tempting."

There were lights burning down at the centre of the theatre, braziers releasing a dim light and a faint smell of lotus, not strong enough to affect Csorwe's senses but enough to make her uneasy. This was the theatre, clearly. This must be where they had brought Shuthmili. Csorwe squinted, waiting for her eyes to adjust to the flickering light. Further on, Tal stopped abruptly, his hands falling limp at his sides.

"The pool," he whispered. "Fucking gods alive, Csorwe, look at the pool."

In the gardens of the palace of Tlaanthothe, where Sethennai kept his private residence, there was a pool like this that stood beneath magnolia trees, and every summer the blossoms fell and bruised on the tiles. Here, in place of petals, bodies littered the steps.

There were more than a dozen, fallen in orderly rows at the water's edge. Oshaaru women, in yellow habits: all followers of the Unspoken.

Csorwe's breath caught. She had seen death before, but these corpses lay so peacefully, as though they had discarded their bodies like clothes and slipped into the pool to bathe. She found it hard to stomach the quietness of it, the fact that there had clearly been no struggle. They seemed to have walked down in neat lines to the deepest heart of the monument, and knelt by the pool, and cut their own throats, just as calmly as Csorwe should have gone to her own death at the Shrine.

"There she is," whispered Tal. "Alive. I think."

Submerged to the shoulders in the pool, floating in a corona of yellow robes like a water lily, was Oranna. Her hair trailed around her in a soft cloud. A shoal of white petals floated in the water. Her lips were parted, her mouth and tusks stained dark as though she had drunk from the open veins of an oblation.

The pollution of the waters, the vessel and her corruption, the secret darkness in the deepest parts of the earth. All these things were familiar—from *The Book of Unmaking* and the rites of the Unspoken—and familiarity turned Csorwe's shock to comprehending disgust.

The water rippled as Oranna rose up out of the pool. Csorwe and Tal froze, but she didn't seem to have noticed them. She moved off into darkness, out of the light of the nearest brazier. Csorwe and Tal edged around, darting from shadow to shadow, column to column, trying to get a better view.

Between the pool and the pillar there was a stone chair, and curled up in the chair, wrapped in her crumpled robe, was Shuthmili. It was difficult to tell whether she was alive or dead, but then she shifted, drawing her legs up into the chair to hug her knees.

It should have been a relief to see her alive, but Csorwe's chest tightened, as if an iron cage had closed around her beating heart. Another factor. Another distraction. She ought to have known better than to let herself talk to this Adept at all. She took a deep breath. At heart this was just another job, and she was a professional, and if she was good at anything it was putting things aside.

Oranna left her wet habit by the side of the pool and dressed calmly in a clean gown, which Csorwe recognised as the ceremonial vestment of the librarian. It had a train of brocade worked in saffron and gold, which made Csorwe think of the little rooms in the outland villages, the women stitching by lamplight: so much work for a ritual they would never see. It trailed behind her, strewn with embroidered flowers, bloodless and open like severed hands.

"You're awake again, then," said Oranna to Shuthmili. Despite the distance, they could hear every word clearly.

"God, I hate this shit," said Tal under his breath. "Shall we kill her?"

"No," said Csorwe, although it took some effort. "We don't know what's going on here. Wait."

"Have you thought any further about what we discussed?" said Oranna.

"There is nothing to think about," said Shuthmili. "I will not help you."

Oranna lit a torch from one of the braziers and approached the pillar. Until now, they had seen it only in outline. Now Csorwe saw every detail of the chained figure, and of the box chained in his hands.

"Oh, shit," whispered Tal. "Is that it?"

"Yeah," said Csorwe, little more than a breath. "That's it."

She hadn't expected the Reliquary to be so *little*. All of Sethennai's wandering—Csorwe's entire existence—rested on this one small thing that wound trouble upon trouble wherever it went.

"The Sleeper is so far gone that tribute will no longer suffice," said Oranna. She looked back toward the bodies by the pool with regret, though without remorse. "We are going to have to shift for ourselves. It cannot be reasoned with."

"Nor can I, ma'am," said Shuthmili. "I will not help you."

She was looking out into the shadows, directly at Csorwe and Tal. Csorwe shrank back automatically. If Shuthmili saw her, she might think they were there to help, and that seemed too cruel for words. They couldn't risk rushing in now, before they had the facts. Csorwe had learned her lesson about that, and she had the gold tusk to prove it.

"That's a shame," said Oranna. She clicked her fingers, and a group of revenants came out of the shadows, carrying a large man-shaped bundle upside-down on their shoulders. Their bony feet clicked on the flagstones.

It was Daryou Malkhaya, limp and heavy as death. Blood trickled down his cheekbone from a wound on his temple.

"Warden—" said Shuthmili.

"He lives," said Oranna. "And he fought fiercely, but without your help I'm afraid he could not match my revenants a second time."

Csorwe winced. They needed the Reliquary. Their best chance to get it was simply to wait. But she didn't want to sit through this. Even Tal had looked away.

Shuthmili half rose from the chair, but the revenants warned her back. "Warden, can you hear me?" she said.

"He is under lotus," said Oranna.

Shuthmili shook her head. "This wasn't necessary. Leave him alone."

"Well, it's not as though I *want* to drown him in the pool," said Oranna. "That would be a waste, and upsetting for both of us. But the choice is there."

"I'm sorry, Malkhaya," said Shuthmili, softly. "You were right. We should have left."

"Open the seal for me," said Oranna. "Retrieve the Reliquary, and I will guarantee his safety."

Shuthmili looked from Oranna to Malkhaya without a word.

Then she stood up. "If that's the choice I'm given," she said, removing her gloves. "Show me."

*

For almost an hour, Shuthmili worked on the binding. Most of the time she sat on the ground, looking up at the pillar and muttering. Once or twice she got up and went to look closer at the chains.

"I wouldn't touch them," said Oranna. "If I were you."

"I see that," said Shuthmili. "This would be easier if I had pen and paper, you know."

The revenants had dropped Malkhaya at the edge of the sacrificial pool, where he still lay, twitching occasionally as the lotus began to wear off.

All that time, Tal and Csorwe crouched in the dark, waiting for their moment.

"All right," whispered Tal. "As soon as she opens the binding, I give the signal. You kill the priestess. I get the Reliquary. We deal with the revenants if we have to, and we go."

"We could try and take her with us," said Csorwe. "The Adept, I mean."

Tal frowned. "What? Why? She'll be fine. Her Warden can take her home. Anyway, you heard the priest talking. They think it's a Qarsazhi artefact. We have to get it out before they realise and make a fuss."

"All right. Fine."

"Stay and make sure all your little friends get out safely if you want," said Tal. "But I'm taking the Reliquary home."

"I said *fine*," said Csorwe. She didn't know why she had even suggested it. Of course Shuthmili would be safe with the others. "I know the plan. As soon as Oranna has the Reliquary."

Down in the arena, Shuthmili stood before the pillar, not quite touching it. There was almost nothing to see. On the edge of Csorwe's hearing, the dull thunder of magic boomed, like the beating of a vast monstrous heart.

Csorwe tightened her hand around the hilt of her sword. She didn't usually have so much difficulty slowing herself down before a fight, reaching that place of calm and ready decision. Something was throwing her off.

At times a dark aura flashed around Shuthmili: coiled roots and tendrils, delineated in darkness. Beyond that, nothing but the endless song of the god, apparently oblivious to what was happening in its resting place.

By now, Shuthmili was shivering like a flame flickering in a draught. She prayed out loud much of the time. "Friend of the Dead, you who watch over the gates of life, I pray that you watch over Warden Daryou Malkhaya. Lord of Wisdom, you who keep us in clarity and rectitude, I pray that you guide my hands."

Then she broke off, turning back to Oranna, who watched from a few feet away.

"There is a problem," said Shuthmili. "I know how to do it. I can remove the binding."

"But . . . ?" Oranna approached, picking a stray petal out of her hair.

"There's no way to do it without awakening the divinity in the pillar. The Sleeper, as you said."

"Ah," said Oranna. "You worked that out. Yes. I suspect the thief was extremely pleased with that. My guess is that they planned to come back and open the seal when they were certain of their safety. Where better to hide it than a dying world?"

"The Sleeper won't be happy," said Shuthmili.

"No," said Oranna. "As anyone might, after some thousand years' captivity, it will be extremely angry."

"Then—what do you think we should do?" said Shuthmili.

"Do it," said Oranna. "Then we'll need to run."

Csorwe and Tal exchanged a glance.

"*Wait*," Tal mouthed. "Stick to the plan. We get the Reliquary and we get out."

"What about Malkhaya—" said Shuthmili. Her eyes were glassy and staring, as though she could not believe quite what was happening. "Tell your revenants to take the Warden to safety. Have them take him to the surface. I can't let him get hurt."

"Very well," said Oranna. She gestured to the revenants, who picked him up again as if he were so much ballast.

"And there is another of my people here—Dr. Lagri—" said Shuthmili. Oranna raised her eyebrows, and Shuthmili's expression hardened. "You know you can't do this without me. As well as Dr. Lagri there are two others, two visitors. Tell your people to find them and make sure they get to safety."

Csorwe winced. It would have been less painful if Shuthmili had forgotten about them.

The revenants carted Malkhaya off toward the far staircase, on the other side of the arena, behind Oranna. Shuthmili ran her hands back through her hair, rearranging her plaits.

"All right," she said, and straightened up.

She stood face-to-face with the kneeling giant, almost nose-to-nose, as if she might lean in and kiss him. Instead, she pressed her forehead to his, and shut her eyes.

The first chain broke with a bright metallic sound. Then another, and more, ringing out a terrible discord. Shuthmili's fists were clenched at her side.

Another chain broke, releasing the arm of the frozen man. And he *moved*. At first Csorwe didn't understand what she was seeing. The hand was square and massive, blue-white with cold. It flexed once or twice in the air, shedding ice crystals, and grabbed Shuthmili's wrist, bending her arm up and back. She cried out once, as if the touch burnt her, but did not move.

Oranna was murmuring something to her, something Csorwe could not hear. Csorwe found herself remembering what Oranna had told her, eight years ago. *She was afraid at first, but when the day came she was quite calm.* Csorwe had really done her best to believe it. She had believed it enough to go up to the Shrine without question. She hadn't known there was any other path but the path of sacrifice. She hadn't known there was a choice to fight.

It might have been easier to bear if Shuthmili had wept. Instead Csorwe and Tal crouched in darkness as Shuthmili shook silently, as if she had gone through pain and into something beyond screaming.

It was Csorwe's fault that Shuthmili was here. She had persuaded the Qarsazhi to stay when they could have run. And Shuthmili had stayed because she wanted to finish her work, to complete the one thing that had been given to her to prove herself.

The links continued to break, one every few seconds. The man in the pillar got his other arm free, and stretched his fingers, shattering their casing of ice. The frozen man cupped Shuthmili's face in his hand, quite gently, as if to comfort her.

Now Shuthmili screamed.

Before she knew what she was doing, as though some deep internal coil had reached the limit of its compression, Csorwe rose up out of the shadows and leapt forward, drawing a knife from her belt. She could not let this happen.

She didn't hear Tal call after her. She heard nothing, and

saw nothing, in fact, but Oranna and Shuthmili, Oranna's thin anxious smile, Shuthmili crying out in agony.

She grabbed Oranna around the waist, dragging her back, and held the knife to her throat.

And then, at least for Csorwe, everything was very simple. Oranna stopped struggling once she realised Csorwe could cut her throat whenever she chose to.

She leant in, speaking clearly into Oranna's ear. Her hair smelled of incense and beeswax. She was dead weight in Csorwe's arms, resistant without struggling. "Tell her she can stop. Tell her it's over. She doesn't have to do it."

"I'm afraid that is not going to happen," said Oranna.

Csorwe tightened her grip, cutting into the soft flesh at the hollow of Oranna's neck. A threadlet of blood ran down the blade.

"Even if you kill me," said Oranna, "you cannot stop it now. Even if you kill *her*. The seal is opening."

"You knew it would hurt her," said Csorwe. Her voice trembled. She hadn't realised how angry she was until she heard it.

"She knew it herself," said Oranna. "She's quite brilliant."

Chains ruptured, like a peal of bells breaking. Metal and screaming.

The seal broke. A wave of power flashed outward from the pillar: invisible, irresistible, cold and pitiless and mighty as the corrupted seas. Time seemed to stop. It felt like a physical blow.

With a crack so deep and painful that Csorwe remembered the root of her tusk breaking in her jaw, the ground began to rupture. Shuthmili crumpled where she stood, and only the grip of the frozen man kept her upright.

Csorwe's ears rang. One moment she stood on solid ground,

the next, it broke apart, like sheets of ice. The foundations of the monument shook.

As Csorwe tried to get her balance, Oranna broke out of her grip, leaping back across a fissure.

"I told you," she said, adjusting her robe. "It can't be stopped. I suggest you start running."

Another concussion knocked Csorwe to the ground. She got upright again in time to see the dead man's hand open, releasing Shuthmili's wrist.

Shuthmili stumbled back, slipped, and fell. The last of the chains shattered, and the frozen corpse came free. It struck the ground, rebounded once, and disintegrated, scattering crystals of petrified flesh. Its chest came apart and the Reliquary bounced across the ground, skidding toward the edge of the rift.

It was so close. Almost within arm's reach.

Csorwe gave up trying to keep her balance, threw herself across the ground and lunged for it. Oranna was closer. She seized the Reliquary in her outstretched hand and slithered back.

The central rift in the floor of the theatre grew deeper and wider with every second. The bloody water in the sacrificial pool drained away into the earth. The Sleeper was waking, and it howled with rage, just on the edge of mortal hearing.

Csorwe was on one side of the rift. Oranna was on the other, with the Reliquary in her fist.

Somewhere in the distance, struggling to stay upright as the ground gave way, Tal was screaming, "*Get it get it get the fucking thing!*"

There was nobody between Csorwe and the staircase to the floor above, far behind her. If she ran now she could make it. The place was coming down any minute now. She had to get out.

Oranna glared back at her. Anger and determination did not mar her handsome face. If anything they illuminated her features.

"Tell Belthandros he *lost*," she said. Then, as the ceiling began to fall in, she ran.

Csorwe would have gone after her. She would have run through falling rocks and spikes of ice to get an inch closer to the Reliquary.

At that moment a jagged block of broken masonry struck the floor near Csorwe's foot and shattered like glass.

Bad news and bad luck swarm around the Reliquary of Pentravesse like flies around a carcass. This could have been bad news, bad luck, or something else.

Csorwe leapt away from the falling rock and saw Shuthmili. She lay motionless, unconscious, her bare hand uncurling beside the toe of Csorwe's boot.

And once again, everything was very clear. Csorwe picked Shuthmili up, hoisting her over her shoulder. She let Oranna and the Reliquary go, and she ran for her life.

11

Entirely Gone Away

NO GOD WATCHED OVER Csorwe any longer, but something must have guided her steps. The Monument didn't fall until they were out.

The bowl-shaped valley crumpled like an eggshell, giving its tombs back to the earth. The boundary wall was falling, and Csorwe ran for the nearest gap, bent almost double under Shuthmili's weight. They emerged onto a stony hillside, where black leafless trees stood, petrified where they once grew.

There was no sign of Oranna, of Tal, of Lagri Aritsa or Daryou Malkhaya. Csorwe and Shuthmili might as well be the only ones left alive.

Csorwe kept running, one hand on her sword and the other keeping Shuthmili steady over her shoulders. She battered her way through the woods, breaking glassy thickets underfoot. Stray branches cut her clothes and scratched her skin. She screwed up her face against the sting and trampled on, stumbling on the edge of panic.

She hacked through a stand of reeds that fell like wind chimes, barely cleared a little frozen stream, ran on down a clear slope, and cleared the petrified woods just as her foot caught on a loose stone and she tripped. They fell headlong down the frozen hillside, her thoughts scattering as they hit the ground at the bottom.

Csorwe struggled to catch her breath, looking dazed at the sky above the branches. It was a bruised and chilly gold.

Shuthmili lay perfectly still, peaceful, as though resting. Csorwe crawled over and checked her over, but she was unharmed. In that respect she was doing better than Csorwe, who had a stinging graze down her hip and thigh despite her thick winter clothes.

What had she done? The Reliquary had been *right there*. All she had needed to do was pick her moment, and she had failed. She had been tested and tempered again and again, and when it came to it, in the moment that mattered, she had weakened. Oranna had the Reliquary.

Shuthmili sighed, settling on the cold earth. The sound was enough to shake Csorwe out of her self-pity. She told herself to get a grip. It would soon be night. They needed rest and shelter, or they weren't going to survive it.

She mustered her strength one last time and lifted Shuthmili, carrying her to a hollow nearby. It wasn't much, but it would protect them from the elements and make them harder to see.

Csorwe curled up beside her, throwing her cloak over them both to try and conserve warmth. She was too numbly tired to take any other precaution. Sleep hit her like a falling rock.

She woke slow and sore. The wrenching pain of her lost tusk, deep in the root of her jaw, returned first to her perceptions, like a small insistent haunting. The rest of the world assembled itself shard by jagged shard.

She was very cold, propped upright against something very

hard and colder still. It was morning, and someone had tied her to a tree.

A few feet away, Shuthmili had laid out her cloak on the ground and was kneeling in prayer, facing the sunrise. It was a relief to see her awake. It took Csorwe a moment to realise exactly what had happened.

"*You* tied me up!" said Csorwe.

Shuthmili straightened up and looked her over. There was nothing even remotely approaching gratitude on her face. She looked as though she were checking that a rabid dog was still securely chained.

"Yes," said Shuthmili.

". . . *Why?*" Csorwe was too baffled and too tired to be angry. She could hardly make sense of it.

"You lied. I know you aren't who you said you were. You obviously weren't students. You—you must have been working for that woman," said Shuthmili.

"*Oranna?*" said Csorwe.

"You must have been," said Shuthmili. She had sounded calm enough initially, but Csorwe saw now that she was jittering as badly as Tal at his worst, pacing back and forth as if trying to remember something she had forgotten. Eventually she went back to the pile of their belongings and started going through Csorwe's bag.

"I should have realised," Shuthmili added. "She must have sent you to undermine me."

Csorwe leant back against the petrified tree trunk. She could almost have laughed. She didn't know how to begin to deny it.

"I rescued you," she said.

Csorwe wasn't sure what kind of reaction she had been

expecting. Surprise, at least. Maybe a thank you. Instead Shuth-mili pushed her hair back out of her eyes and scowled.

"Well, you picked a good moment for it," she said, and went back to rifling through Csorwe's things. "If you were going to rescue me you could have got there sooner."

Minutes passed. Csorwe tested her bonds, reflecting that she was certainly Shuthmili's first prisoner and the knots might not be secure, but she had no such luck.

Shuthmili's hair had fallen into her face again and Csorwe couldn't read her expression, but she was searching through the bags now in a kind of panic, as though she had lost something.

"Don't you have any food?" Shuthmili said eventually, with obvious reluctance.

"There's dried beef in the side pocket," said Csorwe. Shuthmili scrutinised her for a moment, maybe calculating whether this could possibly be a trick. "It's not good, but it's fine," said Csorwe.

Shuthmili wolfed almost the whole packet of beef with absolute, efficient concentration, tearing the sticks apart in her hands. She turned away from Csorwe, as though ashamed of her hunger.

Csorwe was pretty hungry herself, but that could wait. The hard facts of her situation were beginning to make themselves known, like shards of glass in a mattress.

She tried not to think about Tal, and what might have happened to him. He had cheated and betrayed his way out of too many situations for it to seem fair for him to die in a rock-fall. It was hard to imagine he might actually be gone. He had been a grim fact of her life for too long. There was no triumph in beating him like this, anyway, without him around to know that she'd won.

And what had she won, anyway? The Reliquary was gone. She had come so close to Sethennai's heart's desire, and she had failed him. She remembered the old dream, with Sethennai as the heir of Pentravesse and Csorwe as his right hand. She had imagined all kinds of things. That she would learn his secrets, that she would properly understand him, that she would help him shape the world to his design . . . looking back, it all seemed rather pathetic. As if he would trust her again now.

Around them, the frozen hills stretched away, the mountains rose up in silence, the grey sky seethed. All the sinews that held this world together had snapped. No light, no warmth. Nothing to eat in the whole wretched, beguiling expanse.

After a while, Shuthmili brought her a few sticks of dried meat.

"Going to untie me?" said Csorwe.

"No," said Shuthmili.

Csorwe bared her teeth. She was reaching the end of her patience with this. "How do you expect me to eat?"

Shuthmili tore off a bite-sized piece of beef and held it out to her, at arm's length.

"No," said Csorwe.

"That's fine, if you're not hungry," said Shuthmili.

Csorwe's pride wasn't all that refined. She didn't exactly like being fed from the hand like an animal, but she liked it better than starving. Shuthmili tore up the remains of the beef and fed it to her piece by piece. Shuthmili enjoyed this experience perhaps even less than Csorwe did, flinching back every time as if she might get bitten. Afterward, at least, she gave Csorwe a drink from the last of the water.

"Can you make food?" said Csorwe. "With your magic or whatever?"

Shuthmili, who had withdrawn to the other side of the hollow again, shook the last shreds of beef into the palm of her hand and tipped them into her mouth. "No," she said.

"Clean water? Light? Heat?"

"I could purify water—I could light a lantern if we had fuel—but it's not that simple," said Shuthmili. "I can't make something out of nothing."

"All right," said Csorwe. "In that case, I think we're screwed."

"I don't have to listen to anything you say," said Shuthmili.

Csorwe wished her hands were free so she could bury her face in them.

"Look," she said. "I'm not—I didn't lie to you. I had nothing to do with Oranna. I didn't know she was there. But—"

"Why should I believe you?" said Shuthmili.

"*But* it doesn't matter if you believe me," said Csorwe. "We're lost. It's cold. We don't have anything else to eat or drink. Maybe you haven't done this before, so you don't know how quick it can happen, but we will die here if we don't do something."

"If that is the will of the gods," said Shuthmili, eyeing the pile of bags as if she wanted to lie down in them and sleep again.

All Csorwe could do was groan. "You think the gods give a shit what happens to us?"

"Well," said Shuthmili, frostily. "It's one of the central tenets of—"

"If someone was watching us, people would behave themselves better," said Csorwe. "You don't want to die. Your gods made you with a brain, probably."

"But you said yourself there's nothing we can do!" said

Shuthmili. She paced back and forth, perhaps hoping that the Mother of Cities would descend from the skies, smite the heretic, and give her new orders.

Csorwe took a deep breath. Shuthmili hadn't enjoyed the Hollow Monument any more than Csorwe herself. Whatever doubts Csorwe had about Shuthmili's life up until this point, it seemed to have been well ordered and predictable. All things considered, it was amazing that Shuthmili was holding it together even this well.

"We could go and search for the cutter," said Csorwe. "Even if it won't fly, it has food and fuel."

Shuthmili agreed to the plan with indecent haste: in her place Csorwe would have stalled a bit, just out of basic self-respect. Shuthmili unfastened the bindings and immediately tied Csorwe's wrists back together. Csorwe could have taken the opportunity to overpower her, but it didn't take much to imagine how Shuthmili would react to that. And then she'd have a hostile prisoner to deal with.

"Could do with my arms to balance," said Csorwe, without much hope.

"I could do with a bath and a cup of coffee," said Shuthmili. "I'm afraid we're both just going to have to live with it."

It was hard going. The ground had settled, but there were occasional tremors, like the earth's death rattle. The rope chafed Csorwe's wrists, and the walk gave her too much time to think: about Tal, about Sethennai, about the Reliquary and her failure. She tried to concentrate on survival. Uncertainty was a deep pit to fall down, and there were spikes at the bottom.

If the old boundary wall was still standing, and if they could find their way back to it, they could probably follow it round to the landing site. The trouble was that she had no idea where they were. The tremors must have been worse than Csorwe had thought. They had obliterated any landmarks she would have remembered from their outward journey.

"Do you recognise any of this?" she asked.

Shuthmili shook her head. "This is my fault," she said. "The awakening of the Sleeper must have caused a tremendous rupture. An outpouring of energy."

"Is it dangerous?" said Csorwe, not that she needed anything else to worry about.

"Not in theory," said Shuthmili, looking miserable. "Not to us, anyway."

They picked their way through a field of boulders. It was icy underfoot. The wind had dropped, which was a measure of relief, but Csorwe was starting to think someone was following them. She heard—not footsteps, but the tap of pebble against pebble, the sound of gravel shifting.

She tried to imagine it might be Tal, that he had somehow survived just to spite her, but that was a dangerous way to start thinking. She was used to losing things, and wishing never helped.

They passed across an open plateau, clear of boulders. There was something uncanny about this place. Something about the boulders—they were too even, too regular, but Csorwe couldn't place exactly what it was she disliked.

There was a crack like a sheet of slate breaking. It echoed among the boulders on the other side of the plateau.

"Shuthmili," said Csorwe quietly. Shuthmili glanced back at her. "Give me my sword and get behind me."

"What?" said Shuthmili.

A shadow surged up from among the boulders. It was a revenant, the corpse of some dead giant. The ragged shreds of a robe hung about him, like mist around a mountain. He was enormous, misshapen, a blasphemous engine of skin and bone. A broken coronet trailed over his forehead like something left on a grave. His eye sockets were hollow, but a spark burnt within them.

Shuthmili shrank back, retreating into herself. Then she swallowed, straightened up, went to remove her gloves—and found them already gone.

"Mother of Cities," she muttered.

"Give me my sword!" said Csorwe.

The revenant lumbered downhill toward them, swaying like a drunk. He was unarmed, but his jaw hung open, off its hinges, and his teeth were jagged. The stink of rot and dust and embalming salts poured off him.

Shuthmili raised her fist, as if to keep shut the gates of hell with one hand. She was shaking. Csorwe didn't know much about magic, but she knew what it looked like when someone was about to pass out from exhaustion. And, by now, she knew intimately what it looked like when someone made an avoidable mistake by pushing too hard.

"Don't do this," said Csorwe, holding out her wrists. "Give me my sword, for gods' sake, and let me go. I can fight!"

Shuthmili's face twisted, but she unsheathed Csorwe's sword and slashed through the bindings on her wrists before turning the hilt toward Csorwe.

Csorwe flew toward the revenant. He dived after her, snapping his jaw, so close that she could hear the leaky gasp of shrunken lungs reinflating.

Even in the frantic first moments of the fight, it was good to have the sword back in her grip: an extension of her hand, the tool for which she had been made. Csorwe swooped past the man, light as air, drawing him away from Shuthmili.

He snapped at Csorwe, almost lugubrious. She feinted away, leaping to one side to strike at the nape of his neck, but getting her sword back must have made her overconfident. She underestimated his reach. The dead man swiped at her with a colossal hand, flinging her wide across the ground. She hit the frozen earth with a grunt of pain, not far from Shuthmili. Back on her feet at once, she flung herself bodily at the man again, swift as an arc of lightning. Oh, yes. This was what she had missed. This made the world so simple.

Her enemy had been toying with her before. Now he struck in earnest, moving with oily alacrity, grabbing her arm and sinking his teeth into her shoulder. She registered the pain as she registered the stench: something unpleasant to deal with later. Now she was close enough to take her chance. She drove her blade up into his rib cage, and felt dry flesh and sinew yield. It was like stabbing an armchair. He gasped and tipped forward, clutching at the air, and she stepped out of the way, withdrawing her sword. The huge body fell and subsided.

Shuthmili faced her across it, backed up against a monolith. She looked from the blade to the dead man and back to Csorwe.

"What if I ask you really nicely to give back the sword," said Shuthmili.

Csorwe wiped the blade on her trouser leg, leaving an unsightly smear of ichorous resin.

"I don't think so," said Csorwe. She turned the shattered body of the giant with her foot. In true death, without anything else to give him form and weight, he was very light—no more than a bundle of driftwood. The tarnished coronet had fallen off during the fight, and was lying among the pebbles, shedding enamelled petals.

"I suppose you solve all your problems by impaling them," said Shuthmili, still flat against the rock, watching Csorwe like she was about to explode.

"I'm not here to hurt you," said Csorwe, slightly winded from the fight. Her shoulder was beginning to ache where she had been bitten. That wasn't going to be good. "I told you. We didn't lie to you. I'm Sethennai's agent." She stretched her left arm and winced. If they had time, she would stop and deal with it, but it wasn't bleeding too badly, and she didn't want to stay here.

Shuthmili didn't look completely convinced; Csorwe wasn't sure whether to put this down to Qarsazhi paranoia or Churchly sanctimony or a healthy dose of inborn suspicion.

"I know you're panicking," said Csorwe. "You don't need to trust me. That's fine. You just need to follow me."

After a moment, Shuthmili nodded. They went on, leaving the defunct revenant behind.

"Did someone raise that thing?" said Csorwe, her thoughts leaping to Oranna, and to the possibility that the Reliquary might still be in reach.

"I don't think so. I couldn't feel any magic on it," said Shuthmili. "I think it must have been . . . natural. If that's the right word for it."

Csorwe peered out across the field of boulders. They were worn down and broken by the elements, but there was something artificial about the way they were placed, in rows and columns, for miles, receding into the mist.

"This is a graveyard, isn't it," said Csorwe.

She expected to get something like, *This whole world is a graveyard,* but Shuthmili just nodded.

The mist drew in, like a white curtain closing. They kept moving. The crunch of their footsteps on the grit echoed among the boulders, keeping Csorwe on her guard. Revenants tended to move in packs, and it was worrying that the first one had got so close before she'd noticed it.

There was another crack of breaking stone. Csorwe grabbed Shuthmili's arm to stop her.

She narrowed her eyes, peering out at the mist, hoping she was wrong. Nothing at first. Just the ranks of gravestones, miles of them, baffling the eye. Graves enough for a whole city.

She blinked and looked again. Something was moving, out in the distance, like worms coming out after rain. Two or three figures, crawling up out of the mist. More, out of sight, as far as Csorwe knew.

"Shuthmili," she said, in a low voice, trying not to frighten her. "We need to keep moving, just as slow as we're going now. This place is waking up."

Shuthmili stared, swallowed, then nodded. "Yes. That would make sense," she said, which was nice, because things had stopped making sense to Csorwe at least eight hours ago. "The Sleeper was keeping this world from declining. Now that it's awake . . . all that energy has been unleashed and things are going to decline very fast indeed."

She broke off and stared out into the mist, her eyes glazing. It would be a hell of a lot easier to do this without dead weight, but Csorwe was damned if she was going to leave Shuthmili to die *now,* after everything she had done to get her this far.

"All right," said Csorwe. "Don't panic. If we run—if we have to start running—they're going to start chasing us. Once we run we can't stop." Talking Shuthmili through it made it much easier to deal with her own impulse to bolt.

Shuthmili nodded, but looked as if she was just picking her moment to bolt as hard as she could.

Csorwe bit her lip. She wasn't used to dealing with anyone else's fear. She hurried Shuthmili on down the slope toward another clearing in the gravestones. She could see the figures rising in the mist, at the very edges of her vision. Dozens of them by now.

"You've done so well," she said, trying to be soothing. "We're nearly out."

"You can't possibly know that," said Shuthmili, clearly on the brink of panic.

"All right," she said. "Point taken." Csorwe herself had never had much patience with anyone telling her everything was going to be fine. The revenants were still stiff and jerky, recovering slowly from centuries of sleep. That would change as soon as they had something to chase.

"Why don't you tell me about something nice?" said Csorwe, trying another tack.

"Something *nice*?" said Shuthmili. Disbelieving scorn was an improvement on terror, at least.

"Yeah," said Csorwe, who would rather have fought another corpse than try to make small talk. "I don't know. What do you . . . like?"

"I don't see how that's relevant," hissed Shuthmili. "I like not being stalked by the walking dead. I like wearing clean clothes and getting a good night's sleep. I don't think you're in a position to supply any of those things."

"You know, it was a lot easier to deal with you when you were unconscious," said Csorwe, although anger was also better than terror, and after years of working with Tal she was entirely used to it.

"Yes, that's what I'm told," said Shuthmili. "I'm fine. I'm not going to run away. You don't have to jolly me along. I don't need distracting."

Out in the graveyard, the dead were rising fast. More of them than Csorwe could count, now, in every direction. Csorwe's skin prickled, and every instinct, natural or ingrained, prickled with it. There must be thousands of them. The urge to run was almost irresistible.

"Are you sure?" said Csorwe. "I quite like a distraction, myself."

"What do you think is *nice,* then," said Shuthmili, though she sounded a little warmer.

"Breakfast," said Csorwe, hopelessly aware that this made her sound like a yokel. "It sets you up for the day. Wouldn't mind getting a chance to clean my sword, either. Your turn?"

"I wish you hadn't mentioned breakfast," said Shuthmili, though she finally sounded less tense. "I can't think when I last had a proper meal—"

Csorwe scanned the horizon as they walked. At last, at the bottom of the hill, beyond the edge of the graveyard, she saw the wandering line of the boundary wall, and the ridge, and the silhouette of *Prosperity*.

Out in the graveyard, something broke into a run. It was like the fall of ice that starts the avalanche. The dead began pouring down toward them.

"Shit," said Csorwe, grabbing Shuthmili's arm. "Let's move."

She broke into a sprint, and the dead pursued them.

Even running, the crowd of revenants did not move fast. On her own, Csorwe could have outpaced them, but after a few minutes Shuthmili was wheezing. She was going to collapse if she kept going.

Csorwe rarely worked with other people, unless you counted Tal, which she didn't. She wasn't used to matching her pace to anyone else's. She and Tal operated on the principle that if you fell behind, you were left to rot.

Still. Shuthmili was not Tal, and Csorwe was not prepared to let her die. If she could draw the revenants off for a second, Shuthmili would have a moment's rest, and Csorwe would catch up to her afterward. Never mind that that would take Csorwe directly into the path of the revenants, perhaps close enough for them to reach her.

Some of the fear and failure that had weighed on her since the Monument melted away. She had lost enough, but she could still do this much.

"Catch your breath," she called. She darted away from Shuthmili at a sharp angle, waving her sword and yelling. "Hey! Hey! Come and get me, you leathery fucks!"

Glancing back she saw the dead, a shambling train flowing down the hillside toward them, like water settling into a groove. One or two of the nearest broke away from the line and started following Csorwe instead. Once they were properly drawn off, she doubled back and started running in the other direction. A little way ahead, Shuthmili stumbled on, taking great gulps of air.

They weren't far from the wall. There was a narrow gap where the tremors had shaken it apart, making a kind of tilted doorway.

Csorwe caught up to Shuthmili and seized her arm. They were getting to the wall if Csorwe had to drag her there.

All around them the ground shifted as the graveyard gave up more of its dead, as hands came up from the earth like reaching roots.

Shuthmili was still trying to run, like someone in a dream whose legs stop working. Csorwe slowed her own pace to keep level with her. The dead were close enough now that she could see the cobwebbed gratings of their ribs, the horror of their crumpled skulls and shattered jawbones.

The smell of funeral oils. Myrrh and camphor and balsam, bone and ash and dust.

The closest revenant grabbed at the hem of Shuthmili's surcoat and she screamed, a breathless sound, like an animal caught in a trap. Csorwe kicked through its bony wrist, scattering metacarpals, and shoved Shuthmili through the gap in the wall. She grabbed the revenant by the neck and smashed its skull against the wall, again and again, until it stopped struggling.

"*Run*," she yelled to Shuthmili, and took up her place in the doorway. They were coming down the hill in a thick crowd. Csorwe didn't try to calculate how many she could take before she fell. She knew an undefeatable enemy when she saw one. Perhaps this was just as well. She had failed. She saw, with clarity, that she would rather die fighting than admit to Sethennai that she had failed him.

"I can't," said Shuthmili, crumpling on the bare earth, just a few yards ahead. "I'm sorry, I can't—"

Csorwe turned back to face the dead. They kept coming, all fleshless limbs and faceless heads. Csorwe stabbed and cut and thrust and stabbed, holding her ground as far as she could. She heard herself screaming somewhere in the distance. The world closed in. Only this doorway was real: this three-foot gap, and the hemisphere beyond. Shuthmili and the ship, Talasseres, the Reliquary, and everything else beyond the wall faded into shadow.

This was it. This was the end. This was the door in the hillside and the darkness beyond.

She fought on as long as she could. They surrounded her, now. They were grabbing at her limbs, her clothes, tearing at her hair. It didn't hurt too badly and perhaps never would.

"STOP."

Shuthmili's voice was cracking under strain, so distorted that Csorwe barely recognised it.

The dead heard her. They froze, their hands locking uselessly in bony half-cuffs around Csorwe's limbs. With a final effort, Csorwe broke out of their grip and stumbled back, kicking the revenants' legs out from under them.

"STOP NOW. LEAVE."

Shuthmili was swaying on her feet, still only a few feet away. Her eyes were vacant, her mouth hanging half open, her hands limp at her sides. She looked like a revenant herself. The voice that came out of her was not her own.

"STOP. SLEEP. END. REST."

The closest revenants began to disintegrate, shredding themselves to splinters. Farther up the hill, they were still coming in crowds, but as they got close to Csorwe and the wall, they started to trip over the ones who had stopped, forming a drift of tangled bones.

Csorwe backed away, slowly at first. Then she threw Shuthmili over her good shoulder, and with the last of her strength, she ran on up the hill toward the ridge.

Perhaps Shuthmili was right. Perhaps the gods did care what happened to them. Perhaps they had worse ways in mind for Csorwe to die, on some bad day in the future. She cleared the ridge, and *Prosperity* was there, undamaged, whole, and skyworthy.

Csorwe dropped Shuthmili over the side and leapt after her. By now the dead had trampled past the blocked doorway. They lapped up against the sides of the mazeship, a sea of hands and mouths.

The Qarsazhi had rigged the ship for a speedy departure. Csorwe beat away grasping hands to sever the mooring-ropes, and kicked the alchemical engine to life. *Prosperity*'s canopies filled and she began to rise.

From above, the dead looked like an immense swarm of rats, flowing over the landscape, away from the sinking ship that was the fallen monument. Csorwe checked the ship's instruments. A dial with a face of smoked green glass indicated the direction of the Gate. Csorwe did her best to point the cutter in that direction, her hands trembling on the controls.

The wheel was slippery with blood. Csorwe's first thought was that the ship must have been wounded. Her left arm and the front of her coat were stained dark. When she moved, a fresh stream trickled down her sleeve. She couldn't feel her left shoulder at all, as though the whole joint had been bitten away.

She began peeling off her coat, and then thought better of it, sinking back into the pilot's chair.

It must have been the first revenant, the big man. The others hadn't managed much more than scratches.

She sat there for some time, leaking blood. Her mind worked terribly slowly, each thought swinging into place as though lowered from a crane. If she kept losing blood she was going to pass out. If she passed out, there was nobody to steer the ship. She alternated from one thought to another, as her hands slipped one by one from the controls and she slid from the chair to the deck.

Her vision blurred. Everything was cold and vague, like sinking through clouds. From a great distance she felt someone dragging her body away.

Nobody to steer the ship! she thought, and tried to struggle away from them, but her limbs wouldn't obey.

She felt a deep, stabbing ache in her shoulder, then a spreading heat that mingled with the pain and smoothed it away. It was good, in fact, like coming back to a warm bed on a cold night. It spread through her body, faintly tingling.

Either death was more pleasant than advertised, or something else was happening to her. With a great effort she opened her eyes.

She was lying on her back on the floor of the cabin. Shuthmili was kneeling over her, pinning her bare shoulder with both hands. Her face was a wide-eyed mask, the pupils dilated into black wells. Csorwe twisted, trying to look at her shoulder, and felt another wrench of pain. She cried out loud.

"Stay *still*," said Shuthmili. She obeyed, and once again the pain ebbed away.

"What are you doing?" said Csorwe. She regretted asking. Shuthmili didn't answer, and whenever her concentration broke, the pain returned. The pain itself wasn't so bad, but it came with the awful wrong feeling of something cut and ruptured inside her.

Shuthmili's white robes were bloody to the elbow. As the minutes passed, she seemed to return to herself. The vacancy in her eyes was replaced with a clear, chilly focus. She prodded at Csorwe's injured shoulder as if it was a joint of meat. Sometimes this hurt. Csorwe bit down on her sleeve, trying not to cry out.

At last Shuthmili sat back on her heels, and swiped back a lock of hair, leaving a streak of blood on her forehead. The pain seeped back in, but it was *old* pain somehow, the ache of a long-healed wound. Csorwe twisted to look at her shoulder. There was a silvery crescent of tooth marks there, already scarred over.

Shuthmili wavered, blinked, then threw up a gout of tar-black ichor, courteously managing to avoid getting it on Csorwe. The substance smoked where it hit the boards, eating away a jagged hole in the polished wood.

Shuthmili wiped her mouth. "Sorry," she said.

"Er," said Csorwe.

"You would have lost the arm," said Shuthmili. "*Very* corrupt." Her lips were blue and her eyes bloodshot, but she looked pleased with herself.

"What happened?" said Csorwe. "What—who's steering the ship?"

"Nobody," said Shuthmili. "I landed her." She leant over Csorwe again and buttoned up her coat over the ruined shirt underneath. "I'm not supposed to know how," she said. "But it's not very complicated if you pay attention."

"I've seen what you can do," said Csorwe, crawling to one

of the benches and hauling herself upright. "Doesn't seem like stopping you learning to fly a ship is going to help much."

Shuthmili shrugged. "If you had someone on your hands who could do what I can do, you might want to keep them on the ground."

"Are you all right?" said Csorwe.

The black ichor had all but dispersed now, leaving an oily scar etched on the floor of the cabin, among smears of Csorwe's blood.

Shuthmili looked uneasy. "I am quite hungry."

"But are you . . . I don't know. Are you . . ."

"Have I lost control of myself? Is the Dragon of Qarsazh planning to manifest her revenge upon the mortal realm through me? Am I going to speak in tongues and yank out your viscera?" said Shuthmili. "I am not." She spoiled the effect by shuddering, and adding, "At least, I have no conscious intention to do so. I should . . . I must return to Qaradoun as soon as possible. They have all kinds of tests. They can make me safe."

"You don't look corrupted," said Csorwe.

"Nobody does," said Shuthmili. A sad pause. "I suppose I'll never make the Quincuriate now. And all my inscriptions are gone. Thousands of years, gone in a day. Such a waste."

By now Csorwe understood far too well how it felt to lose what you had worked for. She had no idea what she could say to make Shuthmili feel better. She didn't see how it could ever be better.

"You did your best," said Csorwe eventually.

"I hope so," she said. "It would be nice to think so. I would never have done as she asked, not willingly, if not for the Warden—if not for Malkhaya. It would have been more correct to let him die before giving in, but he's always been quite kind to me. He feels sorry for me."

"I probably ought to have left you to die as well, if we're having regrets," said Csorwe.

Shuthmili laughed, a raspy little cackle. She still hadn't got up, and the effort of laughing knocked her back on the ground, into a puddle of bloody robes. "Well, it's not too late," she said. "By my estimate we've got about thirty seconds before I pass out again."

"What?" said Csorwe.

"My lady Zinandour is generous," said Shuthmili. "But she exacts steep interest. I went too far. Well, at this point *too far* is a fading dream. I am so much further than far. I am *entirely gone away*." She laughed again, shaking like a branch in the wind, and lay down, resting her head in the crook of her elbow. "Goodnight, Csorwe."

Csorwe crawled over to her, ignoring the ache in her shoulder. She pulled Shuthmili closer to the alchemical engine and turned up the heat.

Shuthmili had landed the ship on a cliff top, beyond the reach of the rising dead. Outside, the sky turned red, then black, as if pigment was seeping through the clouds. The hills lay beneath a blanket of frost, quiet at last in death.

Csorwe found blankets in the locker. She dimmed the ship's lanterns and put a cushion under Shuthmili's head. She lay down beside her, curled around her like one hand cupping another. At last, in the warm shadow of the engine, she slept.

12

Salvage

TALASSERES CHAROSSA HAD LIVED an interesting life with many periods of unconsciousness, but this was the first time he had been jolted back to reality by someone physically shaking him. This person was holding him by the collar of his jacket. He kicked out automatically, and felt his knee connect with some solid body. The person gave a grunt of pain, and dropped him.

Tal landed on a pile of rubble and lay there in triumph for some minutes, thinking, *That's right, arsehole.*

It was a large man whom Tal had never seen before. He wore a filthy yellow habit over work boots, and looked down at Tal as if he was considering leaving him to die.

"Got a live one, ma'am!" called the man.

Light footsteps on stone. An Oshaaru woman drifted over. Tal recognised her, with resignation, as the mad bitch from the bottom of the Monument. The bloody train of her dress hissed on the gravel like surf on sand, and she looked down at Tal with distant curiosity.

"Take him out to the ship," she said.

If the fates had possessed any kind of grace or mercy when it came to Tal, he would've passed out. As it was, he remained conscious throughout the whole humiliating process, as the big bastard tied him up, hoisted him over his shoulder, and dropped him into the bottom of a cutter like he was the catch of the day.

He lay there, sore and uneasy, as the little ship hummed to life. His stomach dropped as it rose into the air, but he had other things to worry about before travel-sickness.

Just about any misery or discomfort was bearable if you had something else to concentrate on, and just for once it appeared that the universe had thrown him a bone. That woman had the Reliquary. Maybe just this once Csorwe hadn't definitively ruined everything.

The bilges of the cutter were cold and full of splinters. Tal's arms were bent behind his back at a painful angle, and he had no idea where he was being taken, but his imagination was already blossoming with warming visions.

He had always known he'd get a chance eventually. There was always a chance, if you were prepared to wait and didn't have a lot of pride about surviving in the meantime, or leaping on that chance when it came along.

Even if—purely for example—you were a younger son who had failed out of the Tlaanthothei Academy for Boys. Even if you'd done some things you weren't particularly proud of. You just had to survive long enough and eventually you'd get your opportunity.

Everyone in Tlaanthothe would prefer to see him fail, to preserve their view of the world and Tal's place in it: *Niranthe's youngest, not very bright, lucky for him that he's good-looking, lucky for him that she got him a place with Chancellor Sethennai, because I don't see what he would have done on his own, such a shame what's become of the Charossai these days . . .*

None of *them* had been at the fortress during Olthaaros' last years. They didn't know anything about what Tal was capable of doing on his own. But they would know his value sooner or later.

He would get the Reliquary back, escape somehow, and return to Tlaanthothe. Csorwe would be furious. She would have assumed he was dead. Too bad for her. He would stumble back into the School of Transcendence—and Sethennai might have feared he was dead too, so maybe he'd be relieved to see him—and then Tal would hand over the Reliquary, and—

And, well. It wasn't even gratitude he wanted. Nobody liked having to be grateful, Sethennai least of all. Tal didn't care to put words to the magnitude of what he wanted from Sethennai, even in his head. It was pretty mortifying to concede that kind of power to anyone.

The cutter jolted, resounding once or twice against some rigid object. Tal tried to sit up and see. They were docked against a much larger ship that floated on a cushion of mist. The big man carted Tal on board, and as they passed he saw the name of the ship painted on the side, an Oshaarun word he didn't recognise: *Ejarwa*.

There weren't many people on board. The crew seemed to be limited to the big man, and a few others like him, all wearing perfunctory yellow habits over something sturdier. Tal was relieved to see that the crew were all *alive*, at least. He was sick of revenants; the living were easier to manage and mislead.

None of them paid any attention to Tal. The big bastard marched him down a gangway and into a long cabin with a row of bunks.

"Well, this is pretty forward of you, but all right," he said to the man, who dropped him on one of the bunks. No response.

"Hey, your boss seems like a fun character," he said. "What's the appeal there? You two fucking or what?"

The big man picked him up again, holding Tal face-to-face with him. He now saw that he wasn't that old. Same age as Tal, or younger. This gigantic boy had a great hairless jaw and little mad eyes, like a potato.

Tal never took one bite of a bad idea without polishing off the whole chunk. He winked at the boy.

"You are not fit to *look* at the Lady Oranna," said the boy, in a thick backcountry accent, like Csorwe when she was drunk. Then he punched Tal in the stomach.

Tal doubled up, all rational thought blotted out. When he recovered, the boy was gone and the door was locked.

There were no windows in the cabin, and nothing he could use as a weapon. His sword was gone, either confiscated or left in the dying world. The fibres of the ship were trembling with the faint vibration of an alchemical engine running at full power.

In short, he was trapped on board a ship in flight, with only the Lady Oranna and her colossal goons for company. At twenty-three he was absolutely too old for this shit.

What would Sethennai say? Plan and consider, then act with precision. Or at least think a *little* before you wade in, Talasseres. If he was lucky, an affectionate smile, a seasoning of irony. Tal remembered the smile so vividly he felt like he'd been punched in the gut again.

All right. Oranna wanted the Reliquary, but she didn't want him dead. She was keeping him alive, either for information or as a hostage. Tal would rather slash his wrists than spend any more time as anyone's hostage, so he needed to get moving.

Once he was certain the enormous child wasn't coming back,

he wriggled over on his side and started working at the bindings on his wrists. The boy had tied him up with enthusiasm but not much expertise. He freed himself, extracted one of the emergency knives stowed in his boots, and crouched in the darkest corner of the cabin to wait, keeping himself entertained by thinking what he might say to Sethennai when he gave back the Reliquary.

Sorry to keep you waiting . . . Better late than never . . . I think this is yours? That last one was good; Sethennai would like that.

The next person through the door was Oranna, as Tal had hoped. This was his reasoning: the gods are bound to the earth. Their essence, like water, finds its way downward. In the sky, a wizard's powers begin to fade and fail. Sethennai didn't like to leave Tlaanthothe if he could avoid it. Olthaaros had always hated travelling by ship, even within the Siren's domain. Also, Oranna was a necromancer, and as far as Tal could see, there weren't any dead bodies lying around. She was less than five and a half feet tall and if she didn't have magic, Tal was pretty sure he could take her.

She took one step into the cabin and stopped, noting the empty bunk. Tal propelled himself up out of the corner, ready to drive his knife into her belly.

The cabin surged with power, crackling in every nerve. In mid-air, Tal's vision seared white. When he came back to himself, he was on his knees, with a throbbing pain in his temples and the taste of iron in his mouth.

Nobody had ever accused Tal of knowing when to stop. He was still holding the knife, so he went for her again. The same thing happened.

Oranna looked down at him through heavy-lidded eyes, disappointed but unsurprised.

"Your body is a grave, as all bodies are," she said, in impeccable Tlaanthothei. "There is plenty of dead matter inside you. More than enough to choke on. It would be more sensible to stay on your knees."

Tal's bones ached as though something had sucked out the marrow. He didn't want to do as he was told, but he couldn't get up if he tried. *Oh, fuck.* This was going so wrong.

"We need to talk, Talasseres Charossa," she said. Wizards always thought it was so novel and threatening when they could pull your full name out of thin air, as though they could do something to you with it.

"Yeah, why not," he said. "My friends call me Tal."

"I'm afraid we are not going to be friends," she said. "However, I think we should be able to handle this without fuss. You're working for Belthandros Sethennai, of course."

"Who's that?" said Tal.

Oranna sighed. "The only intelligence you are insulting is your own," she said. "Who else could possibly have sent you?"

Tal shrugged.

"I do understand," she said. "It's a matter of pride. You don't wish to give him up. But please understand that I do not have the time to navigate around your self-regard."

"Got time to navigate around my dick," said Tal.

Oranna did not dignify this with a response. She called for the potato boy, and a curly-haired acolyte, who brought a silver goblet, pouring smoke. Tal couldn't see what was in the cup, only smell the strong, half-familiar bitterness.

The boy held Tal down and they put the cup to his lips. Tal grimaced, clamped his jaw shut, twisted his head away, to no avail. The silver rim of the cup bumped against his teeth, and the smoking liquid splashed his chin. His outrage drowned out all fear. This wasn't what was supposed to happen. He refused to believe it.

"Drink," said Oranna.

"Fuck you," he said, which was a mistake. As soon as he opened his mouth the boy forced his jaw open and poured half the cup inside. He choked, spat, bit the boy's fingers in fury, but it was impossible to avoid swallowing some of the mixture. Blood heat, overwhelmingly bitter.

Immediately, the world slowed. Tal felt himself falling, cut adrift from reality, swallowed up in darkness. It wrapped around him, severing mind from body, reason from will, thought from consciousness. Every particle of his being was dispersed, isolated, and analysed. And it *hurt*.

He was a professional. Getting kidnapped, beaten, stunned with magic, forced to drink poison, et cetera—that was nothing. This felt as though something had laid open his heart with a blade of ice and was picking over the pieces.

It took only a few seconds. Then he landed back in place. He was an empty shell, as if his innards had been prised out and eaten with lemon juice.

"As I said, you are here working for Belthandros Sethennai," said Oranna, as if flicking through paperwork.

"Yes," said Tal. He couldn't help it. He felt another lurch into darkness, and the word dripped from his mouth like saliva.

"You and your accomplice intended to collect the Reliquary of Pentravesse," she said.

"Yes," he said.

"Why did she attack me?"

"Csorwe? I don't know, probably because she's a fucking

imbecile," said Tal, grateful at least to be able to add remarks of
his own volition.

For some reason, Csorwe's name appeared to give her pause,
but she shrugged it off.

"Shall we now assume that I know who you are?" she said.

"It's always nice to meet a fan," said Tal, and winced as
another flash of pain shot through him.

The servants picked Tal up and laid him down on one of the
bunks. He tried to struggle, but he could only shiver. Oranna
came to stand over him.

His vision stuttered and blurred. He saw now that she was
holding the Reliquary. If he could move his arms he could reach
out and take it from her. As if sensing his intentions, she stepped
back, and it swam out of reach.

Tal clenched his jaw and tried to sit up, without success.
"So—so you're really pretty obsessed with Sethennai, aren't
you," he said. If he could get her talking, maybe he could stop
her asking too many questions.

"I found him briefly impressive," said Oranna.

"Yeah, he's an impressive motherfucker," said Tal. "Let me
tell you, though, if you're doing this to me to get to him, you're
not going to get anywhere. He doesn't know who I am half the
time."

"Credible," said Oranna. "Belthandros is not known for his
thoughtful and considerate nature. But, unlike the rest of his
acquaintances, I have no interest in plumbing his psyche. How
do you open the Reliquary?"

Was that what she wanted? He could almost laugh.

"I don't know," he said. "I mean get your goddamn oyster
knife out and get shucking if you want but you're not going to get

anything from me. I don't know. I don't know anything about the Reliquary."

He ought to have known more than he did. He remembered Sethennai trying to lecture them about it, back in the day. Csorwe had paid actual attention, because she was always disgustingly keen, like a little dog that wants a bit of your kebab. But it had been a hot afternoon. Sethennai had put on some kind of rosewater scent and worn his collar unbuttoned. Tal hadn't retained much information.

Residual tremors of power rippled through the cabin, smelling of hot metal. Tal's eyes watered.

"You know I'm not lying," he said. "Give me another sip of that shit if you don't believe me." Whatever it was, it was still working. He could still feel his secrets stirring in him, threatening to tip over.

She looked almost disappointed in him. "You never wondered?"

"No," said Tal. "I don't wonder about anything unless someone's paying me. I don't understand him. He doesn't tell me shit. I don't know what it does or why he wants it. I do what he— I do my fucking *job*, you know. He points me at a problem and I deal with it."

Tal had never been any good at trigonometry or rhetoric or any of the things you were supposed to be good at. He didn't have magic, as his mother had hoped he might. But he *was* pretty good at creeping, lying, and stealing, and Sethennai seemed to value him for it.

"Ah," said Oranna. "You don't seem entirely stupid. What is it that he has offered you for this service?"

"What he's offered me?" said Tal. He was on the verge of something, either laughter or tears, spilling out of him like pulp from a burst apple. "Nothing," he said. "This is what I get. The work. And the money's good," he added. This wasn't untrue, and a lot of people were incurious enough to take it without question, and given that Tal no longer received any kind of allowance from the Charossa treasury, it was something for which he was genuinely grateful.

"Is that so," said Oranna, and tilted her head to look at him. "And that's enough, is it?"

Tal became very aware of them all looking at him, not just Oranna's gaze but the bland regard of the two servants to either side of her. This was one of those questions that Tal kept where it belonged, in an impregnable vault concealed from the light of day. But he could feel the bolts drawing back, all the grimy little corners of his soul unfolding themselves into a staircase. It was so blindly unfair. They weren't going to learn anything from this.

"Yes," he said, the words welling up all at once. "No. It's fine. It's all I'm going to get, so. It doesn't matter if it's not enough, and I'm happy with it, so it's none of your business, and anyway—" Tal realised with distant, wondering horror that he couldn't stop himself saying it. "And anyway, I love him and there's nothing I can do about it."

The two goons didn't react to this in any way. Oranna raised an eyebrow faintly.

He had no idea what he'd find himself saying next, where Oranna's next question would cut him, but she rose, as though snapping shut an irrelevant book, and turned away.

Tal wondered whether he should have pretended to be more useful or important. She didn't open him up again, at least. She looked back at him, half curious, then stalked out of the cabin, taking her people with her, leaving Tal where he was.

For the next few hours Tal curled up on the bunk and tried to sleep. It seemed like the best way to put his head back together. Half drowsy, beyond shame, he tried to imagine that Sethennai might be on his way to rescue him, but even in his imagination it didn't seem all that likely.

A smaller, older potato servant turned up eventually and led him out of the cabin and back to the cutter, where the original big bastard stood at the wheel.

It was a relief to see daylight again, even the cold grey daylight of the dying world. *Ejarwa* was anchored in a valley; up ahead, a Gate burnt green and gold, a disc of fire set into a sheer cliff.

Tal experienced a flare of brief hope, like a struck match. The Gate was a way home, or at least a way out. If he could only get there . . .

They landed the cutter on the hillside. The men were muttering to each other, perhaps assuming Tal couldn't hear them, or couldn't understand their language.

"—she says just kill him quickly and leave him here," said the small man.

The boy chewed his lip and nodded, then turned to Tal. "Up. Out," he said, pointing Tal over the side of the cutter. Tal did as he was told. Once over the edge he pretended to trip on the scree, dropping to the ground to grab the other knife from his boot.

The boy hauled him up with a curse, but he hadn't seen the knife. Tal twisted and stabbed, aiming for his throat, but the blade went wide, slashing across the boy's cheek. The boy howled and dropped Tal, grabbing at his face as blood dripped between his fingers.

Tal scrambled for his life, hoping he'd at least bought enough time to get away. Then he slipped on a piece of loose slate and went down. They were on him in seconds. One of them stamped on his wrist until he let go of the knife.

They picked him up and shoved him against a broken bit of wall.

"Lady Oranna is merciful," said the boy. His face was streaming blood where Tal had cut him.

"We aren't," said the small man. He smiled, showing brown and missing teeth between his tusks. Then he hit Tal in the face.

They kept hitting him. They weren't very bright. Tal thought they would probably kill him by accident before they could do it on purpose.

"Fuck, you might be getting better at this, I nearly felt that one," said Tal. He was pretty certain the latest blow had loosened a few teeth. The boy hit him again.

"Anything smart to say to that?" said the boy.

Tal's head swam. A stream of blood was running down the back of his throat, warm and slimy. He realised, with shame, that he didn't have anything smart to say to that, so he just grinned at the boy and tried to stop his ears twitching. Foreigners were mad about Tlaanthothei ears. Once they noticed them they couldn't keep their hands off them.

The small man kicked his legs out from under him. This was bad. Once you were on the ground you were basically fucked. At this point Tal welcomed oblivion, but he had always intended to leave a beautiful corpse. It was hard to imagine anyone regretfully cradling his toothless carcass once it had been kicked around the landscape and dumped on the hillside. Oh, well.

He curled into a ball instinctively, shielding his head and neck, because his treacherous lizard brain wanted to live more than he did. His eyes were squeezed shut and there were new sounds of fighting, so it took him a moment to register that the next blow hadn't struck home.

At length there was silence, punctuated by groaning. The toe of someone's boot jabbed Tal in the shoulder.

"Get up."

"Ugh," said Tal.

Another jab. With some difficulty he propped himself on his elbows, inhaled a quantity of bloody mucus, and looked up.

"Get up, Tal," said Csorwe.

Tal started laughing, like a gate banging in the wind.

Of course. As if Csorwe was going to let someone *else* beat him to death. The sense of what she was saying didn't really register. If she chose to flip him over and crush his windpipe there wasn't much he could do to stop her at this point. That was how Belthandros Sethennai had killed his uncle. He laughed harder and harder.

Csorwe rolled her eyes and hauled him up, shoving him against the wall. Tal and the wall were becoming fast friends by now.

Csorwe checked him over. How many fingers was she holding up, could he count to ten, et cetera. At least she didn't seem to expect Tal to be grateful. If she had, he would've spat blood in her face.

"You'll live," she said. "We've got a ship. Time to get moving before anyone realises this lot are missing."

From this vantage he could see that the big boy and the small man were flat on the ground a few feet off, unconscious or dead, hopefully in a puddle of their own frozen piss. The ferrety Qarsazhi girl was standing over them, looking disdainful.

"Hope she was worth it," said Tal.

"Fuck off," said Csorwe.

He twisted round, looking back at the cutter. He couldn't see *Ejarwa* anywhere. "She's got the Reliquary. We could—"

"No. Get in the boat," said Csorwe. "We're going."

Daryou Malkhaya lay trapped in the ruins of the tomb-monument for two nights and two days. His right arm was crushed beneath a fallen pillar. At first the worst part was the pain. Then it was thirst.

He lay there as the revenants swarmed in the ancient fields, like an algal bloom—now thickening, now dispersing. His throat was too dry to make a sound. His mouth was sour and full of dust.

Time came apart, like a severed string of beads. Malkhaya, as he had been—Warden of the Church, *Maya* to his friends—ceased to exist. There was only a stuttering awareness, brief flashes of lucidity, like a candle extinguishing itself again and again.

I failed, he thought, when he could think of anything. *I failed in my duty.* He couldn't remember what it was that he had failed to do. He remembered the name *Shuthmili,* though not who it was or what it might mean to him. He tried to hold on to it for as long as he could, and then, along with everything else, it was gone.

Malkhaya's body was still lying in the ruins when the Gate illuminated itself again. It lay there as the Qarsazhi frigate *Reflection in Tranquillity* descended toward the ruins of the

Hollow Monument like an angelfish toward a dying coral. *Tranquillity* flew three pennants: alongside the Nine-Petalled Rose of Qarsazh were the Inquisitorial violet and the white banner of the Imperial Quincuriate.

The five Adepts who made up Vigil Quincury disembarked from their shuttle barge and began to sweep the rubble. There were footsteps and voices, which Malkhaya might have heard if he had lived another day.

And then they brought him back. He felt this as a vivid flash of effervescent heat. He ought to be in agony, but they had taken his pain away, or else perhaps there wasn't enough left of him to feel pain. He had no sensation in his limbs at all.

A purple-black shadow loomed over him, surrounded by ghosts.

"Can you speak? Give your name," said the shadow. Malkhaya complied, in a voice that felt and sounded like sandpaper on the tongue.

Another point of awareness: he was lying flat on his back on bare earth. The Quincury stood around him in a circle. Five pairs of linked hands, bare skin to bare skin. The differences in size and colour of these hands were the only indication that the five members of the Quincury were individuals, or had once been so. In their robes and veils they were ageless, eyeless, and androgynous. Their gauze visors looked to him like the eyes of houseflies.

Shuthmili was meant to become like this, he thought, without any recollection of who Shuthmili was, or how he felt about that.

A woman stood outside the circle, dressed in Inquisitorial regalia, black and purple. Malkhaya tried to say something and came out with a kind of rattle.

"I am High Inquisitor Qanwa Zhiyouri," said the woman. The light from the white sky was somehow too bright, blurring her features. *Qanwa Zhiyouri.* The name should have meant something to him, but he couldn't place it. *High Inquisitor* meant something, though. It meant that Malkhaya should obey.

"I'm afraid you are dead, Warden," said Inquisitor Qanwa. Her voice was cool and clipped, every syllable like a pellet dropping into a saucer. "Soon, Vigil will release you to rest at the Hearth of the Mara. Before then, I'm afraid there is one last thing we must ask of you, to complete your duty."

"Yes, ma'am," said Malkhaya.

"We have found no survivors," said Inquisitor Qanwa. She knelt beside him, the better to hear him. "Tell me, Warden, what was the last you saw of my niece?"

Malkhaya told her all he remembered, about the heretic priestess, the bath of blood, the singing pillar, and all the other horrors they had found within the tomb-monument. His dead voice rasped away as if the story was a mass of timber that he needed to saw through.

The Inquisitor's face never changed, never expressed any interest or surprise. "Unfortunate," she said sometimes, or "I see."

He finished the story, telling Qanwa the last he had seen of Shuthmili. He was aware that he ought to feel something about the things he had seen, or at least about his own death. Daryou Malkhaya had been a man of bright, simple emotions. His friends had teased him about it. He remembered the man he had been as though they had been to school together, and not seen one another since.

"Thank you, Warden," said Qanwa. "That's all we ask of you.

Your body will be returned to your house." She straightened up, her voice becoming brisk. "Vigil, that will do. Cut the connection."

The circle of people around them broke apart, and with it the light faded, and Malkhaya no longer seemed to be anywhere at all.

"A matter of regret that Dr. Lagri's body was damaged so severely," said Inquisitor Tsaldu. He was Qanwa Zhiyouri's new aide, one of the new breed of ascetics who shaved their heads to show their devotion.

"Agreed," said Zhiyouri. She was back at her desk in her own stateroom, rereading the transcription of her interview with Malkhaya's corpse.

Vigil Quincury had tried and failed to revive Lagri Aritsa three times before succeeding on the first try with Daryou Malkhaya. Now both their corpses were stowed in *Tranquillity*'s cold storage, so that Vigil could make another attempt on return to its sanctuary at the Traitor's Grave. She hadn't lied to Malkhaya. His body would be returned to the Daryou house eventually, once it ceased to be of use to the Inquisitorate.

"But the Warden's testimony was clear enough," she said. "I think we know what our next move must be."

"Yes, ma'am?" said Tsaldu. He was at least thirty-five, but Zhiyouri could not help thinking of him as a young thing. He was unusually pale for a Qarsazhi. Zhiyouri assumed he had some provincial ancestry.

"My niece must be found, and soon," she said. "You've read the reports from the Traitor's Grave. Shuthmili is urgently needed to restore Archer Quincury to full function."

Archer Five had died suddenly only a few weeks before, and the four remaining Adepts of Archer Quincury were clinging to life in protective stasis. Unless its numbers were restored, Archer would fail fast, and Shuthmili was the only viable candidate. Zhiyouri had seen her niece's preliminary test scores. There was simply no other unassigned Adept with power and control to match her, none even remotely fit to become part of the most powerful weapon in the Qarsazhi arsenal.

"If Shuthmili is alive it is a fair assumption that she has been— let's be charitable—*rescued* by the Tlaanthothei operatives," said Zhiyouri. "I've already set a course for Tlaanthothe. Sethennai will be cooperative, I've no doubt, since I did him a favour by giving him access to this world. We'll find Shuthmili, stabilise her, and return to Qaradoun to begin the tether immediately."

"Inquisitor, might I . . ." said Tsaldu. "What if she cannot be stabilised?"

"It would be preferable to bring her back to the Traitor's Grave before making any decision about that," said Zhiyouri sharply. She had known Tsaldu was going to make trouble. Most Inquisitors gained a certain flexibility as they matured. Tsaldu was as rule-bound as the day he had graduated from the University.

"Yes, of course, Inquisitor," said Tsaldu. "If it is possible to subdue her in time. But if not, it is a mercy to end such a life. Your personal connection—"

"You are getting ahead of yourself, Tsaldu," said Zhiyouri, mildly. She tapped her fingers lightly on the surface of her desk. "No, I can't say I relish the prospect of euthanising my niece. But you know we cannot afford to waste resources. The School has nothing else of Shuthmili's calibre to offer, and the enemies of Qarsazh are always watching. The Tarascnesc, for instance, already know of the death of Archer Five. Archer is our deterrent. It cannot be allowed to fail. We need her."

Zhiyouri knew what Tsaldu perhaps did not: if Archer was lost, there was nothing to replace it. There were lower-ranked military Quincuries, Sabre and Aegis and the like, but Archer had been shaped and refined over more than a century. It was not just a weapon but a testament to the continuity of the Imperium.

"If she is corrupted she would be worse than useless to Archer," said Tsaldu, who had evidently become very daring. There were two spots of colour on his pallid cheeks. She raised an eyebrow at him. "I am simply trying to explore the possibilities," he said.

It was not the first time on their voyage that Zhiyouri had found Tsaldu irritating, and she was sure it would not be the last. She kept her voice level. "Have you ever seen a corrupted mage, Tsaldu?"

"No, ma'am," he said.

"Over the course of my career I have prosecuted almost a dozen," she said. "On one occasion, the wretched creature got loose in the courtroom. We lost three Wardens and an Inquisitor before he was put down."

Zhiyouri's memory of that day was disjointed, but she remembered the mage, laughing, his teeth picked out in ichor, black spittle dripping from his chin. Death had never seemed more merciful.

"I am fully aware of the possibilities," she said. "And I know what our last resort must be. We prepare for the worst, as always. But I do not want you *hoping* for the worst. Is that understood?"

"Yes, ma'am," said Tsaldu.

Zhiyouri nodded and rose from her desk. "Inconvenient in more ways than one that Archer is out of commission. We need to cauterise the trouble on the surface, and there's really nothing like Archer for tidying up a mess. Still, we have Vigil, and it should be more than capable of stepping in. Come up to the observation deck and we'll see it done."

Important to keep Tsaldu friendly, since she had no prospect of acquiring any other aide for the time being, and he would enjoy watching this.

Tranquillity was still hovering above the Precursor world. From the observation deck they could see the ruins of the monument, and the scuttling grey shapes of the revenants, still pouring out of the ground. It had been difficult for Vigil to hold them off long enough even to retrieve the bodies.

Below the ship, five shuttle barges moved with purpose. Aboard each barge was a Quincury Adept, in black mask and white surcoat.

Zhiyouri gave the signal and each of the Quincury barges came to a halt, forming the points of a pentagon in the air above the broken necropolis. Down in the ruins, the revenants wandered in aimless shoals, as though waiting for something to happen.

"Have you ever seen a Quincury in this formation?" said Zhiyouri to Tsaldu. She handed him a pair of goggles, the lenses coated with black gauze like the visor of a Quincury Adept. "Not many people have. This is a privilege. Just a pity it isn't Archer, or we'd really see some fireworks."

On board their barges, the Vigil Adepts removed their gloves and raised their hands. Qanwa smiled as she tightened the strap of her own goggles. She always liked to see this. There was nothing like the Quincuriate to distil order out of chaos.

Five points of light sparked, one for each Adept. The light

brightened, swelled, blotting out the Adepts and their barges, blotting out everything, as though *Tranquillity* was gliding into the sun.

A shadow of heat from the blast reached them even behind the wards of the observation deck. To Zhiyouri, it felt like the warmth of a summer's day. There was a perfect moment, when she felt as if she was floating in light, a clean white illumination that scoured away all impurity.

The light faded. Beneath *Tranquillity* and the barges, the surface of the dying world glowed like a bowl of molten iron. Then the glow faded, leaving behind a gleaming pool of oil-black glass, twenty miles across. The ruins were gone. No more boundary wall. No more fallen graves, nor petrified trees, nor outlines of forgotten houses. No more revenants. It looked as though the void had taken a bite out of the world.

"This is why our Adepts are so feared," said Zhiyouri. "Corruption is a risk, as you so rightly identify. But even Vigil is capable of glassing a city, and it is a middle-ranked Quincury, honed for fine work, not for violence on the grand scale. Imagine the consequences if an Adept of Shuthmili's power were to fall into the wrong hands. Imagine what our enemies would do with such a weapon. We must find her, Tsaldu. There is no time to waste."

III

The Tether

The Reliquary of Pentravesse resists pursuit as a bank of briars resists the passage of a bare-legged traveller. It forbids the rational mind, it tempts even as it forbids, and ultimately it wounds the heedless.

Olthaaros Charossa, from a letter to
Belthandros Sethennai, prior to his exile

13

No Hard Feelings

BELTHANDROS SETHENNAI KEPT THE windows of his quarters open at night. It was an indulgence, and a show of bravado. The wind freshened, and the Chancellor's palace drank in the black desert night through every heedless pore.

A moth flickered across the balcony of the antechamber and brushed the security mesh with one wing tip. There was a brief fizz of light, a satisfying crackle, and a faint, sad smell of incineration. It could have been worse. Csorwe had seen the same thing happen to a bat.

She was waiting in the antechamber with Tal and Shuthmili. It had been a hard journey back to Tlaanthothe aboard the Qarsazhi cutter. They had stopped at a refuelling station only once, and all three of them were hungry and bedraggled, but Csorwe needed to see Sethennai before she could do anything else.

"Hope you're going to admit this was all your fault," said Tal.

"Remind me why I rescued you?" said Csorwe.

"Because you need me to fucking carry you like I have been for years," he said.

If Csorwe had experienced a moment of treacherous relief when she'd found Tal alive, it had long since faded. To hear him tell it, he'd tracked down the Reliquary on his own, and had practically had his hands on it before Csorwe had snatched it from him and thrown it away.

She was about to snap back at him when she saw Shuthmili's expression, exhausted and apprehensive, and thought she'd better save this fight until later. The last few days must have been punishing for the Adept. Even Sethennai conserved his energy between workings. Shuthmili's face was pinched and drawn.

It wasn't long after this that a footman emerged from Sethennai's private study.

"He says you're to go in and I'm to take your friend to a guest room," said the footman, gesturing vaguely at Shuthmili, who shrank further into her chair. "He says it's late and he'll see her tomorrow."

Shuthmili looked blankly terrified, and Csorwe realised she didn't speak the language.

"It's all right," said Csorwe, translating. "Go with them. It's fine." She had been so eaten up with the thought of seeing Sethennai that she hadn't even considered what to do with Shuthmili. "I'll come to see you later," she added, and Shuthmili let the footman lead her away.

Inside the study, Sethennai was sitting by the fire. He had swapped his chancellarial robes for a green silk nightshirt, and his seal for a glass of resin-wine, but he still gave the impression of sitting in splendour. Whatever was to come, it was such a relief to see him, like coming home after dark and seeing the windows lit up. As they entered he looked up with an expression of genuine pleasure.

"Sir," she said, and bowed. Tal did the same.

"Why don't you come and sit down," said Sethennai. "I'll

have them bring up a new bottle. And perhaps you have some news for me?"

Csorwe had expected him to know somehow what had happened, and to be furious already, but it was worse to realise that she'd have to explain it.

"Sir—" she said. "In the dying world—it was—"

His expression clouded. "What happened?"

Csorwe opened her mouth, but could not speak. What could she possibly say? She wasn't going to get any help from Tal. She looked up at Sethennai, still trying to formulate the words.

"You were right," she said. "The Reliquary was there."

Sethennai's eyes widened, filling with a curious light, an excitement she had never seen before. Before Csorwe could think of any way to soften the blow, Tal cut in.

"Csorwe lost it," he said. "We nearly had it, and—"

"Thank you, Talasseres," he said, tapping his fingers once or twice on the surface of the desk. Sethennai never did anything involuntarily. Csorwe felt cold, as if the breeze from the open window had turned wintry. "You lost it?" he said, turning to her.

"Yes, sir," she said. "I'm sorry, sir."

She couldn't meet his eyes. She made herself stare at the glass of wine, tracing the arcs of light and shadow. If she looked up she was sure she would see the walls and corners of the study beginning to fold in on her.

She explained as clearly as she could. Her memories of the Hollow Monument were blurry in places, written and over-written every time she tried to narrate to herself what had happened, and her account was halting. Sethennai looked at her all the time as though from a great distance.

When she reached the end of the story, he nodded, but said

nothing. The silence stretched beyond the moment and into eternity. This was agony. When she dared to glance at Tal, she saw his expression was studiously blank. It was his turn to explain himself next.

"I sense," said Sethennai, once they were done, "that the two of you may be about to embark on a point-scoring exercise, and I suggest you think better of it."

He rose from his desk and went over to the window, looking out at the lights of the city below.

"So. The Reliquary exists. It has been found. Intact and extant, after all. It was within our grasp all this time. This should be something to celebrate."

Silence; nothing but the crackly song of the security mesh.

"And yet you lost it. Not only did you lose it; you let it fall into Oranna's hands. This should not have happened," he said. "I don't understand quite how you allowed it to happen." Tal began to say something, and Sethennai raised his hand. "Either of you."

Sethennai stepped out in front of the window, making a blind silhouette against the stars.

"I have been seeking the Reliquary for the better part of my life, and training you for the better part of yours," he said, turning to face Csorwe. "And now it is in the hands of an enemy. You must know how deeply I regret this."

"She doesn't know how to open it," said Tal. "She kept asking. I didn't tell her." Csorwe could almost pity him when he got like this.

"Oranna does not have even one scruple," he said. "If she manages to open it—well, we'd better help ourselves, because there won't be anything the gods can do for us."

"Why does she want it?" said Tal. Csorwe wished he would shut up. She just wanted the explanation over with so she could go and jump off a bridge or something.

"I have to assume that a large part of it is spite for me," said Sethennai. "Beyond that, she wants it for the same reason anybody would want it. Pentravesse's legacy. All that knowledge. Oranna hoards up knowledge the way people hoard money. For the pleasure of turning it over in your hands and knowing nobody else has it. But that isn't her only reason. She has an odd theory."

He turned back to them, composing himself. Storytelling always put him in a better mood.

"A practitioner of magic is always in tension," he said. "Even if one's patron is a nice, tame, helpful goddess such as the Siren. On the one hand is the well of divine power. On the other hand are the limitations of one's own frail mortal body. Desire always outstrips reality. We have access to the forces which shape and change the universe, but we are always anchored in flesh."

Sethennai held up his hand and flexed his fingers. "This fragile carcass, this little shell, it tires and ages and suffers, and fails faster with every drop of power you drink. Some find that frustrating. Oranna sees it as a challenge."

It could be said that Sethennai liked the sound of his own voice, but Csorwe had never disliked this about him. It was a good voice. Like a spider, he could anchor his argument in a familiar spot and spin himself out into unfathomable spaces.

"There were always rumours about Pentravesse and Iriskavaal. It was said that they achieved an unprecedented union. That Iriskavaal manifested in his body without possessing him. That the goddess held him in her coils without crushing him."

Sethennai looked down at his hand again, turning it so that his rings glittered in the firelight.

"Oranna certainly believes it was done, and that it could be done again, if one had the right bond with one's divinity, and knew the correct ritual. She believes that ritual is one of the secrets contained within the Reliquary."

The power of his voice was such that, for a second, Csorwe thought everything might work out all right. If she was safe, with him, listening to another story about old dead wizards in ancient times, things couldn't really be so wrong.

She dared to look up, and saw the slight smile wither and vanish.

"If she is right . . . I'm sure you can imagine what it is that she wants, Csorwe. If it could be done, Oranna would remove the last barrier between mage and god. She sees herself as the true emissary of the Unspoken One. She would become its incarnation. Living, walking, immortal, and unconquerable. She would bring it out into the light, with all its ancient knowledge and all its hunger."

Csorwe felt a chill creep up her spine and take a cold grip of her senses. She knew the Unspoken One still existed. But her ability to sleep and live her life had been built on the knowledge that it existed in its Shrine, in the wilds of Oshaar, where she never had to go again.

"Oranna has been obsessed with this idea as long as I've known her," said Sethennai. "And now we'll find out if she can really do it."

"We can stop her," said Csorwe, trying to rise above her growing panic. "We can find her and take it back."

"No," said Sethennai. "I will find her. You two . . . I think you had better stay here at the palace, where you can do no more damage."

"Sir—" said Tal.

"You heard me, Talasseres," said Sethennai. "I have no further duties for you at the moment."

"It wasn't my *fault*," said Tal. "We were so close, and Csorwe fucked it up. Let me go, at least. I can find her. I'd like to show her—"

"No," said Sethennai.

"This isn't fair," said Tal, adding, through gritted teeth and with obvious effort, "*sir.*"

"Perhaps not," said Sethennai. Tal sat forward in his chair, fists clenched tightly at his sides. When it became clear that Sethennai had nothing else to say, Tal stood up, shoving the chair back with a screech, and stormed out of the room.

Csorwe kept her head down, sinking deeper into misery. Sethennai paced back and forth. There was no sound but his footsteps on the floorboards.

Eventually he came to sit down again, in the seat Tal had vacated, facing Csorwe on the same level.

"I am not angry with you," he said. "I share in the blame, really. I made a misjudgment about your capacities. Oranna's presence affected you," he said.

He was watching her with great sympathy; this would have been a consolation if it didn't look very much like pity. He was right. She had run as far as anybody could run from the House of Silence and she was never going to get away from it.

"I still want to help," said Csorwe, managing each word with an effort.

"Csorwe, you understand that I need agents in whom I can

place my absolute trust. You are dear to me, but—in this particular matter—you cannot be relied upon."

She had expected to be punished for her failure. Sethennai
rarely shouted, but he could be cold. She expected to be excori-
ated, humiliated. Instead, this. Anything would be better.

"I really do think," he said, and with him this kind of hesitation was always rhetorical, "that it would be better for you to
remain here for the moment."

Sethennai was not a softhearted man. When he had rescued
her from the House of Silence, it had not been an act of mercy.
Her training was an investment. She had been useful to him.
She had gone some way to repaying her debt, and the act of a
moment had undone it.

It would have been easy to claim, like Tal, that it wasn't fair,
but Csorwe wasn't prepared to indulge herself. Sethennai's
judgment was unbearable, but it wasn't unjust. She hadn't been
reliable. She couldn't be trusted with this. She was less than she
had been to him. Only children and the sick are pitiable.

She hardly heard him dismiss her. She rose, numb, blind,
cold, and left his presence.

Tal made it back to his room without losing it completely, biting
down hard on his lower lip to stop himself shouting or bursting
into tears or whatever it was his fragile carcass thought it wanted
to do.

He would never have made it out of Psamag's fortress alive
if he hadn't got good at this, keeping everything locked down
tightly until he was alone.

He shut and locked the door to his quarters. He took off his jacket and dropped it on the bed. He looked furiously around his room as though one of these mute objects could offer him some kind of consolation, and then, with clinical poise and precision, kicked a hole in the door of his wardrobe.

His whole body was tender from the beating he had survived in the dying world, so he couldn't destroy things for very long. Eventually all he could do was fall over on his bed with his hands knotted in his hair, as if the pressure on his scalp might relieve some of the misery seething underneath.

You heard me, Talasseres.

Fuck you, old man! I didn't even get to tell you half of what happened to me—

Tal actually didn't want to think about what had happened to him on Oranna's ship. With that in mind he decided to get drunk. There was a tavern not far from the palace where they knew he didn't like to be talked to.

On the way out, he ran into Csorwe in the corridor. Her room was next to his, and he had half hoped they might cross paths. Not that he ever wanted to see her, but there was something unpleasantly satisfying about the inevitability of it, like picking off a scab. And despite his various bruises, this was one fight that might actually feel good.

"Pleased with yourself?" he said, squaring up so as to block her path.

"Go to bed, Tal," said Csorwe.

"*Go to bed, Tal,*" he said, taking a step toward her. "Fuck you, Csorwe. Do you think we'd be in this position if you hadn't screwed up so badly?"

"I'm not doing this tonight," she said.

"Oh, sure, you think you're being so *reasonable*. You did this.

You fucking did this. I work so hard and he always favours you. I have to live with all your mistakes."

"Yeah, you and me both," said Csorwe. She turned on her heel, glancing back over her shoulder at him as she stalked away. "Go to bed."

Tal thought about going after her. Instead he went to the tavern and sat in the corner and drank resin-wine until it seemed like time to move on to hard liquor.

It had been a mistake to expect anything else from Sethennai. By now, surely, Tal knew exactly what it was that he got, and there was no point hoping for anything else.

Oh, Tal, you could have died! He tried to think how that would sound in Sethennai's voice. Even imagining it was pathetic. *But then it's not like I really would've given a shit one way or another.*

The thing was, he decided, halfway through his second liquorice spirit, that it wasn't fair of him to expect Sethennai to give a shit, because Tal hadn't really shown him yet what he was worth. Tal wasn't a brilliant scholar or a wizard or a statesman, but he was *resilient,* wasn't he? However many times he was knocked down, he always got up, and always tried again.

The tavern closed, and Tal picked his way unsteadily back up to the palace. The night steward was one of his cousins, another young Charossa who'd decided to throw his lot in with Sethennai rather than stand up for the memory of Olthaaros. A smart move, since all Olthaaros' supporters were now in jail or dead, some at Tal's own hands. Sethennai had strong feelings about loyalty.

"Evening, Talasseres," said the cousin, looking Tal up and down with what he took to be a sneer. "Out on the Chancellor's business?"

"Go fuck yourself, Matheos," said Tal, stumbling back over the threshold and toward the stairs.

He fell back onto his mattress. His thoughts took a second to catch up with his body, but when they did they were perfectly clear. Loyalty, that was the thing. This was a test, as it always was with Sethennai. He needed to prove that he was still loyal, and that he was still worth something. And he knew how to do it.

After avoiding a fight with Tal, Csorwe wanted nothing more than to go back to her room and fall into bed, but she had promised to check on Shuthmili.

Security at the entrance to the guest wing let Csorwe through without question. They were all used to the sight of her coming and going, though she wasn't exactly friendly with them. Most of the palace guards were ex-mercenaries from Psamag's old company, who'd found work with Sethennai after the company had broken up, and she didn't like to think that some of them had probably watched as Morga cut her face open.

She found Shuthmili in the room where they'd put her, sitting by the window and examining a potted aloe in detail, as if preparing to make a scientific illustration. Her hair was damp and newly combed, falling to her waist in dark waves.

"Hope they've treated you all right," said Csorwe.

"Yes," said Shuthmili. "I thought I might never have a bath again." She did look restored by it. Csorwe felt very grubby by comparison. She hadn't washed in at least a week. No amount of finger-combing could get all the blood out of your hair.

They had also given Shuthmili a spare nightshirt to wear. It was much too big for her, and she looked absurdly delicate. Her Adept's robes had covered her from toe to chin and Csorwe hadn't seen her bare arms before: they were smooth and brown and slender, without any of the random scars and calluses that marked most of Csorwe's body. Csorwe looked away hastily.

"I've been thinking about how to get you back to Qarsazh," said Csorwe. Shuthmili was obviously keen to be home, and Csorwe didn't need the distraction of figuring out how to entertain a guest. She'd get Shuthmili onto the next ship back to Qarsazh. And then there would be work to do for Sethennai. She would find something to do—anything to prove that he could still rely on her.

"The mailship is probably quickest," she said. "And it's not too expensive. I'll take you down to the docks tomorrow."

Best to focus on a logistical problem; it helped to take her mind off everything else.

"Oh, dear," said Shuthmili. "I didn't think—I don't have any money. I don't usually—I mean, I'm not usually the one buying things."

"They don't pay you?" said Csorwe. She wasn't sure how Shuthmili's relationship with the Church of Qarsazh worked, but Qarsazh was famously wealthy, and it seemed unjust for Shuthmili not to benefit.

"Well, I'm paid an allowance," said Shuthmili. "I mean, my clothes and books and things are issued by the Church, so there isn't much I'd ever spend it on."

"All right," said Csorwe, not very comforted. "Don't worry. I can cover it."

Csorwe had plenty saved—Sethennai paid well and Csorwe's vices weren't expensive—but another problem occurred.

"Have you travelled alone before?" she said. "Will you be all right?"

"It can't be all that hard. People manage it every day," said Shuthmili, then added, as if surfacing after many hours under-water: "I don't think I've ever actually thanked you properly. For what you've done for me."

Csorwe felt a brief unsought glow of pleasure and gratitude. It was strange to be grateful for being thanked, but she was, perhaps because it happened so rarely. Either way, she snuffed it out as quickly as she could. "Forget about it," she said. "It was an accident, really."

"Oh, yes," said Shuthmili dreamily. "One of those accidents I have all the time, where I accidentally pull someone out of a burning building. It was kind of you."

What could she say? It hadn't been kindness that had driven her, back in the belly of the Hollow Monument. It hadn't really been conscious. A momentary lapse in judgment, which all her training hadn't prevented.

"It was nothing," said Csorwe. It seemed very cruel to say, *It was a mistake,* but Shuthmili seemed to catch the implication anyway.

"Well. I am still grateful that you didn't leave me," she said. She withdrew into herself, leaving her face as a mask, the features set.

"I'll get you home," said Csorwe, feeling she had gone about this conversation all wrong. "You'll be back to Qarsazh and you can forget about all this."

Once she had got Shuthmili safely onto a ship, she could

turn round and take stock of the smoking ruins of her own life. Something to look forward to.

She left Shuthmili to sleep and returned to her own room. She was too tired to do more than splash her face with water, but once she was in bed, her thoughts wheeled like seagulls above a midden, circling and circling around the fact of her failure. After everything. After all that she had done. It was a bitter draught to sip.

Somebody else in her position might offer their services elsewhere. Belthandros Sethennai had no equal, in Tlaanthothe or anywhere else, but every city had its intrigues. They were mad for security in Qarsazh. Every clan-liege in Oshaar needed a bodyguard, or she could go back to Grey Hook and work on the caravans. There were kings and chieftains in every part of the Maze who needed someone to kill, steal, and observe with discretion.

But then, anyone who took her on would value her more for Sethennai's secrets than for anything else she had to offer, and she couldn't stomach that. Anyway, it wasn't so simple. She couldn't just leave. She was his to put aside, and that was a fact she couldn't unmake.

She lay awake, miserable, absently listening for footsteps and voices. The night staff went about their regular watches. Sometime between midnight and the small hours, she heard the latch of Tal Charossa's door, and the creak of floorboards outside her room.

It was hard to say whether it was vindictiveness or concern or pure curiosity that drove her after him.

There was a note on the floor just outside her room, dropped in passing:

No hard feelings.
Jokes! Hope you drown in a sewer.
    Tal Charossa

She rolled her eyes and followed him, silently, up to the hangar where the small ships hung like bats.

She watched from the shadows as he made ready one of the floatpine barges, stowing provisions and following them with a bundle of clothes.

"Leaving?" said Csorwe, as he turned with a hatchet to cut the final rope holding the barge in its berth.

Tal swore. All the sharp lines of his face twisted with anger and relaxed to sullenness in a moment. "I have work to do."

"No, you don't. We've been relieved of our duties."

Tal's grin and the blade of the hatchet reflected his lantern in twin flashes of malice. "Well, don't let me tell you otherwise."

"You're going after the Reliquary," she said, understanding at last.

"Maybe the cosmos has a plan for Talasseres Charossa beyond serving *Belthandros* as all-purpose errand boy." He shrugged, kicking the barge's alchemical engine to life. "Or maybe not."

Csorwe stepped forward reflexively, as though there was anything she could do to stop him.

Tal laughed, a sharp, discordant sound like a string breaking, and he cut the line. "This is a test," he said. "And I'm going to pass. Whatever you do now, you know I'll beat you there."

The barge slipped from its berth and away into the night: a narrow retreating shape, and then just the point of the lantern, winking and vanishing against the glittering sky.

At first Csorwe thought of jumping into another barge and

chasing him. There were several in the hangar. He didn't have much of a lead—she could overtake him easily—and for all his talk, he probably didn't have much of a plan either.

Then she imagined Shuthmili, waking up the next morning, bewildered and alone in a foreign city. Shuthmili could awaken a sleeping god, she could turn back the dead, and she had apparently taught herself how to fly a cutter just by watching other people do it, but Malkhaya and Aritsa would have spoon-fed her every meal if they'd been given the chance, and apparently she wasn't used to handling money. It wasn't fair to pull someone out of a horde of revenants and immediately leave her to fend for herself on public transport. Csorwe had to stay and help her get home.

14

Reflection in Tranquillity

Y OU SURE YOU WANT to go back to Qarsazh?" asked Csorwe, the next morning over breakfast.

She had taken Shuthmili to Kethaalo's restaurant, one of the few places in Tlaanthothe that Csorwe truly appreciated. The place was small, comfortable, and quiet, and not overrun with students, especially at this time of day, when most of them would be attending classes or sleeping off their hangovers. Csorwe both wanted to stay out of Sethennai's way while he cooled down and had hopes that a proper meal might shake loose a better idea than putting Shuthmili on a mailship back to Qarsazh alone.

Shuthmili looked at her as though she had pulled a bug out of her hair and eaten it.

Csorwe shrugged. "I was just thinking. You could go anywhere from here, if you wanted."

"No," said Shuthmili, after a pause. "There isn't anywhere else for me. The Church is my home, and if they don't want me in the Quincuriate anymore, then, well, that's not what the gods intended for me."

"Why wouldn't they?" said Csorwe. "None of this was your fault. And you don't look like the dragon goddess is about to burst out of your chest or anything."

"I hope not," said Shuthmili. "But it's not enough just to be good. The Quincuriate is incorruptible. If they think I'm compromised, because of what happened, then, well. If that's what they decide then it isn't meant to be." It was painful to see how hard she was trying to put a brave face on it, but Csorwe was grateful for the effort. At this point they needed the bravest faces they could get. "The main thing is to get back to Qarsazh as soon as I can, so they know I did the best I could."

The waiter came to the table with ironwort tea and plates of sweetmeats. Shuthmili went through a plateful of pistachio fingers like a brand-new agricultural machine.

"You must have been starving," said Csorwe, guilty all over again for her shortcomings as a host. She hadn't even managed to find Shuthmili clean clothes that fit: she was still wearing the nightshirt, though now with leggings and a jacket for modesty.

"Sort of," said Shuthmili. She chewed and swallowed hastily. "It's not always this bad."

Csorwe raised an eyebrow and ordered more food.

"It's just magic. This is the usual problem, for a mortal body channelling divine power. Magic eats away at you. It breaks down your body, saps your tissues. If you're not very good and you push too hard, it does it all at once and you end up, you know, semi-liquid."

"Oh," said Csorwe, looking down at a smear of apricot preserve on her half-eaten pastry. Sethennai had talked about this before, but it had always seemed so academic for him.

Shuthmili paused to inhale an almond bun. "Luckily I *am* very good. But I have to repair myself. It takes up a lot of energy so I'm more or less starving all the time. Do you know whether they have coffee here?"

"Er," said Csorwe. "I'll ask. Doesn't repairing yourself use the power as well?"

"It definitely does," said Shuthmili, brightly. "But you can balance it, if you're careful. I've been using magic since I was a baby and if I stop now my skeleton will crumble like wet chalk. You can see it's a bit of a bind—are you going to eat that?"

Shuthmili sounded perfectly cheerful about it. Csorwe wondered again whether Sethennai had the same problem. Was this what he meant about desire outstripping reality?

"Looking forward to getting home?" said Csorwe, not at all eager to think about Shuthmili's bones dissolving.

"Yes, I suppose so," said Shuthmili. "You don't have to worry about me, Csorwe." She smiled, covering her mouth with her hand. She was almost expressive this morning. Her smiles came far more readily than before. Csorwe put it down to the effect of a good night's sleep.

"I guess if you've survived this long without exploding yourself, maybe your gods are watching out for you," said Csorwe. All the same, she was glad she had decided to escort Shuthmili in person.

They left Kethaalo's and went back up to the palace to collect Shuthmili's things, such as they were.

It was almost over, Csorwe thought. Soon it would be time to get back to work. The idea made her very tired. It would be nice to rest, for once, just to walk in one of the parks or sit outside one of the teashops in the Corn Market.

She didn't know Tlaanthothe as well as she could. For the past five years she had been busy enough that she had probably spent more time in refuelling stations than inside the city. She didn't have friends here, never mind anything more than that. Taymiri had married her lieutenant and left town after a few years dangling Csorwe by a thread. After that Csorwe had decided it was safer and more comfortable not to bother.

Sethennai's city was a paradise, but Csorwe had never quite loved it the way he did. She never felt at home here, not in the same way that she had in the warrens of Grey Hook. But then, in Grey Hook she had been an anonymous child, free to wander. Here in Tlaanthothe she was the Chancellor's sword-hand, and there was no escape from being recognised.

When they arrived back at the palace, Sethennai was occupying the throne room. Csorwe could hear him from the hall, talking to someone. She couldn't make out the words, but from the pitch and tone of the rumble she gathered that he was half amused, half annoyed, and tilting more toward annoyance the longer this person continued to bother him.

"Come on," she muttered to Shuthmili. "We'll go 'round the back way." Sneaking around like this made her feel both guilty and foolish, but she had no desire to trouble Sethennai in this mood. If they were lucky, he would have forgotten that she and Tal had even brought a guest back with them. After sleeping on it last night, she reckoned that going to Sethennai for help getting Shuthmili back was out of the question. He was likely to work out what had happened, that Shuthmili was the reason Csorwe had failed to claim the Reliquary, and it would reawaken all his anger and disappointment from the night before. And it would be no good for Shuthmili to learn what Csorwe had given up for her. Neither of them needed that kind of obligation. Better if she could quietly get Shuthmili away without anyone knowing more than they needed to.

As they crept toward the back stairs, they heard a clear voice from the throne room.

"Belthandros, I have been as patient as I can. I do understand this is an unexpected request. But I have reason to believe that my niece returned to the city with your agents, and in light of our long acquaintance—"

It was a woman's voice, speaking Qarsazhi, with the calm evenness of one who expects to be obeyed.

Shuthmili flinched back. "That's my aunt, Zhiyouri," she said, barely moving her lips. "She's a High Inquisitor. She must have come to get me back." Her expression tightened, returning to correct rigidity.

This was good news. Csorwe told herself the only reason she felt as if they'd been caught stealing from the kitchens was because she'd insisted on this bit of childish subterfuge in the first place.

"I have heard no such thing from my 'agents,' as you put it," Sethennai was saying. Either he had really forgotten, or he was being obstructive. Csorwe could believe either.

"What should we do?" said Csorwe. The answer was obvious, but she found herself sorry to be letting Shuthmili go so soon.

"We'd better not keep them in suspense, I suppose," said Shuthmili, turning toward the door.

"The Chancellor is in a private meeting," said the footman outside the throne room.

Csorwe ignored him, pushing through the double doors.

"Csorwe, what on earth—" said Sethennai, too surprised to be angry at first. He was sitting on his throne, for once, so he must have wanted to intimidate his visitor, old acquaintance or not.

The visitor—Shuthmili's aunt—was a middle-aged Qarsazhi woman in a dark uniform. She looked as though she had been cut out carefully with scissors. Her hair was the colour of polished metal, worn in a single braid pinned tightly to the back of her head.

"*Shuthmili?*" said this woman.

"High Inquisitor. Good morning," said Shuthmili, stepping out from behind Csorwe, and approaching with far more confidence than Csorwe was able to muster herself.

Sethennai sat back on his throne and gave Csorwe a piercing look. His ears were almost horizontal with annoyance, and the look said, *I certainly hope there's a rational explanation for this.*

A hurried debriefing followed. Shuthmili's story was that Csorwe had rescued her from the Precursor world and had been trying to help her get home. It took Csorwe a second to recall that this was, in fact, the truth.

"I see," said the Inquisitor. "I am glad to see you well."

"Listen," said Shuthmili. "I realise I may have been compromised. When we get home I can do anything that is required for purification. But Inquisitor, I promise—if that awful woman hadn't got hold of Malkhaya, I *never* would have—"

"I think this is a conversation that can await our return to *Tranquillity*," said Zhiyouri. Csorwe felt a prickle of annoyance on Shuthmili's behalf, but Shuthmili didn't seem to notice the dismissal.

"Do you mean you brought your ship all this way?" said Shuthmili. She sounded both shocked and rather touched.

"Everyone wants you to be safe," said Zhiyouri. "Especially now."

Shuthmili watched her, expectant.

"Perhaps this too ought to wait until we are on the ship," said Zhiyouri. She glanced pointedly at Csorwe and Sethennai, then seemed to decide they didn't matter. "There is a new vacancy within the Quincuriate."

"And they're thinking of me?" said Shuthmili. Her eyes brightened, and then her whole body seemed to light up with pride and readiness. "They're still thinking of me?"

"Of course," said Zhiyouri. "Once you have been cleared of corruption, but I don't imagine that will take so very long. We will assess you on the frigate on our way back to Qaradoun. You should be ready to begin the tether as soon as we reach the Traitor's Grave."

"But what if I don't pass?" said Shuthmili.

"I would not worry so very much about that," said Zhiyouri, with a pleasant smile. "It is a long journey and *Tranquillity* is ready to depart as soon as you are. Let us get you home, shall we?"

Shuthmili nodded, speechless with what Csorwe took to be relief.

"I'll go and collect my things, Inquisitor," said Shuthmili.

"Certainly," said Zhiyouri. "I will be waiting in the shuttle-barge."

Csorwe had meant to follow Shuthmili out, if only to make sure she found her way back to the guest room, but Sethennai raised a hand.

Once the other two were gone, he rose from his throne and stretched. "You've been busy."

"I meant to explain it all last night," said Csorwe.

"I know Qanwa Zhiyouri. She is less actively stupid than most Inquisitors," said Sethennai. "But I don't like unexpected visitors any more than I like any other kind of surprise. Don't make a habit of this, Csorwe."

"No, sir," she said.

He had nothing more to say. Csorwe wondered whether she should ask for work to do, or tell him that Tal had run away, or anything to prolong the conversation and make her feel more normal, but in the end she just left.

She was probably meant to spend the rest of the day in her quarters feeling ashamed of herself, but as she climbed the stairs she found her thoughts returning to Shuthmili. It ought to have been a relief to get the Adept off her hands. As nice as it had been to have a distraction from her immediate problems, she needed to face them eventually. And she couldn't possibly expect her to stay any longer. Shuthmili wanted to go home to Qarsazh, and Qarsazh wanted her back.

Nevertheless, something bothered her.

At first she'd thought the Qarsazhi treated Shuthmili like a child. She realised now that wasn't quite right. Outside the House of Silence, most people raised their children in the hope and expectation that they would grow up into adults. Even the knowledge that Shuthmili could be dangerous didn't explain all Malkhaya's sad looks, all Aritsa's solicitous care in bringing her drinks and blankets. They had treated Shuthmili as if she were dying.

Csorwe blinked. Things fell into place all at once, like the tumblers of a lock aligning. The Quincuriate assessment. Shuthmili's last chance to prove herself under her own name. And now one of the Quincury Adepts was dead, which meant Shuthmili's number was up, and Zhiyouri was clearly eager to rush it all through on the ship before Shuthmili had any chance to think about it. What the hell were they going to do to her?

She strode back down the corridor, kept from breaking into a run only by the presence of guards and footmen, and pelted down the stairs.

Qanwa Zhiyouri's shuttle-barge was hovering above the long palace drive. Csorwe could see her sitting inside under a canopy, next to a uniformed guard. Csorwe hopped up into it and sat opposite her.

"Hello," said Csorwe. The guard bristled, reaching for her weapon.

"It's all right, Warden," said Qanwa Zhiyouri. Maybe it was Csorwe's imagination, knowing they were related, but Zhiyouri did look rather like Shuthmili. They had the same curious, unblinking stare. "I have this person to thank for rescuing my niece, I think."

"That's right," said Csorwe. She hardened her posture, drawing on her thickest Grey Hook accent. "Daryou Malkhaya said he could assure me of the Church's generosity."

"Daryou Malkhaya is dead," said Zhiyouri.

Csorwe squashed any reaction she might have had to that. She would have known it if she'd taken the time to think about it, but she'd been avoiding doing so. "I don't care," she said. "I saved her life. You owe me."

In fact, she had forgotten about the reward until that moment, but people were always ready to believe in greed.

"I'm afraid I can't say I'm carrying a great deal of cash at the moment," said Zhiyouri, as if Csorwe were a beggar who might leave if discouraged.

"Then I'll come with you," said Csorwe. With every minute she was more convinced that she was right, and less willing to take her eyes off the Qarsazhi.

Zhiyouri's expression conveyed the blank outrage of a machine thrown off its track. For a moment Csorwe thought this woman might actually be about to strike her.

Then they heard footsteps on the gravel outside, as Shuthmili approached, and Qanwa Zhiyouri sighed.

"Very well," she said. "I am sure my aide will be happy to attend to you."

It took Csorwe one minute in the company of Inquisitor Tsaldu to identify him as a miserable bastard.

The Qarsazhi Inquisitor was a stock character in the theatres of Grey Hook and Tlaanthothe: relentless in pursuit, sinister in motivation, very keen on wrapping himself up in a huge black cloak and giggling cruelly. Tsaldu had the look of disdain down perfectly, but he was not one of life's gigglers.

"And how much did Dr. Lagri promise you?" he said, peering at her over his desk.

The frigate *Reflection in Tranquillity* was anchored in the foothills outside Tlaanthothe. Two or three Tlaanthothei security vessels were watching the ship at a discreet distance. Csorwe did not doubt that, in each turret of the ancient wall, Sethennai's war machines were stirring in their sleep. A Qarsazhi frigate was not a trifle, but it seemed they really had sent it just for Shuthmili.

Csorwe yawned. "I don't remember. Lots," she said. It was wonderful what you could achieve by acting dense and looking violent. She also had the sense that she'd been fobbed off on Tsaldu because Qanwa Zhiyouri had better things to do, and it didn't encourage her to be polite.

"Well," he said. "We're certainly grateful for the effort you expended keeping Adept Qanwa alive."

They had taken Shuthmili away as soon as they got on board: two of them, veiled and visored as though Shuthmili might be carrying the plague. Csorwe had been forced to remind herself that she'd known Shuthmili for less than a week. She couldn't assume on nothing more than a hunch that she knew better than Shuthmili's own people what was good for her. Still, if she'd had a choice she wouldn't have left Shuthmili alone with them.

"Mm," said Csorwe. "I got hurt, you know. Messed my shoulder up pretty badly."

"I see," said Tsaldu. "Name your price, then."

Csorwe named a ludicrous sum. Tsaldu didn't look even a little amused. Before he could answer, a messenger arrived. Apparently he was wanted by High Inquisitor Qanwa.

Csorwe followed, keeping an insistent few inches behind Tsaldu, hoping she was exuding greed rather than suspicion. The interior of the ship was all polished wood, lacquered panels, icons in niches, and deep, thick red carpets which swallowed up noise. There must have been hundreds of people aboard the frigate, but all that conversation was reduced to nothing but a pervasive rustling.

They came to a windowless chamber belowdecks, and Csorwe elbowed her way in after Tsaldu. This room was one part chapel, one part workroom, one part dungeon, with candles burning before a large tin-glazed icon, glass instruments set out on the benches, and a hospital cot fitted with shackles.

Shuthmili was sitting on the edge of this cot, dressed in a plain shift. Her eyes were bloodshot. Perhaps they had told her about Lagri Aritsa and Daryou Malkhaya, and she'd been weeping for them. She didn't meet their eyes as they came in, only looked blandly at the icon on the opposite wall.

Next to the bench was Inquisitor Qanwa, flanked by two people in androgynous white surcoats and veils, their faces covered by masks of black gauze. The only flash of colour on either of them was a ribbon-thin sash, embroidered blue on white. Csorwe took them to be priests, until they began to talk.

"I have completed decontamination and the first stage of aptitude testing." They spoke, and this was no metaphor, with one voice: low, calm, musical, and sexless. "I find that Adept Qanwa is free from corruption and in principle fit for the tether."

"The Mother of Cities provides for us," said Inquisitor Qanwa with satisfaction. She seemed pleased enough that she didn't object to Csorwe's presence.

"You're certain on the matter of corruption?" said Tsaldu.

"If Vigil is certain then we are certain," said Qanwa sharply, clearly referring to the strangers in white.

"Inquisitor, with the greatest respect," said Tsaldu, "I thought you said this was something which ought to wait until our return to the Traitor's Grave—"

Csorwe listened to them babble on about indices and basal impurity and all kinds of other nonsense, and wished Shuthmili would look up.

"It is clear enough," said Inquisitor Qanwa, cutting off the conversation. "When Shuthmili passes her assessment, she will be suited for integration into Archer Quincury."

Shuthmili looked up at last, her eyes flashing with some strong emotion; pride or triumph, Csorwe guessed. This was what Shuthmili had said she'd hoped for, after all. But Csorwe still felt the edges of a creeping dread.

"It is truly fortunate that we have such a fitting candidate ready to replace Archer Five," said one of the Vigils.

"Tsaldu," said Inquisitor Qanwa, "I will oversee the secondary phase of testing. I will need you to step in and cover my outstanding duties in the meantime."

Tsaldu accepted, just about managing to do so with good grace, and shuffled out with the Vigils. They moved in a cascade of white silk. Even their footsteps matched.

"I would be willing to begin the tether today, if it were possible," said Shuthmili, in the old chilly monotone, sitting up so straight she might have been a painted cutout of a woman.

"Of course, Shuthmili," said Inquisitor Qanwa. "We are very glad to have you back."

"Yep, well, you can thank me later," said Csorwe, earning a satisfying look of disgust from Qanwa. "Your little friend and I didn't finish discussing my reward."

She glanced at Shuthmili in case she was amused, hoping the Adept was just pretending not to know her for her aunt's benefit. Shuthmili paid no more attention to her than you'd pay to a fly buzzing in another room.

"I've made up my mind," said Csorwe. She propped her hands on her hips and looked up at Qanwa with all the studied insolence she could muster. If she'd had a straw she would have gnawed on it. Actually, her mind was chewing up and spitting out this latest piece of lunacy just as fast as she could talk. Best just to go along with it. "You're heading back to Qaradoun, right?"

"Well, yes," said Inquisitor Qanwa.

"Great. Let's say I want to make my fortune in the big city. Take me back to Qaradoun with you and we'll call it evens."

*

They showed Csorwe to a passenger cabin. This was as immaculate as the rest of the ship, with the same low sloping ceiling and dark red panels.

A Warden made it clear to her that if she knew what was good for her, she'd stay in her cabin and not bother everyone with her presence. Eventually someone brought her dinner: poached eggs and noodles and shreds of mushroom in a sweet-savoury broth. She had to admit it was better than what you usually got on board ship.

Once she'd eaten and had no further distractions she began to realise just what an enormous mistake it had been to follow through on this idea.

Sethennai had explicitly told her to stay at the palace. Even if Tal was right, and it was all a test, and they were *supposed* to take the initiative, she should have taken a boat of her own and gone hunting for Oranna. Instead, she was on board a foreign ship that would soon make way for the Qarsazhi capital, a dozen Gates from Tlaanthothe.

The smart thing would be to bail as soon as she could. They'd have to stop to refuel eventually. The Qarsazhi could do awful things to each other on their own time. In theory, Csorwe had her own shit to deal with.

In practice, she couldn't stop worrying about Shuthmili. Half the time she could believe that Shuthmili had been quiet because she wished Csorwe would just leave. If that was so, Csorwe couldn't blame her. It had been an uncomfortable episode and she was ready to forget about it herself. But then—she couldn't quite shake the suspicion that the Inquisitors had *done something*—given Shuthmili more drugs or laid some kind of magic on her—to make her so silent and compliant. Shuthmili had looked just the same when she was Oranna's prisoner, down in the Hollow Monument.

She lay there and listened as the frigate broke away from its orbit of Tlaanthothe and traversed the Gate. They were on their way. No use now wondering whether she'd made the right choice.

The lights in the corridor dimmed, and the crew moved to night watches. Once she was sure most of them had turned in for the night, she slunk off to look for Shuthmili.

The Adepts' dormitory had room for a dozen people in bunks stacked three high, but contained only Shuthmili, tucked neatly into a cot at the far end, staring at the opposite wall. She heard Csorwe coming, and unfolded herself.

"Do you people make all your beds tiny on purpose?" said Csorwe.

"I suppose they don't want us to get any ideas about sharing," said Shuthmili, looking pensive, and wrapped the blanket around her shoulders.

"In case hitting your head on the doorframe all the time really puts you in the mood, I guess," said Csorwe without thinking, then wished she hadn't. Shuthmili probably, technically, knew the facts of life, but the Qarsazhi could be delicate about these things.

"I didn't know you wanted to go to Qaradoun," said Shuthmili, who didn't actually seem too fazed.

"Yeah, I have to add to my collection of useless child-size furniture," said Csorwe, sitting on one of the bunks opposite Shuthmili. "What was it like, the testing?"

"Tiring," said Shuthmili. "But I think I passed muster. Archer Quincury is a military division. It's not quite what I expected."

She smiled thinly. "I had been revising alchemy, mechanics, anatomy—I hadn't thought they'd want me for this."

"What does Archer do?" said Csorwe.

"It's more about what it doesn't do," said Shuthmili. "For instance, it doesn't turn forests to ash. It doesn't boil rivers dry. It doesn't reduce cities to puddles of glass. If you're a neighbour of Qarsazh and we've taken advantage of you in some way, and you don't feel friendly towards us, and you're thinking of getting back at us, you might first think carefully about how much you enjoy it when Archer doesn't do anything."

"Oh," said Csorwe. "Wow."

Shuthmili frowned and bit her lip, perhaps wondering if she'd said too much. "Archer is vital to the stability of the Imperium," she added. In Csorwe's experience you couldn't argue with people once they started saying things like this, so she didn't.

"But you're all right?" she said, instead.

"Yes," said Shuthmili, still frowning, now with concern. "I'm fine, Csorwe. I'm back where I need to be."

"I'm sorry about Dr. Lagri and Malkhaya," said Csorwe. "Did they tell you?"

She nodded. "I am sorry too. May they rest at the Hearth of the Mara," she added hastily. "I've never really said that for someone I knew before. It's—it's almost too much to believe. But in other ways, it isn't a shock. I knew, I think—back in the Precursor world—that they hadn't escaped. I'll write to their families, when we get back to Qaradoun, if my aunt permits it. If she thinks they would like to hear from me. I should do that before I am tethered, at least."

"Look, what does that mean?" said Csorwe, already one hundred percent certain she was going to hate the answer. "The tether. Getting tethered. What is it, really?" *What are they going to do to you?* was what she wanted to ask, but it was still possible she had misunderstood, and she didn't want to put Shuthmili on her guard.

Shuthmili took a deep breath and folded her hands in her lap. "The Imperial Quincuriate is—how to put this—uniquely stable. Quincury Adepts are trusted. They are virtually immune to corruption, so there's no risk. They don't suffer from the same physical decline as ordinary Adepts. That's because of the tether."

"It doesn't sound completely terrible," said Csorwe. "What's the downside?"

"It's not meant to sound completely terrible," said Shuthmili. "It's an honour. It's a privilege."

"Mm," said Csorwe. "You can say that about a lot of things. Where I grew up it was an honour and a privilege to sew up your mouth and starve to death."

Shuthmili looked horrified, and Csorwe immediately regretted bringing it up. Whatever her feelings on the House of Silence, the last thing she wanted was to hear someone else's opinion on it.

"It's nothing like that," said Shuthmili. "Each Quincury—er, that's a unit of five—shares the same tether. They share a single consciousness. The process of tethering and integration binds a new Adept into the Quincury."

"A single what?" said Csorwe. Shuthmili didn't seem to hear her.

"That's why they're so stable. With five minds working together, the strain is spread equally. Apparently you don't even need to *think* about repairing yourself. It's just handled."

"A single consciousness."

"Yes," said Shuthmili, briskly. "Each Quincury has its own personality. Imagine one person with five separate bodies."

"No thanks," said Csorwe. "So . . . when you're . . . tethered, you won't be yourself?" The worst part was that it made sense of how they treated Shuthmili. She saw that now. Like she was a very expensive and important part of a very expensive and important automaton.

"I will continue to exist," said Shuthmili. "My conscious mind will merge with the shared mind of the Quincury. I will certainly be different."

"But then . . . you won't be you, yourself."

"No," said Shuthmili. "Not anymore, I suppose."

"And that's what you *want*?" said Csorwe, pushing away the urge to scream. "But that's just dying," she said. "If you won't be there anymore, that's the same thing—"

Before Shuthmili could answer, the door slid open. Inquisitor Qanwa Zhiyouri stood in the doorway, turning on them the affronted look that people usually reserved for Tal Charossa. Shuthmili shrank back into her bunk.

"You were told to stay in your cabin," she said to Csorwe, controlling herself. "You have no right to come in here and bother Adept Qanwa."

"What the fuck, *Auntie Zhiyouri*," said Csorwe. "You know exactly what they're going to do to her."

"I haven't the faintest idea what you mean. Leave of your own volition or I will summon a Warden to remove you."

"Don't touch me," said Csorwe. She doubted Qanwa Zhiyouri would expect a punch in the stomach. She was prepared to fight over this, right here and now.

"Csorwe," said Shuthmili. "It's all right—we can talk another time—" She sounded utterly tired and, unless it was Csorwe's imagination, utterly hopeless.

Csorwe saw then that there was no point attacking Inquisitor Qanwa. It would just get her kicked off the ship or thrown in some kind of grim Qarsazhi jail. With reluctance, she went limp and nodded.

"Fine. Sorry," she said. "Just checking on her."

Qanwa Zhiyouri made no response, her mouth set in a thin line.

"It'll be all right, Csorwe, I promise," said Shuthmili. "Aunt, she didn't mean any harm—"

Shut back into her cabin, Csorwe felt suffocated, as if she were being pressed to death between layers and layers of velvety red upholstery.

Maybe it was just a Qarsazhi thing. Maybe this really was normal there. Maybe they all loved to meld their consciousnesses with each other. Maybe the only reason Csorwe was even getting herself involved was that she had salted and burnt the rest of her life and she had nothing else to distract her.

No. Whatever the reasoning, it was a pointless shame and a waste. The word she was gradually catching up to was *outrage*. Eight years ago Csorwe had gone willingly to her own death because it had been expected of her, because she had been told it was an honour, because she hadn't known that she had any choice.

She should never have let them take Shuthmili. The worst part of it was that nobody here knew what they'd be losing. Shuthmili had lived with these people her whole life and none of them seemed to know her, or like her, even a little bit. Csorwe wanted to know how Shuthmili had ended up so strange and entertaining, when she'd grown up with a bunch of pencil-sharpening wankers who probably alphabetised their thumbscrews.

Shuthmili deserved to live, and Csorwe deserved to buy her another breakfast, and that was a fact. With that in mind, Csorwe planned her rescue.

15

The Life of an Adept

CSORWE STAYED OBEDIENTLY IN her quarters, keeping note of the watches, and of the Gates as they passed them by. They were only a few days out from Qaradoun. She needed to move sooner rather than later. A rotation of Wardens had been stationed at the door to the Adepts' dormitory. They were very clear about the fact that Adept Qanwa needed to meditate and prepare herself for the tether.

The Warden of the third watch left the door to the Adepts' dormitory at the third hour of the morning, according to the ship's internal clock. There was then a minute's delay as the Warden of the fourth watch finished his morning cigarette. In this time, Csorwe picked the lock and slipped inside.

Shuthmili was asleep on the same bunk as before. She was frighteningly still, the blankets pulled up to her chin, her plaits coiled on the pillow on either side of her pinched little face.

A perfect face, Csorwe thought, and frowned, taken aback by the thought. That wasn't why she was doing this.

"Shuthmili," she whispered, shaking her lightly by the shoulder. "Wake up!"

It took Shuthmili a long time to surface. "Csorwe?" she murmured. "Why are you here?"

"Wanted to talk to you," said Csorwe, suddenly embarrassed. The plan she had devised relied on Shuthmili agreeing with her quite quickly, but she hadn't thought much about what she was going to say.

"You're still here," said Shuthmili, rubbing her eyes. "I'm glad. I thought you might have gone."

"They wouldn't let me in," said Csorwe, ignoring the spark of warmth that kindled in her chest at the news that Shuthmili was glad to see her. "So—listen—we have two hours before the guards change position again. The next guy will probably look round the door to check you're all right. And I think by then we should be gone."

"What do you mean?" said Shuthmili. She sat up in bed, gathering the sheets around her.

"We'll need to steal a shuttle-barge from the bay on the deck above," said Csorwe. "But I know which way we can go and avoid the guards—"

"Are you—are you asking me to run away with you?" said Shuthmili. Mostly disbelieving, maybe a little amused. Then all amusement faded. "This is about the tether."

"Yes," said Csorwe. "Did you really know what it meant? You've really known all along?"

"I did," said Shuthmili.

"But you said you've wanted it since you were little. You worked for it. I saw you *studying*—but you'll die."

"I won't die," said Shuthmili. "It's not the same thing."

"But you won't be able to think for yourself," said Csorwe,

doing her best not to raise her voice. If the guard overheard them then none of this would matter.

"Thinking for oneself is an overrated luxury," said Shuthmili. "As a part of Archer Quincury I will be safe from harm, and safe from accidentally harming others."

"That's not enough—" said Csorwe.

"It is," said Shuthmili, with patience. "I don't want to spend the rest of my life picking over every passing thought for signs of corruption and staving off organ failure. Every time I use magic it takes a little more from me. If I don't join the Quincuriate I'll live to be forty, if I'm lucky, and once I die that's it. There will be no rest for me at the Hearth of the Mara. The old Archer Five died peacefully at *ninety-five*."

"So that gives you what, seventy-plus years as . . . that," said Csorwe. She remembered what Shuthmili had told her about Archer, and it didn't sound pleasant. "Running a protection racket."

"Seventy-plus years protecting the Imperium," said Shuthmili. "Preventing war. Making sure millions of people continue to live safely in Qarsazh. That's important."

She didn't sound any more convinced by this than Csorwe was herself.

"There is a whole world out there, you know," said Csorwe. "There are other things. Other places. You could do something else."

There were so many worlds, so many possible lives, and she couldn't imagine how to conjure up even one that would appeal to Shuthmili. She didn't remember Sethennai having to work very hard to persuade her, all those years ago. She didn't even remember everything he had said. Maybe she had just been a coward.

"Is it so hard to understand why I might choose this?" said Shuthmili. "To be a part of something greater. Not to doubt yourself all the time. Always to know where you belong and what you need to do."

"Because you wouldn't have any choice."

"I don't have any choice now," said Shuthmili, as though this were blindingly obvious. "The life of an Adept is the life of an Adept, and there is nothing for me outside it. My family gave me up to the Church when I was a child. It's pure chance that I know my Aunt Zhiyouri, and I don't remember my parents at all. I won't ever marry or do any other job. I belong to the Church. Where I live, when I sleep, what I wear, what to eat, what to say, what to think. None of that is my choice."

"And if you join this Quincuriate then you just won't know that you ever wanted anything else," said Csorwe.

"Yes, exactly," said Shuthmili. "I will be where I am meant to be and wanted for the first time in my life. I will never be unhappy, and I will never be alone."

"Well," said Csorwe hopelessly. "I guess nobody else can promise you that. It just seems like a shame." She wished she had better words to describe exactly how much of a shame it would be.

Shuthmili rubbed her eyes again as if hoping this might be a dream. When she spoke again, all her earlier assurance had faded. She sounded as if she were finding her own way in a mist.

"Everything I said—I always believed that. I do still believe it," she said. "But it was odd—when I thought I must be compromised, that they'd never want me for the Quincuriate—I started thinking . . ."

"Yeah?" said Csorwe, doing her best to disguise her eagerness.

"I thought, well, I'll just go back to research, I don't need to be tethered for that, I can still contribute something. And it would be in my own name. I almost liked that idea, even if it would feel like a failure."

She paused, ruefully, picking at her fingernails. She didn't meet Csorwe's eyes as she went on.

"And I liked seeing Tlaanthothe with you. It was interesting to go somewhere new. Once I'm tethered there won't be many new places to see."

She looked down, seeming to withdraw into herself, and Csorwe realised she was ashamed.

"I don't know," said Shuthmili. "I just don't know. Maybe I'm weaker than I thought I was."

"No," said Csorwe. "I don't know what you are, but you're not that." She glanced back at the door, where the silhouette of the guard's head was dimly visible through the carved screen in the door.

"Even if I wanted to change my mind," said Shuthmili, "just for the sake of argument. I'm not saying I will. Could we really just go? Just get up and leave?"

"Yeah," said Csorwe. "Easy."

It was, in fact, embarrassingly easy. Shuthmili called the Warden. When he came into the room, Csorwe unfolded from behind the door, clamped her hand over his mouth, pulled a pillowcase over his head, tied him up, and shoved him into the bunk.

"My word," said Shuthmili, "I hope he'll be all right." She bit her lip, but she didn't exactly linger in the cabin.

They crept down the corridor, following the route Csorwe had planned to the shuttle bay. Maybe Shuthmili's nasty dragon goddess was keeping an eye on them. They weren't seen. She gestured Shuthmili toward the nearest shuttle-barge and cranked open the doors to the bay.

"Are we just going to *take* it?" said Shuthmili, though she didn't hesitate to climb in to the barge.

"Didn't they teach you how to steal a ship at wizard school?" said Csorwe. There was no alarm from the innards of *Reflection in Tranquillity*—no sign at all of pursuit. She leapt into the barge after Shuthmili, pulled the release lever, and they fell away into the sky, like a leaf borne along on the surface of a stream.

Qanwa Zhiyouri did not allow herself many pleasures. The fewer, the sweeter, she felt, and delaying one's rewards helped to focus the mind. On this occasion, she permitted herself a glass of wine. Specifically, a seventeen-year-old apricot wine from her own estate outside Qaradoun, which looked like liquefied topaz and tasted like the tears of a divinity.

The vintage was appropriate. It had been seventeen years since the power of the Traitor-Dragon had first manifested in Shuthmili. Qanwa's brother Adhara had sent for her in a panic. From the incoherent scrawl, Zhiyouri had at first assumed his daughter had fallen out of a tree and injured herself.

When she had arrived at the townhouse, she learned the truth. The five-year-old Shuthmili was lying under a blooming cherry tree in the courtyard, surrounded by piles of blossom and fruit that were already beginning to decay. It was midwinter. The tree should not even have borne leaves. It certainly should not have been able to loop its roots so tightly around Shuthmili's limbs that it became difficult to tell what was bark and what was flesh.

It was lucky for Shuthmili that her aunt had arrived on the scene so swiftly. Zhiyouri was already a fully trained Inquisitor, and had been able to remove the child safely from the tree without her little heart exploding. It could have been embarrassing for Zhiyouri—perhaps it didn't say much for her professional acumen that she'd failed to notice her own niece was a half-realised mage—but the whole thing was kept very quiet. Only a few weeks later, Zhiyouri had delivered Shuthmili to the School of Aptitude herself.

As for the cherry tree, it was not created to cycle six months in a day. It had generated a full harvest of cherries and driven them to ripeness. Even if it could have ridden out the shock to its system, Shuthmili had sheared it from its place in time, and it was dead within the month.

Zhiyouri had witnessed the heartache that followed. There were few people, on this earth or any other, for whom she had much pity, but her younger brother was one. Shuthmili had been Adhara's treasure. To learn that something you valued had been corrupt from the beginning was not pleasant.

In addition, in every office of the Imperial Registry, in every copy of the Genealogy, the page that listed the living members of the Qanwa house—the page where Zhiyouri's own name appeared!—was now amended with a notice of Shuthmili's poisonous aptitude. The Traitor's curse ran in the blood. The prospects for advancement and marriage of every Qanwa were stunted, and would remain so for a generation or more. It had been a blow to Zhiyouri both personally and professionally.

Seventeen years later, Zhiyouri was doing very well for herself, and the sting had been soothed by her promotion to High Inquisitor. She didn't blame Shuthmili, except in the way you couldn't help but blame a wild dog for biting. It was nevertheless a great relief to know that the tether was close at hand. Once Shuthmili was shuffled away into the Quincuriate, her name would be written out: no longer a Qanwa, no longer a citizen, but a Quincury Adept and instrument of the Imperial will. The Genealogy would be amended and the whole sorrowful chapter would be closed, for her, for Adhara, and for the rest of the family. All the better because Zhiyouri would have a hand in closing it.

She sipped her wine and closed her eyes, thinking on the pleasant neatness of this. The apricot wine was made with the aid of a grey mould that grew upon the fruit and shrivelled it, sweetening the flesh inside even as it rotted the skin. It was the finest achievement of civilisation to take that kind of ugliness and transform it into something useful and beautiful.

A thunderous knock at the door disturbed her reverie. It was of course Inquisitor Tsaldu, the destroyer of all peace. She was irritated, to a degree that she recognised as irrational. It was just such a pity to waste this one luxury she'd allowed herself, before she could even enjoy it.

"Inquisitor Qanwa!" he said, his ghostly face gaping with horror. "Inquisitor—the Oshaaru passenger has gone, and—well—it seems she's taken your niece with her."

He told her everything. She gripped the edge of the desk to steady herself.

"Summon Vigil," she said. "And the officers. We must change course immediately. *Go,* Tsaldu! At once!"

It had been a mistake to permit Sethennai's lackey on board. Zhiyouri had nobody to blame for that but herself, but she spared herself only a few seconds of fury and recrimination. Anger was itself a pleasure, and it was easy to overindulge.

She sat at her desk, hands flat against the cool mahogany, and took a deep breath. This was a substantial annoyance, but if resolved quickly, it was not a disaster. It might almost be enjoyable to have a little diversion on their way to Qaradoun.

Zhiyouri doubted that the Oshaaru girl had any master plan. In all likelihood the scheme had been invented on the spur of the moment when she realised that Shuthmili was valuable.

It had been a long time since Zhiyouri had enjoyed a proper chase. Not since her work as a prosecutor, in fact. A chase, like a puzzle, had its protocols. At first, the hunter always appeared to be at a disadvantage. Inevitably, though, the quarry scattered and panicked. The hunter watched, waited, assembled her forces, and—at the last—closed the trap.

Shuthmili peered over the side of the barge, her fingertips pale where she was clutching the edge. Beneath them was a misty canyon, threaded with fine silvery rivers, little streams of light painted on the blue-black void.

"Of course," she muttered. "Of course. Why *would* I plan half a minute into the future? Csorwe, I think we've made a mistake."

"Yeah?" said Csorwe, who was sitting at the wheel.

"They aren't just going to let me run. They'll come after us as soon as they realise I'm gone. They're probably already coming after us. You don't know what they'll do to get me back."

"I can guess. They sent a frigate to Tlaanthothe for you already," said Csorwe.

"Once they catch us they'll kill you and they'll take me to the Traitor's Grave. And if they think for some reason that I came voluntarily, if they think I've gone rogue, they'll kill both of us.

Do you know how my people execute rogue mages?" said Shuthmili. "It's—they have this monster—"

"Don't think about it," said Csorwe. "Doesn't help to panic."

She slowed the barge, steering it into a quiet spot under an overhang. This was going to take her full attention.

"Listen—we should turn back," said Shuthmili, clutching the side. "Take us back to the ship. I'll explain everything, I'll try to make them understand that you were trying to help, but I'm *fully* committed to the tether, and—"

"If that's what you want," said Csorwe.

"It doesn't matter what I want," said Shuthmili. "You shouldn't get yourself killed."

"Neither should you. I couldn't just let you walk into it. But if you want me to take you back to die, I will."

"I won't die," said Shuthmili, as if this, of all things, had pushed her over the edge of losing her temper. "I told you. That's not what it is."

"All right. If you want me to take you back to tit around in a mask for an unnaturally long time, I will."

"Whereas, if I stay to *tit around* in this dinghy with you, we will last perhaps half an hour before *Tranquillity* blows us out of the sky," said Shuthmili.

"We've made it this far," said Csorwe. It had been about half an hour. "The fourth watch isn't due for another hour and a half, so they won't know you're even gone until then, and after that they won't know which way we've gone. Once we're past the Peacock Gate they'll never be able to track us."

Shuthmili fell silent for a moment, considering. The peaks and crags of the Echo Maze drifted by, blue and blurred in an indistinct false-dusk, and the wind flicked Csorwe's hair back from her face.

"But then where do I go?" said Shuthmili, as if only just realising that she couldn't go back to her inscriptions. "Do you have a plan in mind?"

"Sure. Come with me," said Csorwe. It really might be that simple.

"I mean, after that," said Shuthmili. "Come with you *where*?"

"Wherever," said Csorwe.

". . . it's kind of you to offer," said Shuthmili, as though presented with a particularly ugly birthday gift. "But you have your own work."

"I'm serious," said Csorwe.

"You can't be," she said. "Not really."

"Deadly serious," said Csorwe. "I thought it all through. You saw the Reliquary, you were there. Oranna has it and I need to get it back before she does something terrible. So I'm going to steal it from her and you should come and help."

Shuthmili's anger gave way to doubt. "Last time I was worse than useless. What if she captures me again?"

"I'm not going to let that happen," said Csorwe.

"It's easy to *say* that—" said Shuthmili. "And more to the point—she killed all those people. What's to stop her hurting you, or worse—"

"A lot of people have tried to hurt me. And you *would* be useful. I don't know magic, and you do. You'd be more than useful. You could help me stop her."

Shuthmili looked unconvinced. Maybe it was time to try a different tack.

"Listen, what do you know about the Reliquary?" said Csorwe.

"I know the *myth*," said Shuthmili. "It seems awfully convenient that it's resurfaced now. It doesn't make sense that the actual
Reliquary of the actual Pentravesse would have survived."

"And if it was real?"

"If it were real it would be one of the greatest discoveries this
century, in historical significance alone. And if any of the myth
is true—if it's not broken, or empty—if the texts weren't exag-
gerating—it would be unimaginable. Unimaginably valuable,
unimaginably powerful, unimaginably *desirable*—" Shuthmili
trailed off, realising Csorwe was grinning at her. "What?"

"No, no, go on," said Csorwe.

"Pentravesse was certainly a real person who really lived, but
you have to admit it sounds a bit unlikely that he really stored up
this impossible knowledge in a special box."

"Sethennai thinks it's real," said Csorwe, and paused to let
this sink in. "If we got it back for him, he'd take me back, and
you too. There'd be work for you. He could help you, teach you,
whatever. If anyone can hide you from your aunt and Tsaldu,
Sethennai can. He helped me and he'd help you too."

"Do you actually think it's possible?" Shuthmili looked out at
the dark landscape, trailing her hand in the breeze.

"Sure," said Csorwe. "I do this kind of thing all the time." She
hadn't meant it to sound impressive, but found herself hoping
that Shuthmili would be impressed all the same.

"Inspiring," said Shuthmili, hiding a sliver of a smile behind
her hand. "And Belthandros Sethennai would really take me
in?"

"He doesn't do charity," said Csorwe. "But he took me in when
I was little, and he doesn't let go of anything useful. He misses
having other wizards around. There are some in Tlaanthothe but

none of them are any good, or something. He'd like you, I bet. And it's got to be better than Archer."

"No," said Shuthmili. "I can't."

"All right. So tell me to turn the barge around. Tell me to take you back. You're right. If we turn back now, they won't even notice you've been gone. It can all start up again."

Shuthmili closed her eyes. "So—but—how can I? How can I possibly . . ."

"Betray your Church? Leave your people? You can, I promise. You miss it for a bit. It's hard for a bit. But if it's stay and die or leave and live, Shuthmili—"

"I can't do it," said Shuthmili. "I won't survive for five minutes."

"I get it. It's hard to run alone," said Csorwe. "But you won't be on your own."

All around them, the Echo Maze resounded with the voices of wind and water. Csorwe didn't meet Shuthmili's eyes. She didn't want to influence her decision, or maybe she just couldn't face her. Then she felt Shuthmili's hand on her wrist, very light, like a breath.

"All right," Shuthmili said. "Let's go."

Under the overhang, they drifted in a pocket of stillness. Mist folded and faded in the canyon.

"I was worried you'd say that," said Csorwe, after a minute.

"What? Why?"

"Because I know how we'll find Oranna, and I don't like it."

16

Handmaid of Desolation

IT WAS EARLY SPRING in northern Oshaar. Snow still covered the little town in great heaps, as though the sky had decided a mercy killing was the only thing for it, and was trying to smother the place with a pillow.

"What is this place?" said Shuthmili, pulling down the hood of her coat.

"This is my hometown." The streets were glossy with ice, and a sharp wind was blowing down from the mountain. It was three o'clock in the afternoon and already starting to get dark. The two moons of Oshaar loomed toward each other across the sky. "You ever heard of the Followers of the Unspoken One?" she said.

"The Unspoken is a god of prophecy, I think," said Shuthmili. "It's one of the major cults of northern Oshaar. The Church classifies it as a low-priority threat. We don't approve of their sacrificial practices but they're relatively stable and content to stay in their own little— Csorwe, do you mean they're *here*? And you grew up here?"

"Yes."

"So you were—you subscribed to the heresy?" Shuthmili's hands were buried in her coat, but Csorwe suspected she was twisting them together anxiously.

"Wouldn't say I actually sent off for anything," said Csorwe. "I was a child. Don't worry. It was a long time ago. I don't worship anything these days."

"I'm in no position to judge anyone," said Shuthmili. "I'm just trying to work out whether—whether Dr. Lagri and the Warden would be more upset to learn I'd run away with a heretic or an atheist. It's sort of funny. Poor Aritsa. Poor Malkhaya."

"They would have got on just fine in the cult of the Unspoken," said Csorwe. "We had a lot of sticklers."

"Oh no," said Shuthmili. She could have been laughing or crying or just breathless in the cold. "Oh, no, those poor men. Both of them. They didn't deserve it."

They trudged on up the glassy streets and out onto the high road. Csorwe told Shuthmili about the House of Silence and the rites of the Unspoken, leaving out anything that pertained to Csorwe's own actual history. She liked Shuthmili. She hoped Shuthmili might like her, as long as she believed Csorwe was competent and successful. All that old stuff, everything about being the Bride of the Unspoken, it was both too private and—because Sethennai and Talasseres both knew—too public. It was nice to talk to someone who didn't automatically know about Csorwe's first and worst betrayal.

From the House of Silence, they came on to the subject of Oranna. "I think she must have broken with the Followers of the Unspoken Name," said Csorwe. "The ritual of oblation—everything we saw in the Hollow Monument—it's too extreme. They would never have given her authorisation to leave Oshaar and chase the Reliquary."

"But you think she might come back here now that she has it?" said Shuthmili.

Csorwe had done her best not to think too hard about it, but it was only fair for Shuthmili to know what she was getting into. Reluctantly, she explained what Sethennai had told them about Oranna's aspirations to union with the Unspoken.

"That's deeply blasphemous," said Shuthmili, sounding almost impressed. "Qarsazhi mages have spent hundreds of years learning to limit the connection between practitioner and divinity—to make it safer—the idea of opening up like that . . ." She shivered, no longer sounding impressed at all. "But I don't think it can be done. It would take too much power. It would shred you from the inside out. But if she thinks there's some secret technique in the Reliquary . . ."

"Yeah. I just hope she hasn't managed to open it," said Csorwe. "If she was really asking Tal, she must be desperate."

Csorwe looked up ahead, above the trees. It was too dark to see the sacred mountain, but by day the steps to the Shrine would be dimly visible from here.

"This is where her power is. She may have come back here. And if not . . . there is another way to find her." Csorwe disliked the idea so much that she'd delayed explaining it to Shuthmili, but it was time. "If we have to, we can claim the pilgrim's boon of prophecy. We can ask the Chosen Bride."

The great doors of the House of Silence were always shut, and these words were inscribed above the lintel:

Hail the Commander of Legions! Hail the Knight of Abyss! Hail the Overseer of the Eaten Worlds! Hail the Unspoken Name!

The breaking of all worlds is foretold, and the ending of time. May we bear witness, for desolation is its watchword.

A young lay-sister was waiting at the side gate with a lantern. She was surprised to see Csorwe and Shuthmili, and then delighted when she learned that they were pilgrims. "The Lady Prioress will want to meet with you," she said, ushering them inside.

The House of Silence was just as it had always been. This shouldn't have been a surprise. It had been exactly the same for a thousand years or more. Incense and ashes of lotus, beeswax and woodsmoke. A bone-deep chill, rising up from the crypt. Soft footsteps on the stairs, and at every corner of every hallway, the flutter of yellow hems disappearing.

Csorwe's throat tightened as they waited to be shown into the Prioress' study. She had hoped it would feel smaller and easier to understand. Your childhood fears were supposed to shrink away and become laughable. The House of Silence was still as dark, still as grand, still a spreading, intricate void of mystery and doubt.

She steeled herself. She had nothing to fear from the Unspoken anymore. Her gold tusk, her scarred face, and all the training and tempering of the past eight years had marked her beyond recognition, and in any case none would remember the child she had been. The Prioress' study was an enormous vaulted room that the small fire could never warm. It seemed to take an eternity to cross the expanse of cold flagstones to the desk. When they reached it, Csorwe didn't recognise the Prioress, and it took her a second to realise that this wasn't just the effect of time. She was looking at a completely different woman.

The new Prioress raised an eyebrow, marking Csorwe's surprise.

"I—ah—I hadn't heard that Prioress Sangrai had retired," said Csorwe, trying to cover it.

"Prioress Sangrai lies among the eminent dead," she said. "I am Prioress Cweren."

Now Csorwe remembered her. Cweren had been the choirmistress in Csorwe's day—a small, plump, pale woman, now a touch greyer and a touch thinner. It was the way of the House of Silence that things became greyer and thinner over time.

"I was hoping to meet with Oranna," said Csorwe, feeling out what Cweren might or might not know about what Oranna was up to. "She was the librarian in Prioress Sangrai's time, or—or so I've heard."

"I know who she is," said Cweren, after a moment. "Oranna left us. I am sorry to disappoint, but she is not here."

Csorwe probably ought to have been disappointed, and did her best to look like it, but she could only feel relieved. At least when she did have to face Oranna, it wouldn't be here, in the heart of her power.

"When Sangrai announced her retirement, there were those who felt Oranna should succeed," said Cweren. "Sangrai announced her selection—that is to say, me—and Oranna was terribly angry, I think. She had never expressed overt interest, but she had amassed a little following of acolytes, some of the younger priestesses, who made her case for her . . . for a time I thought she might challenge me."

"To a *duel*?" said Csorwe.

"It would have been an honourable death for me, but a certain one. Oranna is an outstanding practitioner. On a good day, I can convince a handful of knucklebones to dance. She would have cut me down on the mountainside and made a martial sacrifice of me." Cweren reached carefully for her cup of wine and took a long sip. "I could have enforced her loyalty. I could have demanded that she pledge oaths in blood. I did not. I let her go. Alas, she did not go empty-handed. She took several lay-brothers and -sisters. Most of the promising acolytes. *All* the best young priestesses. Every important book from the library, and an entire case of silver candlesticks. We have not seen her since."

"I see," said Csorwe.

It was just as she'd expected, then. Oranna had gone, and convinced her favourites to go with her, and—

The realisation hit Csorwe like a handful of ice down the back of her neck. By now, most of those who had gone with her were dead.

They had died in the Hollow Monument, bleeding into the sacrificial pool on Oranna's orders. If Csorwe had looked at their faces, she would have recognised some of them, could have put names and histories to those anonymous bodies.

There was a knock at the door, and Cweren got up to answer it, conducting an inaudible conversation with whoever had arrived.

Csorwe stood there, numb, staring out of the window. It was utterly dark outside. Beneath the windows of the House were lakes of illumination, in which you could see the snow falling again, the flakes scattering with frantic urgency.

Shuthmili nudged Csorwe's elbow and whispered. "They don't know where Oranna went?"

"Don't seem to," said Csorwe.

"Are they lying?"

Did Cweren know what had become of her promising acolytes? Better for her to imagine that they were off rampaging with Oranna, not mangled corpses under the ruins of the Monument.

"No," said Csorwe. She ran a hand back through her hair, trying to clear her thoughts as they spiralled. *This whole place is withering on the vine,* she thought. *They're halfway slid into the grave already.* "No, I—"

We ought to go, she wanted to say. *I've seen enough, I want to leave.* In that moment it seemed that nothing could be worth staying in the House of Silence a second longer.

Before she could say anything, Cweren returned, accompanied by a round-faced child in a novice's habit.

Cweren took her seat again behind her desk, and the child stood behind her, shifting her weight restlessly from one foot to the other and clearly waiting for some kind of cue. The girl was young enough to stare openly at Csorwe's scars, but too old to say anything about it. Csorwe wondered whether this could be Cweren's own child; it would be unusual but not impossible.

"So," said Cweren. "If we are finished with the preamble, I take it you are here to ask the boon of prophecy."

Cweren said it so plainly that Csorwe was blindsided. She swallowed, then nodded. "I'd hoped Oranna might be able to help us. But since she's not here, then, yes, I suppose so."

"Very well," said Cweren. "I see no reason to delay. Evening prayers take place in one hour. Will it suit you to pose your questions to the Unspoken then?"

Csorwe nodded again. They couldn't avoid it, so it did seem best to get it over with.

"Good. Tsurai, dear, have you had your dinner?"

"Yes, miss," said the girl. Csorwe noticed she had a gap in her front teeth.

Cweren smiled. "Tsurai is our Chosen Bride. She's been prophesying for two years now. We all value her guidance."

Csorwe felt colder still. Of course. Just as there was another Prioress, here was another Chosen Bride, hunting alone round the House of Silence, just as Csorwe had done. She'd known it, on some level. It had been at the edge of her mind as soon as she'd contemplated asking the boon of prophecy. But she hadn't thought far enough to remember that the Chosen Bride these days would be a child.

"How old are you, Tsurai?" she said.

"I'm eight, miss," said Tsurai.

Eight years since Csorwe had left. Of course. The wheel turned slower and slower but it still drove them down into the Shrine.

Csorwe took a deep breath, conscious of all the eyes on her— not least Shuthmili's—and forced herself to be calm. She was still going to ask for the prophecy, even though it meant demanding that this child channel the Unspoken for her benefit. Csorwe had prophesied so many times—she could almost believe it was not so bad. It was survivable, at least. She herself was the proof of that.

Either way, it was no good having scruples now. They could find Oranna, and recover the Reliquary before she could work out how to open it, and win back Sethennai's trust—or they could give up, and let her inflict the will of the Unspoken on a world that had not yet learned to fear it.

"We'll be glad of your help," she said to Tsurai. "Thank you."

Tsurai just stared at her, and Csorwe remembered with a bitter pang how she had felt when Sethennai had thanked her for the prophecy, all those years ago.

"Excellent," said Cweren. "We will convene in the great hall in an hour, then. Is there anything else you wished to ask, before we go to ready ourselves for the prophecy?"

She had been all too ready to leave, but there was one last thing she owed to the past. "My, er, cousin is a lay-sister here. I'd like to speak to her if I can. Angwennad."

"Oh, dear," said Cweren. "Yes, I knew Angwennad. I'm afraid to say that she died last year. She is interred in the crypt if you wish to pay your respects."

Long ago, Csorwe had entertained a dark fantasy that if she ever saw Angwennad again, Angwennad would know her, and forgive her. She had never seriously believed in the daydream, never actually fed it and given it room to sleep, but it was nice to imagine that Angwennad had hoped in secret for Csorwe's survival, even knowing that if Angwennad had actually recognised her, she would have been horrified and then outraged. Anyway, now she would never know, and Csorwe would never know, and that was that.

Candlelight banked and subsided in the great hall of the House of Silence, like a gleaming at the crest of a wave. The smell of lotus was thick in the air, dizzying, choking. Even once Csorwe steadied herself she could feel it softening up her senses. She had been gone so long now, it was hitting her twice as hard as she remembered.

"Chosen Bride, I most humbly ask a boon of the Unspoken One," said Csorwe. Even half drunk on the fumes of black lotus, there were some formulae you never forgot.

The Chosen Bride sat on her throne in the robes of yellow

brocade that had once belonged to Csorwe, and looked out at the assembly through the swirling clouds.

"What is it that you desire?" she said. It was the voice of an eight-year-old in pitch and timbre, but cold as the grave and about as welcoming.

The Unspoken One had not changed. It was not in its nature to do so.

"Knowledge," said Csorwe.

"Knowledge of that which has passed away, or that which is to come?" said the Unspoken One.

The moment stretched itself out dizzily as Csorwe tried to convince herself this was going to work.

"Knowledge of that which lives in the present moment," said Csorwe.

There was a sharp intake of breath from the crowd. Every eye in the room was fixed upon her. It had been eight years since Sethennai's visit to the House of Silence. She had hoped they might have forgotten him.

"Speak, then," said the Unspoken One.

"Unspoken and Unspeakable One, where is Oranna, once your priestess?"

She had talked this through with Shuthmili. The Unspoken Name was usually prepared to answer two questions, possibly three.

Tsurai fidgeted, just as if she were a real child trying to think of the answer, and not the vessel of a god.

At last: "She seeks the key to the Reliquary of Pentravesse."

"And what is that key?" said Csorwe.

"The key is not an object but a place," said Tsurai. Csorwe ought to have seen that coming. The Unspoken did not lie, but gods had a strange way of thinking about things. Tsurai was watching Csorwe through the smoke with hard, attentive eyes. Even when she tilted her head, those eyes did not seem to move. She seemed to be trying to place Csorwe, to work out how she recognised her.

Still, this gave them almost nothing to go on. She had to dare another question.

"Where is that place, Unspeakable One?"

"In the domain of the Lignite Spire. Before the earthly throne and mansion of the Lady of the Thousand Eyes."

"And where—" said Csorwe, but Tsurai cut her off.

"The one called Oranna is my priestess yet. She is loyal. She serves in devotion. But *you*—" Tsurai rose up from the throne. Her whole body was shaking, but her eyes stayed on Csorwe. "You I know, faithless child. Why have you returned to me now?"

Prioress Cweren swooped up onto the dais. Whether she was trying to calm Tsurai down or planning to order her acolytes to set upon the traitor, Csorwe did not wait to find out. The wrath of the Unspoken began to sound in the hollows under the mountain; soon it would overflow into the hall. The last thing she saw was Tsurai, crumpling to the floor like a paper doll. Csorwe took Shuthmili's arm and, once again, they ran.

They grabbed their bags from the outbuilding where they'd stashed them, and they fled down the road to the town below. The stolen barge was waiting where they had hidden it. The forest sank away beneath them and they rose into the starless sky of Oshaar.

"Your god is more powerful than I expected," said Shuthmili, settling into her seat and rubbing her hands together to warm them.

"Yeah," said Csorwe. "The Unspoken is as old as hell and everything here has been the same for six millennia or however long. It's a dumb piece of shit and it just wants to sleep in the mountain and eat a child every fourteen years. And that's all I've got to say about it."

"I see," said Shuthmili. "But of course, it can't hear anything you say up here."

"Mm," said Csorwe. "You're right." She slowed the barge and leant over the edge. A thousand feet below, the pine forest was as black as the sky. "You can't hear me, can you, you old bastard?" She laughed, bitterly, the cold air catching in her throat like a mouthful of ice water. "We got away again. How does that feel, friend? You're ten million years old and see and hear everything but I guess you're slipping in your old age because you didn't *fucking watch me close enough.*"

She fell back in the bottom of the boat and laughed with sheer, idiot relief, until she thought she might be going mad. In the cold air her laughter came out of her in great wheezes, like a leaky bellows.

Eventually she could open her eyes again, and saw Shuthmili leaning over her, holding the lantern. She blinked away tears of laughter, expecting Shuthmili to look either arch or disapproving. Actually, she was smiling, the same unhappy, unconvincing smile Csorwe had seen before.

Csorwe realised, now—and in fact she must have been pretty dense not to see it before—that Shuthmili was unspeakably beautiful. That everything about her was perfect and that it would be worth doing almost anything to coax a genuine smile out of her. Csorwe lay still where she had fallen, lightly stunned.

"Is something wrong?" said Shuthmili. She brushed her hair back out of her eyes in a way that made Csorwe want to take her face in both hands and kiss her.

"No," said Csorwe, pleased with herself for how impressively normal her voice still sounded. "I was just thinking."

"Oh, do tell me how that goes," said Shuthmili. "I've heard it's not as good as people make it out to be."

"I don't recommend it," said Csorwe. She swallowed, sat up, took her place, and started the engine again. Her cheeks were hot despite the cold wind. She had never been so grateful that it was dark.

Shuthmili peered over the side, looking down at the shadow-woods below. "I'm sorry that we didn't get much we could use."

"What d'you mean?" said Csorwe.

"The Unspoken One was just laughing at us, don't you think?" said Shuthmili. "The Domain of the Lignite Spire."

"Before the earthly throne and mansion of the Lady of Fuck Knows, yep," said Csorwe, though her skin prickled as she remembered the statues of Iriskavaal that she had seen in Echentyr.

"It's a myth, isn't it?" said Shuthmili. "Iriskavaal is gone. Her throne was shattered three thousand years ago, and her earthly mansion was in Ormary, and that's been gone since Pentravesse's time—it must be—or half swallowed by the Maze . . ."

"The Unspoken One doesn't lie. If it says this place is the key to opening the Reliquary, then it exists."

"I suppose it makes about as much sense as anything else I've seen this week," said Shuthmili.

"You heard what the Unspoken said," said Csorwe, raking the fingers of both hands back through her hair. "Oranna is still loyal. We have to assume she knows as much as we do, or more. I'll bet she's already on her way to the Lignite Spire."

They might already be too late, Csorwe thought. She might already be there. How would it look, when Oranna became the incarnation of the Unspoken? What would it do? *Living, walking, immortal, and unconquerable.* Ready to devour new worlds. The possibilities whirled like falling snowflakes.

"In that case, I don't believe the plan has fundamentally changed," said Shuthmili, wonderfully matter-of-fact. Her voice called Csorwe back from the edge of another panic. "We will find her, and if we are very lucky she will destroy herself in an attempt to commit this appalling blasphemy, and if not, we will stop her ourselves. Someone told me you do this kind of thing all the time."

"Someone may have been getting ahead of herself," said Csorwe.

"In any case, it seems to me the real question now is how we're going to find this imaginary place," said Shuthmili, evidently in no mood for objections. She sounded almost enthusiastic. "I've never seen it marked on any map, and our education in geography at the School of Aptitude was just as rigorous as the rest."

Csorwe was grateful, at last, to have a question she could really answer. "The refuelling station at the Peacock Gate. A friend of mine from back in the day runs a shop there, selling charts. If the Lignite Spire is a real place, she'll have the map. It's two Gates away, so you'll probably want to get some sleep."

*

The night was still. The barge's engine hummed, a thin icy wind made Csorwe grateful for her winter coat and gloves, and Shuthmili breathed softly in her sleep. There was no other sound.

Once their course was set for the nearest Gate, she allowed herself to look back at Shuthmili, and let the terrible new realisation that she'd felt earlier settle over her like a thin snowfall.

The Gate was visible from miles off, casting its light across a network of frozen rivers. They passed into the Maze, where a golden false dawn bloomed, and Csorwe narrowed her eyes against the light.

Shuthmili was the most beautiful and interesting person she had ever met. That didn't mean she needed to do anything with this information—not yet, or ever. It was just something nice to hide away and think about from time to time.

For now there wasn't anything to do but keep moving. She didn't have time to reckon with this along with the rest— Sethennai doubting his faith in her, the Unspoken One still clawing its way after her out of the past—and Shuthmili seemed to have plenty going on too. Gods knew they were both going to need their wits about them for this next part.

She hadn't lied to Shuthmili about the Peacock Gate. There *was* a refuelling station. A woman who lived there really did sell rare charts of the Maze—charts with a reputation for accuracy, no less—and Csorwe really had known her, back in the day.

Calling Big Morga a friend was a bit of a stretch, though.

Last time Csorwe had seen Morga, she'd cut Csorwe's face open and thrown her into the snake pit. Once Olthaaros was out of the way, Morga and Sethennai had struck a deal, in which he would give her a huge amount of money and she would go away forever, just in case anyone decided to start making trouble about the counter-usurpation.

Well, she'd decide how to handle that particular awkwardness when they got there.

The hours wore on. Shuthmili stayed fast asleep. At first Csorwe planned how she'd convince Morga to give them the map. Then she just daydreamed about the possibility of getting a hot meal at the station. She had a deep weakness for station food, even the seaweed candies they kept in suspicious vats.

They were already so far from the House of Silence, and its chill had faded. That place had nothing to do with who she was anymore. This was her real life: the boat, the wind, the lonely inner reaches of the Maze, and a certain quarry to chase.

Three white canopies moved under an arch of ancient stone, like seabirds returning. The shadow of the mazeship *Ejarwa* rippled across the blanket of fog below as she passed.

Ushmai was at the wheel. Oranna stood on the ship's viewing deck. The air of this world was chilly and full of dust. It tasted like salt on the tongue.

She should really have been used to the cold by now, but she kept thinking about her library, back in the House of Silence. That had been the last time she had really been warm.

Mortification of the flesh is an offering to the divine, adding salt to the meat of sacrifice. It sharpens a practitioner's ability. Oranna had no desire to sew up her lips or put out her eyes, but she was far from the Shrine of the Unspoken and she needed to squeeze out as much power as she could. Constant, low-grade cold and hunger seemed to be doing it so far.

It helped that they had run out of money a month earlier, shortly before they travelled to the Hollow Monument. Oranna tended naturally toward a pleasant roundness, but in recent weeks her cheeks had hollowed as their supplies had run low. The last of the House of Silence candlesticks had gone to fuel for *Ejarwa*, and that was almost all used up. The last of the lay-brothers was dead, sacrificed in the Maze to fuel Oranna's navigation spell. She was burning through the dregs. Only Ushmai was left, and even she would find her ultimate use in time.

Everything was rushing toward its end. The only solid object was the Reliquary, safely tucked into an inner pocket of her robe. Its hard edge bumped against her thigh whenever she moved.

The rush of the end wasn't as exhilarating as Oranna had hoped. She was exhausted in body and soul. There was no joy in her work anymore, and no spark of dark elation when the Unspoken answered her call. There was just more to do, and more danger to guard against.

It would be worth it, she told herself. She had spent such long years in the House of Silence, cold, bored, and deprived of any worthwhile company. She knew how to bear the hard slog. Belthandros' visit had provided the spark that she needed—a taste of the bright world outside—and since then she had gone so far beyond what he'd been prepared to teach her.

The mage's death lies always just ahead of her, as if she stands with the sun behind her and looks upon her shadow. Another principle she had learned in the House of Silence, where they were always so keen on your acquiescence to death, and so fearful of any challenge. When the Unspoken One accepted her as its incarna-tion, she would no longer know weariness or weakness or doubt. She would have its power and its knowledge, and she would have life. So many years of life. A whole future, to write and rewrite the world.

Early on, she had thought of taking back the House of Silence—making her library whole, teaching Cweren the consequences of usurpation, and turning the place she had hated for so long into her own fortress—but it was almost beneath her now. If she was going to build a citadel for the Unspoken, there were other places. She had heard, for instance, that Belthandros Sethennai had a city that was dear to him, and it might be amusing to make him give it up.

At last, they rounded a corner, and she saw the tower. It bit the fog like a single jagged tooth, cutting with its serrated edges into the sky itself. It was a broken bone, a shattered spur, a claw.

It was real. The earthly mansion of Iriskavaal had survived. It was within her grasp. Everything she had worked for, everything she had suffered and struggled and killed for. The Lignite Spire was still standing, and it held the key to the Reliquary.

Oranna clung to the rail and laughed. The wind carried the sound away.

"Ushmai," she called. "Take her in. We're here."

17

Young Blood

THE PEACOCK GATE WAS set high up on the flank of a canyon. Every now and then the Gate flashed as a vessel passed through, sometimes a bitten-off rhythm of flickers as an entire convoy arrived.

The station had begun as the hulk of a single merchant tanker, colossal and derelict, anchored to the rock just below the Gate by great chains to serve as a place for the trade ships to refuel.

Since then it had grown and grown again. Broken ships from a hundred different worlds had been tethered to it in tiers, laced with covered walkways and pontoons, canopies and bridges and floating outposts, so that now the whole place looked less like a flotilla and more like a single monstrous organism, a tumour of maze-oak and canvas. Out of this chaos it had become something more than a refuelling station and more than a trading post: a floating town, a home to hundreds of people.

The lower part of the station was porcupined with mooring-trees, where hundreds of newer ships floated at anchor. Csorwe took the barge in cautiously, navigating through the cloud of small cutters, barges, and shuttles that buzzed around the station. Shuthmili watched over the side, chewing her nails.

It was difficult to pick out individual ships from the mass, but as they approached, Csorwe saw for the first time: the Qarsazhi frigate *Reflection in Tranquillity* was here, battened on to one side of the station like a gigantic flea.

"Shit," she said, dread rising in her like sickness. The brief sense of purpose and freedom she had experienced out in the Maze drained away. "Your aunt's here already."

The Peacock Gate was one of the busiest in the Maze. She should have anticipated this. Almost everyone had to pass through it eventually. That was the whole reason Morga had set up her shop here, but it also meant that if you were hunting a fugitive you could do worse than waiting and watching at the station.

Shuthmili worried at the corner of her nail and shoved her hands into her pockets. "How many people are there on the station?"

"Maybe a thousand," said Csorwe, her eyes still fixed on *Tranquillity* as if she could will it into nothingness. "Hard to say. Lots coming and going all the time."

"Do you think we can do this? I mean, if we try to sneak in and get to your friend without being spotted? In your professional opinion?"

Despite the cold fear in her belly, Csorwe grinned. She enjoyed the idea of having a professional opinion.

"We can do it," she said. "Station security is pretty territorial. They won't be any friendlier to your aunt and her people than we are. And I know some back ways around the station. But I can't ask you to risk it, if you're not sure."

"No," said Shuthmili, "I'm sure. We've come this far. And it can't be much worse than the revenants."

"Let's hope," said Csorwe, noticing with some pride how much bolder Shuthmili seemed now than even a few days ago. She thought of the first time she'd struck out on her own, back in Grey Hook, and wondered whether Sethennai had noticed it. Had he felt a similar sort of pride? She hadn't seen it at the time if he had, but then, it would have been the least of the things she hadn't realised about him.

The shuttle barge they were flying was conspicuously Qarsazhi, so Csorwe landed it out of sight and stashed it in a crevice of the rock. Then they joined the rest of the foot passengers on their way up to the station.

The Inquisitors would be looking for two women, one Oshaaru and one Qarsazhi. They were much too obvious. Shuthmili was wearing Csorwe's coat over her nightshirt, which was less recognisable than her Adepts' robes but still odd-looking. Possibly they could buy some new clothes once they reached the station. It would be good to buy food, too, and other supplies. Csorwe had itemised her possessions, and all she had left was a stack of dry flatbreads, a half-charged alchemical lantern, and a handful of rude notes from Tal Charossa.

All the same, she thought their best bet was to get in and out as quickly as possible. She put her dream of a hot meal aside for now. If all went well, perhaps they could go shopping after they got the map.

Behind the relative order of its security barriers, refuelling bays, and public gangways, the station was an organised shambles: broken-down ships stacked on top of each other in loose tiers, chaotic but more or less stable. The air was hot and thick. The smell varied from tier to tier, but was always bad. Latrines, algal vats, dirty laundry, and fermented anchovies. Csorwe had visited the station many times on business for Sethennai, but it was still difficult to find the way.

The noise and chaos hit Shuthmili hard. As they were buffeted by the crowds, her eyes became ever wider and glassier. Csorwe remembered the early days in Grey Hook all over again.

"So, look, we don't have enough money to afford the map," said Csorwe, taking her arm firmly to distract her. "Morga knows she can charge. Especially if she figures out how badly we need it. But I have an idea of how we can convince her."

"I thought you said she was a friend of yours," said Shuthmili.

"Well," said Csorwe. "The last time I saw her she tried to kill me. But it wasn't anything personal."

Shuthmili nodded, slowly, staring as if nothing could surprise her any more.

"Don't worry. People try to kill me all the time," said Csorwe. Putting on a little bravado for Shuthmili's benefit had the advantage of making her feel slightly better.

Then she realised Shuthmili wasn't staring at her, but at something in the crowd of people behind her.

"Don't look," said Shuthmili in a choked whisper. "Don't draw attention."

Csorwe nodded and pretended to keep talking, steering Shuthmili toward a nearby market stall to give them some cover. When she got a chance she half turned her head and caught a glimpse of a person all in white, with a black visor and a white veil completely covering their head, and a thin sash of blue braid.

"One of the Vigils," said Csorwe. When she'd seen them on the ship they hadn't seemed so very frightening, but the ghostly way the pale figure drifted through the crowd chilled her blood.

"Yes," said Shuthmili in a whisper, knotting her hands

together. "Vigil Quincury is the Inquisitorate's bloodhound. I should have known they'd send it after us—"

She stopped talking abruptly and shrank back behind the market stall, behind Csorwe. It was almost an involuntary movement, like shutting your eyes against the sun.

Two Qarsazhi soldiers were coming across the market toward the Vigil Adept. Csorwe drew back into the shadows after Shuthmili, shielding her from their sight, and crouched down behind a stack of boxes. She couldn't have drawn breath if she had wanted to.

The two soldiers and the Adept exchanged a few inaudible words, then left together. The crowds parted for them and they went on down the corridor without even looking in Csorwe and Shuthmili's direction.

Shuthmili was still crumpled behind the boxes.

"Are you all right?" said Csorwe, inadequately. Now that the immediate danger was gone, her own fear returned with a vengeance. They were virtually defenceless, crouching in the bowels of a remote station, surrounded by enemies and far from any help. Shuthmili didn't respond, and for a second Csorwe just wanted to run, anywhere, even if it took her into the path of danger—anything was better than waiting to be found.

Then Shuthmili got up, brushing discarded wrappers out of her skirts.

"Yes," she said. She set her jaw. "I'm fine. I'm not panicking. We can do this."

"Do you recognise those soldiers?"

"Not their faces. They're Wardens from *Tranquillity*," she said.

"Shit. All right," said Csorwe. She peered out into the trunk gangway, but it was deserted. "We just have to get as far as Morga's shop. You're still all right with the plan?"

Shuthmili paced the width of the tunnel, like a tiger in a cage measuring the span of its captivity. "I don't have a lot of experience with this kind of work," she said. "For most of my life the most exciting thing that ever happened was when we heard they might be planning to serve a different kind of coffee at breakfast. But if I can't even *try* then I should just go back to my aunt and turn myself in."

Morga's shop was only ten minutes' walk away under ordinary circumstances, but the Wardens were everywhere, red-jacketed like biting ants. They must have been doing a full sweep of the tier. Csorwe and Shuthmili had to dodge painstakingly from passage to vent until they reached their destination.

Morga's shop was set up in the stern of an ancient Oshaarun warship, bitten in half in some forgotten conflict and now bolted to the very edge of the station's armature. Csorwe couldn't imagine how big the warship had once been. It dwarfed the little yacht moored to its side. The only way to reach the entrance was by a rope bridge strung across empty space, which swung like a pendulum, some thousand feet above the canyon floor.

"Morga certainly looks eager to welcome new customers," said Shuthmili, with a nervous little laugh. Csorwe's heart swelled with some kind of painful new emotion at the prospect that something might happen to Shuthmili, and the knowledge that she wouldn't ever be able to forgive herself for it.

The bridge swayed unpleasantly when Csorwe stepped onto it. As she neared the middle, the wind from the canyon blew her back and forth, like a spider hanging from a single thread.

But she reached the other side without difficulty and Shuthmili followed after her.

On the other side of the rope bridge was a flight of steps, leading up to a door cut into the hull of the warship. Beyond the door was a narrow wooden gangway, but here any resemblance to a ship ended. The gangway gave on to many windowless rooms, each one lined with pigeonholes, and each pigeonhole was stuffed with rolls and books and bundles of paper. The only light filtered in from the door, and the whole edifice was filled with the sound of creaking timbers and papers rustling slightly in the breeze.

"I suppose you don't think we can just find the map and go?" said Shuthmili, peering at the index labels on the nearest pigeonhole.

Csorwe shook her head. "She won't keep anything valuable here—wait. Shh."

Csorwe stood stock-still, wondering if she'd misheard. Perhaps she was now so tense she was imagining things. But no—that was a voice. Sound always carried strangely on board a station. It was the voice of Big Morga, echoing down from above.

"Yup, I heard you," Morga was saying, in Qarsazhi. It would have sounded like a friendly business-as-usual drawl, if you didn't know that in a previous life Morga's business had been efficient killing. "Heard that part too, and you already know I don't give a pint of piss about your Imperial Mandate. I haven't seen your fugitives."

A pause.

"Yeah, yeah, I heard. Inquisitor Ballbag's orders. Don't know anything, sorry. 'Fraid you're going to have to get out of my shop. There we go. That's it. Turn around, and out you go. Good boy."

Floorboards groaned overhead. Csorwe pulled Shuthmili hastily into the farthest corner of one of the archive rooms as a Qarsazhi officer came down the stairs, doing his best to exit with dignity.

"Slimy little fuck," Morga muttered, in her own language, and they heard the clink of a bottle on the edge of a glass.

When Csorwe dared to look, she saw the officer's back, receding across the rope bridge. She stepped back out onto the gangway, beckoning Shuthmili after her. At the far end of the gangway was another flight of steps, leading up to the deck above.

"Ready?" she said.

"Let's go," said Shuthmili.

Csorwe strode up the stairs and opened the door to Morga's study.

This had once been the captain's stateroom, but it too had been lined with shelves and pigeonholes and stacks of paper in every corner, like an attic gradually filling with wasps' nests. Sitting at a desk in the middle of the room was Big Morga. By now, she must have been at least sixty, but she was ageing like a glacier: grander with each passing year, and capable of carving through solid rock.

"Good evening, ma'am," said Csorwe, coasting along on a heady mix of sleeplessness and desperation. She was covered in a thin layer of sweat and smelled like a midden. She might've hoped her natural charm would carry the day, if she'd had any natural charm.

Morga sipped her whisky and observed the two of them at

her leisure. "Evening," she said, eventually. "So. You'll be the fugitives, then."

Csorwe nodded.

"You know, if there's one thing I hate, it's *comedy*," said Morga. "If either of you is a boy in a wig or hiding a parlourmaid under your skirts or any of that bollocks, just let me know now so I can show you the quickest way to the bottom of the canyon. Can't stand it."

Morga gestured to the enormous gallery window. Beyond it, the canyon yawned, swallowing ships like a whale sieving krill. It would be a very long way down. Csorwe swallowed. If ever she had possessed a grain of Talasseres' daring, she needed it now.

"No, ma'am," said Csorwe. "We need your help."

Morga propped her chin on one hand and observed them with the boredom of a crocodile. She didn't show any sign of recognising or remembering Csorwe, but then, that didn't mean anything either way.

"We need a map. We're looking for the Lignite Spire," said Csorwe.

"Mm," said Morga. "And the Qarsazhi are looking for *you* because you've stolen one of their war-mages. That'll be you, hmm?"

"Yes," said Shuthmili. Her gaze was fixed on the wall, as though looking straight through its substance to the outer void of the Maze. Shuthmili's character, as part of the plan they'd discussed, was the high-eldritch fallen sorcerer who tended to star in the same type of drama as the stock Inquisitor. She had pulled up her hood, and her fingers were laced together over her sternum.

Morga saw nothing to interest her, and her attention flicked back to Csorwe.

"So what you're telling me is that all Morga needs to do is hand you two over to the nice man in the pretty red uniform, and he'll take his soldiers and bugger off? And, you know, bit of a reward for my trouble? You must have something pretty compelling up your sleeve, friend, because that's exactly what I'm going to do if you don't."

Csorwe licked her lips. *Just stick to the plan.*

"Shuthmili's a mage," said Csorwe. "She could be useful to you."

"I don't like mages," said Morga.

"You don't like them when they're not on your payroll, ma'am," said Csorwe.

Morga smiled. Most Oshaaru wore caps on their tusks, or scrimshawed them with patterns. Big Morga's were as bare as knives, and one was chipped.

"What can you do, then, sweetheart?"

All right. Showtime.

"You got a blade?" Csorwe said, wriggling out of her jacket. She had at least three knives on her already, but whipping out a concealed weapon in front of Morga would be an efficient method of suicide.

Morga raised an eyebrow and pushed a small knife across the desk. Csorwe tested the blade on her thumb, as though inspecting it for purchase. It wasn't really more than a letter opener. This wasn't going to be fun. Unfortunately, there was no room here to stall for time. It needed to be abrupt and startling or there was no point doing it at all.

She bit down on the inside of her lip to stop herself screwing up her face, and in one quick, vicious movement, drove the blade into the soft part of her left forearm.

The black blood ran in streams into the crook of her elbow. She watched it drip onto the surface of the desk. The floorboards shrieked as Morga threw back her chair and leapt to her feet. The pain was bad but distant. In many ways the anticipation had been worse.

Csorwe pulled out the knife, saw a sliver of wax-white fat before the blood welled over, and as she did, everything faded to background noise—the plan, the map, Shuthmili—and all she could see was Morga holding up her broken body, over the table in Psamag's hall. She could feel Morga's hands, one in her hair, one under her arm, showing round her mutilated face for the lieutenants to see.

She blinked hard, again and again, as though the blood was running in her eyes. The room came drunkenly in and out of focus. This was it—she had made a terrible mistake, her arm was useless, Sethennai didn't know where she was, and nobody was coming to get her. The bloody knife slipped from her nerveless hand.

Then there was that stirring bone-deep warmth again. Shuthmili remembered the plan. Csorwe should never have doubted. She had Csorwe's arm firmly in both hands; her expression was utterly focused, dizzyingly lucid. The cut was narrow but deep. The blood dripping on the desk looked like ink. Csorwe shivered, and Shuthmili glanced up at her. As she broke concentration, Csorwe felt another stab of pain, like a shard of glass working free from her arm.

"Don't look at your arm," said Shuthmili. "Look at me."

Csorwe swallowed. It was worse to be given permission to look. Without the pain she had nothing to distract her from all *this*. Shuthmili's lower lip, caught between her teeth. Her black eyes, narrow with focus. Maybe it wasn't too late to stab herself again.

At last Shuthmili released her hold and sat back in her own seat, swaying. Csorwe's arm was whole again, wiping clean the events of the past two minutes.

"You all right?" said Csorwe.

Shuthmili pinched her nose and straightened up. She was breaking character a little, but Csorwe couldn't fault her for anything. "Mm. That was easy. You're surprisingly cooperative."

"So I'm told," said Csorwe weakly.

"Do not pull a stunt like that with me again, thanks," said Morga. She grabbed Csorwe's forearm in one enormous hand and pulled it back and forth, prodding the skin with a sharp nail as if checking for possible tricks.

At last she grunted and let it go. "Your mage is not a total charlatan, I'll grant. So, let's bargain. What was it you wanted, again?"

Csorwe wanted a glass of water and to be left alone for one goddamn minute, but there it was.

The whole study was lined with shelves, most filled with loose papers and folders. They must have been indexed according to some scheme. It only took Morga a minute or two to find what she was looking for: a leather scroll case, battered and perished as though it had been lost at sea. She opened it without care, shedding flakes of leather like dandruff. Inside was a roll of thin, crumpled paper. Morga slid it out onto the desk and unrolled it with the side of her pen.

It was a chart of the Maze. Parts were familiar: the Gates of the Greater Tlaanthothe-Kasmansitr nexus, linked like a huge constellation. A dashed line indicated a road by land; a solid line meant a viable route through the Maze, although what was meant by *viable* might depend on how much the owner of the ship cared for his crew.

Csorwe peered at it, trying to make sense of what it was saying, and whether it could possibly be legitimate. The Great Gates were ringed: *Free City of Grey Hook, University of Tlaan-thothe,* and all the rest. There was the Peacock Gate, on the outer rim of the nexus, just underneath the arrow labelled *To the wilds of Oshaar* in spidery Qarsazhi calligraphy.

There were other lines, needle-thin, reaching away in great arcs to the inner and outer Qarsazhi provinces, to Tarasen, Salqanya, and—Morga traced one branching line to the other side of the chart and tapped it with her forefinger—*Domain of the Lignite Spire.*

"That's your road," she said.

"This is an antique," said Csorwe.

Morga's lips curved up in a smile of great condescension. "You're the one that wants a way into a dead zone. Guess you'll have to hope the Maze doesn't change on you."

Csorwe passed the map over to Shuthmili. "You know about . . . old things. Is this legit?"

Shuthmili turned it over and inspected the lettering minutely. At one point she sniffed the paper, wrinkling her long nose. "May I see the case?" she said.

Morga chucked it across the table. "Don't see what good it'll do you. The case is just what it came in. Wouldn't lick it if I were you." She shrugged and turned back to Csorwe. "It's legit. You think I could do business if my charts weren't good?"

"Stranger things have happened," said Csorwe. "But if Shuthmili thinks it's good, we'll take it."

"Good for you," said Morga. "What are you offering me? What have *you* got that's better than Qarsazhi gold? And don't give me another load of arse about healing. I'm an old woman. I'm out of the business. I don't need anyone to mop my forehead."

"Do you remember," said Csorwe, "what General Psamag used to say, about the certain things in life?"

Morga's eyes narrowed. "Remind me."

"No man can escape the death that's set down for him," said Csorwe. "Yes?"

"Yes," said Morga, giving her a sharp look. The wheels were turning very quickly. Csorwe reckoned they didn't have much time, and gave Shuthmili the signal.

"How old are you, Morga?" said Shuthmili. Csorwe had coached her on this as they climbed up through the tunnels.

Morga gave a throaty splutter of laughter. "Older than you, sunshine."

The next line was the same, whatever Morga said: "I can give you ten years." Shuthmili was really very good at this. She stared into the middle distance as though the void was revealing its horrors to her even now.

"You threatening me?" said Morga, leaning toward them. She was one of the few people who could loom while sitting down.

"No," said Shuthmili. "In the old country they called you Morga the General, didn't they? You spent too long in service to a lesser man. Your heart slows in your chest. Your bones are brittle. The time that Psamag took from you is gone. I can return to you ten years of life, to live again on your own terms."

Morga didn't immediately laugh. She sat back in her chair and folded her hands. "Really."

"The Emperors of Qarsazh live beyond the span of mortal man," said Shuthmili. "Surely you know this?"

This could even have been true, for all Csorwe knew about the Emperors of Qarsazh.

"And you want me to believe that's because they've got sorcerers pumping them full of young blood when they start drying up?"

Shuthmili smiled an impeccable smile: aloof, superior, infused with sinister glee. "Yes, quite so," she murmured. Csorwe tried not to think about kissing her.

"No wonder they're itching to get you back," said Morga. "How long's it take?"

Shuthmili laced her hands together and stretched. "We may begin whenever you choose. Though you may wish to go somewhere more private."

"What's the risk?" said Morga.

"As with any complex spellwork, the risk to the practitioner is significant," said Shuthmili. This part certainly had the ring of truth. "But the process has been refined over the centuries. The greatest risk for you is that it simply does not work."

Which was the crux of it. As Shuthmili had made very clear, she couldn't actually rejuvenate anybody. ("Time damages the body like nothing else. The best I can do is tighten up the skin, give the cardiovascular system a bit of a sluicing, repair a little wear-and-tear on the joints. She'll *feel* better, so I imagine it should be fairly convincing.")

This wasn't even nearly the most ill-founded and dangerous plan Csorwe had ever been involved with. All things considered, it should have worked.

It *was* working.

Their demonstration had gone off perfectly, and she had been right about Big Morga. The old mercenary couldn't resist the temptation to dance on Psamag's grave for another ten years. If ambition wouldn't do it, spite would. Morga was just deciding when it would be seemly to agree, and whether she could squeeze any more out of them.

Morga stood up and paced the length of the room, turning the scroll case over and over in her hands. Every now and then she stopped to run a huge flat thumb over the seam. "Well," she said, at last. "I still think it's a load of crap. But I suppose we can come to some kind of—"

This was the point at which—with the inevitability of a dropped brick—something ran at high speed into the gallery window and annihilated itself in a cloud of shattered glass.

Csorwe pushed Shuthmili behind Morga's desk. Morga leapt in the opposite direction, moving with startling speed and grace. A stray timber hit Csorwe, sweeping her aside. She hit a wall and fell.

In the moments of screaming disorder that followed, Csorwe lay half stunned on the ground, and Shuthmili tried to drag her into the lee of the desk.

The window was gone. The room yawned, open to the howling wind. Morga's papers whipped through the air like startled game birds. The only thing that stood between them and thin air was the wreckage of a cutter, wedged crossgrain into the wreckage of the study.

Out of this disaster leapt a tall thin man, covered in shards and splinters. He had a knife in one hand, and in the other, a loaded crossbow. It was Talasseres Charossa.

A moment like this belonged to whoever was upright and could put one word in front of another.

"All right!" said Tal. "This isn't a Grey Hook whorehouse, don't just stand around with your mouth open. I want a map." He had the crossbow fixed firmly on Morga. Maybe he hadn't seen Csorwe and Shuthmili.

Morga pushed herself up, raised her eyebrow a hairsbreadth, and glanced around her office. "You got any particular one in mind?"

"The Lignite Spire," he said. "The Domain of the Lady of the Thousand Eyes."

Morga laughed, the deep, hollow laugh of a person who by now expects this kind of thing. "Well, shit me sideways," she said eventually. "It's Talasseres."

"Funny," said Tal, levelling the crossbow. "Have we met? I don't remember."

"Maybe you were too busy polishing Psamag's boots, but— oh, put that thing down. If you shoot me you're not getting your map, are you?"

Morga was still holding the leather scroll case that contained the map. Csorwe slunk down behind the desk next to Shuthmili.

"What now?" Shuthmili mouthed.

Csorwe grimaced. It was only a matter of time before the rest of the station realised what had happened. Already there was noise outside. Even over the wind she could hear people shouting on the other side of the rope bridge.

They could wait it out. If they had infinite time and nobody on their tail, they could follow Tal and get back the map. But there was no time. The Wardens were catching up to them.

"Forget it," she said. "We have to get out of here."

There had been a slim chance, and now there was no chance at all. They could cry about it later. All they could do now was get out alive.

"So, Talasseres," Morga was saying, quite calmly. "I *sell* maps. So I'm pretty sure you must be here to *buy* this map, because nobody would be thick enough to come here and try to *rob* me."

There was no way to the door without being seen. Csorwe waited for Morga to reach a natural break in her monologue, then stood up, holding up her empty hands to prove she was unarmed. Tal spotted her immediately. He had begun to look less certain of his plan, but at the sight of Csorwe and Shuthmili, delight broke upon his face like a sunbeam.

"Oh, perfect," he said. "I bet you were so close, as well."

Morga looked from one of them to the other, an ugly suspicion forming, almost visible in the air. Still, with Tal's crossbow trained on her, there wasn't much she could do.

The scroll case was right there in Morga's hands. The universe seemed to take a special delight in letting Csorwe get *so* close but no further.

"We're going," said Shuthmili. She sounded about as tired as Csorwe felt. "We don't want any trouble." They sidled toward the door. Tal, unwilling to take his eyes off Morga, let them go.

The door opened with perfect timing, like those on a cuckoo clock, revealing an outraged Inquisitor Tsaldu.

Behind her, Csorwe heard Tal say, "Oh, fuck this," and the sound of a crossbow firing. She didn't look back. Instead, she lowered her shoulders and charged the Inquisitor. He hadn't expected to find them here. He hadn't expected to be attacked on sight, and he certainly hadn't expected a headbutt in the stomach. Csorwe threw him back down the stairs and pulled

Shuthmili down after her into the gangway, stepping over Tsaldu's crumpled body.

Shuthmili glanced back. "Is he——?"

"Doesn't matter," said Csorwe. "Probably fine. Keep moving!"

She had hoped the rope bridge would be clear, but as they reached the outer door she saw they hadn't been that lucky.

There were already six Qarsazhi Wardens on the bridge.

Csorwe reached for her sword and stepped out to face them. If she could fight some of them off she might give Shuthmili a few extra minutes——

"Csorwe, look!" said Shuthmili breathlessly, grabbing her arm.

Morga's yacht was anchored to the hull of the broken warship, below and slightly to one side of the bridge. The Wardens had seen them, and now they were running. It would be over in a matter of seconds.

"Go!" said Csorwe.

Without hesitation, Shuthmili climbed up on the rail and threw herself into the yacht. It was close enough that Csorwe could have made the jump without thinking about it, but her heart was in her mouth as she watched Shuthmili land in the cockpit.

"Stop!" barked one of the Wardens, but Csorwe was already in the air.

She hit the deck of the yacht with an impact that jarred her bones in their sockets and forced the air from her lungs. As soon as she could draw breath, she scrambled up and into the pilot's chair. The Wardens were almost level with them now, sizing up the jump.

Csorwe thanked the Unspoken that the controls were

configured in a style she recognised. She pulled the lever to release the mooring and gunned the engines.

The yacht shuddered as it pulled away. For a horrible moment Csorwe thought maybe it wasn't skyworthy after all, and the damn thing was about to shake itself to pieces. Then it lifted up and away, and swooped out into the free air. Nothing now could stop them reaching the Gate. They had failed, but they were alive.

Beyond the Peacock Gate, Csorwe took the yacht through a series of quick little Gate-jumps, Maze to world to Maze, like a row of running stitches. If the Qarsazhi could track them through that, they deserved to be found.

Their last Gate was tiny, almost defunct, scarcely big enough for the yacht to pass through. They came out into a region of the Maze even less familiar than most: a huge still lake, entirely surrounded by cliffs. It was like being at the bottom of a gigantic well. The surface of the lake was silvery-dark and cloaked with a fine mist that parted behind the ship like a wake. The other Gate was on the other side of the lake, a slow and easy voyage.

Csorwe sat back in her seat and let herself take a deep breath. Her heart gradually stopped racing. Once her body calmed down enough to let her feel anything, she felt empty.

She had no idea what they were going to do. They were out of money. The Qarsazhi had found them once, and they would eventually find them again. The yacht was horribly recognisable and plenty of Wardens had seen them go. She didn't see how they were even going to survive until the next day, let alone pursue Oranna. Every plan she could think of came with a *but then* or an *unless,* and she couldn't think straight enough to work through them.

Shuthmili knocked on the doorframe and climbed down into the cockpit.

"Csorwe, I don't mean to interrupt you, but when was the last time you slept?"

She couldn't honestly remember. The idea of pawing through cupboards for sheets was the most tiring thing she could imagine. It would be easier to stay awake forever.

"Hmm," said Shuthmili. "I've been exploring the ship. Based on some of the things in the lockers, I don't think I would have enjoyed Morga's parties. But I did find bunks and bedclothes. Anyway, we're passing over a little archipelago. Do you think we might moor the ship and get some rest?"

Csorwe nodded and began to take the ship down. "It's just a shame," she mumbled.

Shuthmili looked at her with some concern.

"About the map. That we didn't get it. I'm sorry," said Csorwe.

"Oh!" said Shuthmili. Not surprised but delighted, as though someone had given her an unexpected present. "But—oh—" She scrambled up into the co-pilot's seat and began rifling through her coat pockets. "I thought you'd realised. We did get it."

She pulled out a single roll of paper. It was crumpled into the shape of a battered cigar, but it was intact.

Csorwe stared at it. These things simply did not happen. She unrolled it and flattened it out, refusing to believe it. *"How?"*

"I didn't think Morga would go for our offer," said Shuthmili. "I found an old paper in your coat pocket. When she let me look at the map I just swapped them."

"God alive," said Csorwe. "If she'd opened the case . . ."

"I know," said Shuthmili. "I thought I'd better take the risk."

"You're a lunatic," said Csorwe, with immense pride.

Shuthmili looked down at the map and smiled. The collar of her coat was hanging open, exposing a two-inch triangle of bare skin at the hollow of her neck. Csorwe let herself imagine how soft it might be for one full second before telling herself to stop noticing these things.

She landed the yacht on one of the islands, increasingly worried that Shuthmili would insist on going to the trouble of making up bunks. When she left the cockpit, though, she found that Shuthmili had dragged all the pillows she could find into one cabin and laid them out on the floor. She was already sprawled across the pile in her shift.

Under other circumstances Csorwe might have had some kind of reaction to the sight of Shuthmili's bare legs, but as it was she was so tired she could scarcely stay upright.

Shuthmili clearly had no concerns about sleeping next to Csorwe. Still . . . things had changed since their escape from the Precursor world. She didn't want Shuthmili to suspect anything, and she didn't want to torment herself. She wasn't going to be like Tal Charossa, always limping tragically after someone who wasn't interested. She curled up on the heap of pillows at a discreet distance and pulled a sheet over herself.

Just as she was dozing off, a stray thought pricked her awake.

"What old paper?" she said, but Shuthmili was already asleep.

Tal made it out of Morga's station in one piece. One bruised and exhausted piece, hiding in the cargo hold of the Qarsazhi frigate, between barrels of wine and sacks of rice. He was bleeding from a long cut above the eyebrow, and it was possible that Morga had broken his nose.

It didn't matter now. He was safely away, and he had the map. That was the only thing that mattered. This was what nobody understood about Tal. They could beat him down. They could humiliate him. But he was never going to stop, he was never going to give up, and in the end he was going to win.

He crawled in between the barrels until he found a place where he could sit down comfortably. He struck a light and perched on the edge of a crate. Only then did he crack open the leather scroll case. Inside was a flimsy sheet of paper. He unrolled it carefully, and recognised his own handwriting.

> *No hard feelings, you piece of shit.*
> *Tal Charossa*

Oranna took the Reliquary out of her pocket, turning it over in her hands. "I have contemplated taking a hammer to it," she remarked.

"Just to find out what's inside?" said Ushmai, blowing on her fingers to try and stay warm.

"It might be worth it," said Oranna.

They had been inside the Lignite Spire for some time now. It might have been hours or days. The place was a barefaced violation of geometry, and Oranna had spent so long trying to commune with the Unspoken One that she didn't have a very clear handle on space or time.

Her patron was not forthcoming. Oranna had burnt lotus three times a day, and taken a measure of agaric, although she never enjoyed its side effects. She had spent half a day quivering in the tower's antechamber with nothing to show for it but a troublingly sensual hallucination about the so-called Prioress Cweren. All that the Unspoken had to say on the matter was: *The Reliquary opens before the throne and earthly mansion of Iriskavaal.*

They had reached the tower, and the Reliquary failed to open. They had entered. They had searched. No luck.

She ran her fingertips over the lid of the Reliquary. It gleamed as though freshly polished. Belthandros' reaction would be something to see if she destroyed it. He had a good way of holding himself apart, as if he was a passing visitor in the world, amused by the locals but ultimately not *involved*. Frictionless. The mistake people made was trying to stick to him. A burr, after all, is something you brush off your coat. Breaking the Reliquary would certainly get his attention, if she decided his attention was something that interested her.

She was immediately ashamed of herself for thinking it. Her lips thinned. Destroying a source of power she could use herself, purely to spite Belthandros? Unworthy. No better than the priestesses back at the House of Silence, who had nothing to do but feud and fixate and squabble. She had enjoyed Belthandros' company and correspondence for a brief time, but he was, in essence, irrelevant. She had more important things to do.

"The earthly mansion of the Unspoken is the Shrine in the mountainside," said Oranna. "And the throne lies within it, although we are not permitted to kneel before it . . . this world is all that remains of Old Ormary. The Lignite Spire, where we now stand, was once the earthly mansion of Iriskavaal. But her throne was destroyed. It no longer exists, here or anywhere else. Surely it isn't possible that the Unspoken One was wrong?"

Ushmai gave her a look of wild terror, then realised that this had been a rhetorical question, and that she was not required to have an opinion.

"No," said Oranna. "The throne must be here, whatever that means. We are on the right track. We are being tested. It is a question, as always, of what we are prepared to give up."

18

A Machine for Prophecy

Q ANWA HAD BEEN STARING at her charts since she had
awoken that morning, trying to trace the fugitives' route
through the thick web of Gates around Peacock Station. She
had learned from plenty of mistakes over the course of a varied
career, enough to know that Peacock Station had been a minor
blip rather than an irrecoverable disaster—but it was nevertheless embarrassing.

Assuming she was intending to sell Shuthmili, where would
the Oshaaru woman take her, logically speaking? This was
another opportunity to solve order out of chaos. Once you had
all the information aligned correctly the solution would emerge
with glorious, self-evident clarity. She wanted to be left alone to
plan their next move.

Instead, here was Tsaldu, convinced he had something urgent
for her attention.

"By the Nine, Tsaldu, are you unable to deal with a stowaway
yourself?" she said. Tsaldu winced at the mild profanity.

"It's not quite that, Inquisitor Qanwa—" he said.

"This is what we have cells for," she said. "Detain him now
and put him off the ship when we next stop to refuel."

"Oh, come on!" said a voice from the corridor. Qanwa peered

out and saw a skinny Tlaanthothei boy in a torn shirt, with a Warden clinging to each arm to hold him back. He looked like the usual station dregs, out for what he could get. "Tell her what I told you!"

"Inquisitor Qanwa, he says he has information—" said Tsaldu.

Qanwa sighed. If Tsaldu had been as competent as he was fastidious, she would have liked him better. "Of course he does," she said. "And of course I have nothing better to listen to. Tsaldu, it is imperative that we retrieve my niece before she can be sold on—"

"I know where your wizard's gone," said the boy. "Let me go and I'll tell you."

"*Excuse me?*" said Qanwa.

"Your Adept, whatever," he said, making a token struggle. "Two plaits. Looks like a weasel that's just bitten into a nice refreshing lemon. I know where she's gone and if your fancy Imperial maze-charts are any good at all you'll be able to get to her."

The Gate flashed as the yacht passed through—tides of jade and gold rippled across its surface—and then a pulse of pure golden light washed over the hull, and they passed into the dead zone.

Morga's chart had been easy enough to follow, with Shuthmili at hand to decode the annotations. This was the last Gate marked on the map. They had found it in a forgotten valley of the Maze, far from the trade routes, far from any station, in the farthest reaches of the nexus.

The world turned in on itself, dissolving and reforming like wet clay. And then the Gate spat them out.

A shallow black basin lay under a shimmering half sky. It was just as Csorwe had seen in Echentyr, but worse. The sky split like the bud of an opening blossom, giving way to inverted mountains, upturned valleys, gigantic columns and arches of stone.

This was a world half swallowed by the Maze. In the basin before them, cracked obsidian stretched far into the distance, piled and shattered, like the vitrified ruin of a city. Haze swirled and banked as if moved by the wind, though the air was lifeless. Rising from the thicket of mists, still many miles away, was a coal-black tower, stark and static against the endless swirl of the sky.

Csorwe heard a distant shrill whooping cry, and saw a flight of something like birds take off from one high turret. They kicked off into the high air, moving in formation with a precision that was almost beautiful. The hairs on the back of her neck rose.

She brought the ship in to land near the Gate, and they disembarked.

"I've just looked through the lockers again, in case we'd missed anything useful," said Shuthmili. "But I don't suppose we'll have any use for chocolates or whisky."

"You never know," said Csorwe. "How are you doing? You ready for this?"

"I won't tell you I'm fine," said Shuthmili, "as it didn't seem to make any impression the first ten times. Also, it would be tempting the gods to punish me for my deceitfulness, because I'm terrified."

"Shuthmili—"

"I know what I'm doing," she said. "This was my choice. I'm not going to turn back. I like to finish things once I've started them. And if I wanted to be safe, I could have stayed."

She lifted her chin, resolute. Her hood was pulled up against the chill, so her face was haloed by a circle of soft fur trim, and the wind blew escaped strands of hair across her face. Csorwe felt a terrible rush of fondness. In other circumstances it could have been a gentle feeling, a quiet warmth, a desire to tuck the stray hairs back behind her ears, to touch the back of her neck—as it was, it gripped Csorwe's heart with the cold urgency of a threat.

"Maybe we should bring the whisky," she said.

It was a long walk across the plain to the base of the tower, exposed to the cold and to the gaze of anyone who might be watching. The ground was ruffled in places with faint waves, like ripples in sand frozen into the rock.

"Do you see that?" said Shuthmili, stopping to look at something on the ground: a feathery swirl the size of her palm, barely distinct from the rock itself. "It's a starfish. What a beautiful thing. I think we're at the bottom of the sea." She smiled to herself in private delight. *"Much is lost, but much lasts . . ."*

They needed to keep moving, but Csorwe couldn't bear to call her away from this. She looked so happy. This was something fear couldn't touch.

Csorwe remembered the night they'd met, the intensity of Shuthmili's focus on her work, the arcs the brush made in the air, the dark glitter of her eyes in the firelight, and wondered how it could have taken her so long to realise what she was feeling.

"Oh, it would really be something to document this place," said Shuthmili, straightening up. "But don't worry. I know we don't have time."

"It's all right," said Csorwe. "What does that mean? *Much is lost . . .*"

"It's from one of our philosophers," said Shuthmili. "About

whether it's worth trying to preserve the past, when all worlds eventually fall into decline."

"They used to talk about that in the House of Silence," said Csorwe. If it had been anybody else, she would have kept this to herself, but she found herself wanting Shuthmili to know her better. "We were just there to watch as everything slid away and got eaten up by the Maze. That was what the Unspoken One wanted. *Desolation is its watchword.* Think I like your version better."

"Well, our man also wrote a long book about how he didn't mind dying because the state of Qarsazh would prevail, so I think he was probably a bit weird," said Shuthmili.

Csorwe still couldn't help but regret leading Shuthmili into danger, but she had said it herself: this was her choice, and she had her own reasons. They could not predict what Oranna might do with the power of the Unspoken, or what the Unspoken might do once it acquired a mortal body, but Csorwe doubted anything so fragile as a dead language or an ancient sea creature would survive it.

"What happened, in the House of Silence?" said Shuthmili. "Why did you leave?"

Csorwe tensed, reaching instinctively for a way to brush off the question and sweep it into the far distance. Then again, she had never told anybody about it on her own terms before. Sethennai had explained her to Tal before she'd ever had a chance.

"You remember the little girl. Tsurai," she said. "That was me. I was her. The, uh—" She had to scrabble for the words in Qarsazhi; it was hard enough making herself explain without having to reach for vocabulary. "The—betrothed bride of the god. It's not as bad as it sounds."

"It does sound . . ." said Shuthmili.

"No, it was all right. I wasn't unhappy there. They treated me well." She didn't know why it seemed so important to make Shuthmili understand this. She hadn't been raised among monsters. That wasn't it. "They were all kind to me. Up until the last minute. I don't blame them. It would have been hard to do anything else, when they could just let it happen and let life go on."

"Yes," said Shuthmili. "I see."

"I mean, I just let it happen myself," said Csorwe. "I knew what was going to happen and I still went. I could have run away myself, and I never did. If Sethennai hadn't come for me, then—"

She swallowed and looked away, fixing her eyes on the grey horizon. It was very quiet. In the Maze proper, you had the sound of wind and water. Here there was nothing at all: no birds, no insects, only the crunch of their footsteps in the dust.

She told Shuthmili the whole story: she had been born in the same year the last Chosen Bride had been sent to the Shrine. She had been orphaned by plague as a baby. They had clothed and fed and educated her at the House of Silence, which was more than some plague-orphans could hope to get. After fourteen years she was to answer the summons of the Unspoken, and go up the mountain to the Shrine.

"And then . . . ?" said Shuthmili.

"And then I don't know," said Csorwe. "Nobody knew. It was my personal mystery to unravel, but we were all pretty clear that I was going to die. And in the end I never found out how it was supposed to happen, because Sethennai got me out at the last minute. I know this sounds bad, but it was just . . . ordinary."

"No, I know," said Shuthmili. She paused, biting her lip. "I lived at the School of Aptitude until last year, when I was assigned to Aritsa's research group. Nobody at the School was unkind or unpleasant. And it helped to have an ambition. That's what the Quincuriate was to me. I thought I understood what the tether would mean, and I thought I wouldn't mind it. So I do know. Truly."

"Yeah," said Csorwe. From anybody else she couldn't have tolerated this, but there was nothing about Shuthmili's expression that was mocking, nothing that suggested she was storing it up to use against her. Csorwe just hoped it hadn't changed Shuthmili's opinion of her. "That was how the world worked. I didn't know anything else."

She walked on, looking at her feet. Once you started seeing the feathery little starfish they were everywhere, scattered across the rippling stone as though the sea had only just retreated. "Do you wish I'd never said anything?" she said, quietly.

"What?" said Shuthmili.

"Do you wish I'd just let you go? So you'd be in Qarsazh now, getting tethered or whatever?"

"No," said Shuthmili. "It would be good to be safe, but I'm beginning to see now that I was never safe there, not really. I'm glad to be here." She paused, a flicker of shock in her eyes. "Do you mean you wish Sethennai had never come for you?"

Csorwe thought about it, then smiled despite herself. She was grateful to Shuthmili for saying it out loud so that she didn't have to, and now the thought was gone. "No. Of course not."

"Good," said Shuthmili. "I, too, am glad that you survived until adulthood. Travelling with you has been fun." She noted Csorwe's incredulous look, and smiled. "No, I mean it. Though

I'm beginning to worry that I may not be as sensible as I always thought I was. My suspicion is that I like you."

She gave Csorwe a curious look, not unlike the way she had looked at the starfish.

Csorwe's heart flapped like a moth trapped in a lantern. Shuthmili was clearly waiting for her to say something. By the time she remembered how to produce words, it was clear that she had paused too long and it would be better to pretend she'd never meant to say anything. She shoved her hands in her pockets, stared at the ground, and kept walking.

Idiot! she thought to herself. It shouldn't have been so hard. Not after she'd already gone on about the House of Silence.

Shuthmili started up again, in what Csorwe recognised as a heroic effort to break the silence. "What's it like, working for Belthandros Sethennai?" she said. She always called him by his full name, as if he were a figure of legend.

For once Csorwe was glad to make conversation, but this was almost as hard to answer as the proposition that Shuthmili liked her. She didn't know how to explain the last eight years. The work, the weariness, the isolation, and the way it was all made bearable when Sethennai seemed pleased with you.

"It's all right. I mean, it's pretty good. He's not bad to work for."

"Giving me the hard sell, as always," said Shuthmili. "Do you like him?"

Shuthmili seemed to think this, too, was something a reasonable person could answer.

"He's not the kind of person you can like or dislike," she said eventually. "We're not friends. He doesn't confide in me, or anyone. He's never expected me to tell him my secrets. But, you know. He didn't have to save my life. He didn't have to do anything for me. And he never wanted me to go on about how grateful I am either."

"I'm just trying to imagine what it'll be like to meet him properly, if we can pull this thing off," said Shuthmili. "If I'm going to be working for him."

"You'll like him," said Csorwe. "He's funny."

Sethennai had little tolerance for failure, and none for disobedience, but he believed in results. If she returned with the Reliquary, he would forgive her. At least, she had to hope so. And he would see how useful Shuthmili could be, how smart and how brave—they could work together . . .

She had been so focused on their immediate survival that she hadn't had much time to imagine what it would be like, if Shuthmili worked for Sethennai. It was almost painful to acknowledge what a difference it might make to have someone to talk to on the road who was friendlier than Tal.

"When you work for him we can travel together, if you'd want that," said Csorwe. "You could try all the bad station food. There's a lot, especially if you don't mind eating mealworms."

"My goodness," said Shuthmili. "No. In fact I think I insist upon it. A mealworm tour of the Echo Maze." She beamed. "How glamorous."

"And when we get back we can see Tlaanthothe properly," said Csorwe. It felt dangerous to speak this out loud. She had imagined a bright future in Tlaanthothe once before, and the city had disappointed her, so slowly that she'd scarcely noticed her hopes diminishing.

"It does have good parts," she went on. Showing Shuthmili

around would be different. "We could have dinner at Kethaalo's. And Sethennai's got a big library, you'll like that."

Csorwe waited for Shuthmili to say something, unable to look at her directly. It had been pleasant to imagine all these things in the quiet of her own head, but somehow the prospect that Shuthmili might actually be interested made them seem further away. She had always been so bad at this. She should have figured out how to deal with it when she was sixteen instead of learning how to kill people.

And then Shuthmili took Csorwe's hand in hers. Csorwe could feel the warmth of her skin even through the gloves. She squeezed Shuthmili's hand lightly and released it.

They went on in a curious silence. Without looking, Csorwe was very aware of Shuthmili's presence beside her: each footstep, the fluttering of her skirts in the wind, the way she chewed her lip when she was thinking . . . she wondered, for the first time, whether Shuthmili was thinking the same thing about her. It made her self-conscious, but not uncomfortably so, just very aware of all her limbs and the startling possibility that there was something to admire about them.

They didn't stop walking, and the tower on the horizon came closer. Too soon the ground began to slope upward, from dry seabed onto pebbly shore, and they came into the shadow of the tower. Though ruinous, the Spire was enormous; taller and broader even than the Gate-fortress in Tlaanthothe. On one face, turned slightly away from the seabed, was a doorway, fully thirty feet high. A broad flight of steps led up to the door, flanked on each side by statues on plinths.

Csorwe edged along the shoreline, trying to get a better look at the door. Some instinct told her to keep low. The light here was strange—misty, flickering with shadows—but it was too bright to rely on darkness for cover.

The still air shifted, and like a buoy moving with the tide, the shape of a mazeship drifted out from the side of the tower, several stories above.

"That's Oranna's ship," said Csorwe. Despite herself she had to stop and take a breath.

Shuthmili slipped her hand through the crook of Csorwe's elbow. Even through the many layers of shirt and jacket, the pressure was comforting.

"When she spoke to me, in the Hollow Monument," said Shuthmili, "I think I was more frightened than I'd ever been in my life. Obviously, my life's got a lot more exciting since then," she added, glancing up at Csorwe with a brief flash of amusement. "But she's just a person. At least for now."

"I hope so," said Csorwe. "But now she's here, she could get the Reliquary open. D'you think—"

Shuthmili bit her lip. "I don't know," she said, after a second's thought. "I would guess she'd need to return to the Shrine of the Unspoken before it could manifest in her—but—I really don't know. I'm breaking doctrine even imagining whether it would be possible."

Csorwe took another breath and shut her eyes. The air tasted faintly of salt, as though the memory of the lost sea lived on in the atmosphere.

"Well," said Shuthmili. "If we do meet the Unspoken One I wouldn't mind the opportunity to give it a piece of my mind."

She tightened her grip on Csorwe's arm, then released it, and they crept closer to the tower. The masonry had once been intricately carved, set with many niches, buttresses, balconies—now most of this detail had fallen or been eroded away, as though the tower had spent long years underwater. The statues on either side of the steps were shaped vaguely like people, but it was hard to tell what they had been; in most cases there was nothing left but a crumbling pillar or fragmentary torso.

The doorway they had seen was empty. There was nothing to stop them walking straight into the tower. Beyond the doorway, Csorwe glimpsed a passageway, which seemed to broaden into a larger hall. She glanced back at the broken landscape, thinking again how small they were, how exposed, and how little they knew about what they were getting into. Shuthmili followed her gaze.

It wasn't going to get any easier. There was no use hesitating. She stepped into the doorway.

The interior of the tower didn't bear any resemblance to the outside. Shuthmili started murmuring about lenition as soon as they entered.

There were colonnades, staircases winding upward, great galleries stacked upon galleries. Ornate scrolls of stone trailed in the air like pondweed. Sometimes it felt as though they were struggling through a submerged garden, sometimes as though they were navigating the slums and rooftops of a ruinous city. It was as though someone had killed a palace by stabbing it through with another palace.

Csorwe felt what she had sensed before, in the crypts of the House of Silence and the depths of the Hollow Monument. This was the place of something ancient and knowing, which tolerated their intrusion because they were insignificant.

What she couldn't spell out, and didn't want to admit anyway, was that the place was enticing. However cold and dark and bewildering, there was a terrible rightness about its angles. She had been born for places like this. There was something familiar, like a long-healed injury, about returning to the domain of an old god.

Tal had been pleased with himself at first. If you couldn't get to the Reliquary on your own two feet, there were worse ways to travel than going by Imperial warship.

He had actually enjoyed the first few days on the frigate. He should have recognised this for the bad sign that it was. Everyone on board *Tranquillity* hated each other, they had hated each other for a long time, and they were barely trying to hide it. Buttoned-up Qarsazhi resentment bubbled all around him, and he slipped blissfully into it, as if into a hot spring. The naval officers and crewmen who belonged to the ship loathed the Inquisitors. Inquisitor Qanwa disliked the ship people and plainly despised Inquisitor Tsaldu, who distrusted her in return.

The Adepts of Vigil Quincury were the only ones who didn't seem to hate anyone. Their silent omnipresence gave Tal the crawling shivers, which got worse once Inquisitor Qanwa gave orders that one of them was to follow Tal wherever he went. The way their soft slippers hushed after him made him want to scream.

After three days on board, Inquisitor Qanwa summoned him back to her stateroom. Four Vigil Adepts were standing before her desk along with a group of four Wardens. Tal's babysitter showed him into the cabin, then took its place beside them. Tal had the choice of making eye contact with Qanwa or looking at the Adepts. The Adepts were creepy, but whenever he looked at

Qanwa he had to bat away an unwelcome recollection of how General Psamag had looked whenever he'd had the opportunity to feed someone to the snake. All that bright mad enthusiasm.

"We are now one Gate away from the Domain of the Lignite Spire, which, according to the testimony of Mr. Charossa, is where we will find our missing Adept," said Inquisitor Qanwa, acknowledging Tal with a smile that made it clear there would be hell to pay if he had lied. Even knowing that he hadn't, it made Tal uneasy.

"One has to wonder what the fugitive intends to do with my niece in a place like this," said Qanwa. "Any ideas, Mr. Charossa?"

"No," said Tal. This part was a lie. He knew exactly why Csorwe was there, and he was prepared to bet that Shuthmili was with her by choice, but he didn't like Qanwa enough to want to help. He didn't give a damn whether they managed to retrieve her or not. All he wanted was the Reliquary. Then he could finally go home.

"I will be going down to the surface of the world myself to retrieve Shuthmili," said Qanwa. "Wardens, I'd like you to accompany me to the tower, along with Vigils One to Four. Vigil Five will remain on board *Tranquillity* to provide communications. Mr. Charossa, I understand you are eager to join the party."

That was putting it a bit strongly. Tal didn't want to spend any more time with any of them, but he could put up with it to get to the Reliquary, and if Qanwa's people could deal with Csorwe and Oranna and any other fucker who got in his way, so much the better.

"Sure," he said.

"Understand, Mr. Charossa, that I have recently had some

disappointing experiences with foreign passengers. If you hinder our operations in any way, I will not hesitate in ordering Vigil to stop you in whatever manner it thinks best."

Tal promised he would be a good boy, and this was how he found himself in the Domain of the Lignite Spire, surrounded by Qarsazhi who hated him as much as they hated each other.

Qanwa was about as friendly as Csorwe ever had been on this kind of expedition, which is to say that she ignored Tal completely and strode on ahead, with two Wardens and an Adept, taking readings from some kind of instrument and checking her map of the dry seabed. Two Warden-Adept pairs fanned out to scout the surroundings, one on each side. The last Adept was left behind to escort Tal.

"So, you must be the unlucky one," he said. It was Qarsazhi-sized, so about a foot shorter than Tal, but beyond that he could tell nothing about its mood or age or gender. Everything about it was neutral.

"I do not understand," said the Adept. This was a simple statement of fact. It did not invite clarification, but Tal didn't need inviting.

"Since they've left you behind to babysit me," he said. "Bet you're the one that always has to make the coffee, too."

The Adept said nothing for a moment. "This is nonsense," it said, with the same objective finality.

"Oh, you tell yourself that, but I bet it stings," said Tal.

"Do you write with your right hand, Mr. Charossa?" said the Adept.

"What?" said Tal. "Yes."

"It does not follow that your left hand is less favoured. Do you prefer one of your eyes?"

The Adept's voice was as flat as ever, but there was still something about the way it said this that made it sound as though it was threatening to take away whichever eye Tal liked the least. Despite his best efforts, his ears twitched as he shook his head.

"Both eyes have value," said the Adept. "This body ensures that you do not obstruct Inquisitor Qanwa, while my other bodies perform higher functions. Perhaps this is a clarification."

Tal grimaced. "You're all the same person," he said. A thought occurred to him. "Do you ever—"

The Adept turned its blank face to him, and Tal thought better of it.

He gave up on looking for entertainment from Vigil after that. He walked on in silence, watching the Lignite Spire grow larger on the horizon. Inquisitor Qanwa had given him back his sword. He was sure he would need it before the day was done.

After an hour or so, the Adept walking beside Tal stopped in mid-stride. It was so still that it looked less like a person than a tall bottle wrapped in white silk. Tal waved a hand in front of its eyes, or at least the region where he assumed its eyes had to be, behind the mask.

"Hey, you," he said. "What's going on?"

No response from the bottle. He didn't quite dare to take it by the shoulders and give it a shake.

It came to Tal that this was the first moment he'd enjoyed without scrutiny since he'd let the Qarsazhi discover him aboard *Tranquillity*. Qanwa and her crew were visible up ahead, but they wouldn't see him now if he struck out by himself. The urge to get away was on him like an itch, that familiar restlessness prodding him to slip his bonds and run, like he was back at school and desperate to avoid an exam he knew he'd fail.

He knew his own interests better now. Running would just guarantee pissing off Qanwa before they even got to the Spire.

"Hey, Inquisitor!" he yelled, instead. "Your wizard's broken!"

They didn't turn back immediately. They had stopped too, in fact, and he realised the same thing had happened to the Adept who had been walking with them. Before Tal could do anything, the Adept beside him screamed.

It was like the scream of an animal or a child. Tal had been through some shit but at least he usually knew what was happening to him and how long it might last. The Adept sounded like it had never experienced suffering before. The one up ahead was screaming too, sending up plumes of rage and agony to the shifting sky.

After a second or two the noise was unbearable. Tal covered his ears with his hands and shouted to the others again, but they clearly couldn't hear him over the screaming. Then a Warden came running up to him.

"Can't we shut them up?" said Tal.

"Inquisitor's trying to calm it down," said the Warden, bellowing over the noise.

Then, as abruptly as it began, the screaming stopped, and the Adept crumpled to the ground. The silence rang almost as loudly as the sound, drumming in Tal's ears. He felt as if he'd been slapped.

"Trust the fucking mages," said the Warden to herself. She hoisted the defunct Adept over her shoulder and strode back toward Qanwa. Tal took it that he was supposed to follow.

Up ahead, Qanwa had got her Adept sitting upright. Its mask was lifted a few inches, enabling it to sip water from a flask. Tal peered, fascinated, and caught a glimpse of a withered chin and a mouthful of uneven teeth. As Tal approached, it set down the flask and snapped the mask back into place.

"The Spire has defences, Inquisitor," it said. Its voice cracked like a mudflat in a drought. "It detected my scouts and disabled them."

"How?" said Qanwa. Tal almost admired her composure. She sounded as though she was upbraiding a servant for bringing her soup cold.

"It is ancient, Inquisitor," said Vigil. "When it was built there was no Quincuriate. It thinks I am a little divinity. A threat."

"How can it still be working?" said Qanwa. "This is a dead world."

"The Lignite Spire is, or was, the seat of Iriskavaal the Thousand-Eyed," said Vigil. "Her power lingers."

"I see. And when you say disabled, what do you mean, exactly?" said Qanwa. She looked up, noted the presence of Tal and his group, and nodded to the Warden, who set down the still-unconscious Adept.

"I do not know," said Vigil. "I have lost contact." It sounded almost like a person, now. It had the blank, uncomprehending manner of someone trying to understand a knife to the gut.

"All right," said Qanwa. "This body is alive, as is Vigil Two. It is safe to assume that your other bodies survive and that the Wardens who accompanied them will take them to safety." She closed her eyes, thinking, then gestured to the female Warden who had come for Tal. "Warden Balshu, you will remain here, with Vigil One and Two. Vigil, when you regain full commu-nication, instruct your Adepts to assemble here and return to the ship with Balshu and the remaining Wardens. It would be irresponsible of me to risk Vigil's safety any further."

Qanwa sighed and pinched the bridge of her nose hard between her fingers. Tal intimately recognised the look of somebody wishing Csorwe had never been born. "Warden Zilya, you will continue with me to the tower. And you, Charossa, I suppose."

If Tal had been Warden Zilya, he might have asked whether it was irresponsible to risk *his* safety. However, Zilya just nodded.

As for Tal himself, his sense of self-preservation had dried up and dropped off long ago from lack of use.

"Let's go," he said. "Can't wait."

The throne room of the Lady of the Thousand Eyes was illuminated with the light of a perfect sunset, red-gold, frozen in the instant before darkness.

"The sun of Old Ormary shines on us," said Oranna. "Three thousand years after its death."

"All worlds fade. All strength fails. No spirit perseveres. Nothing may be preserved." Ushmai quoted scripture when she didn't know what else to say, but in these circumstances it was not inapt.

"Desolation is its watchword," said Oranna. The Unspoken was very far from her now. Its voice had faded as they navigated deeper into the tower. This had frightened her at first, but the Unspoken had been with her as long as she had been capable of thought, and she knew it would come back to her. It knew what she intended, and what she needed, and what she would give in return.

The throne room was as austere as the rest of the tower. A huge, high, bare room of cool grey stone. It had no ornament, and bathed in that bloody light, it needed none.

Pentravesse had walked in this hall as a young man. Here he had received Iriskavaal's patronage, and she had made him great. She had nourished him without draining him.

Pentravesse and the Lady of the Thousand Eyes had been more than an aberration. It had worked once. It could happen again. They had made the modern world. With the knowledge preserved in the Reliquary, Oranna and the Unspoken would remake it as they chose.

Under the apse at the far end of the room was a long table. On the table was a chalice. Oranna withdrew the Reliquary from her pocket and set it on the table. She didn't dare to imagine it might open of its own accord, and, indeed, it did not.

Above the table, set into the wall like a mirror into a frame, was a great stone slab, polished to a reflective shine. Oranna had seen something similar in the Hollow Monument, but that had been obsidian where this was green chrysoprase. All such shrines respond to the same syntax. The altar, the offering vessel, the reflecting glass. This was a machine for prophecy. All that was needed was a suitable offering.

The Qarsazhi fed their gods on bread and milk and other things you might give an infant. Other lesser deities survived on honey and seawater. But the Thousand-Eyed One had been a goddess in the old style, as old as the Unspoken, and she required more serious sacrifices.

"Ushmai," said Oranna. "Would you come here? It's time."

When Csorwe and Shuthmili entered the throne room it was bathed in a light like the end of the world. A curly-haired girl sat by the altar as if it were a dinner table. Her head rested on her folded arms. She might have been napping. You had to come a little closer to see the pool of blood, and realise that she was dead. In this light, her yellow robes were the colour of roses.

At the other end of the table was Oranna, with her back to them. Her head was bowed. She had rolled up the sleeves of her robes, and her forearms were open, dripping blood like ink into a silver cup. She was as pale as a raindrop, and shivering. On the table beside her was the Reliquary.

Csorwe strode into the hall. Shuthmili caught her sleeve and pulled her back just as a curse-ward detonated, lacing the hall with streams of light and heat. Csorwe's hair singed, and she flinched back, but Oranna did not seem to notice. She was looking up at a great panel of green stone. In the stone, her reflection bobbed like the head of a cobra.

"Be careful," Shuthmili whispered. "There are more wards."

Oranna started laughing. "What do you want?" she said in a low voice. Csorwe and Shuthmili exchanged a glance, but Oranna wasn't talking to them. She reached toward the Reliquary and brushed it with her fingertips, smearing blood on the lacquer. "Lady, what more can I give you? You have had everything from me."

Shuthmili gestured to the pillars that ran the length of the room. Each was inscribed with a curse-ward in blood. The wards grew messier and less exact as they got closer to the altar, as though Oranna had started by drawing them with a fine brush and ended by daubing with her bloody fingers.

"Let me see what she's done," Shuthmili murmured. "Don't walk anywhere before I tell you."

Csorwe nodded. She was watching Oranna's face in the green stone. She looked desperate. Csorwe had prepared herself for a fight. She hadn't expected to see her enemy already on her knees.

Shuthmili moved to the first pillar and carefully began to scour away the ward. The blood blackened and fizzled under her bare hands, then came away in dry flakes.

"Yes, I can handle this," said Shuthmili, with a certain quiet satisfaction. All the same, Csorwe didn't enjoy standing and watching. With every pillar, Shuthmili moved closer to Oranna, who remained oblivious, swaying in unison with her reflection.

It was very quiet in the throne room. Every drip of blood and every sizzle of magic was audible. Every now and then they heard Oranna utter another miserable, incoherent prayer. Csorwe didn't trust any of this.

"This quarter's clear," said Shuthmili eventually. "You can come up to where I'm standing."

Csorwe approached. "What's wrong with her?" she said. "Is this a magic thing?"

"Yes. She's gone too far. If she was an ordinary practitioner she would be a sad little pile of burst organs by now," said Shuthmili, leaning in to whisper again. "She's trying to draw on a god besides her patron. Iriskavaal is not answering. And Oranna's feelings seem *very* hurt," she added, with pleasure.

Shuthmili cleared another ward and Csorwe followed after her, feeling useless. Oranna showed no sign of noticing them, but they stayed in the shadows of the pillars and kept their voices down.

"When you get the last one, I'm going straight for her," Csorwe murmured. "If she puts up a fight you stay back. I'll handle her. Once I get the Reliquary, we just run, all right? No point hanging around to talk."

"I think I've enjoyed enough of her conversation." Shuthmili gave a taut smile, and Csorwe felt a flare of determination: to make it out of this, to live, to find out whether Shuthmili would like to be kissed.

One by one the curse-wards fell. The shadows in the throne room seemed to lengthen, as if the dead sun was setting into eternity. Csorwe paced, fondling the hilt of her sword and resisting the urge to drum her fingers on something.

"This last one is . . . sticky," said Shuthmili. The final curse-ward, on the pillar nearest to the altar, didn't look like much more than a smeared splash of blood to Csorwe, but Shuthmili narrowed her eyes at it and muttered, "Oh, she thinks she's so *smart*." She pressed one fingertip carefully against the bloody marble, then the flat of her palm. "As soon as I start to defuse it, it'll try to go off. I can protect myself, but you should stay well back. And I'd better contain it too." She came a few deliberate steps away from the pillar, back toward Csorwe, then knelt and traced a line on the ground. A shimmering blur appeared in the air, a barrier like a heat haze, separating Csorwe and the rest of the throne room from Shuthmili and the pillar and the altar beyond them. "There. That should give me enough time to erase the control sigil. But I can't stop this once I start. Be careful."

"Take your time," said Csorwe. "I'll keep an eye on her."

Up at the altar, Oranna had fallen silent. She was leaning over the chalice, holding her bloody arm in one bloody hand. Her eyes were wide open and unseeing.

As Shuthmili got to work on the final curse-ward, the pillar began to smoke. It was subtle at first, like breath condensing on a cold day, except that it was red. The space behind the barrier began to cloud scarlet. Farther behind Shuthmili, Oranna and the altar were silhouettes in red fog.

"All well in there?" said Csorwe, not sure whether Shuthmili could even hear her. The barrier held back the fumes as if it were solid glass.

Shuthmili made a noise of assent, gritting her teeth. "Nearly there," she said.

And then the doors to the throne room opened. Standing in the doorway were Inquisitor Qanwa, a Warden, and Tal Charossa.

"Csorwe!" said Shuthmili. She couldn't move. Her palm was still flat against the pillar.

The new arrivals stopped dead, struggling to take in the scene. It took Csorwe a second, too, to understand what had happened. Tal had thrown his lot in with the Qarsazhi. A dull wall of rage came down before her, blotting out everything else. Just as they were close—just as she had begun to see something better—of course Tal was here out of pure spite and obstinacy to take it away from her.

"Shuthmili, we are here to take you home," Inquisitor Qanwa started. Then she seemed to see what Shuthmili was actually doing, and faltered. "By the Nine—"

"Stay out of this," said Csorwe, stepping out in front of Qanwa, her hand clenched on the hilt of her sword.

"The mind boggles," said Qanwa, "at what you think you are doing. You have one chance to surrender your sword before we remove it from you."

"Go to hell," said Csorwe. On the periphery, Tal was trying to drop back into the shadows. "I can see you too, you piece of shit, stay where you are."

"Aunt Zhiyouri," said Shuthmili, straining to look back over her shoulder without losing focus on the curse-ward. "It's all right, please—we can talk in one moment—let me defuse this."

"Warden, deal with this," said Qanwa.

In the red twilight Csorwe had somehow lost sight of Tal, and before she could look for him, the Warden charged. Csorwe's instincts took over, smoothly, like a visor clamping down, and she went for her sword.

The Warden looked as if he would be slower than Csorwe, but his reach was clearly longer and he would hit hard. Csorwe dodged away from him, darting around the nearest pillar, but he came up quicker than she expected, and for an awful moment she was boxed in between him and the wall.

With a burst of effort she managed to slip out of the trap, and disarmed him with a lucky side step. His sword clattered on the tiles and she kicked it off into the distance. She forced him back, grabbed his head in her left hand, and cracked it against the pillar like an egg against the edge of a bowl. He went down. She didn't have time to see whether he was dead.

Qanwa was going to do something to Shuthmili. She was only a few feet away from the barrier.

"Oh, no !" said Shuthmili. She didn't seem to be talking to Qanwa. Csorwe snapped round to see Tal, dodging past her. As she'd fought with the Warden he must have looped around the throne room and come up behind them. Of course. He didn't care about Shuthmili—he barely knew who she was. He only wanted the Reliquary. And now the only thing between him and Oranna was the barrier.

"I told you, Csorwe," he said, turning back with a skull-like expression of triumph. "Whatever you do, you know I'll beat you."

"Stop!" said Shuthmili, still stuck to the pillar, but he didn't even hear her.

Tal threw himself at the barrier. He passed through as easily as if it were a film of soap, and the final curse-ward detonated with an eruption of red smoke. There was a flash and a noise like cannon fire. Csorwe leapt back automatically, tasting blood at the back of her throat, as the light obliterated her vision.

When everything stopped flickering, Inquisitor Qanwa had been flung back several yards and lay prostrate. Tal was flat on his back on the floor, shaking. There was blood running from his nose, tracing a contorted path up over his cheek.

As often as Csorwe had wished Tal would get what was coming to him, she found that this was not enjoyable in the slightest.

Shuthmili drew slowly back from the pillar and brushed a lock of hair out of her eyes. It left a smear of ash across her face.

"Csorwe—" she said. Her voice was terrifyingly shaky and uncertain, and she was swaying slightly. She must have been touching the curse-ward when it went off. Csorwe ran to her, wrapping an arm round her waist to hold her up. On the ground, Tal sighed and went still.

"Csorwe, be careful—" said Shuthmili. "Be careful—she's waking up—"

"Oranna?"

"The Lady . . ."

19

The Chrysoprase Door

THE LIGHT IN THE hall of Iriskavaal is the colour of a dying ember. A petitioner kneels before the altar, crouched over the chalice, shielding it. Her bones ache. Her veins are empty, draining slowly into the cup. Her life burns low. Even now she does not look away.

Please, Lady, all I ask is this. I have offered you everything I have. The blood of my servant. My body, my blood, my breath . . .

She is weeping. A teardrop runs down her cheek, holding in its facets the red light of the dead sun and the green glow of the chrysoprase door. It falls into a chalice that already brims over with her blood. The surface ripples.

All I ask is this. Where is the throne? Where is the earthly mansion, if not here?

The Lady of the Thousand Eyes answers.

Over Shuthmili's shoulder, Csorwe saw the green stone slab begin to light up. At first, nothing but points of light, smaller than candle flames. The points clustered and spread until the whole stone was glowing, glowing and moving, with a liquid fire like—

—like a Gate.

Oranna rose up from where she was standing like something returning from the grave: bent and boneless, remembering in slow sequence how to operate the pulleys and counterweights of her sinews. Her head was bowed, and her arms hung loose at her sides.

Gradually, as though the strings that bound her were tightening, she straightened up.

"I . . . I see you're all here," she said, to nobody in particular. She picked up the Reliquary, tucking it into a pocket. Csorwe let go of Shuthmili's waist, moving unconsciously toward her. "This is quite a reception. But I'm afraid . . . I'm afraid . . . it seems I have to go." She turned her back on them and stumbled toward the new Gate.

Csorwe broke into a run. There was the Reliquary, there for the taking. She was so close. "Shuthmili, come on!"

No reply. She turned back. Like a wave rising from the sea, Qanwa Zhiyouri had come up out of the shadows. She had Shuthmili. The Inquisitor had one hand clamped over her mouth, and the other held a knife to her throat. Her face was rigid with anger.

"Let her go," said Csorwe. Shuthmili drummed her heels against her aunt's legs, trying to shout despite the hand clamped over her mouth.

"You are under arrest," said Qanwa. Her eyes were bloodshot, and a dark stripe of blood trickled from her nose to her chin.

"Let her go!" said Csorwe.

"Sheathe your sword now and things will be much the better for you," said Qanwa.

Seeing the knife so close to Shuthmili's throat, Csorwe obeyed, but Shuthmili was still wriggling for all she was worth.

Csorwe took a step toward the Inquisitor. Qanwa was just one woman.

"No, I think not," said Qanwa.

She removed her hand from Shuthmili's mouth long enough to pull out a pair of silver bracelets, and snapped the first one-handed round Shuthmili's wrist.

"No!" said Shuthmili, trying to bite her. "I don't—"

Painstakingly, but without gentleness, Qanwa slid the other bracelet onto Shuthmili's other wrist. At once Shuthmili went still and rigid, slipping down in Qanwa's arms as if the Inquisitor had caught her fainting.

"Let her *go*," said Csorwe. She couldn't think. There wasn't time to argue. Oranna was bent over and staggering, but she had already reached the steps to the Gate. "I know what you want to do to her!"

"You ignorant girl," said Qanwa. "Was this intended as an errand of mercy? In that case you have done Shuthmili the worst possible favour."

"I know what the tether is. I thought she was your family!"

"If you have corrupted her she will face far worse than the tether," said Qanwa, then broke off, movement catching her eye.

Csorwe followed her gaze and saw Oranna, struggling up to the Gate, every step painfully halting. She was taking the Reliquary away with her. If there had been more time—if she had been more careful . . .

Shuthmili's eyes were still open, fixed on Csorwe but impassive and expressionless as the mask of a Quincury Adept.

If the Qarsazhi thought Shuthmili had broken faith with them they would kill her. *Do you know how my people execute rogue mages?*

Oranna stood before the Gate. She was about to pass out of Csorwe's reach, again, perhaps forever, taking the Reliquary with her.

She could let Oranna go. She could kill the Inquisitor and take Shuthmili and run.

And how long would they have? she wondered. How long would it take Oranna to open the Reliquary? How long before the Unspoken One came up from its Shrine? There would be nobody to save her, or Shuthmili, when it did.

She had made this mistake before. There would never be another chance to put it right. A few days' friendship set against everything she owed to Sethennai—she remembered the warmth of Shuthmili's hand, less than an hour before—but Sethennai had taken her hand once too . . .

She could not forget what she owed him, or what was at stake. She turned her back on Shuthmili, and followed Oranna through the mirror.

Infinite darkness, thick and rustling, like drifts of black feathers. The sense of stairs descending. At the bottom of the stairs, a lantern burning in a bracket, illuminating rough-cut stone with an oily, glistening light.

Above them, the Gate blinked out. There was no going back. They had come into some kind of cellar. There were other doors up ahead, but Oranna couldn't go much farther.

She didn't move to defend herself when Csorwe caught up to her. She had to struggle for every breath, one after another like a ragged string of flags.

"Give me the Reliquary," said Csorwe.

"No," said Oranna. "I don't think I will." She propped herself against the wall, the Reliquary clasped in both hands. "Csorwe, isn't it?"

"It is," said Csorwe. If this had been almost anyone else, Csorwe would have knocked her on the head and taken the Reliquary then and there. However, there was some part of her that still baulked at punching the librarian.

Oranna hauled herself fully upright, licking her dry lips. The Reliquary looked strange in her hands: heavy and ornate where Oranna was so insubstantial and so harmless.

"You will lay down your weapon," said Oranna, quietly. Unless you were listening very carefully you might have missed the note of command. "It is too heavy, isn't it?"

Did Csorwe really need her sword? It was bulky, ugly, without subtlety . . .

"Inflexible," Oranna murmured. "And unnecessary."

Csorwe flinched back, recognising the insidious pressure of magic. Still, she really did want to put down her sword. It was such a weight in her hand.

"You are tired," said Oranna. "You have worked too hard for too long. Even you have limits. It is very cold here. You need to rest."

All true. Her hand grew numb at the hilt of her sword, and uncurled, and it dropped from her hand. She scarcely heard it hit the ground.

"I have heard about you," said Oranna. She tore off the sleeves of her dress and began binding the wounds on her arms. She looked stronger, brighter. They were out of the Maze and back into the living earth, within earshot of the living gods. "Whenever people gossip about Belthandros these days, they talk about his shadow," said Oranna. "Belthandros' monster. Belthandros' stalker in the dark."

Oranna bent to pick up Csorwe's sword from where it lay on the ground. Csorwe could have stopped her, but there didn't seem to be any point.

"You're his bastard child, perhaps, or something he created himself out of dust. I've always enjoyed the stories," said Oranna. "But there's nothing like the cold light of day to kill a legend. Where did he find you?"

"In the House of Silence," said Csorwe. There wasn't any use concealing it.

Oranna's smile never faded, but it glimmered like a candle in a draughty room. Now it brightened to such poisonous whiteness that Csorwe could see all her teeth.

"Of course," she said. "Of course it's you. Of course . . . and that's the day he left. *Csorwe.* And you served him all that time . . ."

"I serve him still," said Csorwe.

"Oh, no," said Oranna, laughing with surprise and growing delight. "No, you don't. You serve the Unspoken One, and you have always done so."

"No," said Csorwe, with difficulty. It seemed Oranna wasn't going to let her speak unless she wanted a specific response.

"Belthandros does not believe that the Unspoken One deserves anyone's worship. Belthandros would disbelieve in the sun if it didn't serve his own self-regard. But the Unspoken's power cannot be denied. It served at the right hand of the Abyss. It is as ancient as it is unspeakable, and its hunger is as great as its power. You serve the Unspoken Name and you have done so through all the worlds of the Maze, and you will do so for as long as you live, and perhaps even beyond that."

Csorwe could not speak to deny it, and in her own head, any argument sounded thin and unconvincing.

"Belthandros and I disagreed on many things," said Oranna. "And particularly on this. Because the House of Silence is ridiculous he thought that so too was the power which we served there. I suppose that by stealing you from the very mouth of the Unspoken One, he intended to make some kind of point. Belthandros has no respect for the gods. He keeps a piece of the Thousand-Eyed One in his chapel, and he thinks it is something that can be owned. He uses her power, but he does not serve her. You may believe that he took you from us because he needed a servant, or because he found you remarkable in some way. You are wrong. He intended to prove a point in an argument with me, which he will lose."

Csorwe said nothing. For all she knew, it might be true.

"Do you remember the day they found you?" said Oranna. "Perhaps not. You were very young. Winter in Oshaar is a cruel time, but it hides its cruelty in beauty. I was there." Her voice became softer, more distant, and there was a light in her eyes, as if she was looking at something bright and far away. "We found you in a little house out on the hillside. It was snowing. There were many bodies, too many for the house. *Plague shall come to the house but thou wilt not sicken.* And there you were, sitting in the middle of the floor, untouched. I suppose you must have been two or three years old. The Unspoken One watched over you. You were chosen. You are chosen still. There is no escaping it."

"No," said Csorwe.

"You know," said Oranna, "I should tell you something. I

don't believe anyone else knows this, though Prioress Sangrai may have suspected, and Belthandros perhaps guessed some of the facts. You are not the first Chosen Bride to stray. I was chosen, as you were. Twenty-two years ago, my sister went to the Shrine in my place."

Her eyes were distant. She didn't look to Csorwe for a reaction. If she had, she wouldn't have seen one. Csorwe remembered: *We were novices together. She was afraid at first, but when the day came she was quite calm.*

"Afterwards I became terribly sick. I had studied magic all fourteen years of my life. I owe the House of Silence that much, for nurturing my gift. The magic had corroded and sustained me in equal parts for as long as I could remember, and I knew I would die painfully if I refused to draw on it. But I was afraid that if I called on the Unspoken, it would know what I had done. My body began to destroy itself, and it was only when I realised I was dying that I dared to call upon my patron. The Unspoken had not forgotten me, nor had it forgiven me, but I made it a new promise. Not my death, but my life in its service. They are wrong, in the House of Silence. They are blind. They send us up to the Shrine because it is the only service they can conceive, and they imagine that the god will be angered if they fail to prove their devotion with blood. As if the Unspoken has some particular taste or purpose for the sacrifice of innocents. I promised that I would grow rich in knowledge and power, and I would bring whatever I gained back to the Shrine as my tribute, and I would further the ultimate intention of the Unspoken. This has been my purpose. I suppose Belthandros promised you happiness, when he took you away?"

No, Csorwe thought. He had only ever promised her the work.

"You are unhappy because you have relinquished your purpose. Belthandros cannot give you purpose. You are not even a servant to him. You are a tool for accomplishing some end that you do not understand."

"What do you want from me?" said Csorwe. She had meant to sound defiant, but it came out more like an offer of service.

"The demands of the Unspoken One may be delayed, but never forgotten," said Oranna. "You will come away with me. You will serve a greater power, at last."

Csorwe heard the command clearly, like another voice, layered over Oranna's: *You will go. You will carry the sacrifice. You will climb the stair to the Shrine. You will never know doubt, nor fear, nor pain, and you will never be alone.*

"Yes," said Csorwe, and bowed her head.

Oranna reached out and brushed Csorwe's cheek with the back of her hand.

It was difficult to throw a punch at this angle, but Oranna was not a fighting woman and had not been expecting the blow. Csorwe's fist slammed into her belly and knocked her back. A poor stance, a weak blow, but it gave Csorwe the chance that she needed. She spun on tiptoe, drove her foot into Oranna's stomach, followed the blow with another, swift, automatic, methodical. Oranna's robes tangled her ankles, and she slipped on the damp flagstones and fell flat on her back.

Csorwe stood over her. In the sharp clarity of the struggle, all she could think of was how to kill Oranna. She could find some blunt object and smash her skull. Then she realised—with a sort of bitter amusement, like the husk of laughter—that her sword was here for the taking. It would be cleaner. If she was Belthandros' monster, she was not the kind that killed with a bludgeon. She bent down, turned Oranna to unbuckle the swordbelt, and took her sword from the sheath. Oranna lay dazed, hardly moving.

She was conscious of a distant relief that Shuthmili wasn't here to see this. She rested the point of the blade at Oranna's throat.

There was nobody to hear what she might say in explanation or apology, and it was her own doing. After all, she had left Shuthmili to die. She might already be dead.

It's hard to run alone. But you won't be on your own. Everything she had promised had been a lie. She couldn't blame that on Oranna. It had all been her own doing. She couldn't escape from that any more than she could escape her other debts.

Her sword-hand was numb with cold, clenched so tightly that it no longer felt like a part of her body. Something in her twisted, or came loose, and she fell to her knees. The sword fell beside her, with an empty ringing.

She was so tired. She felt the days piling up, like snow settling. Not so much at first, and then days became years and the weight became unbearable all at once. She had served for so long. Did it really make so much difference whether it was Sethennai or the Unspoken? Either way, she had come to this.

Sethennai might want Oranna alive. Or he might not. He could make up his own mind. She had nothing left in her.

She sheathed her sword and bound Oranna's hands. She took the Reliquary and slipped it into her pocket. It was done.

Oranna was still unconscious. Csorwe hoisted her over her shoulders and left the cellar. The rooms beyond were empty. There was no indication of where they were, except that it was deep underground, perhaps the very depths of a huge compound of cellars.

Csorwe felt nothing. Quiet and hollow as a withered stalk of grass on the point of blowing away. The Reliquary was safe in her pocket. It was just as she had imagined it: heavy, smooth, lightly cracked with age, richly embellished. It might have been a jewellery box or the case of a small instrument.

She had never contemplated Sethennai's motives for saving her. It had happened. He had treated her well. There had been no point wondering.

She wondered now. He hadn't done it out of charity, nor out of mercy. Belthandros Sethennai did nothing unless it brought him some benefit or amusement. She knew she was useful to him, and maybe it entertained him to be kind to her.

It didn't matter why he had chosen her. It didn't matter who she was, what she was, where she had come from, what she had done, whether she had abandoned her friend. She had done what he asked her. She had fulfilled her purpose. The Reliquary was the proof.

She dragged Oranna out into a corridor, with rows of doors in both directions. There was something familiar about this place. In the semi-darkness it was difficult to say what it was . . .

Oranna stirred. Csorwe needed to get out of here before she could wake up.

They reached the bottom of a flight of stairs. Wherever they were, surely the way out was *up* . . . and still Csorwe recognised the place, as though she had been here when she was very young.

A door opened at the top of the stairs, flooding the cellar with harsh, white sunlight. Csorwe narrowed her eyes against it. There were figures up there in the light, looking down at them.

"Hey, mate," said a voice. Csorwe identified it, against all likelihood, as a *Tlaanthothei* voice. "You want to come up here and tell us what you're doing in the Chancellor's Treasury?"

*

They brought her up to the palace, dosed her with strong wine, and wrapped her in warm blankets. When she was young and new to Sethennai's service, she had always resented this, and insisted on licking her wounds alone. Now she couldn't make herself care enough to resist. They had taken away her prisoner early on. She sat where she was put, by the fire in the upper parlour.

Sethennai came into the room in a single billow of green and gold, like an oak tree. To Csorwe's great shame her eyes blurred with tears.

"Csorwe?"

"Sir," she said. She dug into her pocket and pulled out the Reliquary. There didn't seem to be anything else to say.

She had never known Sethennai lost for words, but as he reached out to take the Reliquary he said nothing, only clasped Csorwe's hands in his.

"Oh, brilliant creature," he said. "When have you ever failed me?"

He took the Reliquary and turned it over, running his hands over the surface of the box as if he couldn't quite believe it was real. Then—as easily as if it had never been locked at all—he opened the lid. Csorwe couldn't see what was inside, and after everything she had been through, she couldn't muster much curiosity.

"Ah," said Sethennai. "Of course. Oh, of course." He stared down at the contents of the box as though Csorwe and everything else had faded to nothing. "My god. How long has it been? What a fool I am."

Eventually he seemed to come to terms with what he saw. He closed the lid again and slipped the Reliquary into the inside pocket of his robe.

Csorwe saw immediately that something had changed in him, although it was nearly impossible to pin down exactly what. There was no physical difference. He had been like this when they returned to Tlaanthothe, she remembered. As soon as they had stepped inside the city, he had been quicker, sharper, more vital, more certain of himself. And now the same change was worked again ten times over. There was an unsettling brilliance in his eyes.

Though he had never done so before, he bowed to kiss Csorwe's forehead, a little to the right of the scar that Morga had left there. He straightened up again, a delighted gleam in his eyes, and patted the breast of his robe where the Reliquary lay safe under layers of brocade. "Where did you find it?"

"Oranna still had it, sir. We found her in the earthly mansion of Iriskavaal, at the Lignite Spire."

A faint shadow, like recognition, fluttered across his face, but he just nodded.

"You knew each other, in the House of Silence," said Csorwe, unable to articulate all the other things Oranna had said.

"We did," said Sethennai. "She's a dangerous woman. You must know what it means to me to have this recovered out of her hands. Oh, Csorwe. Best and dearest of my servants. You have returned me to myself. Thank you."

Csorwe lowered her eyes. All this had the quality of a remembered dream: unreal, unsettling.

"Sir, Tal is gone. Somewhere." He had run straight into the curse-ward. She didn't know whether he'd survived it. "Injured, badly. And I don't know how we got into the Treasury. It doesn't make sense."

"Hmm," said Sethennai, standing before the fire. "Yes, it's odd, isn't it?"

She let it go. The Maze of Echoes was a strange place; these things happened.

"I will ensure Talasseres is found. Don't worry about him. Won't you tell me how it all happened?" he said, settling into a chair opposite her.

Csorwe swallowed. "Yes, sir," she said. She could still feel it, that settling weight of snow, that tiredness. She felt half buried in it. The last time she had slept she had been on the stolen ship with Shuthmili. "I wanted to ask," she said. She knew if she didn't voice this now she never would. "Oranna told me that you took me from the Shrine to—to prove a point. Is that true?"

She could almost see the snow now, the white flakes blurring her vision. She couldn't meet Sethennai's eyes. She heard his voice from far away, as if carried on the wind, and before she could understand his answer, she had passed out.

IV

The Traitor's Grave

Let my name be forgotten; let my house forget me, for I shall live in the deeds of my Quincury, for the glory of the Emperor and the Nine.

Oath of the Quincury coadunate

20

The Sword Has Its Regrets

THERE WERE NO CHAINS in the Traitor's Grave, whatever its reputation. There was no wheel, no rack, no furnace. Or at least, not in the portion of the Inquisitorial fortress where High Inquisitor Qanwa Zhiyouri had imprisoned her niece.

Zhiyouri glanced in through the observation window. Shuthmili had been given her own room, comfortably appointed with books and a bed and an icon of Linarya the Radiant above the hearth. The room was quiet, but not silent, perpetually washed by the sound of wind and waves. You would hardly know the door was barred from the outside.

Shuthmili was sitting by the window, looking out at the grey expanse below, just as she had done every day since Zhiyouri had brought her here. It wasn't possible to see individual waves from here. The sea rose and fell as one body.

Zhiyouri shook her head and turned to her guest, a Quincury Adept. It looked exactly like Vigil, except for its sash, which was red on black. This was Spinel, one of the higher research Quincuries. It was unusual to see a single Quincury Adept without its counterparts nearby, but the rest of Spinel was at work in a library or laboratory elsewhere in the Grave.

"I'm afraid that what you've asked is impossible, High Inquisitor," it said.

"I don't see *why* it should be so impossible," said Zhiyouri. It had been more than a week since their return to the Traitor's Grave, and every successive setback made her fizz with frustration, like a fuse burning another inch closer to catastrophe. The events at the Lignite Spire had left her battered. The lingering poison of the curse-ward prickled in the blood long after the initial attack. When she moved too quickly, her nerves snapped and flared, throwing her off-balance. "And I don't see how you can be so certain when you haven't even examined her."

"It is unnecessary to do so. I could have told you this before you brought me here. The union of a coadunate with the Quincury—the process known as the tether—requires the willed exertion of effort from all involved. If the coadunate is unwilling you will not be able to force her to comply." Spinel's voice was as smooth and uninflected as Vigil's, but with a whining note that plucked at Zhiyouri's nerves.

"Could she be drugged?" said Zhiyouri. She wouldn't have put it so bluntly, but this whole operation had been characterised by inefficiency and delay. Sometimes subtlety was not available to you. Sometimes you just had to keep going until it was done.

"No, High Inquisitor," said Spinel. Zhiyouri registered no disapproval in its tone of voice. She didn't know whether the tether carved away the possibility of dissent, or just the ability to express it. "Anything of that nature would make it extremely difficult to complete the tether," Spinel added.

"Do you know, Spinel, I thought you were supposed to be in the business of creative solutions." Zhiyouri raised an eyebrow. Spinel, perhaps, looked back at her. It was hard to tell. The black gauze mask never changed. Zhiyouri never thought she would miss her early career, prosecuting thieves and vandals in the Petty Court, but at least thieves and vandals showed their feelings on their faces.

"That is correct, High Inquisitor," it said. A long pause. "I assure you that I have given the matter serious thought."

"I am so glad to hear it," said Zhiyouri, with no pretence at sincerity.

She dismissed Spinel, and it stalked away down the corridor like a great white crane. Inside the cell, Shuthmili seemed—as always—oblivious to her observer. Zhiyouri suspected she was faking it out of pure wilfulness, and had to leave before her anger overwhelmed her. This wasn't the kind of anger you could pick up and put down recreationally. It was a constricted feeling, as if her throat was closing up.

Back in her office, Zhiyouri stared down at the lacquered surface of her coffee table, cursing the day she had saved Shuthmili's life. If her niece had died in the cherry tree they could, in all likelihood, have hushed the matter up. It would have been a loss of sorts to the Empire, but a clean grief for her brother: something that could heal over, not the unspeakable ulcerating sore that it was.

Adhara occasionally asked her how Shuthmili was faring. Zhiyouri suspected he would have asked more often if he thought it proper. He did not yet know about the latest escapade. She wanted it resolved before she told him anything: Shuthmili tethered, Archer restored, the Qanwa name cleansed of impurity, Zhiyouri herself left to get on with her Nine-blessed job. Not that she would phrase it that way to her brother.

Your daughter is far happier now than she ever was. She has a true purpose, sanctioned by the Emperor and the Nine. I assure you, she is grateful.

No need to mention that the last time Zhiyouri had actually visited Shuthmili in her cell, the little fool had all but spat in her face.

She sighed. It would have been wonderful if Spinel could have provided some convenient magical fix, but in Zhiyouri's experience magic often caused more problems than it solved. People were like locks. All resistance, until you discovered the precise formation of teeth that would open them up. All Zhiyouri's success as a prosecutor had rested on this technique, and Shuthmili was no hardened criminal. Zhiyouri would find the key sooner or later—and she rather suspected it would be sooner.

Perhaps it was time to pay another visit to her old friend Belthandros Sethennai.

Sethennai's hunting lodge crouched on the side of a wooded hill like a bracket fungus.

On Csorwe's first morning at the lodge, one of the game-keeper's daughters came to Csorwe's room to sweep and light lamps. Csorwe hadn't asked for this, but didn't want to offend her by sending her away. In the evening, the girl brought a dinner tray with resin-wine, stuffed vine leaves, and little cakes jacketed in powdered sugar.

Csorwe intended to hunt for what she needed, out in the forest. She thought it might make her feel better, or at least would do something to distract her from the empty road that stretched out before her. That was, after all, why she'd left Tlaanthothe only a few days after returning the Reliquary. Everything in the city was the same as it had always been. She needed something else to think about. If she thought about Shuthmili—but even finishing that sentence was too dangerous.

She went out into the woods on her second day at the lodge. Sethennai had no interest in sports, and kept the hunting lodge only for the sake of appearances, but his gamekeeper had taught Csorwe the basics. Though it had been a long time since she had done this, her training was sound. Move silently through the pines—sight the doe nipping at a bramble bush—bend the bow and loose the arrow—and then at the last instant the doe startled. The barb struck her in the belly. It should have been a clean kill, a quick puncture, but the doe survived, floundering among the brambles as if mired in mud, screaming.

Csorwe tried to fit another arrow. Her hands were shaking. Before she could complete her work she found herself rising from the bushes, crashing through the glade toward the doe. Small birds rose rattling from the brush. The whole forest resounded in panic. As Csorwe blundered closer, the doe tried to run from her, falling through the thickets.

"Wait—" she said, meaning to take the doe in her arms, at least to cut her throat cleanly, but she was already gone, leaving crushed vines, dark spots of blood, empty air buzzing with cries of pain. She might have chased her down and finished her, but Csorwe found she could not. Weary sickness struck her like a bolt and she fell to her knees among the trampled brush, careless of the thorns. After that she left her bow hanging in its place, and ate the food they brought her.

The next day, a letter arrived from the city. She knew it was from Sethennai even before she recognised his crisp handwriting, or the Chancellor's seal. Inside was a message in the usual cipher, dated a few days past.

> *Csorwe,*
>
> *Forgive me for the lateness of this message.*
>
> *The Qarsazhi are not at all pleased with us, but they are bringing Talasseres home. He is doing well and will live. I do understand that this may come as a disappointment.*
>
> *As for what you asked me: I knew Oranna for what she was almost from the moment of our first meeting. She is a monster, and she lies. To herself more than anyone, but compulsively and with malice. She excels at imposing unkind interpretations on perfectly innocent or coincidental events. Her account of my motivations in taking you from the House of Silence is pure fantasy.*
>
> *I do hope you are feeling rejuvenated. Your wages have been deposited with the Bank of Tlaanthothe as usual.*
>
> *Regards,*
> *Sethennai*

Csorwe read the letter through twice or three times before folding it away. Some strong feeling welled up in her, as though she were an unsteady vessel full to the brim.

It had been unrealistic to hope for more. Sethennai's letters were always brief and infrequent. This was the longest she had ever received from him, and it offered a believable explanation, and she should have been satisfied with it. He was busy, and it was unreasonable to wish he might have come in person. If she had wanted to talk to him, she could have stayed in the city.

The gamekeeper's girl was watching, so Csorwe stuffed the

letter into her knapsack and tried to forget about it. She shouldn't have thought so hard about what Oranna had said, let alone told Sethennai about it. Like he said, she was lying, and in any case, it didn't matter. She'd brought him back the Reliquary. That was what really mattered, even if she struggled to feel any kind of satisfaction. That, and she'd stopped Oranna from opening it—but dwelling on that only reminded her that the Unspoken One still existed and would never die and never forget her.

She cringed, now, remembering how often she'd imagined handing over the Reliquary to Sethennai. It wasn't that she'd hoped for a cheering crowd, or heaven forbid a bloody medal, for that or for capturing Oranna. She didn't know what it was that she'd wanted. For him to trust her, to recognise her—he did, didn't he? He trusted her as far as he trusted anyone. It had to be enough.

She didn't reply to the letter, and for the next few days she heard nothing more from Tlaanthothe. She tried to get used to sleeping in the huge canopy bed. She exhausted herself walking in the forest, but lay awake at night, listening for the voices of the dead. She woke from dreams of half-remembered violence. Tal and Shuthmili were there, often, dying by her own hand or another's, two among uncountable crowds. She had killed many without thought, from Akaro onward, whenever that had been what Sethennai needed. It was what he had expected of her. It had been a part of her education, part of her attempt to run as far and as fast from the House of Silence as she could, to become something other than what she had been—and she'd succeeded.

The sword knows neither pity nor regret. So Sethennai had told her, unless it had been one of her teachers, or a line from some cheap Grey Hook tragedy. Every night she lay still, eyes fixed on the heavy drapes above her, reasoning away a new horror.

None of this reasoning made any difference to her dreams of Shuthmili half alive, struggling to breathe, to stand and face her, to hold together a body torn beyond repair.

She would wake, sucking in gulps of the cold air as though drowning in it, and try to put what she had seen in order. This was a passing weakness. She had seen people lose their nerve before. She reassured herself that she would recover in time.

Then she would remember Shuthmili again.

This was my choice. I'm not going to turn back.

When she reached this memory there was no use trying to get back to sleep. One morning, a few days after the letter had arrived, the maid arrived with the dawn to find Csorwe already dressed and beginning the work of sweeping the spotless hearth.

That day she walked down to the village on the edge of the forest. Little white houses, curls of woodsmoke unscrolling across the white sky, skinny Tlaanthothei children wrapped like puffballs against the autumn chill. It reminded her too much of the town below the House of Silence. She bought a bottle of liquor, and turned back without speaking to anyone.

She had never really liked strong drink, but it made sleep a little easier, and dulled the edges of the dreams. She wondered whether lotus would help, but even if she could get hold of some, that wasn't the oblivion she needed. The black lotus sharpened your perceptions as it knocked you flat. She didn't want to see anything in the dark.

She drank herself into a murky sleep almost before the sun began to sink in the sky. She was awoken, slumped on the floor, by the sound of boots on stone. Not the gamekeeper or his daughters. Someone else. Alarm pierced the haze that surrounded her and she snapped upright, groping for her sword. Not there. Nowhere close to hand. She had left it with the hunting bow, untouched. All this passed in a moment, and by now the stranger was standing over her, silhouetted against the last light of evening in the doorway.

"You stink," said Talasseres Charossa. "What is that, grain liquor?"

Csorwe sat dully against the wall, looking up at him. Her eyelids were hooded with sleep, and it hurt to look at the light.

"Think it's from potatoes," she said, as he came slowly into focus.

"Oh, the *good* stuff," said Tal. He offered her a hand up and she took it, too bleary to be really ashamed about it. "You're a mess, aren't you?" he said. "Sethennai said you were going away to clear your head."

She leant hard on his shoulder to pull herself upright, and he winced. "Sorry," she mumbled, a flash of guilt piercing the haze of potato spirit.

The maid had already been, and left the tray of dinner. She would have seen Csorwe in her stupor. When she was back in her right mind she would be ashamed of that.

The wind picked up, whistling in the fireplace. On the dinner tray was a pot of ironwort tea and a bowl of lentils, both already cold. Tal began to pick at the lentils with suspicion.

"Why are you here?" said Csorwe.

She felt a barrier reassert itself between them. As her head cleared she remembered she hated Tal and that he had every reason to hate her. She had brought back the Reliquary. He wasn't going to forgive that.

"Sethennai sent me," he said. He sounded just as bitter as she expected, but for once he seemed to be controlling himself. "He wants you back. He thought you'd be home by now."

"Well. Tell him I'm not ready to come back," she said.

"When, then?" said Tal. With an uncomfortable lurch she realised that she hadn't thought about it. Maybe hadn't intended ever to go back. Maybe she had meant to lose her mind here altogether, to drink and lie awake until she didn't know herself.

"I don't know. I'm not in a good state to work," she said.

Tal shrugged. "Sober up on the journey. He wants you back in Tlaanthothe."

"What for?"

"How should I know?" said Tal. A flicker of anger, like a fire long banked up under the earth, eating away slowly in darkness. "He wants his favourite bodyguard back."

Csorwe ground her knuckles against her temples as if she could rub away the fuzzy feeling of a headache coming on. "I don't think anybody's his favourite except when it suits him," she said.

Tal looked at her, almost alarmed, his cynical grin fading, only to be replaced by a scowl steeped in an even deeper bitterness. "You'd think. You haven't seen him with that woman. Oranna."

"What?" said Csorwe, remembering the letter from Sethennai.

"Well . . ." said Tal, wrestling with the words. He would not meet Csorwe's eyes, and his ears drooped with misery. "Since you so helpfully dragged her back to Tlaanthothe she's been kept in the deep cell. But she comes up to his room most nights." His gaze flicked up, unable to resist the chance to gauge Csorwe's reaction. "For discussions."

"I did wonder, once," said Csorwe. "But I'm pretty sure they hate each other." Whatever it was, she had been certain it had ended in Echentyr.

"Oh, yeah," said Tal. "They hate each other. But they've got plenty to talk about."

Csorwe thought of the sliver of light under the library door, and a small fragment of the past came suddenly clear, as if she had wiped away the mist on the window. *She hasn't ever forgiven me for leaving her in the House of Silence,* Sethennai had once said. Csorwe hadn't really understood that at the time, but of course, Oranna had been as lonely at the House of Silence as Csorwe herself. Sethennai had come, and then he had left, and he hadn't taken Oranna away with him.

Plenty to talk about.

"Well," she said, and looked over at Tal. He ran a hand through his curls and propped his face in his palm, still not meeting her gaze. "You're not having fun without me, then," she said.

Tal buried his face in both hands and pretended to laugh.

"I've been sleeping with him for three years, you dumb shit," said Tal. He sounded close to tears. "You just didn't notice."

Csorwe found herself lost for words.

She couldn't get round it by mocking him. He wasn't lying to her. So there was just this . . . fact.

Was it really possible she had missed something like this? If they had been keeping it a secret deliberately, she had to admit that it was. Just this fact, and all the implications that flowed from it, like ice water from a melting glacier.

"Don't get jealous," said Tal, with a grotesque laugh. "Now she's here, I might as well have been washing his fucking cravats."

Csorwe drew the flask of potato liquor from her coat and held it out. He took it, laughed briefly, and shoved it into his own pocket.

"If you're thinking about pitying me, don't, I'll fucking vomit," he said. He straightened up, putting on languor like a threadbare jacket. A pause to compose himself. Csorwe was grateful for the opportunity to do something with her own face, make it blank and orderly again. "Stop sulking, get a grip, and pack your stuff," he said. "We're going home."

Her first thought was to refuse. She didn't want to face Sethennai, and she didn't want to walk round Tlaanthothe as though everything was the same.

Then again, there was no peace for her here. She had hoped it would be good to have some time alone with her thoughts, but it turned out she didn't like their company much. As Shuthmili had told her, thinking wasn't as good as people made it out to be. At least Sethennai could give her work and purpose, and that would be a distraction.

"Come on," said Tal. "What else are we good for?"

Whatever it was they were good for, it wasn't small talk. The journey back to Tlaanthothe was a full night by cutter, conducted in near silence.

It worried her that she'd got Tal so wrong. His yearning had been so painfully obvious that she hadn't bothered to imagine there was anything more to it. She'd always assumed that what Tal wanted was to be noticed, desired, favoured. But clearly such favour wasn't enough. No, she saw now. It wouldn't be enough. Not for Tal, anyway.

She probed her own feelings carefully, testing the ropes before she could trust them with her whole weight. No. She couldn't think this through now.

The dull glow of Tlaanthothe in the distance swelled up out of the darkness like a sea creature surfacing. Tal was tired, and Csorwe was by now entirely sober, so she took his place in the pilot's seat.

Time to get back to it. Tomorrow she would be back to the old grind, and this would be over. She tried to conjure up some gladness for it, but she just felt weary.

Tal dozed under a blanket. She wondered whether he saw the same ugly visions she did. Did he see Olthaaros choking to death? Did he see the corpse of the oblation, bled dry in the Hollow Monument?

He opened one eye a crack and looked at her.

"I saw her, you know," he said, slurring as though he stumbled on the edge of sleep. "On the ship."

Csorwe went very still. "Who?"

"The girl. The Qarsazhi girl. Sh'mili."

"What do you mean?" said Csorwe. She sat up straight, alert, as if she had been waiting in ambush all this time. "How? When?"

"The Qarsazhi must have taken us both back to their ship after what happened at the Lignite Spire. I woke up in the brig, and she was there too, in another cell. Alive. They were arguing about what to do with her. Didn't think I could hear."

"What?" said Csorwe. Her voice sounded strained and unfamiliar in the darkness. "What did they say, Tal?"

"I was hurt pretty badly. I thought I was dying. It wasn't the main thing on my mind," said Tal. She could hear the grimace in his voice.

"What did they say?" said Csorwe again. She tightened her hands on the wheel.

"Usual Qarsazhi stuff. Oh, she's too dangerous to live, she's too valuable to execute. But in the end they decided they want to keep her for the Quincuriate," he said. Csorwe took a slow breath. She hadn't let herself hope. Surely if Tal had invented this to hurt her, he would have mentioned it sooner.

"I didn't tell you before. I wasn't going to tell you. I don't know—I didn't—" It was uncanny hearing Tal sound ashamed, like watching a cat walk around on its hind legs.

She shook her head. "Forget it. Go to sleep."

This was the least malicious thing Tal had ever done for her, so it was inevitable that it hurt like mad. She had spent the last couple of weeks shoving things down a well. Here was Tal with a good long stick for stirring.

If Shuthmili wasn't dead, she was in a Qarsazhi dungeon, or she had already been given over to the Quincuriate. And whichever it was, death or captivity or oblivion, she knew up to the last what Csorwe had done. She had trusted Csorwe, and she had learned what that got her.

But all the same, it was like opening a window in a stuffy room and feeling the cold wind hit you, full of the scent of trees and water and all the living things outside that you had forgotten. Shuthmili was alive.

Tal took over flying the cutter as they came down into Tlaanthothe. It was early morning, and the city had a freshly washed look, as though the wind off the Speechless Sea had scoured it clean. As they passed over the docklands, a flash of red caught Csorwe's eye.

A Qarsazhi frigate was moored at the upper quay. Its canopies were furled, but there was no mistaking that shade of crimson. In a dream, you can run from your pursuer as long as you like, but as soon as you stop to catch your breath, there he is, waiting for you behind the door. It was *Reflection in Tranquillity*.

Csorwe only realised she had gasped out loud when she heard Tal laughing at her.

"You knew about this," she said.

Tal shrugged, then winked. "Might've."

"Ugh. What are they here for?"

"Looking for you, obviously," said Tal. "The only reason they didn't put *me* on trial in Qarsazh instead of bringing me back is because I took their side at the Lignite Spire. They think Sethennai sent you on purpose to suborn their Adept. And, well, let's be honest, I saw how you looked at her. You would've suborned her like *that*."

"Hilarious," said Csorwe. Where was Shuthmili now? Could there be some chance the Qarsazhi had brought her with them?

"Oh, come on. As if Sethennai's really going to let them arrest you." Tal grinned at her.

"Fuck off," she said, without heat. "Who is it? Qanwa?"

"Yeah, and the one who looks like a big egg. They want to lodge an official complaint about you, which I didn't know was possible, or I would've got in on it."

"How's Sethennai? I mean, is he upset about it? He doesn't like surprises."

Tal's expression clouded. "No. He loves it. He's got all his toys back, anything that happens now is just another fucking sideshow for him to lord over. Why do you think he wanted you to come home?"

Csorwe took a deep breath and exhaled slowly. "Well. Guess we'd better go and find out."

Sethennai was sitting on a terrace by the lily pond, wearing his old, hideous coat over his robes, and smoking a cigar with quiet satisfaction.

"Come and sit down, Csorwe," he said, as if pleasantly surprised that she had decided to turn up. "I hope you enjoyed your holiday."

She hadn't seen him alone since she had handed over the Reliquary, and she wondered how she could acknowledge it without actually talking about it. When it came to it, however, he didn't mention it, and neither did she.

"As I'm sure Tal has informed you, Zhiyouri is here kicking up a fuss. I don't entirely understand her problem—she has her Adept back, I have my Reliquary, everyone is happy—but as a favour I've agreed to let you speak to her, since she was so obliging about letting you and Tal join the expedition in the first place."

Maybe now was Csorwe's chance to ask about Shuthmili. The idea of asking for help made her nervous, but she had no other resources left to her. She had brought back the Reliquary, after all, so her credit with him was as high as it was ever likely to be.

"Sir," she said. "I was wondering."

"Oh, yes?" he said.

"Shuthmili—Inquisitor Qanwa's niece—the Adept I met before . . ."

"Ye-es," said Sethennai. "I'd almost like to meet her, since she's been such a continued thorn in our collective side."

"Do you know where she is? Did they bring her?"

"I don't think so. I'd be surprised if they had," said Sethennai. "The Qarsazhi are very strange about their mages, all that purity-and-danger nonsense."

"Don't you think there's anything we can do for her?" said Csorwe.

Sethennai appeared to consider it. "I doubt it. Why do you ask?"

She owed him honesty. "We got to know each other a bit. I like her."

That didn't even cover it, but she didn't know how to explain it to Sethennai in a way that wouldn't make him laugh. A nasty voice in the back of her head told her that, in the end, it didn't matter much what was or wasn't happening in her idiot heart, because she had left Shuthmili to die, and you couldn't come back from that.

"I see," said Sethennai. "Well, they're acting as though you abducted her on her wedding night." He gave her an enquiring look, which she ignored. "I assume she is presently shut up in some kind of walled garden. But frankly, getting involved would be a waste of a favour."

He was already moving on to other things. If Csorwe wasn't prepared to push him now she might as well reconcile herself to never knowing.

"Sir—do you know what they do with their mages?"

"The Quincuriate? Oh yes. It's rather an elegant approach," said Sethennai. "Distributing the entropic burden—and it lets them do incredible things with telecommunications. It's half the secret of their success."

"But if it was you," she said, "you wouldn't do it. Would you?"

"Would I give myself up to something greater?" He sounded interested. "For all that knowledge and power? For what amounts to immortality? I might."

"It just seems like a shame," she said.

Sethennai smiled. "Csorwe, of all the grief in all the worlds there are, it is strange to pick out the suffering of the Quincury Adept for your sympathies. They live long lives, in luxury. They study and perfect their art—at public expense, might I add—and they are valued for it."

"But Shuthmili—"

"Don't worry about your friend. She is to be envied."

There was no point arguing. Csorwe should have been angry about it, or upset, or some kind of feeling, but the numbness was so big by now that she could hollow it out and get inside it. Walk up and down arcades of emptiness, looking at nothing and thinking about nothing.

"Don't worry about Qanwa Zhiyouri, either, when you speak to her," said Sethennai. "She's a reasonable woman. She has more perspective than most Qarsazhi. Just remember: you were acting on my business. That's your line."

Csorwe nodded.

"All right. Good. I'm glad you're back and we can get this over with. Anything else?"

"Sir, what happened to Oranna?" She didn't mean, and wasn't ever about to ask, what was going on between them, except if Sethennai accidentally said something that proved Tal was lying about the whole situation, then maybe she could relax.

"She's in the deep cell," said Sethennai. "Thrice warded and thrice bound. If she can get out of that, she deserves her escape."

"What are you going to do with her?" said Csorwe.

He raised an eyebrow. "Well . . . we've plenty of time to make up our minds about it. Don't worry. I'm not going to let her out to go rampaging again."

"She killed almost everyone—" said Csorwe. "Should she go back to the House of Silence to—to—uh, to face justice?"

Sethennai's eyes creased up with bemused wonderment. Then he started laughing. "Exalted Sages, Csorwe. If there ever comes a day when anyone faces justice, then you and I had better hope we're both far, far away."

Oranna had never been in prison before, so it was difficult to know what to expect. One thing she had not anticipated was a huge stone bath, endlessly refilled with hot water and rose petals.

This wasn't *her* fantasy, nor was it a romantic ideal belonging to Belthandros, as far as she knew anything about him. She had decided it was a joke, not at her expense but at the expense of sentimental gestures in general.

The rose petals materialised from nowhere, never bruised or crushed, floating like blots of fresh blood on the surface of the water. After a while they seemed to dissolve. She couldn't imagine how much it was costing him to maintain this from a distance.

Possibly not a joke, then, but a display of superior force. She had one thing, which was plenty of time to think. She no longer needed to know what was inside the Reliquary. Several things had become clear to her about Belthandros. One of them was that—now he had the Reliquary back—his power was almost unlimited. He could do whatever he wanted.

Well, the bath at least was very warm. She had survived the

pointless economies of the House of Silence and she wasn't going to argue herself out of an opportunity to bask, at least for a little while.

She had already itemised the furniture. Featherbed, silk sheets. Paper lanterns in the shapes of swans. Ivory game board. Tray of sweetmeats, endlessly replenished. Jug of resin-wine, likewise. Bookcase, well stocked.

It all reminded her of a tasteful bordello. There were no windows. The room was suspended within a shell of air, warded with salt, resin, and ashes. On the table, with the tray and the jug, was a piece of rock crystal, big enough to toss from hand to hand. This stone was taken from the Shrine of the Unspoken. It provided an umbilical cord between Oranna and her god. A thin trickle of power, enough to keep herself happily alive, so long as she didn't use it for anything else.

He had left no other restriction. She could starve herself of it, let the poisons thicken in her blood, spin herself out to the edge again, and try to save up enough power to puncture the membrane of the cell. Or she could live here in dull and perfect luxury.

"I leave that up to you," he had said. "Feel free to experiment."

Comfort, safety, and boredom; freedom, risk, and suffering. Oranna did not trust anyone who offered her a choice. A choice was just another prison. Not, of course, that she had ever been inclined to trust Belthandros.

She got out of the bath in a cloud of rose-scented vapour, and picked up the rock. She felt the power in it as a latent chill, as though it had been just lately brought up from a deep cellar. When Belthandros wasn't around, she slept with it tucked up against her chest, as if the cold might seep into her breastbone. It was a good reminder.

She knew what she had to do. The longer she left it, the more likely it was that she would just surrender to all this luxury. Belthandros had a way of cultivating a dumb, unthinking devotion that Oranna found particularly distasteful.

She knelt by the side of the bath. Belthandros hadn't left her anything like a weapon. He had cut her nails himself, gently and with something like affection, when he healed her injuries, and she didn't fancy trying to do real damage with her tusks and teeth.

She laid her left hand flat on the edge of the bath, and traced an arc with the rock, from shoulder-height down to the knuckle of her little finger, just pricking the joint with the point of the crystal.

Belthandros' mistake was believing everyone was like him. He was too vain to do permanent harm. In a trap like this, he would lie back and feel sorry for himself. He had never met anyone who couldn't be bought.

She raised the rock above her head.

This I do in your Unspeakable name. Give me strength.

She brought it down.

Her finger was somehow still attached to her hand. It took another three blows to make it come away, mashing flesh into stone. Then she threw up.

Skidding down a bloody slope to unconsciousness, her first instinct was to kill the pain. There wasn't much you couldn't cauterise if you burnt hot enough, but she needed all the fuel she could get. The pain and the sickness were the sacrament as much as the blood, the flesh, the bone.

She steadied herself. Hard to stay upright. She leant over the edge of the bath, bending almost double, and dropped her smashed finger into the water.

The roses shrivelled away at once, like paper touching a flame. The surface shimmered and tightened. She saw her own face, haloed with wet hair, grotesquely lined with pain.

The blood had soaked into the cracks in the stone. It pulsed cold, numbing her mutilated hand. The power welled up in her, a dark potentiality, promising many things—the power to warp, to watch, to open ways previously closed . . .

And she knew immediately that it wasn't enough to break out of the cell. Belthandros was many things, but he wasn't an imbecile. There wasn't anyone left to help her. This was the trouble with sacrificing all your acolytes. She wasn't getting out of here on her own resources. She would need an accomplice.

Napping in her own quarters for the first time in weeks, Csorwe dreamt of the library at the House of Silence, warm, bright, and quiet. The fire burnt high, rustling in the grate. There was a new row of shelves that she had never seen before, and every bookcase was stocked with new books, bound in leather the colour of wine. She was certain she would find the answer she needed in one of those books, but she was being watched.

The librarian sat in her chair by the fire, warming her hands. Her old yellow habit was nowhere to be seen. She was wrapped in a silk dressing gown of Tlaanthothei design, and she held a piece of rock crystal in her right hand. Her left hand was clenched in her lap, and it bled, staining the silk with a pool of black blood. The blood ran and pooled on the floor. It made a path for Csorwe to walk.

The librarian smiled. "If you want to know where she is, you had better ask one who knows."

21

Thrice Warded and Thrice Bound

BEFORE SHE CALLED FOR Csorwe, Qanwa Zhiyouri spent some time setting up the arena for her interrogation. It would be just the two of them, like old friends, sitting in garden chairs on a balcony overhung with flowering vines. She had brought a Qanwa coffee service with her from the family townhouse—blue and gold irises on porcelain—and it looked very fine set out on the balcony table. She intended to get what she wanted without giving the Nine-cursed girl any cause to complain to Sethennai.

She had foregone her Inquisitorial robes. Instead, she was wearing a light shawl over a summer dress, and had taken the time to style her hair into elegant braids rather than pinning it up and forgetting it. Better if Csorwe could be made to forget the last time she had seen Zhiyouri, snarling over Shuthmili's shoulder with a knife to her throat. Zhiyouri was eager to forget it herself; she really would have preferred not to have had to resort to violence.

When Csorwe arrived, she too seemed to have dressed in her best clothes, and even to have combed her hair so it more or less lay flat. They were both to be on their best behaviour, then. Zhiyouri could almost have smiled. She certainly hadn't forgotten how Csorwe had looked in the Lignite Spire: wide-eyed with shock and anger, much too raw to be feigned. Zhiyouri had seen, and remembered, and she intended to put it to use.

"I do appreciate your agreeing to meet with me. I know our last encounter was not quite this civilised," said Zhiyouri, gesturing her into one of the garden chairs before sitting down herself.

"But I'm sure we can get to the bottom of all this, for Shuthmili's benefit," Zhiyouri went on. "All I need from you is a clear picture of what happened, and I think it might be best that we go back to the beginning. My colleague Inquisitor Tsaldu believes that you arrived in the Precursor world with the fixed intention of kidnapping my niece."

"No," said Csorwe. "I had no idea she was going to be there. I was just there on Sethennai's business."

Zhiyouri listened as she gave her story. No, Csorwe hadn't known what they would find in the dying world. No, she didn't really remember how she and Shuthmili had got out before the collapse.

Zhiyouri recognised the sound of a defendant feigning ignorance. It was amazing how often people thought this would work, as though they were the first ever to try it.

"Then you brought her back to Tlaanthothe, handed her over to me, and negotiated your passage to Qaradoun, as well! Very commendable." Zhiyouri gave her a gentle, practiced smile, and noted the answering flash of rage in the girl's eyes with a checkmark of satisfaction.

"None of that was on Sethennai's orders," said Csorwe. She had obviously been trained to say this, but Zhiyouri believed it: it wasn't in Sethennai's nature to order something so absurd. "Dr. Lagri said there'd be a reward, so I thought, why not,"

Csorwe went on. "I didn't figure she was so valuable. Realised I should've asked for more."

"And yet," said Zhiyouri, "before we were even halfway to our destination, you—and this is really the part that makes no sense to me—you coaxed or coerced Shuthmili into a barge and vanished." Zhiyouri was still sore about this: that it had happened, that she had allowed it to happen, that it had already absorbed so much time and trouble and still was not resolved.

"Yeah," said Csorwe, with studied insolence. "I was going to ransom her back. Took her to Peacock Station to get the bidding started. If you lot weren't going to come for her, I figured someone else would."

"You know, you aren't painting yourself in your best light," said Zhiyouri. "Avarice, like aqua regia, dissolves all resistance, yes? I'm surprised Sethennai let me talk to you at all."

Csorwe shrugged. "Not much you can do about it now, is there? You've got her. I didn't get anything except a lot of trouble. So it goes."

Csorwe knew exactly what she was doing. There was nothing to lose by playing the dumb thug if you had Sethennai's protection. Zhiyouri knew this defence well enough, and knew too how to break it. She smiled and set down her cup.

"Do you really think I am so stupid, girl?" Zhiyouri said, in Oshaarun.

Until now they had been talking in Qarsazhi, which Csorwe seemed to speak almost perfectly, but it was time she learned that Zhiyouri could meet her on her own territory. She was one of the few Inquisitors who had considered it worth learning the Oshaaru language, and while she had never mastered it, she knew enough for these purposes.

Csorwe's guard came up quickly, but Zhiyouri did not miss the instant of shock. *Got you there*, she thought, and couldn't help grinning.

"I forgive you for this," said Zhiyouri, "because many of my colleagues are utterly stupid. But do not lie to me. It is insulting."

"Maybe that's the point, Auntie," said Csorwe.

"We saw you with Shuthmili," said Zhiyouri, still in Oshaarun. "I was wrong, before. You did not force or take her. She went with you. You worked together."

That was the crux of it, the matter Zhiyouri had missed the first time around. Zhiyouri didn't know the exact nature of Shuthmili's feelings, and it would be worse than useless to try and coax her niece into admitting anything, but she could guess. It had been Zhiyouri's own prejudice, perhaps, to see Sethennai's Oshaaru sword-hand as a ruffian first, and only to realise after the fact that she was also a girl Shuthmili's own age; more specifically, a girl with bright eyes, long limbs, and a graceful confidence of movement that spoke of high training and commitment to practice. Zhiyouri could guess very well how it had been; she only wondered whether Csorwe had reciprocated. Sethennai had not seemed entirely clear on the matter.

"If that's what you think, that's what you think," said Csorwe. Her tone was as lazy as before, but the pose of callous arrogance was gone. All the muscles in her shoulders had tensed as if ready for action. Given how this girl had dealt with Warden Zilya, Zhiyouri ought to be afraid. Instead she felt the old quickening of excitement. She had her quarry boxed in, and all that remained was the coup de grace.

Zhiyouri dropped back into Qarsazhi, and leant back in her chair, watching Csorwe, still smiling. The smile was beginning to hurt. She could feel the corners of her mouth drawn tight over her teeth. "There's no need to be on your guard. I've no wish to harm you or Shuthmili. She is my brother's daughter, after all. I know you are trying to protect her. I want to know why."

"Seems like you've got your story already," said Csorwe. "Don't know why you need me at all."

"Because we can't integrate her," said Zhiyouri, feigning frustration. Or rather, her frustration was real, but she would never have displayed it without expressly intending to do so. "She will not accept the tether. I want to know why all her years of conditioning have failed. I want to know what you've *done* to her."

This got the reaction Zhiyouri was looking for. Once you got past the scar, and the tusks, and the determined facade of stoicism, Csorwe was easy enough to read. Shock, followed by relief, followed by something that looked much like *joy,* if Zhiyouri was not mistaken.

Csorwe tried, with only partial success, to compose herself before speaking. "Bad luck."

"It's unfortunate, isn't it?" said Zhiyouri. Perhaps she had control of the situation now that she'd broken Csorwe's composure, but she couldn't relax yet. She had the girl on a hook, but if she made the wrong move the fragile line would snap.

"Unfortunate, in fact, for everyone who is concerned for Shuthmili's welfare," she went on, smoothly. "I don't know if you know much about the average life expectancy for an untethered practitioner compared with a Quincury Adept, but—"

"No, I know," said Csorwe.

So there was no use trying to frighten her with that. Still, an immediate threat might do the trick.

"Rather more urgently, there are those at the Traitor's Grave who feel it would be more fitting for Shuthmili to face trial, and they are beginning to lose patience."

Zhiyouri thought she had managed that quite well: dropping the name without seeming to do so.

"Do you know how rogue mages are dealt with in Qarsazh?" Zhiyouri went on.

"Seems like you want to tell me," said Csorwe, her lip curling.

"The general public finds it hard to believe that a mage can be effectively killed with a blade. It isn't true, of course, but justice must be seen to be done. The Inquisitorate commissioned Spinel Quincury to devise a new method of execution. The Mouth of Radiance is what they made. It's quite something to see it in action."

Mentioning the Mouth usually got a reaction—shock or squeamish fascination. Csorwe just gave her a long stare.

"I bet," said Csorwe. "Sorry. I didn't do anything to her. I can't help you."

"Oh?" said Zhiyouri. "Interesting. Chancellor Sethennai tells a different story. Based on his information I have to assume that you persuaded my niece to doubt her calling."

Csorwe went very still. When she spoke, it was with awful hesitation, like a child admitting to some misdeed. "He . . . told you that?"

"He was very forthcoming," said Zhiyouri. She had spoken to Sethennai only that morning, and Csorwe's reactions had confirmed all he had told her and more. Zhiyouri doubted he would have said anything at all if he'd guessed how she intended to use the information.

"Well, good luck working it out, then," said Csorwe. "I'm not helping you. She won't ever agree to it. There's nothing you can do." There was renewed anger in her eyes, a steel wall of stubbornness closing off any other emotion. It hardly mattered.

"That's all right," said Zhiyouri. "You've been very helpful. I think I have what I need."

Csorwe slammed the door to the balcony. The numbness inside her felt more like an ache, the ache more like rage. She had meant to go back to her own room, but she found herself heading for Sethennai's office before she knew what she was doing.

Tal was lounging against a pillar outside. "Went well with the Inquisitor, then?" he said.

"Get wrecked, Talasseres," she said, throwing open the door to the study.

Sethennai was sitting at his desk over a ledger.

"Good morning, Csorwe," he said, without looking up. "This isn't like you. Is something wrong?"

"What did you tell Qanwa?" she said. "About Shuthmili and me?"

"Nothing more than you told me," he said.

"And what's that?" said Csorwe, stepping up to the edge of the desk. She felt the blood rushing in her head, like the wind rising as it blew across the sea, building toward some disaster she couldn't anticipate.

"That you and Shuthmili had got to know one another, that you liked and pitied her. That you must have persuaded her to doubt her calling."

The exact words Inquisitor Qanwa had used. It was true. Csorwe clenched her jaw to stop herself shouting. Sethennai wasn't finished.

"That you yourself have an unusual background that perhaps affected your impressions. Nothing more sinister than that." He held her gaze, calm and still. He never lost his temper, which made it so easy to believe that he was being reasonable and you were a petulant child.

"I didn't say anything like that," she started, but knew it was no use getting into what had or hadn't been said. "You didn't have to tell Qanwa."

Not only about Shuthmili but also about her *unusual background,* as if it was nothing. She knew she wouldn't be able to explain it to him, how it felt to be interpreted to a stranger, as if all her feelings and actions could be deciphered with this simple key. How it felt to realise that this really was Sethennai's idea of who she was.

Sethennai was all mild bemusement. "Zhiyouri is not our enemy. It made no sense to withhold something so harmless. They are leaving, there is no damage to our relationship with Qarsazh, and nobody is agitating for you to be arrested any longer."

"It's not harmless," she said, stumbling over the words in her anger. She had to try one last time to make him listen. "I thought we were on the same side."

That wasn't how it worked, of course. She was on Sethennai's side. His enemies were her enemies. It didn't work the other way.

"I know it is not nice to have your feelings discussed publicly," he said, "but I suggest you rise above it. Go and get some sleep, please, and get yourself under control."

Sethennai tapped the surface of the desk with his fingertips. His rings flashed, green and gold. On the desk beside him was an eight-sided box of polished and inlaid wood. The sight of the Reliquary kindled a brief flicker of understanding in her—*Of course he keeps it by his side*—answered by a flash of contempt—*And what was the point? Did I think something would change?*

That had always been the hope, not that she had put it into words, even to herself. If she could bring back the Reliquary, if she could prove her value and her commitment, he would see her as she was.

That had been the dream that had kept her going, through exhaustion and loneliness, through toil, through interrogation. She had betrayed Shuthmili for it, and it had never been anything more than shapes in smoke.

Tal had left when she emerged from the room. She realised she had been hoping he'd still be there, maybe so she could pick a fight with him, or else because he was the only person in the world who might understand.

So she did what she rarely did, and went to Tal's room. It was neat to the point of sterility: he had a display of knives hanging on one wall, and a full-length mirror on another. A bottle of scent stood on the washstand next to his shaving gear. Beyond that there was no sign that this was anything more than a guest bedroom, except for Tal himself, who was doing exercises in front of the mirror with a practice blade.

"Your form is terrible," said Csorwe. She sat down on the edge of the bed.

"Piss off," said Tal, pleasantly enough. "What do you want?"

"Qanwa's leaving, I think," she said. It was too painful to start with any of the things that were actually bothering her.

"Thank fuck," said Tal. "Count yourself lucky you didn't have to sit through any more of her. The way she stares. And

Sethennai's spent the whole time buttering her up. *Oh, tell me about your vineyards, tell me about your summerhouse.* Makes me sick."

Csorwe could see how it was unfair. Sethennai had no patience for chatter. Tal had spent five years getting more clipped and pertinent, concentrating more acid into fewer words.

"You ever wonder what he'd have to do before you'd say something?" she said.

"Sethennai, you mean? What would I say?" he said.

"I don't know," she said. Even talking to Tal, who knew what it was like as well as anybody ever could, it was hard to put into words. "That you've had enough. That you know he's never going to believe you're—you know—"

"A real person?" said Tal, examining his face in the mirror.

"No, I—" said Csorwe. The words were like three shards of ice—difficult to hold, painful if you touched them for too long.

"Are you just realising this now?" said Tal.

"Do you really think he's like that?" she said. "But you're—"

"Still fucking him?" he said. "Well, yeah. I live in hope. Also, have you *seen* him?"

"Ugh," said Csorwe.

"Do I ever think about walking out and finding another job?" said Tal. "I used to think I should. But then again . . . I disappointed my family. I didn't do anything with my education. I helped Sethennai murder my uncle . . . you've got to stick somewhere or you just keep slipping. I'm reconciled. And he's like that with everyone, so you know it's nothing personal. Nobody's a real friend to him."

Csorwe sighed and flopped back on the bed. She had left the House of Silence, left Grey Hook, left Shuthmili. She couldn't think of a single person who'd treated her nicely whom she hadn't left behind or abandoned or betrayed.

Maybe Tal sprayed his possessions with some kind of essence of self-pity.

"When you were on the Qarsazhi ship, did they ever talk about where exactly they were taking Shuthmili?" she said.

"Not really," he said. "I wasn't paying attention."

Csorwe rolled her eyes. "I should've known. You didn't get anything at all?"

"No. I didn't care once they said they were going to bring me home."

Csorwe couldn't blame him. A month ago she would have felt exactly the same way. It had been worth trying. But soon Inquisitor Qanwa would be on her way back to Shuthmili, knowing whatever it was that she knew.

She strode back toward her room, her thoughts swirling, anger and grief and a strange elation mixed as one. Eventually, a single idea crystallised out of the mess. Shuthmili was alive, and Csorwe knew where she was—*the Traitor's Grave,* whatever that was—and that meant Csorwe could find her and get her back. After all, she'd been expensively trained for many years. She had a refined expertise in getting things back. Shuthmili might hate her forever—it was possible that she had screwed that one up comprehensively—but she had to try.

She rifled through her room, sweeping everything back into her travelling bag. Clothes, knives, charts, money, papers. She'd bribe a Qarsazhi guard, or hide on board their ship, or dangle Qanwa over the balcony until she admitted exactly where they'd put Shuthmili.

This happy thought lasted until she emerged from her room

to the news that the Inquisitors had already left Tlaanthothe. They must have packed up and gone immediately after Csorwe's meeting with Qanwa. Csorwe cursed herself for hastiness. She should have stayed civil and tried to squeeze more information out of Qanwa at their interview. Instead, Qanwa had slipped away, taking the strongest lead on Shuthmili's whereabouts with her.

Csorwe silenced the little voice that said, *It's no use, you're too late, just give up.* She had spent days and fucking days feeling sorry for herself at the hunting lodge, when she could have done something. She should never have left it so long, but she had no excuse for leaving it any longer.

But what should she do now? Where was the Traitor's Grave? She didn't know Qarsazh well enough even to make an educated guess.

You had better ask one who knows, she thought, and for a moment couldn't remember where the phrase had originated.

Then the dream came back to her, as vivid and unsettling as if she was living through it all over again. The waiting oracle, the path of blood . . . She had learned about such dreams in the House of Silence, and she knew they were an old and unreliable magic. *Ask one who knows . . .*

She couldn't remember the face of the librarian from her dream, but she had no doubt where the vision had originated. She didn't enjoy the idea of Oranna wriggling into her sleeping mind, but it was an offer of help. She was certain of that, and equally certain that Oranna would expect something substantial in return.

She would have tried any other possibility before facing Oranna again. It wasn't just that she personally disliked her. It would be a betrayal of Sethennai to ask his enemy for help, and she knew Oranna would ask for more than she wanted to give.

And yet . . . she had imagined Shuthmili locked up in a dungeon alone. She knew Inquisitor Qanwa better than that, now. Qanwa would keep Shuthmili somewhere nice, and treat her well, and surround her with people who'd all tell her what a good thing it would be to accept the tether. They would tell her what an honour and a duty it was to be eaten up by the Quincuriate, and how lucky she was to have been chosen. Csorwe knew all about that. Nobody's resolve could last forever under those circumstances.

If there had been infinite time she might have had another choice, but there never was. Time narrowed to a point, and she was entirely out of other ideas.

The guards outside the deep cell all knew who Csorwe was. They didn't even ask her what she was doing there. It was embarrassing. Sethennai was careless. Csorwe had always worried about his carelessness.

The deep cell was shaped roughly like a peach pit, built from the same timbers as the hull of a mazeship and reinforced with silver and iron. It was suspended on chains from the roof of a natural cave, dangling like a locket above a black chasm. The guards were stationed on a walkway that ringed the cave above the crown of the cell, watching the chains. Each link was the size of a man's chest, and covered with a verdigris of wards and seals.

A narrow staircase, without handrails, wound down from the walkway like a screw thread. Water boomed in the chasm below.

None of the guards seemed keen to accompany Csorwe down to the bottom of the staircase, where a rope bridge extended across the void to the door of the deep cell.

The door was locked, but then, Csorwe had access to the palace strong room. She had the run of the whole place. She had Sethennai's complete trust. An enormous, encompassing thing. Csorwe had never thought before about how *breakable* it was. When she first started practising with a real sword, she hadn't been able to stop thinking about how easy it would be to cut flesh and skin. She was about to do something appalling. In her pocket, her fist was clenched around the key to the deep cell. The metal was warm.

The guards had gone back to their own conversation, now that Csorwe was out of sight. She almost wished one of them would say something. If they did, she'd have to account for herself, instead of turning the key in the lock and opening the door.

Inside, the deep cell was warm and humid, like a greenhouse. Oranna was sitting in an armchair. The pink-and-gold light made her look like a strange flower, a huge orchid from some unknown world. Then she looked up at the door, at Csorwe, and the strangeness fell away. She was a deeply tired woman, too close to the end of her resources to look relieved.

She was still wearing the bloody dressing gown, and Csorwe knew she had been right about the dream.

"You called for me," said Csorwe.

"I had to call for someone," said Oranna. Her hand was bandaged up in a torn pillowcase, rather than bleeding freely on the tiles. "You are an easy connection. You were Chosen as I was. And you broke my nose, not so long ago."

"I'll break it again if you start up on all the Chosen Bride stuff."

Oranna laughed. "I am not wrong. And you will get nowhere by pretending I am. But I can put it aside for now. Since you have answered me, you think I have something of value to tell you."

"Yes?"

Oranna held up her bloody hand to her face and passed it across her left eye, leaving a smear like black ash on her cheek. "I have watched you since you came back to Tlaanthothe. If Sethennai paid you a moment's attention he would see what he does not. That he is losing your fealty. With every drop of blood I shed, you forget him."

"No," said Csorwe. "It's not like that—"

"He has been lying to you. He is not what he says he is. You owe him nothing."

"I owe him *everything*," said Csorwe.

Oranna laughed again. "But to owe is not enough. You wish to reach out and take something for yourself. For the first time, your desires outstrip his intentions. And he will not be pleased to learn it. Trust me, I know how it works."

"It's not like that. It's not the same as whatever weird grudge you have against him. It's not about him. It's not about *me*."

"No," said Oranna. "It's about Qanwa Shuthmili. Isn't that right? You want to trade in your loyalty for something that cannot last. I am thirty-six years old and just about beating the odds. Qarsazh trains its Adepts to burn like oil lanterns, a little at a time, eking out a limited supply for a few brief lights. But Shuthmili burns like a forest fire. I only had to see her workings once to recognise it. She is magnificent, and she will be dead within a decade."

"I don't care," said Csorwe, which wasn't true, but she didn't have time to think about it now. Any of them might be dead within a decade. "You wouldn't go to the Quincuriate, would you, if they tried to make you?"

"I did not die to serve my own divinity," said Oranna. "It goes without saying that I would not give up my mind to make a vessel for the Dragon of Qarsazh."

"You know where they're keeping Shuthmili," said Csorwe. "You do, or you wouldn't have called for me."

"Perhaps."

"The Traitor's Grave."

"Look long enough and you will certainly find such a place," said Oranna, "but it is also the name of a Qarsazhi prison-fortress."

"Do you know how to find it? How to get in?"

"No," said Oranna. "At least, not exactly. I know very little for certain. But I know where we can obtain certainty."

A little certainty was better than none. "Swear you'll help me rescue her. Promise me that and I'll get you out of here."

"Mm. You don't *want* to betray Belthandros?"

"No."

"But you'd better face up to the fact that you're doing it anyway. He will have no difficulty recognising it. Don't flinch. You have run from one who loved you before. You will find a cold, hard centre to yourself. You must let it be your compass."

She remembered falling in the market at Grey Hook, Sethennai picking her up and putting her back on her feet. There must be something very cold and hard in her if she was truly thinking about doing this.

"I won't flinch," she said, dully.

"Then we can work together," said Oranna.

Csorwe rubbed a hand over her face, squashing her cheek

against her nose, as if she could recognise herself again by feeling the bones of her skull, the familiar smooth numbness of the gold tusk that Sethennai had given her.

Oranna went over to the great stone bath, which was covered by an embroidered cloth, like a sarcophagus. She drew back the cloth, releasing a rising cloud of steam. There was a smell of flowers and dilute blood. From out of the water she picked up the rock crystal Csorwe had seen in her dream, wet and shining.

"Take it," she said. As soon as Csorwe's bare skin touched the stone, she felt a familiar lurch, the old rushing darkness, and for a moment she felt as though she sat on her throne in the House of Silence again, awaiting prophecy.

At that moment she knew exactly where Oranna intended to go to obtain certainty. The Unspoken One would give them the truth. The Shrine called her back again. Every time she thought she was free of it for good, it demanded her return.

"You want us to go back to the House of Silence," said Csorwe.

"Of course not," said Oranna. "If I go back, there will be a great irrelevant fuss and I will have to duel Cweren to the death, which I truly cannot be bothered to do. The House of Silence is dying, and the old cult of the Unspoken is dying with it. I am the first of the new blood."

Csorwe's face must have changed, because Oranna smiled. It was such an unpleasant smile. Csorwe had no idea how she had ever managed to convince the acolytes to follow her.

"You killed all the others," she said, before she could stop herself.

"Is it such a bad thing, to die for what you believe?" said Oranna.

"They believed in you, then. Ushmai and everyone."

"Yes," said Oranna. "They believed in my cause. They believed in . . . eternity."

"Uh-huh," said Csorwe. She remembered Ushmai lying slumped at the table within the Lignite Spire. No eternity for her, at any rate.

"The true power of the Unspoken One abides forever, and in time it will have its incarnation," said Oranna. "You and I will go directly to the heart of that power. To the throne and earthly mansion. To the Shrine."

It took a moment for Csorwe to realise exactly what Oranna was proposing. A cold horror latched on to her, like a leech.

"No," said Csorwe. Her voice shook slightly. Even after all these years. "Never."

"You are afraid," said Oranna. "Afraid, perhaps, that you will find what you have always denied. That you belong still to the service of the Unspoken One. That—"

"Do you *want* to escape from here?" said Csorwe, taking a step toward her. "I wasn't joking. Keep this up and I'll break your fucking nose."

Oranna grinned. "Point taken. But you know there is no other way. The Qarsazhi do not publish the location of their secret prison."

Shuthmili was alive, and suffering, because of Csorwe's own failure. This was no time to be afraid.

She gave the shard of Shrine-stone back to Oranna, who bound it into her robe.

"All right," said Csorwe. "If there's no other way."

"There is none," said Oranna. "Won't you ask how you can trust me? How you can be certain I won't double-cross you?"

"*May the abyss consume the breaker of promises,*" said Csorwe. "*May the maggots eat the flesh of her vessel.*"

"*May her name be forgotten utterly,*" said Oranna, with satisfaction. "Quite right. I may have forsaken the temple but I have never forgotten the law." She went to the wardrobe, which was full of flimsy robes and gowns, and scowled. "You must lend me a coat," she said. "I have had enough cold for a lifetime."

"Yes, fine," said Csorwe. Despite the close walls and the muffled quietness of the deep cell, her skin began to prickle, alert to any sign that they were being watched or overheard.

Once they left the cell they would only have so much time. She would tell the guards that Sethennai had summoned the prisoner. They couldn't rely on having time to get to the docks, so she would need to requisition one of Sethennai's own cutters, moored in the palace hangar. Just as if it was all on his business.

She already had her bag, packed with provisions. She had visited the Bank of Tlaanthothe and withdrawn all her savings. If the bank officials or the quartermistress had any suspicion, it might already be over, but she didn't think that was likely. She walked, spoke, and acted with the shadow of Sethennai's authority. One more day in that shadow. That was all she needed, and then the betrayal would be complete.

The cutters floated at their moorings like a row of swans, cool and pale above the bright heat haze of the city. As Csorwe had predicted, nobody had challenged her. They had scarcely looked at Oranna. The young guardsman at the hangar had wished her a good morning, then looked as if he regretted it, and left.

Csorwe had never quite recovered from the humidity of the

deep cell. Her hands were clammy. She wished she had brought her Torosadni sword, but it remained on her bed in her empty room, along with the other gifts Sethennai had given her. Adding theft to betrayal was, somehow, too much.

"Get in," she said to Oranna, swinging their bags hastily into the cutter.

"It is a good feeling, to lose extraneous things, however much you thought you valued them," said Oranna, stepping down into the cutter. She was still wearing the exquisite dressing gown, with Csorwe's winter coat draped incongruously over her shoulders. "That I can assure you."

"All right, whatever," said Csorwe. There was nobody else in the hangar. She dropped the final bag into the cutter, which bumped against its nearest neighbour with a hollow sound. She winced, but there was nobody to hear.

It couldn't really be so easy to do this. If it had been, she could have left any time. There must be something she had forgotten, some unscalable invisible wall. She couldn't believe the whole natural world was going to let this happen.

And then, footsteps. The door to the hangar burst open, and in came the young guardsman, and with him Belthandros Sethennai.

Sethennai's shirt was only half buttoned, his hair loose, and Csorwe realised that, for the first time, she had taken him by surprise. It didn't make him look any gentler. He looked as though he'd been carved from basalt: hard, precise, unforgiving.

"And what the bloody hell do you think you're doing," he said, striding toward them. His hands and feet were bare.

Csorwe couldn't think or speak. She was horribly grateful when Oranna stood up in the cutter and laughed.

"What does it look like, Belthandros?" she said. "Don't be a sore loser." She still had that lump of crystal clutched in one hand, and now the shadows gathered about her, accumulating like wool around a spindle. She began to reach for the controls of the cutter, but the little mazeship was still anchored to its mooring by a sturdy chain. The switch to release it was mounted on the wall behind Sethennai. Oranna looked to Csorwe just at the moment he noticed she was there.

"Csorwe," he said. "Quick off the mark, as always. I'll handle this. Go up to my study and fetch my gauntlets."

She stood frozen for a few seconds before it came to her: he didn't realise. She had been caught in the act and it didn't even occur to him that she was capable of turning against him. She was unspeakably relieved—*It isn't over, he still trusts me, it doesn't have to be the end*—and maybe this was it. Maybe she'd reached the limit of her defiance. She was going to do exactly as she was told. She was going to fetch the gauntlets. Then she would follow him straight back to her old life, to solitary expeditions and biscuit rations and squabbling with Tal Charossa for scraps of attention. She wasn't going to argue. She was just going to do it.

"No," she said.

Sethennai was already striding down toward Oranna, and it took him a second to understand what he'd heard. "What?" he said, looking back toward Csorwe. A deep frown cast his eyes into shadow.

"I'm leaving," she said.

Sethennai flashed her a taut uncomprehending smile. The young guardsman saluted and scuttled out, presumably going after the gauntlets himself. "That's nonsense. I need you in Tlaanthothe."

"Well . . . I'll come back," she said, lamely, as if she could ever possibly come back after breaking a prisoner out of the deep cell. "I have to go." She couldn't bring herself to speak Shuthmili's name.

"Exalted Sages, what has got into you?" said Sethennai. His smile did not fade, but he looked less amused than ever. "Why would you want to go?"

Csorwe said nothing, avoided his gaze, wondered whether she could really make herself do this.

"Has she made you an offer? We've discussed this, Csorwe," he said. "Nobody else is worth your time and talents. Our friend here certainly isn't. Any wage she's named, get it in writing and I'll double it."

Oranna was still laughing quietly to herself. Csorwe knew she had to leap one way or the other, but couldn't make herself move.

"It's not that," she said.

"If it's a guessing game you have in mind, we can play in considerably more comfort once Oranna is back in the deep cell," he said. "This doesn't amuse me as much as you seem to imagine it might. Today is not the day to test me."

"I'm sorry, sir," she said.

Sethennai sighed. "Whatever this is about, it's going to have to wait. I need you focused."

"You don't understand," said Csorwe. "I'm sorry. I am sorry. But—"

She lunged forward, hooked her foot round his ankle, and drove her knee between his legs. He stumbled back and fell with a startled yelp of pain, curling like a beetle. She leapt past him before he could recover, pulled the switch to release the cutter, and threw herself back into the boat beside Oranna. Sethennai was back on his feet—she heard him call her name—but the cutter was already moving away from the edge, Oranna's hands were on the wheel, and before he could reach her, they were gone.

22

Obligation

THE THAWS HAD COME early in the high mountains that year, and there were clear streams running in the forest above the House of Silence. They gleamed in the first light like new steel. Oranna brought the cutter in to land in a clearing high up on the hillside.

Csorwe's hands were clenched into fists in her pockets to stop them from shivering. Only a few weeks ago she had laughed at the Unspoken with Shuthmili. Remembering that deliberate, childish defiance, she wanted to give her past self a good shaking.

At least Oranna was keeping quiet. After their escape from the palace of Tlaanthothe, she had been ebullient in a way Csorwe found hard to stomach, but the closer they came to the Shrine, the more she withdrew into herself. Now that they'd arrived she was as rigidly tight-lipped and tense as Csorwe herself.

They walked down through the woods in near silence. Little grey birds sang in the branches of the pines, and once or twice they saw a fox streak across their path, a sleek ghost-white shape, to be seen only as it vanished.

Csorwe had no time for any of this beauty. From the memory of her disrespect to the Unspoken she had moved on to her most recent treachery, and felt sick with guilt.

"Shit," she muttered, "I actually kneed him in the balls."

"Not before time," said Oranna, with a brief, thin smile. "I didn't think you would do it, when it came to it."

"Me neither," said Csorwe. "He'll come after us."

"Not here," said Oranna. "The Unspoken One knows Belthandros for what he is. I doubt he will ever willingly return here."

This was no comfort to Csorwe. "The Unspoken One knows who *I* am," she said. "I was here with Shuthmili and it remembered me."

"Of course," said Oranna. "You cannot think it will ever forget you."

Csorwe shivered.

A bare prow of rock jutted out from the dark sea of evergreens, marking the Shrine of the Unspoken Name. Here below them were the narrow steps cut into the rock, leading up from the road in the valley below. Here was the plateau where little flowers grew between the flagstones. Here was the doorway into the hillside.

Oranna's expression did not bear looking at. It was one measure of fear dissolved in a whole sea of anticipation. The light of dawn made her radiant.

"You're really weird about this, aren't you," Csorwe muttered, to no response. It didn't make her feel any better. You could be as brazen as you liked, but mortal audacity made no more difference to the gods than the buzzing of flies.

Oranna dropped down onto the plateau from above, and Csorwe followed her.

Approaching from another angle had made it almost possible to forget where they were. All of Csorwe's shame and remorse were blotted out in an instant by terror of the divine. For the first time in eight years, she felt the true, close presence of the Unspoken One.

At first it was no more than an incurious tide of dark water. Once or twice it lapped at her, then receded, impassive. The absence was almost worse. Up ahead, the empty doorway yawned, and the Unspoken waited.

"I can't," said Csorwe. "I can't do this." She turned. In that moment it made no difference that she had lost everything and everyone else. She couldn't face the darkness in the Shrine. "I have to go."

"No," said Oranna. "Why?"

"I didn't want to die—I still don't—I can't do this," she said, choking on the words.

"You will not die here," said Oranna.

"I left. I abandoned my duty," she said.

"The Unspoken One is merciful," said Oranna, and she truly seemed to believe it. "This is a time of change, Csorwe. In such a time the duty that is imposed on you may not be the purpose that you are truly beholden to fulfil."

"I—I left with Sethennai," she said. Given the choice she would not have spilled out this much misery in front of Oranna, of all people, but she couldn't seem to stop. "And I don't know if he was worth it."

She had believed in him, so deeply, and for so long, but with every year that had passed, the life she had imagined had receded, like a shadow on the wall, always moving away. Whenever she had been happy—with the Blue Boars, with Shuthmili—she had given it up for him, a man who valued her as a sharp edge and gave away her secrets without even recognising what they were.

"Ah," said Oranna. "Well, yes. Belthandros is, forever and

in so many ways, a disappointment." She smiled secretively to herself. The sun was still rising over the mountain and her eyes were filled with light. "A mistake to waste much soul-searching on that man. Remember your reasons for coming here."

Csorwe couldn't remember any reason for doing anything. She was cold and tired and for an instant it truly seemed as though she had come to this place as a castaway, thrown up on to a bare mountainside by forces she could not understand or control. Just following orders as usual.

Unfortunately, that wouldn't wash any longer. She was here by choice. By choice, because she had made a terrible mistake and she needed to put it right. By choice, because Shuthmili mattered, even if she never wanted to see Csorwe again.

She told herself these things and felt infinitesimally braver.

They walked together toward the Shrine, and stepped through the door in the hillside, into the shadow.

"I assume you brought a light," said Oranna.

Csorwe flinched, feeling strongly that it was a bad idea to talk in here.

"Don't be silly," Oranna went on, sounding more brittle and less natural than usual. "We *want* it to know we're here. It's not blasphemy if you're all friends. Light, yes?"

"I thought you were a mage," said Csorwe, rummaging in her backpack for the alchemical torch.

"And I thought you were supposed to be a competent operative— Ah. Thank you," she concluded, as the torch bathed the chamber in a pallid, stuttery light.

It was as Csorwe remembered it: a large round cave, punctured with many passages that sank away into the mountain. In the middle was the pit, with the smooth notch for kneeling.

"We ought to have brought a calf," said Oranna. "Well, no matter, *you* have plenty of blood." On seeing Csorwe's expression she took a step back. "That was a joke." Her voice was shaky. Csorwe had never heard her acknowledge a mistake. It hadn't occurred to her until then that Oranna might also be frightened.

Csorwe swallowed. "No more jokes," she said. "Have you been here before?"

"No," said Oranna. "I have not."

"I've never been further than this," said Csorwe. "Which way do we go?"

"Deeper," said Oranna. "I don't think it matters. The deepest point."

They circled the pit. Csorwe remembered the protocol for conventional mazes, so they took the leftmost path. There was no sound but their own footsteps, their own breathing, and occasionally a drip of water like a glass breaking.

The tunnel split, and split again, into narrow channels that spread and converged at random, wide enough for one to pass at a time, and then only by sidling shoulder-first. Csorwe had the uneasy feeling that they were making no progress, that the paths were only turning further in on themselves.

"Lenition," she said.

"Yes," said Oranna. "Hold fast."

The presence of the Unspoken deepened around them. It made no attempt to encroach on them. It didn't need to. It was like walking into the sea, wading up to the waist and then up to the neck.

After a while, Oranna began to pray.

"The tongue is to be cut out, for the name of all that is praise-worthy is unspeakable. It is correct to seal the mouth and exult in starvation," she said. The Litany of the Unspoken was not cheerful, but at least it was familiar. Csorwe thought Oranna was reciting it for comfort, until they heard the answer.

The voice came rustling out of the darkness ahead of them.

The eyes are to be put out, for there is no use in them. Mortal witness is not to be borne in sight but in annihilation.

Oranna looked up and smiled, as if greeting an old friend. "May we bear witness, for desolation is thy watchword."

And at last the passages opened onto a great cavity, like vessels broaching the chambers of the heart. The light of the alchemical torch burnt low, smothered by the absolute darkness. Instead, they heard and felt the void before them as a change in resonance. There was no sense of freedom or release in the great open space, for something else was there, a paralysing thing, a weight that distorted the space around it.

Csorwe's heart rattled in her chest. The distortion seemed to press down on her lungs. She struggled to get even a mouthful of air. In this room, in the deepest darkness of the mountain, was the throne of the Unspoken One.

The rustling voice faded. At first the chamber seemed very quiet, and then they heard the small, dry sounds that filled the space. Like the beating of the wings of moths, like the whisper of cloth on stone, like fallen leaves.

Oranna raised the light, and they saw that the throne room of the Unspoken One was not empty. All around the edges of the cavern, all waiting in rows on ledges and galleries, all turning to face the intruders, were the dead.

They were uncountably many. The crowds extended beyond the light of the lantern. None of them were taller than Csorwe. The white dresses were almost pristine—a little ragged at the hems—but the faces of the Chosen Brides of ages past had shrunk flat against their skulls. Their eyes were deep pits. Their hair had fallen like dry straw. Only their tusks—some bare, some capped in gold—were just as they had been in life.

Csorwe stopped short, speechless at the sight. So many of them—still dressed for the ceremony—and all so small, so thin—and all of them had died here when Csorwe had fled.

Even Oranna paused. As she did so, the revenants moved. Csorwe's hand went automatically for the sword that was not there, and felt newly ashamed.

They were not being attacked. They were being welcomed.

The dead girls moved at a measured, ceremonial pace, stepping in formation into the centre of the room. They took their places in two columns that stretched on into the darkness ahead.

"The honour guard," Oranna murmured. "Failed vessels. So *many* of them—"

The dead stood upright and unmoving, only shifting slightly to follow Csorwe and Oranna as they approached.

The presence of the Unspoken was everywhere: in the darkness, in the cold, in the empty eyes of the mummified brides. It seemed to have no source, fluctuating around them like wavelets on a still sea.

No—thought Csorwe—it was them. All of the brides were a part of the Unspoken. Sethennai had sent Csorwe once to the shallow lakes of Salqanya to harvest a certain anemone, a sensitive creature between flower and shellfish, with many fronds that moved in unison to taste the water. The dead girls reminded Csorwe of nothing so much as this. Appendages of some unknown and unknowable intellect. It was all of them.

They couldn't turn back now. Bound together by the meagre

light of the alchemical torch, they walked down between the columns. The entrance disappeared behind them, and the light seemed to shrink. All Csorwe could see was the ground just ahead, bordered by the pale skirts and bony ankles of the brides.

And then they came to the end of the room. They came to the throne.

It was a rough shape cut into the wall of the cavern, a deep door-shaped indentation at least thirty feet high. Sitting within it, like a white bird on a window ledge, was another bride, as shrivelled as the rest. A crown of dried flowers still rested on her thin hair.

As they drew near, Oranna made a noise, horribly loud in the silence of the chamber. A choke of suppressed grief.

"Ejarwa," she said.

The girl on the throne watched her without expression.

"No, wait," said Oranna, raggedly. "I was Ejarwa. You were Oranna. We changed places. You remember—"

The girl closed her shrunken eyelids and opened them again, lizard-like.

"I was Oranna," said the girl. She spoke in a soft rasp, carrying all the chill and all the weight that Csorwe recognised. A voice as cold and hard as iron. "I was Ammarwe. I was Serwen. I was Najad. I was Cwenna. I was Anakhrai—"

She stopped mid-word and blinked again.

"I am the Commander of Legions, the Knight of Abyss, the Overseer of the Eaten Worlds. I am that which has passed away and that which is yet to come. But you know me, as I know you. Ejarwa. Csorwe. What is it that you desire?"

It became clear that Oranna could not speak. Csorwe was going to have to do this alone.

"I—I most humbly ask a boon of the Unspoken One," she said. "Knowledge. Knowledge of the present time. I am sorry—"

The throne-bride watched Csorwe, unblinking.

"You return to me, beloved Csorwe," it said. "You recall your loyalty. To those who serve, the prophecy is freely given. What will you know?"

It would be so easy. It was always easy to take what was offered and not think about what they would ask from you, but Csorwe had played this game before. She no longer followed the Unspoken One. Her loyalty had never been freely given.

"No," said Csorwe. "I do not serve." Oranna flinched, and she felt the surge of the Unspoken One's displeasure and incredulity as a physical, crackling rush. "I—I come here as a supplicant. With respect. But not to serve."

The throne-bride said nothing.

"I'll—" said Csorwe, faltering. "I'll make a fair exchange. I'll give my word. What would this knowledge cost me?"

"Your word is worth nothing," said the throne-bride.

Csorwe felt a well of panic opening up somewhere beneath her, but she couldn't let herself fall. She had no intention of pledging herself blindly ever again, and there was no point trying to trick or cheat the Unspoken. Oranna and Ejarwa had tried it and the god had claimed them both in the end.

Perhaps if she *chose* to return to the service of the Unspoken— if she did it deliberately—it might not be so bad. No, it was no use lying to herself. A lifetime serving the will of the throne-bride would be as lonely and rewardless as it had ever been to work for Sethennai. Instead of an empty room at the palace, a hollow grave here in the mountain, surrounded by her own shrivelled sisters.

But there was no other way to find where Inquisitor Qanwa had taken Shuthmili. There was no other choice.

Before Csorwe could say anything, Oranna spoke.

"I will stand as her bond," she said. Csorwe looked round at her in shock. Oranna's eyes were still wet with tears but her expression was as certain and as grim as Csorwe had ever seen it. "Be assured of my loyalty. I will ensure the debt is paid in full."

A long pause. The throne-bride did not appear to be considering it. She sat as still and blank as a doll.

"What does that mean?" said Csorwe. She felt obliged to whisper, although there was no question that the brides could hear her.

"It means that you owe me," said Oranna, articulating each word with bitter clarity.

"*What* do I owe you?"

"A pledge in blood," said Oranna. "If that is acceptable to you, Unspoken and Unspeakable One."

Csorwe did not need to ask what this meant. She remembered well enough. A pledge in blood was a ward etched on the skin, a sign of the seriousness of your intention. It was not a compulsion: you could still break your promise, but you would regret it.

"I accept it," said the throne-bride. "Make your pledge."

"Well," said Csorwe, turning to face Oranna, who was smiling slightly. "What do you want? I'm not going to let you carve me up like you did to Ushmai and the rest."

Oranna laughed. "You *still* don't believe that was voluntary, do you? I do not want you dead, Csorwe. You are much more use to me alive. Very well. What I want from you is—shall we say—a favour. A task. Three days' service, from dawn of the first to dusk of the third day. I believe that is the standard formula."

"I'm not doing it now," said Csorwe. "I have to go and get Shuthmili." She couldn't quite believe this would work, but if it did then she could bring herself to work for Oranna. Three days was nothing, compared to the years she had given Sethennai.

"Very well," said Oranna. "Three days' service, not to be called in before one month has passed."

Oranna was still smiling faintly. Csorwe's stomach felt hollow, as if she was looking down from a high building. Surely— *surely*—Oranna couldn't have planned this from the start?

It was too late now, anyway.

"All right," said Csorwe. "I'll do it."

Csorwe held out her left arm. There was no sign of the incision she had carved herself in Morga's office. It was, more or less, a blank canvas.

"Do I have to say something?" she said, looking from Oranna to the throne-bride and feeling a flicker of annoyance. "I don't know the words."

"Did we teach you nothing—" said Oranna.

The throne-bride rose from her seat and descended toward them. Both Csorwe and Oranna shut up immediately.

The throne-bride took Csorwe's outstretched arm firmly in her own bare hand. Csorwe willed herself still, refusing to flinch or shiver. The dead girl's fingers were papery, like the bark of dry twigs. Her grip was light but immovable.

With a great effort Csorwe made herself look away from her arm and up at the throne-bride's face.

She was a little shorter than Csorwe. The milk-tusks at the corners of her mouth were no bigger than almonds. And though her eyes were long gone, she radiated a blank, chilly intelligence. Her regard cut through flesh and bone, took Csorwe apart, appraised each particle of her body and mind and recorded the precise failings of each.

The throne-bride took Oranna's arm in her other hand. The presence of the Unspoken tightened around them, like a loop drawn shut.

"Your agreement is witnessed," said the throne-bride.

Csorwe felt a stinging pain on the back of her hand, as though she had been stung by a wasp. A small cut appeared below her third knuckle, and sliced down toward the wrist, as if an invisible hand was writing there with a scalpel. The pain grew slowly sharper as a sign traced itself out across her skin, black on grey. Csorwe gave an involuntary twitch and a drop of blood welled up and dripped down over her thumb.

The only comfort was that Oranna was going through the same thing. When it was over, the throne-bride looked at the stump of Oranna's ruined finger like a teacher inspecting the work of a promising student, then let her go.

The sting faded quickly. An identical sign was carved into both of their hands. It was in the old heraldic script, just one of many that Csorwe had never learned to read.

"What does it say?" she said.

Oranna smiled. *"Obligation."*

"Sounds about right," said Csorwe, wondering how soon and how violently she would come to regret doing this.

"Tell me, then," said the throne-bride. "What is it that you so desire to know? For your three days of service, I offer three questions."

Csorwe needed no time to consider her first question.

"Where is Qanwa Shuthmili?" she said.

"She is held within the Traitor's Grave," said the throne-bride.

The vision came a second later. It was as if a curtain was drawn back in Csorwe's head, admitting a beam of steely light. She saw a square grey fortress surrounded by waves.

"Where is the Traitor's Grave?" said Csorwe.

The throne-bride did not speak. Instead, Csorwe knew, as if she had always known it, where to find the prison. The fortress stood on an island in the Bay of Qaradoun, a few miles off the coast of Qarsazh. She knew now how to get there as easily as she knew how to get back to Tlaanthothe. Easier, in fact, because there was no going home for her now.

"I need to get in without being seen. What's it like inside?" said Csorwe.

The blue-grey light grew brighter, dissolving the darkness around them, the spindly figures of the revenant brides, and Csorwe herself.

This was just how it had been in the old days, when Csorwe had been called upon to prophesy. She knew with clarity that she was now inside the memory of a long-dead thief. She followed this person to the shore of the island, hiding behind their eyes as they climbed the cliff to the base of the fortress. The gate was guarded, but there was an abandoned sally port—yes, she saw it now—and the thief got inside without being caught. Once they were inside the fortress, the knowledge unspooled into her, a cascade of floors and rooms and balconies and back stairs. She knew the blueprint of the Traitor's Grave as if she had grown up there.

The vision ended abruptly, dropping her back into the darkness of the throne room.

"What happened to the thief?" she said.

"To those who serve, the prophecy is freely given," said the throne-bride.

Her three questions were used up. She didn't think she would have liked the answer anyway.

She was still reeling from the vision. At least her hand seemed to have stopped bleeding. Surely they were almost finished with their business here. Csorwe was ready to see sunlight again.

"Unspeakable One," said Oranna, hopefully. She seemed to have bounced back from the shock of seeing her sister. Csorwe's heart sank. "I have so much to ask."

"Stay, then," said the throne-bride. "Rest, here. A place is set aside for you."

Oranna's expression flickered briefly. Csorwe was reasonably certain what remaining in the cave would mean for your future prospects.

"I still have things to accomplish in the outer worlds," said Oranna. "If you still permit it."

"You will have your answers in time," said the throne-bride.

"There is so much I could do," said Oranna. "If you would share what you know. My suspicions about Belthandros are almost confirmed—you are not bound here, Unspeakable One— you could walk the mortal earth again, if you chose it—if you remembered—"

The throne-bride said nothing. Oranna watched her for a moment, then bowed her head.

"I understand. In time, then."

And so, to Csorwe's immeasurable relief, they left the Shrine of the Unspoken.

23

The Emperor's Cutlery Drawer

SEVEN FLOORS BENEATH SEA level, Qanwa Zhiyouri stood over a dead body. The morgue of the Traitor's Grave was warded throughout with a lace of silvery sigils, like frost on glass, which kept the place even colder than you'd expect from an underwater sub-basement. Zhiyouri always forgot how blessedly uncomfortable it was, and wished she'd brought a shawl.

The body of Daryou Malkhaya looked even worse than it had when they'd recovered it from the Precursor world. His cheeks and eyes were hollow, and his skin had dulled to the colour of driftwood, fuzzed in places with flecks of ice. Two Vigil Adepts were poised over him, like seabirds about to start pecking.

"Bring him back," said Zhiyouri. Vigil had already confirmed that it could be done. The Warden made an unusually obliging corpse, it seemed.

The Adepts removed their gloves, placing their bare right hands on his forehead and sternum. There was a moment of effort, a semi-visible flash of light, a taste of rust in the back of the mouth, and Daryou Malkhaya drew breath with a clotted, tearing gasp.

His eyes came open one after another, slowly, revealing eyes that were clouded white as if rolled back.

Zhiyouri waited, watching him struggle to suck in air.

"Why does he do that?" she asked. "He doesn't need to breathe."

"The habit of a lifetime," said Vigil, appearing to shrug.

"I-I can't see," said Malkhaya. His body twitched as if trying to shudder, but the muscles were cold and shrunken to the bone. "I can't see—what happened to me—"

"Hush, Warden," said Zhiyouri. "It's all right." She glanced back at Vigil. "Will he know me? We spoke before?"

"I doubt it," said Vigil.

Zhiyouri introduced herself again. Malkhaya calmed down visibly once he understood he was in the presence of someone of rank.

"Inquisitor—my Adept—something happened to her—" he tried.

"Yes," said Zhiyouri. "Don't worry. We have her here."

"She's safe?" said Malkhaya. His unseeing eyes widened.

"I saw her this morning," said Zhiyouri.

Shuthmili remained in her cell, as intransigent as ever. But safe, yes, undoubtedly.

"It's a sad thing, Warden," Zhiyouri went on, "but I've begun to realise I don't know Shuthmili very well at all. You worked with her, didn't you?"

The dead man took a rattling breath. "Yes."

"You were with her in the Hollow Monument," said Zhiyouri. "You've already told us about what happened. But I'm interested in one thing in particular. Shuthmili sacrificed herself to save you, as I recall, when you were threatened by the Oshaaru necromancer."

"Yes," he said. "I am ashamed of it. She shouldn't have been the one to save me." He couldn't manage more than a few words without gasping. This interview was likely to take all Zhiyouri's reserves of patience, not that she had much left after speaking to Shuthmili earlier.

"It was—a waste," he said. "I couldn't honour her sacrifice."

"Yes, very sad indeed," said Zhiyouri. "But I'm beginning to think that must have been the root of our current trouble with her. I want to hear all about it. I hope it may provide us with a way out."

The dead Warden told her everything, in his halting way. Zhiyouri could not help but be amused: despite her niece's stubbornness now, she had clearly given way immediately when Malkhaya's life was threatened. A soft heart, like her father's.

"She is safe?" said Malkhaya, when Zhiyouri finished questioning him. "You're certain?"

"Yes, quite certain," said Zhiyouri.

"Ah," he said. "Good. I'm glad. I'm glad."

He settled, eyes shut, no longer struggling for breath. At Zhiyouri's nod, Vigil severed the connection.

Csorwe and Oranna approached the Traitor's Grave by night, from the sea. The prison island was a blunt grey spike, sticking up out of the waters of the Bay of Qaradoun, like a drowned man's thumb. Beyond it, the capital city was dimly visible: the shadow of a skyline floating on the far horizon, dusted with lights.

"Here we are," said Oranna. "The Emperor's cutlery drawer."

"I'm surprised you're still here," said Csorwe. "Thought you'd leave the minute we got out of the Shrine."

Csorwe hadn't expected or wanted Oranna to accompany her to the Traitor's Grave, but she had to admit it had been useful to have another pilot for the cutter.

Oranna gave an enigmatic smile. "Our original agreement survives the pledge in blood. My promise to assist you still stands. You freed me from Belthandros' oubliette. I have not yet forgotten it."

It was difficult to get a read on Oranna. Csorwe's instinct was to assume she was lying all the time. Sethennai had called her a liar. *She lies compulsively and with malice.* But then, Oranna had nothing to gain by deceiving Csorwe now—or did she?

"And you want to protect your investment, now that I owe you," said Csorwe. This was as close as she could come to an explanation for Oranna's behaviour. The sigil on the back of her hand was almost healed. If she didn't flex her fingers, it didn't hurt at all. "The Qarsazhi will kill me if they catch me. You can't get your three days out of a corpse."

"How certain you are," said Oranna, still smiling.

Csorwe couldn't relax in Oranna's presence, especially when she said things like this—and couldn't help tracking Oranna out of the corner of her eye whenever she moved—but then, it wasn't likely she would have been able to relax anyway, given what she was about to face.

They were coming in very low, close to the choppy surface of the sea. Now and then Csorwe flinched as salt spray was dashed in her face. They carried no lanterns. Nobody would see the cutter from the prison tower unless they were specifically looking for it.

"Have you ever been to Qaradoun?" said Oranna, from the wheel.

"No," said Csorwe. It was reassuring in some ways that Oranna kept trying to make conversation. Csorwe didn't think you'd make small talk with someone you were about to stab or double-cross.

"Pity," said Oranna. "It's a beautiful place. About as much unlike the House of Silence as you can imagine. Warm weather, wonderful food, art, fashion, music . . . just a shame about all the Qarsazhi, really."

Thinking about the House of Silence twisted something up in Csorwe's gut, and trying to imagine Oranna as a person who was interested in music or fashion did something similar to her brain. She ignored it, focusing on the rise and fall of the waves, and the approaching bulk of the Traitor's Grave.

As the shoreline came more clearly into view, Oranna frowned, then turned the cutter sharply, raising scallops of spray as it swerved across a high wave.

"What are you doing?" said Csorwe, clinging to the rail.

"Take the wheel," she said, still frowning. "Don't take us in any closer."

Csorwe did as she was told, and Oranna leant over the side, reaching as if to dip her hand under the surface. Now Csorwe looked, she saw faint lights there, glimmering underwater, like a chain of jellyfish.

"Wards in the ocean," Oranna said. "Perimeters within perimeters. There's no chance we can take the cutter in like this."

"Then what?" said Csorwe.

"I have no idea," said Oranna. "But if we cross the perimeter we'll alert every Warden at the fortress. And once they see the cutter they'll know we're intruders."

"If we go into the city we could steal a Qarsazhi cutter," said Csorwe. "Would that help?"

"If the Unspoken wills it," said Oranna, doubtfully.

"Or we could destroy the perimeter, or defuse it, or—"

"Perhaps," said Oranna. "When I am back to my full strength. Even so, it would take a long time. I don't blame the Qarsazhi for their Quincuriate, you know, even if it is a perversion. There's only so much one practitioner can achieve alone. Mortal flesh is so *frail*."

"Mm," said Csorwe. Even if she could rely on Oranna, it was too much delay. She had to hope Shuthmili had managed to hold out this long, but anything could happen in a day. "It's only a couple of hundred feet. I can swim that distance easily. And it's a warm night."

"What?" said Oranna.

"I'll go by myself. I'm good at sneaking. Can you spell me up so the Wardens don't see me? I don't know, make me invisible or something," said Csorwe.

Oranna was obviously torn between disapproval and curiosity. Csorwe recognised the look, but couldn't think how, until she remembered Sethennai, and Shuthmili. Maybe all mages were like this, deep down.

"You think of magic as a sort of toolbox, don't you?" said Oranna. "Do you have any idea how much study, how much negotiation, how much prayer and sacrifice . . . I have dominion over the hungering dead, over the whole kingdom of death. I am an extremely accomplished necromancer. I cannot *make you invisible*."

"I bet it's possible," said Csorwe.

"It is not," said Oranna. "If I were at my full strength, which I am not, I suppose I could transfigure you permanently into glass, which I doubt you would enjoy. Or, if you wished to avoid a certain person, I could bewitch them to make you inconspicuous to their eyes—although—"

"Yes?"

"I can do nothing about the guards at this distance. But the security perimeter does not see with mortal eyes. It detects certain signifiers—the warmth of your blood, your beating heart—and I might be able to cloak you from its notice, at least temporarily. I cannot promise it will last long enough to cover your return journey."

"I'll deal with that when it's time to leave," said Csorwe. She hadn't got this far by looking before she leapt. In her experience, a plan never survived long enough for an exit strategy to be worth anything anyway.

"And it will be very unpleasant for you."

"I can handle it," said Csorwe.

They took the cutter farther out, and made a long loop around the island. Csorwe stripped out of her outer clothes, and buckled her belt back on over her undershirt. She wished now that she hadn't left her good sword behind. If Sethennai even noticed, he would be disgusted by the pointlessness of the gesture. She had two good hunting knives, though, and if things went according to plan she wouldn't even need them.

"You will want to hold on to the rail," said Oranna, setting her hand on Csorwe's sternum. "This is going to hurt."

At first it just felt cold. Csorwe was more uneasy about the contact than the pain. Then the chill seemed to penetrate her bones, driving spikes of ice through her heart and lungs. She should never have trusted Oranna. This had been a mistake from the first. Oranna was killing her—draining the warmth from her body—she tried to breathe, sucking in great gasps of air, but it did her no good. The cold tore at her insides as if she had swallowed great claws. She tried to pull away, reaching for her knives, but her hands were clumsy, as if they had swollen into clubs, and she couldn't fasten them on anything. Panic swirled and tightened around her.

At last Oranna let her go. The damp heat of a summer's night in Qarsazh wrapped around her. She clutched the rail with both hands, retching.

"You—you weren't joking," she said, when she could speak again. "That hurt like hell."

"Well, it wasn't much fun for me, either," said Oranna. "Living flesh is a nightmare to practice upon. Anyway, it worked. You won't have any difficulty with the perimeter."

Csorwe swallowed and nodded. She didn't feel any different. She would have to take Oranna's word for it. She remembered, uneasily, how successfully she and Shuthmili had tricked Morga.

"Guess this is the last I'll see of you," said Csorwe. "Nothing to stop you taking the cutter, once I'm gone."

Oranna smiled. "As I said, I gave you my word. And you gave me yours."

"Uh-huh," said Csorwe. It had occurred to her that the blood-pledge wouldn't mean much if Oranna couldn't find her.

"Why would I devalue my own currency? Why would you?" said Oranna. "Besides, there aren't many runaways from the House of Silence. We ought to stick together." Csorwe was certain this was intended purely to throw her off balance, and it worked. "We are . . . in a sense . . . sisters, don't you think?" Oranna went on, and her smile became practically phosphorescent.

"You sent your sister to die," said Csorwe.

"Ejarwa did what she wanted to do," said Oranna. "I will remain here with the cutter, circling the island. And you had better hope I'm not lying, because I don't see how else you mean to get away. When you get hold of Shuthmili, bring her to a window and give the signal."

The water was surprisingly cold, but the air was balmy and the waves quiet. Csorwe crossed the first trail of lights with a brief tingle of alarm, but she felt nothing. The light didn't change. That might not mean anything either way, but it was encouraging. She glanced back over her shoulder, and saw the shadow of the cutter moving off, deep black against the blue night sky.

She crossed another two perimeters—still no response—and reached the shallows. She lay on her belly in the water for some time, looking up at the fortress. The beach here was a short fingernail of gravel at the bottom of a steep cliff. There was a jetty, where one or two boats were moored, and a staircase cut into the cliff, only just visible in the moonlight. Two Wardens were wandering up and down the jetty, coming in and out of view. Csorwe couldn't always see them, but their boots slapped on the boards, louder than the hissing of the waves.

She stalked up out of the water. One of the Wardens seemed to notice something, and stopped in mid-stride. She froze, not daring even to look round. A moment passed—two, three—and then the Wardens returned to their patrol.

At last she reached the bottom of the cliffside stair. This was more dangerous. Once she was high enough, she was absolutely exposed.

The stairs were narrow and slippery with spray under her bare feet. The wind cut through her wet clothes as though she were naked. At least she could see the Wardens on the jetty easily from here. As she climbed she watched them trundling back and forth.

She couldn't see what was at the top of the cliff. If someone was there Csorwe would need to deal with them before they could raise the alarm. And what if there were two of them?

She crouched at the top of the steps and listened for talk, footsteps, breathing—anything. Nothing but the sound of the sea below, and the wind blowing in the dry grass.

There were no guards. There was only the fortress, so big that it blotted out the sky, and its great outer wall, and the forgotten sally port that she had to hope still existed.

The stairs in the hillside, said a treacherous voice in her back-brain. *The door in the stone. You're going to your death, Csorwe. There are only two certain things, you know that? Hunger and death. Those are the only things you can rely on.*

She sidled along the edge of the cliff, staying low. There were guards at the main entrance to the fortress, and others on the wall, but at least there was a little cover here in the grass. The sally port was at the far edge, where the cliff had eroded until it was almost flush with the wall. Csorwe had a few nasty moments scrambling out to reach it. It would be pretty funny to come all this way and die by falling over your own feet into the sea.

The sally port was barricaded with planks, but they were soft and swollen with water; it was easy to batter her way through. Not so easy to do it silently, but she didn't seem to have drawn any attention.

The opening gave onto a narrow passage, slanting upward and half-full of loose gravel, which slid and crumbled under her feet.

Once or twice she had to cling on for balance and hope the floor wouldn't give way altogether. Gravel rolled away beneath her, bouncing out of the sally port and cascading into the sea below.

She scrambled out into a slightly wider passage, and then reached a door, latched on the other side. Csorwe finagled a blade past the jamb and, little by little, hitched up the latch. The hinges gave a sad, crunchy little squeak as the door opened, and she came out into the back of a storeroom, full of barrels and boxes. The sea breeze was gone. This place smelled of dust and stale coffee. She crouched behind a gigantic jar of olive oil to catch her breath. If the vision she had been granted in the Shrine was accurate, she should have come out on the ground floor, where they kept the guards' quarters, record offices, that sort of thing.

She scrambled over the barrels and out to the door of the pantry. It wasn't locked, and she didn't hear anyone nearby.

The ground floor was virtually empty. Csorwe agonised over the safest way to pass the open door of a kitchen, but it turned out there was nobody inside but a young man listlessly mopping the floor. He didn't look up once.

She made her way undetected up several stories—administrative offices, a library, a wing of private Inquisitorial studies, and Quincuriate quarters. There were many more guards here, but they patrolled in regular patterns and it was easy to avoid them. There were magical wards too: worked into the doorframes and carved upon the panels, disguised as harmless decoration. Sethennai had taught her enough to recognise and avoid them.

Csorwe waited for the last patrol to pass, then slunk out into the corridor again. From here she could see the stairs up to the next floor. There was nothing left but the top floor. According to the thief, that was the prison level.

Shuthmili was here, upstairs, only just out of reach. Csorwe's nerves, already drawn taut, began to screech in discord. What if she was too late? Shuthmili had already resisted for so long. What if she had given in?

She drew back into an alcove and tried to calm herself. It was such an amateur move to start thinking about things when you were working. She let another patrol pass by, then darted for the staircase.

Stairs were always difficult, and these were particularly bad. Whatever you tried, you were exposed from one side or the other. There was only a tiny blind spot at the top, where an arrow-slit window let in a grey shaft of moonlight.

At the top of the stairs was another corridor. There was no attempt to hide the wards and seals cut into the walls, into every block and every panel. Csorwe could almost feel the press of them: a low buzz at the edge of hearing, a flattened quality of light, a curdled thickness in the air.

The wards didn't seem to respond to Csorwe's presence. She had to hope Oranna's spell was still working.

Csorwe had been in prisons before. She knew roughly what to expect: muttering, shouting, even singing. There was no sound here at all, just the buzzing of the seals, like dust made audible, and a faint draught coming from somewhere.

She didn't see any guards. Maybe it wasn't wise to leave the prisoners any sort of potential sacrifice to work with.

There was no cover here, either, just dozens of doors, all closed and barred. Shuthmili could be behind any one of them, but she needed to be quick. She couldn't risk calling out. For a moment she considered some flashy Talasseres move, like unbolting every door and escaping with Shuthmili in the chaos, but she could see too many ways for that to end badly.

She went on down the corridor of doors, wondering where it ended.

The sound of the draught got louder as she walked. Maybe someone had left an open window, and the wind from the sea was getting in.

It didn't sound like the sea. There was a hiss of blowing sand in it, as though she were back in the Speechless Sea, as though the corridor were a canyon and a storm was building in the desert beyond.

She looked back the way she had come. She couldn't see the stairs any longer, only doors, stretching off into the distance.

The noise waxed, building like a thunderhead into a great rumbling swell of sound, though the feeling of the wind was still soft, only brushing Csorwe's bare skin and stirring her hair. Ahead of her: nothing but doors, and the corridor stretching on and on.

She had time to think, *For fuck's sake, of course it was too easy, of course, that's why it was so empty everywhere. Oh, shit.*

Doors, and more identical doors. They could have locked up a whole city of people in this place. She broke into a run.

As if in answer, the wind whipped about her ears, more forceful now, and getting louder. Fear can be useful. That was what Sethennai said. This fear, she felt as a fog: thick, sickly, paralysing.

At last the corridor reached its end, in a blank wall of bare stone. Csorwe stopped ten feet away. She could no more drag her eyes from the wall than she could have looked away from a predator about to spring. In that blank expanse was a threat she could not articulate. She was trapped here in this dead hallway, only her and the uncanny roar of the desert wind. The fog grew thicker, numbing her responses, slowing her reactions.

The wall changed without changing. Not a barrier but a tunnel, a hollow way, opening before her. The wind was howling in the tunnel and someone was walking toward her, like something coming up out of a nightmare. Someone dressed in white, head bowed, walking against the wind but purposeful, unswerving, relentless.

It was a Vigil Adept. The world dissolved around her, and she felt herself falling.

24

Neither a Blessing Nor a Curse

THE PRISONER IS CONTAINED, Inquisitor," said Vigil. "I'm afraid I made no progress with the interrogation."

Qanwa Zhiyouri made a dismissive gesture. "I'm not particularly interested in anything she'd have to say for herself. Had quite enough of *that* in Tlaanthothe. It's too bad we couldn't take her immediately, but I do not desire Belthandros Sethennai as an enemy. And you would have missed out on the fun of closing the trap."

Vigil nodded. Zhiyouri didn't know whether a Quincury could actually have fun, but she had certainly enjoyed planning the operation: making sure the old sally port was clear, reducing security without tipping off the intruder that something was wrong, and ensuring that she found her way safely to the old prison level where Vigil had set up its lobster pot.

"Let me know if she does say anything," said Zhiyouri. "I don't think she's got what you'd call a very developed psyche, but she might be more forthcoming now she's outside Sethennai's protection."

She dismissed Vigil, called for a fresh pot of coffee and some biscuits, and summoned Shuthmili to her office. Best to give her one last chance to see sense.

"Please," said Zhiyouri to her niece. "Take a seat. Help yourself to a biscuit. They're made with honey from the Qanwa estate, you know. You must be hungry."

Zhiyouri knew this, since she had been the one who had ordered the Wardens to reduce Shuthmili's rations. If Shuthmili was determined to be difficult, she was not going to be comfortable.

"I am fine, thank you," said Shuthmili, though Zhiyouri noted her eyes were fixed on the plate of biscuits.

"Just between the two of us," said Zhiyouri, "don't you think it's time we sorted out this silly mess?"

Shuthmili blinked, folding her hands demurely in her lap, well out of the way of the biscuits. "I'm afraid I've lost track of time a bit. Is there a rush?"

Most mages out of the School of Aptitude were shrinking things, quiet and eager to please. Zhiyouri found Shuthmili's assurance distasteful, but she forced a laugh.

"Well, no real rush, I suppose," she said, "but we've already wasted a certain amount of time retrieving you from various scrapes, haven't we?"

No response.

"I know you have your doubts about the Quincuriate, but I assure you it is no bad thing to have a vocation," said Zhiyouri. "It's a gift to know that you are where you're meant to be, doing what you're meant to do."

"Is that how you feel about the Inquisitorate, Aunt Zhiyouri?" said Shuthmili sweetly.

"Of course," she said. "The work, that's the thing. You would be much happier if you had proper work to do. I certainly always am."

"You don't really believe that, though," said Shuthmili. "You don't think you're like me."

Shuthmili evidently did not recognise that Zhiyouri was paying her a supreme courtesy by implying that they were, in any sense, equals. Zhiyouri felt a growing urge to slap her. Instead she smiled, as if entertaining a child's joke. "Well, not in all respects," she said.

"It would be simpler if I were to enter Archer Quincury, wouldn't it?" said Shuthmili. "Not a single mage in four hundred years of spotless genealogy, and now me. It makes life difficult. I can see that. If I become Archer Five then you can erase my name from the Qanwa record."

"I think that's rather unfair of you," said Zhiyouri. Not to mention rather self-centred. "In the Quincuriate you would be contented and successful. It is a position of honour. At the moment your position can do nothing but damage to the house, and you are plainly miserable."

"Yes. You only want what's best for me," she said. "So I've heard."

"I want to help you," said Zhiyouri. "I understand that you are young and it is never pleasant to make decisions that will alter the rest of your life. But you would make an *exceptional* Quincury Adept, according to every possible assessment. It is an insult to the Nine to waste that kind of talent."

"Careful," said Shuthmili. "It isn't a talent. *Neither a blessing nor a curse, but a duty.*"

"Semantics," said Zhiyouri, snapping off the word. It was a bit late for Shuthmili to turn pious now, but two could play at that game. "In any case, shirking a duty is also an affront to the Nine."

"If the Nine cared what we did, people would behave better," said Shuthmili, with a smile as thin as the sheen on a beetle's shell. "It wouldn't bother you, would it, if I had turned fully heretic? You're so desperate to get me safely into the Quincuriate, it doesn't matter what kind of corruption I might take with me."

"And what kind of life do you think you're going to have outside the Quincuriate?" said Zhiyouri. The fact that Shuthmili was right made her angrier—Zhiyouri's private view of religion was that it was useful for some purposes, and otherwise tiresome, but that wasn't something one could admit to in polite company, and it was uncomfortable to be seen through. "You can't think they'll ever let you out again. No more jaunts with the Survey Office. What does that leave? Tutoring in the School of Aptitude? You'd be a glorified governess and you'd die of the mage-blight. Is that really what you want?"

"I suppose so," said Shuthmili. "Or there's always ship service, not that it really solves the mage-blight issue."

Zhiyouri had to assume this was a joke. Ship service would be an obscene waste of Shuthmili's talents. "Do you really think you'd enjoy life as part of a warship?"

Shuthmili shrugged. "Well, I'm sure my superiors will determine the best placement."

Zhiyouri bit down on a snarl and willed herself to be calm. She held all the cards here. Let Shuthmili have her fun now, and learn later that it did not pay to antagonise Qanwa Zhiyouri. "Don't you see that they already have?" she said, mildly.

"Oh, yes," said Shuthmili. "I'd be an excellent Quincury Adept. I do know that. But it's the only placement I have the capacity to refuse, and I find I'm quite enjoying the experience."

"Yes," said Zhiyouri. "You know, I did think you might be."

You could let your quarry believe that she had managed to conceal her pitiful secrets, that she had won, that she was safe. But the Traitor's Grave had many cells, and Zhiyouri had many strategies, and Shuthmili had no notion what was locked away in any of them.

Csorwe lurched into wakefulness, feeling as though someone had driven nails into her skull. She wasn't tied up, but a heavy fog of weakness pressed down on her. She couldn't move, nor could she see anything more than a diffuse day-brightness. Her ears felt tight, as if she had sunk to the bottom of a deep pond.

All around her was the sound of wind grating on concrete. Gradually, she began to hear voices.

"—brought me up here?"

It was Shuthmili. She was here! Csorwe's heart leapt, despite it all. She tried to uncurl and look for her, but she couldn't make her limbs behave, or even open her eyes. Whatever they had done to her, it was taking a long time to wear off.

"I thought you might like some air," said a woman. It took Csorwe a moment to recognise this as Qanwa Zhiyouri.

"How thoughtful," said Shuthmili.

"Well," said Qanwa brightly. "We don't make good decisions when we're cooped up inside. And I like the sea, don't you?" Qanwa added. *I hold my faith in the Mara, from whom all things derive.*"

"From whom all things *arise*," said Shuthmili. Csorwe had never been so glad to hear someone being an awful pedant. She tried again to open her eyes. No luck.

Qanwa laughed, not pleasantly. "It's been a long time since my Inquisitorial exams."

The wind never let up. Csorwe could taste the sea in the back of her throat. She kept trying to move. If she could only get to Shuthmili . . .

"Let's cut to the chase, shall we?" said Qanwa. "You think that you have some kind of choice vis-à-vis the Quincuriate. I understand that you have had some fun keeping us all hanging. I have now reached the end of my patience, and it's time that you understand the situation."

"I understand the situation perfectly," said Shuthmili. "You haven't had any luck cajoling me into the tether, so we've reached the part where you threaten me. But if you kill me I'm useless to you. You can't give me anything I want, and you can't take away anything I mind losing. Surely this conversation has to end sooner or later."

"I think," said Qanwa, "that you will want to hear me out."

Csorwe heard footsteps on concrete nearby, coming down toward her.

"Thank you, Vigil, if you don't mind . . ." said Qanwa.

Csorwe was lifted and carried up what seemed like a short flight of stairs. Two people, at least. They weren't deliberately rough with her, but they might as well have been delivering a bolster.

"And start waking her up, I think," said Qanwa. Csorwe's eyes and ears cleared, as if a wax seal had been peeled away. She could see where she was, not that it was much of a blessing.

They were on the roof of the Traitor's Grave, a flat grey expanse high above the flat grey expanse of the sea. The wind was even louder here, and colder, biting through Csorwe's shirt to nip at her skin. Two Adepts of Vigil Quincury were holding her up under her arms. The grip felt like two steel vices pinning her upright by the ribs.

Qanwa Zhiyouri leant against the parapet. The collar of her surcoat was pulled up high against the wind. Beside her, looking frighteningly neat and tranquil and ordinary, as if she had accompanied her aunt on a trip to the seaside of her own free will, was Shuthmili.

Csorwe tried to call out to her, but her mouth wouldn't open. Shuthmili's eyes widened, but her expression didn't change from what it had been: a waxen mask of distaste, belonging to someone who had not only seen a maggot, but who was resigned to seeing maggots every day, and had begun to be disappointed in their quality.

"I know the Inquisitorate is your *vocation*, Aunt," said Shuthmili, "but did you ever consider a career in theatrical production?"

"If your father knew how ill-mannered you've become, I'm sure he'd weep," said Qanwa, not sounding particularly offended. She advanced on Csorwe and the Vigil Adepts, and peered at her as if examining a piece of fruit for bruises before purchase.

If Csorwe could have bared her tusks at Qanwa, she would have, but her body remained totally inert. Her heart wandered sleepily on. The wakeful part of her mind was screaming and hammering on the bars, but her body couldn't feel enraged, or even particularly frightened.

"What is the point of this?" said Shuthmili. She didn't come any closer—didn't move, in fact, from the parapet where she was standing.

"She tried to break into the Grave," said Qanwa. "I'm trying to make up my mind what we ought to do with her."

"Ah," said Shuthmili. "I see."

"I'm glad you see," said Qanwa, strolling back toward Shuthmili. "There's no reason this has to be at all unpleasant. All I ask is that you consider my points."

"And if I don't, that's when things become unpleasant," said Shuthmili. "You really are a woman of god, aren't you, Zhiyouri?"

"I have been called to serve as befits my abilities," said Qanwa, piously. Then she turned and Csorwe saw her grin like a jackal. It was the expression of someone much younger, someone who hadn't learned that you shouldn't let your enemy know they were beaten.

Shuthmili laughed, angrily. It sounded like icicles shattering. "Let me see if I've got this right, Aunt. If I do as you ask, and choose the tether, and serve my country, and clear the family name, then you'll let Csorwe go?"

"Of course," said Qanwa. "She's done no lasting harm. There's no need to be vindictive."

Csorwe could see, with bleak clarity, where this was going. *It's all right,* she said to herself. *It'll be all right. I always knew this was temporary.* You could only borrow so much time.

"And if I decide to be stubborn . . ." said Shuthmili.

"The Inquisitorate has never looked mercifully on those who corrupt our Adepts," said Qanwa. "And you were so very promising. Such a shame."

"If I don't do what you want, you'll hurt her," Shuthmili translated.

"As you pointed out, it would be self-defeating to hurt *you,*" said Qanwa. "In any case, you are my niece. But I don't believe you're quite as detached from worldly matters as you'd have us all believe."

There was absolutely no chance that Qanwa would ever let Csorwe go. She didn't even have to wonder about that. Even if Shuthmili caved right away, it was all over for her. She could just about raise her head by now, and she tried to catch Shuthmili's eye, willing her to understand it.

"You seem to enjoy having a choice," said Qanwa. "This is the nature of the choices that we have to make, as adults, in the real world. I can give you some time to think about it, if you like."

Don't listen to her, Csorwe thought. *Don't do it. She's lying to you.*

Shuthmili didn't take her eyes off Qanwa.

Don't do it. Don't do it, Shuthmili. Once she's got you tethered she can do whatever she wants to me and you won't care enough to try and stop her.

"That's all right," said Shuthmili at last. "I've made my choice."

Qanwa unclenched her hands, relaxing minutely into her victory. Perhaps she didn't see the set of Shuthmili's jaw, or didn't recognise what she was seeing.

"I won't," said Shuthmili. "I'm sorry. I will not."

The relief felt, to Csorwe, like being dipped into a hot bath. At last the joints of her fingers and toes began to loosen.

"She promised she would help me, and she left me," said Shuthmili, matter-of-factly. "I was happy before I met her. I never thought of anything else. She convinced me to leave, and then she left me behind. She ruined my life. I owe her nothing."

It stung. But it was true. Csorwe's promises and good intentions meant nothing. When the time came she had abandoned Shuthmili out of pure selfishness, chasing down Belthandros Sethennai's dream of power. She had left Shuthmili worse off than before.

Hate me if you hate me. Just don't give in, thought Csorwe.

Qanwa watched her. "If that's the case, then . . ." She made a gesture, and the Vigil Adepts hoisted Csorwe up, holding her high, and carried her toward the parapet. Csorwe couldn't so much as wriggle. The most she could do was claw her fingers at them.

"I suppose we may as well drop her over the side," said Qanwa.

The Vigil Adepts walked her out to a gap in the parapet, where the roof of the Traitor's Grave dropped away into the sea.

"I don't want her to suffer," said Shuthmili. Csorwe couldn't see her face any longer, but her voice hadn't changed. "But if that's what you're making me choose, then I prefer to live."

Csorwe dangled like bait on a hook. Her pulse was starting to race, as though her heart had finally caught up to the situation. The fog was finally lifting. She could move her wrists and ankles, not that it was going to do her much good. All that Qanwa had to do was order her Adepts to open their hands, and that would be the end of her.

Csorwe had always imagined she would die in a panic, in some kind of fight, and she had always hoped that she wouldn't know at the time what was happening. But this wasn't so bad. It really wasn't. Eight stolen years and one short drop into the abyss.

"Shuthmili," said Qanwa. "On some level I admire your stubbornness. I really do. But you've been saying this girl's name in your sleep for weeks. Are you really going to let this happen?"

"Do you ever think you ought to find some kind of hobby outside work?" said Shuthmili. "It sounds as though you need an outlet. You're beginning to see conspiracies."

The Adepts dragged Csorwe back from the edge, brought her

over to where Qanwa and Shuthmili were standing, and dropped her on the ground. Her legs collapsed beneath her immediately, and she fell back on the concrete.

Qanwa looked down at Csorwe, and prodded her shoulder with the toe of her boot. "You know the choice you have to make, Shuthmili."

"And you know my answer," she said.

Qanwa sighed. "You make life very difficult for those around you," she said. "You say that you don't want her to suffer. Vigil."

One of the Vigil Adepts loomed into view. The mask looked like a hole in the sky.

All at once, as though a blanket of numbness had been lifted, Csorwe could feel all her limbs again, but she couldn't get up. She was bound in place, but not by ropes. Something looped and scuttled around her wrists and ankles, and where its barbs cut her skin, she felt the beginnings of the numbness returning. The crawling thing coiled around her neck, pinning her head back against the concrete.

"Stop it!" Shuthmili was saying. "Tell them to stop it!"

"Are you prepared to reconsider?" said Qanwa.

"Go to hell," said Shuthmili.

"Shuthmili," said Csorwe, struggling against the crawling thing and the panic as if they were one substance. "Don't—"

Inquisitor Qanwa peered down at her, a misty silhouette against the sunlight. Csorwe growled through clenched teeth.

Nobody was coming for her. And Psamag had showed her exactly how long this could go on.

Qanwa nodded to the Vigil Adept. "Again."

Csorwe felt something wriggling in her throat, something extending legs and feelers as though breaking out of its chrysalis.

She gagged, struggling for breath, and felt the thing begin to crawl upward, scrambling toward her mouth. Vigil stood and watched her choke.

Csorwe's breath began to fail and her vision darkened as the crawling thing scuttled out between her lips. Then it was gone, wriggling away across the concrete, and she gasped for air.

"Try something else," said Qanwa.

One of the Vigil Adepts knelt beside Csorwe, and laid a hand quite gently on her forehead.

Csorwe took a deep breath. The cool air stung her mouth. *Don't listen,* she thought, as if Shuthmili could hear. *It's not worth it. Remember how I left you.* She was terrified to speak. What if Shuthmili thought she was begging for mercy, or for help . . .

Then the pain swallowed up the world in a terrible radiance. Csorwe was eyeless, voiceless, nameless, a single unravelling skein of awareness, flayed open and dissolving in fire. She was dying—she was already dead—no mortal thing could survive this kind of pain.

All she could see was the mask of Vigil, like a single gigantic eye, and then the world blurred into smears of ash.

Csorwe heard herself screaming. Flat against the ground, limbs splayed as though she had been pinned for display.

When her vision returned, she saw that Vigil was holding the crawling thing in its hands, something jointed but sinuous, like a great centipede. It struggled in Vigil's grip, curling and uncurling. Its front parts had feelers like little bent horns. The Adept pinched them in gloved fingertips, first one then the other, and twisted them away, quite casually.

"Shuthmili—" she said. As she spoke she felt another crawling thing, ridged and spined, tighten around her neck, cutting off her voice.

Qanwa strode toward Shuthmili. "If I'm wrong, and you're not lying to me, and she means nothing to you—then *why is she here?*"

"I have no idea," said Shuthmili. This had the ring of truth. "She must have come to look for me of her own accord," she went on, and faltered for a moment. "Aunt. She hasn't done anything wrong. There's no reason to do this."

"That's entirely up to you," said Qanwa.

"Zhiyouri," said Shuthmili, with perfect self-possession. Her eyes were very dark. "Let her go."

"You know what you have to do," said Zhiyouri.

"Fine," said Shuthmili. "If that's how it is."

Down at her side, out of Zhiyouri's sight, Shuthmili made a slow gesture in the air, her fingers curling and uncurling, tracing a pattern like smoke, and clenched her fist.

Then she moved. She swivelled on her heels, reached into the air, and out of nowhere drew a blade of silvered glass, as though breaking off a piece of the sky. Light flashed on the blade like a spray of water—and with impossible speed she thrust the sword into the chest of one of the Vigil Adepts. It wriggled for a moment, audibly gasping for breath, and then fell still.

The other Adept screamed like a wounded horse and stepped back, clutching at its own chest as though trying to pull out the blade. Then its white robes darkened: white to red to a livid grey, like ink spreading through water, black and translucent. Then it was nothing more than a statue of grey crystal, fixed in position.

Shuthmili drew her sword from the chest of the dead Adept, then turned, blank as a sleepwalker, and made a sweeping motion with her other hand. The statue shattered.

All this took perhaps a second. Directly overhead the sky

seethed and coiled in a closing spiral. Clouds swarmed toward the epicentre, as though scenting blood. The surface of the sky began to pucker and twist.

"Shuthmili—" said Qanwa. "What are you *doing*—"

Csorwe had seen carnage before, in its aftermath and in its full rage. What followed was like a dream of butchery, an illuminated vision, a howl of agony at the edge of fever. She couldn't make sense of it. High Inquisitor Qanwa's tongue became a crystal pendulum and pearls discharged themselves from her eye sockets. Shuthmili's glass blade slashed open her belly in a single stroke. Each living organ became a gleaming lump of precious stone, tumbling from the torn flesh under its own weight.

It was hard to say at what point Qanwa Zhiyouri died, or whether she died at all. Her body was racked by tides of transformation. If Shuthmili's expression had been anything other than bland, this would have seemed horribly playful. Dark coils flashed and flickered in the air around her, and Csorwe remembered: *Zinandour is trying to find her way back to the mortal worlds. I could be the gate through which she returns.*

Csorwe didn't care about the dragon goddess, but that didn't sound like something Shuthmili could survive. Despite her screaming nerves, she managed to tip herself over onto her stomach and prop herself up. She had no sense of how long this took, seconds or minutes or hours.

At last Qanwa was done with dying. The corpse lay unrecognisable on the flagstones, laced and encrusted with jewels, wounds inlaid with gold. Shuthmili stood over her, perfectly still but breathing hard. Her glass sword lay discarded on the concrete; at some point she seemed to have decided that she preferred to use her hands. She was surrounded by a halo of shadowy tendrils that writhed whenever she moved.

Csorwe sat up, willing Shuthmili to turn toward her, to say something—even just: *Go away, Csorwe*—anything at all to prove that she was still herself.

At last Shuthmili opened her mouth, half formed a word, but said nothing. She was trembling. When she spoke at last it seemed to be a prayer.

Csorwe managed to get to her feet. As she did so, she saw movement on the other side of the roof. Someone was coming up the other stairs. White robe, black mask, blue sash—another Vigil Adept.

"Shuthmili!" she called. "Look out!"

Shuthmili's eyes darkened, perhaps in recognition, and she readied herself again.

Csorwe lunged for the glass sword, and rose with it in hand. She could almost keep her balance now. She couldn't lie there and let Shuthmili fight alone, even if there was nothing she could do against such an enemy.

"Traitor," said the Adept, in a voice distorted by unimaginable pain. It walked unevenly, one hand clawed to its chest in memory of the wound.

As it spoke, Qanwa's mutilated body began to stir. It came crawling across the floor toward Shuthmili—faster than Csorwe could have imagined was possible, bending its limbs in ways they could never have moved in life—and dragged itself upright, trailing ropes of pearls like guts.

"I'll take her," said Csorwe, and stumbled into the fray.

At least this was a fight that she understood. Her body ached, and the shape and weight of the glass sword was bizarre, but here was an enemy who could be struck, knocked back, beaten down. The revenant was slow, heavy, and half formed, and Csorwe couldn't be certain that it would even stay dead, but at least she understood what she was doing moment to moment. It was nothing to the fight between Shuthmili and Vigil.

Csorwe had seen a wizards' duel before, but Sethennai and Olthaaros were politicians, and they'd had an audience. Nothing about this fight was ostentatious. Neither of them was trying to persuade anyone of anything. They faced one another, not speaking, scarcely moving, never breaking eye contact. No retreat was possible. The slightest weakening meant death.

There were two other Vigil Adepts out there. Csorwe and Shuthmili needed to end this before they could arrive, or else before the effort drove Shuthmili over the edge.

Csorwe struck Qanwa's shoulder. The blade struck a plate of mother-of-pearl at an odd angle, and as she tried to recover, she felt a blow to her midsection, and heard Shuthmili cry out.

Qanwa's corpse had punched her in the stomach. Its hands were golden claws, as sharp as knives. The corpse withdrew the claw, shining with blood, and drove it in once more. She felt the pain remotely, dully, and her head began to spin. She struggled, slashing wildly with the glass sword, but the world was receding—her vision darkened—her hand slackened—the sword slipped from her grip, and she fell.

25

Glass and Ashes

THE UNSPOKEN ONE COULD sanction many things, but not the breaking of a bargain. Oranna reminded herself of this as dawn broke over the Traitor's Grave. Apostate, deceiver, killer, yes, when necessary, but she had never been a breaker of promises. Nor did she intend to lose out on the favour Csorwe had pledged to her.

Still . . . she had been looping the cutter in circles all night, like a nervous vulture sizing up the suspect carcass of the prison island. Now the sun was up, she had already used the cutter's spare fuel supply, and it was only a matter of time before someone spotted her. She didn't intend to spend any amount of time in a Qarsazhi jail. If Csorwe didn't signal in the next few minutes, she would have to leave.

Satisfied with the reasonableness of this decision, she settled herself at the wheel. A moment later, she was startled halfway out of her seat by an unearthly shriek of rage. It came to her beyond sight and sound, on the same level that she heard the whisperings of the Unspoken.

Oh, good grief, thought Oranna. *She's killed a Quincury Adept.*

She wheeled the cutter at once, turning in toward the prison. No use worrying now about setting off any alarms; she doubted they would register high on the guards' list of priorities just at that moment. The scream went on and on, rising in spikes of outraged intensity, wailing wordlessly of mutilation and loss.

As she neared the Traitor's Grave, it became clear that things were worse than she had imagined. Some kinds of magical conflagration were visible from miles off, like the pillar of ash cloud before the volcano coughs up its poison.

Once or twice, Oranna had seen a practitioner deliberately burn out. Most of her kind who lived to adulthood were good at moderation, always careful to maintain their resources, weighing out each expenditure carefully against the desired result. Sometimes, though, someone would decide that the desired result was a gigantic explosion, and never mind that the price was more than they could pay.

The screaming ended abruptly.

At the same time, the engine of the cutter began to cough. Oranna checked the fuel gauge and cursed: the hand of the dial was pressed almost flat against the edge. She had only a matter of minutes before the vessel fell out of the sky, and only one place she could possibly land.

That was her decision made for her, then. An interesting situation had always been her weakness.

Unspoken and Unspeakable One, if this is to be the day of my death, don't think I have forgotten the bargain we made, she thought. She remembered the silence, the quiet girls lined up to form an honour guard, her sister enthroned in darkness. *I am yours.*

The sky above the Traitor's Grave shimmered as she brought the cutter in. There was a scorched and oily haze in the air. The roof of the prison was distorted beyond recognition, whipped up in glassy sheets and spikes like rose petals curled in around the heart of the flower. These petals were scattered with corpses, some in lively states of disassembly. One Quincury Adept was pierced through with a spike of stone, and now dangled a foot above the ground, robes fluttering in the wind.

The only one still upright was a thin girl in white, on the last piece of flat ground at the centre of the devastation. She was kneeling over a crumpled body that might have been Csorwe's.

Ah, thought Oranna. *Aha.*

She landed the now-useless cutter and leapt out, feeling the charge of recent death in the air, the veins of power beneath her feet. She couldn't help thinking how easy it would be to give up all control, to let the power crackle through her, to let her cells return to dust. The urge to self-immolate must be contagious.

Qanwa Shuthmili looked up at her. Her eyes were dead black. Her face and robes were smeared with blood, though probably not her own. The power poured off her like smoke. Oranna abruptly recalled the nature of Shuthmili's patron.

If the poor girl was possessed it would be an additional complication that Oranna had not predicted, as much as she would be interested to meet the Dragon of Qarsazh in the flesh.

"So who am I talking to?" said Oranna. No point mincing her words.

"Go away," said Shuthmili.

Still mortal, then. She was very close to the brink, but holding steady. Like a cracked glass, nothing but the potential to shatter. The Traitor was not gentle with her vessels.

Before Oranna could answer, the body on the ground twitched, giving a dry, ugly gasp. Csorwe looked the way corpses always looked, but her body still sparked faintly with the defiance that distinguished living flesh from dead matter.

"I can't fix her," said Shuthmili. She was trembling. She kept her dead eyes fixed on Oranna, as though she couldn't bear to look down. "I've got nothing left."

Csorwe's belly was torn open as though some kind of wild animal had got hold of her; her shirt was dark with blood and ichor.

"I stopped the bleeding," said Shuthmili. "But I can't—"

"You *have* flown close to the sun," said Oranna.

"I'm not leaving without her," said Shuthmili.

"If you try to lift her, your rib cage is going to explosively decompress," said Oranna, omitting to mention that there was no way for them to leave now, anyway. "I do not need that. Sit down. I'll see if I can help her."

Shuthmili's Church training paid dividends: she sat down among the corpses and stared into space. Thank goodness for indoctrination.

Oranna knelt over the body. It really was a shame to get more bloodstains on this nice gown. Csorwe was still breathing, but Oranna could feel the outrage of ripped tissue and ruptured organs, the body struggling to manage without the blood it had already lost. She chewed her lip. She'd never studied medicine. Anything she tried might make matters worse.

Csorwe groaned faintly, as if she was far away from her body, and still receding. Nearby, Shuthmili twitched. Power sparked in her fingertips, writing itself across Oranna's perception like after-images of the sun.

"Don't even think about it," said Oranna. She suspected that if Shuthmili tried to channel now, her heart would burst, or the Dragon would come slithering out of her, or both.

No response. Oranna had never been good at dealing with young people.

"Don't be a fool," she said. "You need to eat, at the very least, before you try anything."

"I know," said Shuthmili. "Can't you—"

"I can give her an easy death, if it comes to it."

"No," said Shuthmili. The skin around her mouth was cracked and bluish, and her eyes were turning milky. She looked almost as bad as Csorwe, falling faster than anyone could pull her back.

"If you're sure," said Oranna. "A stomach wound is a bad way to go. It would be a mercy."

"*No.*" Another surge of power crackled and faded as she spoke. Oranna let it go. Not a good idea to goad her.

Shuthmili shouldn't have survived what she had done to the prison and its inhabitants. But then, Oranna hadn't expected her to survive the workings in the Hollow Monument, either. Did Qarsazh know what it had lost? The girl had destroyed at least three-fifths of a Quincury, so if they didn't know before, they did by now, and there was no chance they'd let her run. So, the Inquisitorate would be here soon, and in the meantime, Oranna was trapped in the middle of the ocean with the most dangerous practitioner she had encountered since Belthandros Sethennai.

Their prospects were not bright, but despair was not in Oranna's nature. The shard of rock crystal bound into her bosom bled power into her like a cold heartbeat, and it was a waste not to use it. It was even more of a waste for a Chosen Bride of the Unspoken to die far from home, to nobody's benefit.

"Let me look at her again," she said. Shuthmili was kneeling over the near-corpse herself, like a beast of prey guarding its kill. "Maybe there's something I can do—at least keep her alive until you're back up to strength."

Death was the caress of dry sand and cool water. The waves swelled, crashed, receded. Thought and memory slipped away like little fishes.

After some time it came to Csorwe that this was a dream, and that she must wake. She was flat on her back on the ground. She could feel her wounds healing. Skin and flesh simmered as they mended.

The seething sensation of the healing wound began to fade, giving way to the likelihood of pain. Cautiously, Csorwe felt under her shirt. Someone had bandaged her up. As long as she didn't move, it scarcely hurt at all. She could hear wind and waves, and the sound of someone crying, not far off, and trying to be quiet about it.

Csorwe swallowed a sluggish clot of blood and tried to lift her head. She was very stiff, but not so much worse than you'd expect after sleeping on a stone floor.

It was Shuthmili, curled up on the ground nearby, at the base of a jagged spike of concrete. She was holding the bloody sleeves of her dress up to her face, clamped over her nose and mouth to dampen the sound of her sobbing.

Watching any longer seemed indecent. Maybe she would prefer to be left alone. Csorwe was trying to decide whether to say something when she managed to twist the wrong way and had to bite down on a cry of pain.

Shuthmili heard the noise and turned, lowering her sleeves.

Her eyes were hollow and red with weeping, her whole face gaunt. She said nothing at first, her lip twitching as she tried to compose herself, until Csorwe spoke her name.

"Csorwe!" she said, coming to sit beside her. "How long have you been awake?"

"Only just now. You healed me?" said Csorwe, wishing she'd had time to prepare for this conversation.

"Me and Oranna. You're going to be fine. It'll hurt badly for a while, that's all."

"Where are we?" It was hard to see much without moving. They were surrounded by a crown of concrete spikes, each much bigger than Csorwe and tapering to a vicious point.

"Still on top of the Traitor's Grave," said Shuthmili. She followed Csorwe's eyes to the nearest spike. "After you—after I thought you were—I lost control for a while. But your cutter ran out of fuel. Oranna had to land before she crashed. She's just . . . uh . . . just attending to the bodies."

"Are you all right?" said Csorwe.

Long pause. "Gods preserve me, Csorwe," said Shuthmili eventually. "You saw what I've done."

"Yeah."

Shuthmili bit down on her lip to keep it from trembling. "Death is better than corruption," she said. "I was going to throw myself over the edge. Once Oranna was gone and you were safe. It would be the honourable thing to do. But I can't seem to make myself do it."

"Well . . . good," said Csorwe, feeling all over again like the bluntest of blunt instruments. "You don't—you don't *want* to die, do you?"

"No, I don't," said Shuthmili. "That's the worst part. Or—

no—the worst part is that I don't even feel very bad about it. I hated Zhiyouri."

"I can't say I was too sad to see her go—" said Csorwe.

"But I killed her," said Shuthmili. "And the others. And it felt good to do it—I mean, not the killing, that was nothing, it was like picking flowers, but I can't help thinking it proves they were right about me, all along."

"Right about what?" said Csorwe.

"That I'm just—all this time—whatever I do—" When she broke off, she stared at Csorwe in defiance for a few seconds before rubbing her eyes with her sleeve again.

"Look," said Csorwe. "I know about living with something you've done. However it happened."

"I just wish I could feel guilty at *all*, but I . . . I don't know what else I could have done."

"I know," said Csorwe.

"You must think I'm some kind of monster," said Shuthmili.

"Shuthmili," she said. "Whatever kind of monster you are, so am I." Before she could think about it too much, she reached out and took Shuthmili's hand in hers.

She had expected Shuthmili to pull away, either in shock or out of awkwardness, but she didn't. Neither of them said anything, and the moment went on.

"You can let yourself live with it," said Csorwe eventually, not daring to meet her eyes.

"I hope so," said Shuthmili.

A long moment passed. Shuthmili's fingers uncurled, little by little, and she traced her thumb over Csorwe's knuckle.

Before Csorwe could think how to respond to this, Shuthmili sprang back. Oranna was approaching. "You're awake," she said to

Csorwe, with rather less interest than if she had been commenting on Csorwe's haircut. "That's for the best. We don't have long. I suspect our time here will be numbered in hours rather than days, and a small number of hours at that. It seems Shuthmili did not have the wit to exterminate the guards as they fled this place."

"My apologies," said Shuthmili, sourly.

"It is done. We must assume that word will reach the mainland soon, if it hasn't already, and that a whole pack of Inquisitors will be here before nightfall. The only choice left open to us is to fight or surrender. I hope it is clear which path I favour."

Shuthmili's features set, like wax, into an expression of strain. "I thought perhaps the two of you might be able to get away, if the cutter might still float on the sea."

"Without you, you mean," said Csorwe. "No."

"Please," said Shuthmili. "They'll chase me forever. But they won't bother looking for you once they've dealt with me."

"No."

"Csorwe, you don't have to do this. You can't fight like this."

"I can't *walk* like this. But I'm not leaving you again," she said. She thought—hoped—that Shuthmili looked faintly relieved, just for a second.

"Then you should surrender," said Shuthmili. "Both of you. Tell them I put a compulsion on you."

Oranna laughed. "I've seen how your people treat their prisoners."

"If you run and they catch you, they will kill you," said Shuthmili.

"I was raised for death, and death has been my lifelong study. I have no fear of the end," said Oranna, as though that settled the matter.

"Csorwe?" said Shuthmili, becoming desperate.

"Think I spent long enough with your auntie to figure out how much I'd enjoy a Qarsazhi jail," said Csorwe. She reached out and took Shuthmili's hand again, no longer caring whether Oranna saw it or not. "All three of us were raised for death. I'd rather we chose it."

After a moment, Shuthmili nodded. "Well, then," she said. "I'm glad, I suppose. That we're all here together."

"You may be glad," said Oranna. "I am significantly pissed off." She grinned. "Well, *all strength fails*. But not just yet."

As Csorwe rested, Oranna took Shuthmili to ward them in. If the Qarsazhi intended to take them alive, rather than scouring the roof of the Traitor's Grave in cleansing fire, Oranna meant to make their lives difficult.

They moved from one concrete spike to another, scoring lines with shards of rock. Shuthmili picked up the technique almost immediately. She really was capable. Oranna reflected that it was pleasant to be able to rely on someone else's work, for once.

The Quincury Adepts lay in a neat row. One of their masks had come loose, and before Oranna replaced it she had seen the face of a woman no older than herself, fair for a Qarsazhi, with a dusting of freckles. At the end of the row was a pile of jewels and glass and feathers in the vague shape of a corpse.

"This one made you angry," said Oranna, indicating the heap. There were two real diamonds in it, each the size of an eye. Oranna pocketed them.

"Yes," said Shuthmili, tracing a line with clinical precision. "My aunt."

"Ah," said Oranna. "Family."

Oranna cast around for something else to talk about, feeling strongly that she had borne enough silence, and didn't intend to spend her last hours in stoic contemplation. Before she could think of anything, Shuthmili spoke up.

"What is it that you wanted from the Unspoken? I mean, once you'd achieved your unprecedented union or whatever it was?"

"Oh, you know about that?" said Oranna. She supposed it didn't matter who knew, now that it was never going to happen. She needed to resign herself to that. "Why? Are you considering an approach to the Dragon of Qarsazh?"

Shuthmili looked shocked, though not actively disgusted. "No. Csorwe told me. And I don't think it's possible."

"I think Pentravesse managed it. But I suppose it's the dream of a child, really. The Unspoken One and me, conquering in eternity, never dying. So it goes."

They went on around the roof of the prison, making a garland of wards among the ruined parapets. Shuthmili was a very inventive practitioner. It really was a shame they were never going to get a chance to compare notes properly.

"I could have stayed in Tlaanthothe," said Oranna, tracing her final control sigil. "Belthandros would have kept me kindly for as long as I could outlast the mage-blight. It would have been very pleasant. I suppose there is some version of me who could have been happy with him. Consider it a cautionary tale, if you wish," she added. Csorwe and Shuthmili had been holding hands, after all. Not that it was likely to end well for them. The gods made no allowances for young love, but perhaps it was worth having it while you could.

"You wanted immortality, then," said Shuthmili.

"Oh, yes, that was the grand plan. And I wanted to see how he would react," said Oranna. "It's funny, isn't it, to end up here, after all this? After Ejarwa. After everything else I've lost." She caught Shuthmili's sceptical glance. "Yes, much of which I ruined of my own accord. I always intended to take my place in history. I'm beginning to think I might be a fool."

"I don't blame you for wanting to live," said Shuthmili, though her tone made it clear that she thought it was a stretch.

Oranna shrugged. "Well, there's living and living. Perhaps I should have stayed in Belthandros' gilded cage. I wonder whether he'll be sad to learn about this. And that really is enough of my secrets. I intend to take the rest of them to the grave. But you really ought to say something to Csorwe."

"What?" said Shuthmili. "What kind of thing?"

"Whatever it is people say to one another," said Oranna. "Oh, don't be prim. I've seen how you look at her. I lived in the cloister for long enough to understand how these things work, and *you* are certainly smart enough to figure it out. Though I must say I have my doubts about Csorwe. Say something, or don't. We'll all die anyway."

Night fell. Csorwe could just about sit up by now, which gave her a whole new position in which to do nothing and feel useless. Oranna had somehow managed to go to sleep. Shuthmili was checking the perimeter again.

Csorwe supposed she should have taken the chance to get comfortable with mortality, but in fact she found it very difficult to think about anything other than her fear that Shuthmili was avoiding her.

At last Shuthmili approached, carrying a lantern they had salvaged from the cutter. In that light she looked tired, but not despairing.

"You're still awake?" she said, creeping over to Csorwe.

"Yeah. Aren't you tired?"

"I don't want to sleep," said Shuthmili. "Listen." She knelt down next to Csorwe. "I'm sorry about, you know, before, when Zhiyouri . . . That I let it go on so long. I didn't know what to do. I know that sounds pathetic. I'd been scared of her for so long I didn't realise I could stop her."

Csorwe could almost have laughed. "I've spent this whole time thinking how to say sorry to *you*. I thought probably you meant it, what you said to your aunt."

"What did I say?"

"Nothing—" No, it was no good not saying it now. She had to know, even if it was true. "That you were happy before you met me and I ruined your life."

"No!" said Shuthmili. "No—I was just saying things—I hoped Zhiyouri would believe it." She gave a taut smile. "Csorwe, before I met you, my idea of happiness was, I don't know, going to bed early."

"Guess I can see how I didn't help much with that," said Csorwe.

"And waking up thinking only pure thoughts. No. You didn't." This smile was the genuine one, half-hidden behind her hand like a concealed blade. Shuthmili had a way of saying things like this, then moving on without giving them time to sink in, but this one she seemed to be content to leave, just dangling.

Csorwe watched her, grateful for the opportunity to just look, for as long as she wanted, to take in all the details she had seen before in passing. The flecks of gold in Shuthmili's dark eyes, the long nose and firm chin and the eyelashes that fluttered down as she smiled again. The little creases at the corners of her mouth.

"Stay still," said Shuthmili. "Don't try to move. I'm going to kiss you and I don't want you to tear your stitches."

Csorwe did not try to move.

Shuthmili's lips were wind-chapped and dry. She was tentative in a way that suggested maybe she hadn't kissed a girl with tusks before. At first Csorwe could still notice this kind of detail, and then—it wasn't that she forgot immediately about her injuries, and their enemies, and all the rest—but for a moment everything else faded into the distance.

"Was that all right?" said Shuthmili, drawing back for a moment.

"Uh-huh," said Csorwe. She realised she was smiling, for the first time in a long while. "Can probably do it again if you like."

She did. Not so cautious this time. She ran her fingers up the back of Csorwe's neck and raked them through her hair, scratching lightly in a way that made Csorwe feel as though she had been taken carefully apart and put back together a little stronger, a little braver, a little more complete.

Csorwe leant forward as best she could and buried her face in Shuthmili's neck, so that her nose brushed the hair behind her ear, where her plaits had begun to come undone.

"What are you doing?" said Shuthmili, laughing.

"You smell nice," said Csorwe, unable to keep it to herself.

"Are you sure? I'm covered in blood," said Shuthmili. Csorwe had forgotten about the blood. After a while you did stop noticing it.

"Not that—" said Csorwe. Shuthmili smelled like people usually do, sweat and worn clothes and a trace of soap, but also somehow right and good and perfect. "Just you."

Despite it all, they slept for a few hours, curled up on the concrete, sheltered by the web of wards. They were woken by Oranna's voice, low and urgent, not panicked because there was no point now in panicking, and besides, they had all known what was coming.

In the sky above were the lights of an approaching ship. It would be overhead in a matter of minutes.

"That's *Tranquillity*," said Shuthmili, confirming what they had all guessed. The three of them sat and watched, astronomers waiting for the falling stars that would waste the world. There was nothing left to do. Csorwe was grateful for Shuthmili's hand in hers.

As the frigate drew nearer, it slowed, and new lights spilled out of it: five of them, shuttle-barges that spread out to take their places around the Traitor's Grave. Csorwe's heart sank as she noted that they didn't even come close to the perimeter that Shuthmili and Oranna had created. It really had been for nothing. In each barge was a figure in a white robe and a black mask.

Then there was a brighter light, and they heard the voice of Inquisitor Tsaldu, Qanwa Zhiyouri's underling. He was standing upright on a sixth barge, flanked by Wardens with bolt-throwers.

"Qanwa Shuthmili," he said. His voice boomed across the sky, magically amplified. "As you see, we have this place surrounded."

"Go home, Inquisitor," said Shuthmili in a tone of imperious boredom. After what they had all been through, Csorwe was impressed she could manage anything other than a shriek of rage. "Turn around and fly away. You know what I can do."

"Ah, yes," said Tsaldu. "I must warn you that if you act rashly, Sabre Quincury will reduce the Traitor's Grave to glass and ashes."

"You're lying," said Shuthmili. Her tone of voice scarcely wavered, but Csorwe knew this was more in hope than in belief. The ghostly figures on the barges certainly looked like Quincury Adepts. "They wouldn't send a military Quincury for me."

"Look at what you've done, Adept Qanwa. People like you are why we need these weapons in the first place. Your aunt made a mistake with you. She was too close to the matter. To her, you were still a girl."

"Am I not?" said Shuthmili.

"You may use a sword to cut bread," said Tsaldu, with the confidence of a man who had never handled a sword. "That does not make it other than a weapon."

Shuthmili's lip curled, visible only to Csorwe. "What do you want, Tsaldu?" she said. "Why are you telling me this? Give the word and watch us burn, if that's what you're planning. There's nothing I can do to stop you."

"Come quietly," said Tsaldu. "Break your wards and surrender to me."

"I hope," she said, "that you're not going to suggest I might like to join Archer Quincury after all."

"That is certainly no longer a possibility," said Tsaldu.

She sighed. "A trial, then, prosecuted by my aunt's old friends, and then the arena. Inquisitor, do you think I want to face the Mouth of Radiance any more than I want to be evaporated? At least Sabre would be quick."

"If you come with me, of your own volition, your friends will be safe," he said. "We have no interest in them. We will offer them safe passage from the Grave."

Csorwe's heart clenched in her chest as she came to understand the implications. "No," she said, unable to hold it back.

"Let me think about it," said Shuthmili.

"You have fifteen minutes," said Tsaldu.

Shuthmili knelt at Csorwe's side again. "I think I have to do it," she whispered, as Csorwe had known she would.

"No," said Csorwe. "I won't let you. Not for us."

Shuthmili smiled. "Are you going to steal me away again?"

"If I have to," said Csorwe, although she knew the hard facts well enough: she couldn't move, and there was no way out. "You can't do this. And he's lying to you, isn't he? He's never going to let us go—"

"If I don't go with him, he's going to give the word to Sabre, and that will certainly be the end of all of us. I want you to have a chance. Stay and die or leave and live, as you once said to me. I want you to live."

"Shuthmili, you're not *seriously*—"

"I am."

"Don't tell me you deserve it. You don't," said Csorwe. "Not for your fucking aunt, or anyone."

"No. But my life is mine," said Shuthmili. "Mine to spend, mine to burn, mine to waste. Mine to give away."

"It's not fair—" said Csorwe.

"I know. Awful, really," said Shuthmili. "When you could have been the one to sacrifice yourself. Try not to resent me too much."

"But you should've had a chance. Just a chance. And I wanted to take you to places."

Shuthmili leant over and kissed her again. She shut her eyes.

"I've made up my mind, Csorwe. I'm sorry. I just wanted to say goodbye."

"Let me go with you."

"You'll be with me all the way."

Shuthmili told Tsaldu what she had chosen, and he brought the shuttle-barge of Wardens down to meet her as she severed the wards at the perimeter. The shuttle took an impossibly long time to sink toward the edge of the Traitor's Grave, and Csorwe watched it all. She watched every step Shuthmili took toward the shuttle, as if by looking she could reach through time and hold her still: Shuthmili, in her ragged dress, with a magelight in her hand.

Shuthmili stepped on board the shuttle-barge and the Wardens grabbed hold of her. Csorwe cried out, then, as if they were about to tear her apart—but all they did was shove her into a seat, and then the barge moved away, darting back toward the frigate. The Quincury barges followed, and the door of *Tranquillity*'s shuttle bay slid down with the finality of an executioner's axe.

Csorwe lay back on the ground, burying her face in her hands. It was too much to bear.

"They're leaving," said Oranna, sitting beside her. "Though I must say, I give the Inquisitor's promises no more credence than you do. I cannot believe they would simply let us leave. This is some sort of trap."

Csorwe said nothing.

"It's done. She was brave," said Oranna. "But if you carry on groaning like that I'm going to put a bag over your head. You can cry later. We quite urgently need to decide what we're going to do."

"I don't care what we do," said Csorwe.

"Don't be a child about this, Csorwe," said Oranna. "When someone gives up their life for yours, the *least* you owe them is to try and make the most of what they've given you. We need to think. We need to— Oh, by the twelve hundred Unspeakable names, what in hell is *that*?"

The startled outrage in her voice was such that Csorwe looked up. There was another ship in the sky. It had been above and behind *Tranquillity*, almost invisible in the half-darkness. Csorwe recognised it: the graceful shape of the hull, the white canopies like pieces of the moon.

"It's the *Thousand Eyes*," she said, dully, unable to make any sense of it. "It's Sethennai's corvette."

"The *Thousand Eyes*," said Oranna. "Truly, he has never been a subtle man." She sighed, rubbing a hand across her face, in the first gesture of weariness that Csorwe had ever seen from her. "Then I suppose we must choose again whether we run or fight."

"I can't," said Csorwe. She could probably stand, by now, if she tried, but even if there was new strength in her body, there was nothing left in her spirit. She couldn't fight Sethennai. She couldn't do anything. And the *Thousand Eyes* was fast approaching.

"I cannot beat him in a fair fight, and I do not intend to throw myself into the sea for him," said Oranna. "Oh, futility." She got to her feet and shook out her skirts. "A tactical retreat, then, I suppose. There are worse places than the deep cell."

She helped Csorwe up. The sigil *obligation* flashed on the back of her hand. Csorwe grasped her arm and hauled herself to her feet, wincing only a little.

"You know you're never going to get what you want from

him," said Csorwe, as the shadow of the *Thousand Eyes* fell over the shattered roof of the prison.

"There will come a time when that isn't up to him," said Oranna. "He's not omnipotent, you know. He's very old and very clever. But he has his weakness. Everyone does."

A door opened in the side of the corvette's hull, discharging a gangplank that lowered to the roof of the Traitor's Grave. A figure was dimly visible in the doorway, haloed by light within.

Oranna raised both her hands, one still clasping Csorwe's. "Very well, my dear, we surrender."

"Great," said Tal Charossa. He stood at the top of the gangplank, hoisting a bolt-thrower bigger than his own torso. "You're both under arrest, and you'd better not give me any fucking trouble."

26

The Throne and Earthly Mansion

TAL DID NOT CARE for the city of Qaradoun. The *Thousand Eyes* had been at anchor above the Qarsazhi capital for more than a week, now: the Inquisitorate had asked Sethennai to stay and assist with their investigation, and for reasons beyond Tal's understanding, Sethennai had agreed. Tal had tried to go ashore for lunch several times, never with much success. Today they had sold him some kind of pickled garlic dumpling, and he was sure he still reeked, although he had bathed with orange-blossom water in preparation for tonight, and put a dab or two behind his ears.

He wasn't above this kind of thing, although he tried not to think about it as one cogent strategy, because when you put it like that it sounded kind of pathetic. He had visited a barber down in the city. He had put on a handsome shirt, and left the top button unfastened. He had stopped short of wearing some earrings Sethennai had given him, so as not to seem desperate. Taken independently, these were the rational actions of a man in control of his destiny.

He was running a comb through his hair when he realised he needed to take Csorwe her dinner. He found her, as ever, gazing out through the bars of her cell as though she had forgotten what her eyelids were for.

Once Oranna had been installed in the *Thousand Eyes'* isolation cell, Sethennai had looked Csorwe up and down, shrugged, and told Tal to put her in the brig. She had been there ever since. Sethennai spent most days in town with the Inquisitors, and showed little sign of remembering Csorwe was there. Tal had volunteered to feed her, because—well, he could claim that he wanted to laugh at her, but he had to admit that he really had no reason other than pity.

He slid a tray of bread into the cell, followed by a half portion of garlic dumplings. Someone might as well have them.

He didn't say anything. He knew by now that insults got no more response than friendly enquiry. It was nothing to him, anyway. She'd wait until he was gone, eat the food, and go back to staring.

Today, though, as he turned to go, he heard her speak.

"Tal. I need you to do something for me."

He laughed, out of force of habit. "You don't think I owe you any favours, do you?"

"I'm asking nicely," she said.

"You aren't," he said. "What do you want?"

"In Qaradoun, they have these printed sheets you can buy with everything that's happened this week—"

"I know what a bloody newspaper is, you illiterate," said Tal. "What are you going to do, fold yourself a little hat with it?"

"It's published tomorrow. Go into town and get me one. I need to know—"

"I'll think about it," he said. "If I can be bothered," he added, because it was just unnatural to concede anything willingly to Csorwe.

Back on the upper deck, he checked the study, just in case

Sethennai was back yet, and glanced at himself in the big mirror. He looked good. He always looked good. He was a good-looking man.

Eventually, the word was passed that Sethennai's cutter had arrived back at the ship. Tal's pulse fluttered in the embarrassing way it always did. He waited in his own cabin for a self-respecting amount of time before going to look for him.

In the study, Sethennai had taken off his surcoat and put his feet up on the desk. Underneath, he was still in his Tlaanthothei clothes. His eyes were heavy-lidded, with sleep or contemplation.

"Sir," said Tal. "How was town?"

"Talasseres," said the wizard, and waved him to a chair. His tone of voice and his look were sleepily amused, even affectionate, but this didn't necessarily mean anything. The man would have looked sleepily amused at a wake. "Town was tiresome. I am losing patience with Qarsazh. Zhiyouri's family want me to come to this rogue Adept's execution, and I don't see how I'm going to get out of it. And then I suppose I will have to pay my respects at Zhiyouri's funeral, assuming they've collected up enough of her to burn, and then I think we will go home."

Tal didn't try to disguise how much of a relief this was.

"Yes, I thought you'd be happy," said Sethennai. "I suppose Csorwe hasn't said anything much yet?"

"Mm," said Tal, surprised that he had asked. For some reason, he didn't feel like mentioning Csorwe's request for the newspaper.

"Strange," said Sethennai. Weary, not as angry as he had seemed before. "Why do you think she did it?"

Tal didn't know what to say. After a minute Sethennai set out a sheaf of papers and started going through his notes on the day's business with the Inquisitorate, with occasional questions to Tal.

Sethennai's daily debriefings were some of the dullest shit imaginable, but Tal didn't hate this, sitting in the quiet cabin above the city as the ship listed slightly in the wind. And then there was Sethennai's voice, the effects of which were indescribable, even when he was talking about what Inquisitor What's-his-tits had said to the Lord High Whatever-the-fuck.

After a while, Sethennai reached out and ran his hand through the short curls at the back of Tal's neck, in a way that made him forget what he was saying altogether. Sethennai laughed, and suggested that they retire to the stateroom.

"It's been a while," Tal said, half hoping Sethennai might not actually hear, because it was only a step away from admitting that Tal had missed him, which was altogether too close to claiming some kind of obligation.

"It has," said Sethennai, wrapping his arms around him. He laughed again, in a kind of seismic rumble that sent tremors through Tal's sternum.

Tal scrabbled for the door handle and fell backward into the stateroom, no longer much caring whether he looked like a man in control of his destiny, or, in fact, like a fool with weak knees and his shirt half off.

He felt Sethennai stop dead and turned to see what was wrong, although some wretched part of his brain was already crowing *Told you so, Talasseres.*

Of course—of course—Oranna was there in the room, sitting in the window seat. If she had been a cat, her tail would have flicked back and forth, but since she was just a terrible bitch, she smiled.

The smile suggested: *I know about your orange-blossom water, I know about your new haircut, I know about your handsome shirt. I know exactly what you've done to get here, Talasseres Charossa, and I want you to understand that I don't even have to try to be better than you.*

It took Sethennai longer to accept the inevitable. He let go of Tal and stormed past him into the cabin, muttering an invocation and reaching for his gauntlets. Tal tasted the familiar tang of blood in his throat as the air began to hum.

Oranna held up one of the gauntlets between finger and thumb, and smiled. The other was already on her left hand. Sethennai was a bloody moron who must have left them in his room. At least the Reliquary was where it always was, locked away in the safe in the ship's strong room.

"Good evening, Belthandros," she said.

Sethennai stopped where he was. The crackling haze of energy in the air didn't exactly subside, but it folded itself in and around the wizard, sharpening up its edges.

"Oranna," he said. "This is a pleasant surprise."

"Thank you," she said, swinging her legs.

"And how in the name of the Exalted Sages did you get out of the isolation cell?"

"I don't want to embarrass your security," said Oranna. She didn't even look at Tal. "Maybe you ought to select them on some basis other than pliant disposition."

She got up from the window seat in a cascade of skirts, pulling on the remaining gauntlet as she did so, and smoothing out the wrist.

"Please, stand down," she said. "I'm just here to talk." She didn't come any closer, just stood gracefully and watched.

"If you were here to talk you wouldn't have worn that dress," said Sethennai.

Apart from the gauntlets, she was wearing a long gown of wine-coloured silk. Tal didn't see anything so special about it, except that it was expensive, but then, he had never had much interest in the kind of assets on display.

"Always the gentleman, Belthandros," she said. "Let's discuss this in your study, shall we?" She strolled past him, her gaze gliding smoothly over Tal as though he was an unexceptionable footstool, and took the wizard's seat by the fire. Sethennai followed her.

Tal said nothing, and stayed where he was. There didn't seem to be all that much point in getting up. Once they were out of sight, he curled up on the floor where he had fallen, wrapping his arms round his knees.

He really should have expected this. The only thing he believed with certainty about the universe was that it was just incapable of giving Talasseres Charossa a break. He didn't need any more evidence to support this hypothesis, but oh yes, there it was: the door, ajar, did nothing at all to block the sound of the conversation taking place in the study.

"I'm not here to coax it out of you, *Belthandros*," she was saying. "Surely you recognise that you're not in a very good bargaining position. I have your gauntlets, and you won't channel without them."

"Is that so?"

"I worked that much out years ago. They're a prophylactic." Sethennai snorted, but she went on. "A shield. That's the first part of the secret. I knew that in principle before I even met you.

You need something to protect your body from the power. Am I wrong?"

"If you're sure of your reasoning, you don't need me to tell you one way or another," said Sethennai. He got up; Tal recognised his footsteps moving from one side of the study to another.

"What are you doing?" said Oranna.

"I'm sure you'll come to the point, given time," said Sethennai. "In the meantime, I am lighting a cigar."

She laughed. "Someone ought to have murdered you years ago."

"Are you certain you're not here to coax me?" said Sethennai. "I think I might prefer to be coaxed."

Tal looked around uselessly for exits, but there was no way out without passing through the study, unless he felt like leaping out of the window: all things considered, not an unappealing prospect.

"I know what you are, Belthandros," she said. "It amazes me that no one else has figured it out. Does nobody ever ask you where you come from? Or about your family? Where you made your money, or learned your magic? Not in Tlaanthothe, that's for certain, and yet you've been Chancellor there for more than forty years, give or take a spell in exile."

"I've studied all over the place," he said. Tal, paying attention despite himself, heard the faintest caution in his voice.

"Before that, you were an astronomer in Salqanya. A hundred years ago you were an advisor to the clan-liege of Damogad. A hundred years before that, Tlaanthothe had its first Chancellor Sethennai. I have documentation for all this, and more."

"You've been busy," said Sethennai. Tal got up and crept to the door of the study, peering into the room, where they sat facing one another, heads lowered as if readying themselves for a prizefight.

"So have you, it seems," she said. "If I'm wrong, open the Reliquary and prove it."

Sethennai took a drag on his cigar. "Haven't you heard? It opens only before the throne and earthly mansion of the Lady of the Thousand Eyes."

Oranna laughed again, high and tense. "I know. The Lignite Spire fell into ruin after the fall of Old Ormary, several thousand years ago, and yet it has *a back door into your estate.*" She got up from her chair and walked toward him, as if daring him to challenge her.

"You know, I always wondered," she said. "If the throne of Iriskavaal was truly shattered, what had become of the shards? A thousand fragments, each struggling to understand what it had lost, each possessing a shadow of her power and her rage."

"There is the Siren, of course," said Sethennai. "And I hear you released some unfortunate creature from the Hollow Monument—"

"No," said Oranna. "Two fragments explain nothing. She should have left shrapnel in every world. We could never have healed of those wounds."

"So, what are you saying?" he said. "That the throne is intact?"

"Not as it once was," said Oranna. "Iriskavaal knew that her people had betrayed her, and that her enemies were hunting her. So she came to the most trusted and beloved of her followers, and together they made their plan. Am I wrong, Belthandros?"

"My dear, how should I possibly know—"

"I had assumed, as you did, that the Reliquary was created to save Pentravesse from his own mortality. But what if they both intended to cheat death?"

"What if, indeed?" Sethennai stubbed out his cigar. He no longer sounded entirely amused.

"When all the world hunts you, you pretend to die, and you hide away, and perhaps you forget."

Oranna reached out and laid her gauntleted hand on his chest. "Iriskavaal never truly died. She lives still in you. You are the throne. You are the earthly mansion. You are Pentravesse."

Tal crouched behind the door, listening. He could no more have looked away than he could have cut off his own hand.

"Yes," said Sethennai at last, in what must have been defeat. Tal had never heard him sound like this before. "I suppose you are right." He wasn't smiling, but there was an unfamiliar surprise and delight in his face. "I had forgotten so much. It took the Reliquary itself to remind me. It's an interesting new world to wake up to."

"Isn't it, just?" said Oranna.

"But then, you must know the Reliquary will do you no good. Iriskavaal has her incarnation already, and she is no friend to the Unspoken."

"Oh, the Reliquary is yours. I'm not interested in taking it from you any longer, and I have my own patron. I just want to know how you did it. *Both* of you."

"Having difficulty seducing the Unspoken, are you?" said Belthandros. "Well, I can't help you with that, I never did understand what it wanted."

"It is forgetful," said Oranna. "It doesn't realise what it is. What it could be. What it could do in the world."

"Ah," said Belthandros. "Well, that I do understand."

They went on talking, in softer and softer voices, about things Tal didn't comprehend. The horror of it all broke around him in waves. He could never have been enough. There was really nothing he could ever have done.

When he got his head above water, he realised that he missed Csorwe. She was both the most boring and the most unfriendly person he had ever met, with all the personality of a prison shiv, but he wanted to get drunk and pick a fight with someone.

He wondered what her breaking point had been. Something must have given way. Had it happened all at once? Had she just turned a corner one day and thought, *Fuck you, Belthandros, this wasn't what I wanted from my fucking life? This wasn't how I thought it was going to be. You never promised me anything and I never asked for anything because I didn't want to humiliate myself, and yet here I am, sitting in a dark room listening to you with* her, *and it turns out to be pretty fucking humiliating.*

Certainly something like that.

Csorwe stared at the wall of her cell, counting reasons not to despair. Maybe there was still a chance. She didn't know how long the trial would take. She would know more if Tal brought her the newspaper. Maybe if she could get away from here she could find where they were keeping Shuthmili again . . .

But then, she had only got into the Traitor's Grave because they were waiting to trap her. She had no power here. She didn't know the city's pressure points. She didn't understand the Qarsazhi or their Church. A huge, alien machine, dealing in signals she couldn't decipher. There was no time, and even if there had been, she didn't know where to begin.

Tal didn't bring her breakfast. Maybe, she tried to believe, it was because he'd gone into town to get the newspaper.

When he finally turned up, he was dressed in outdoor clothes. There was something like an apology in his look, something vaguely guilty, and against all evidence and likelihood, her heart rose.

"Did you get it?" she said. "The newspaper? Was there anything about the trial, or the, the—" She couldn't bring herself to say the word *execution*.

"What?" said Tal. "No, obviously not." He glared through the bars at Csorwe with a brief kindling of defiance, followed by a smile of hard, brittle brilliance as he withdrew a key from his pocket. "I can do you one better. We're getting out of here."

"What is this?" she said. "This is some kind of—Sethennai put you up to this."

"No," said Tal. "I'm leaving him."

"What?" She hadn't thought there was anything that could still surprise her, but this did it.

"I'm leaving him. I've quit. I've cut ties. I'm a free agent. I've returned his letters. Is any of this getting through? Do you need me to speak slower?"

"I don't believe you," said Csorwe. "Go away. Tell him—tell him I'll talk to him, if he wants to talk to me, if—"

"He doesn't," said Tal. "Because he doesn't give a shit about you, or about me, and he never has."

She shook her head. "I don't believe you. Go back and tell Sethennai I—"

"I'm not telling him anything, because I'm not going back to him, because he's a pompous fucking prick and I hate him." All this quite brightly. With relief, even. "Fuck me, Csorwe, is it really so hard to believe?"

"Prove it," she said.

"I can, actually," he said.

He unlocked the cell door and came inside, thrusting something else toward her, wrapped up in a bundle.

Csorwe knew what it was before she opened it.

"*Really?*" she said, looking down at the Reliquary. Wrapped up in one of Tal's shirts it almost looked ordinary.

Tal giggled. "Brought your sword, too."

She made a derisive noise, but buckled it back onto her belt. It wouldn't do her any good, but she felt somewhat more complete. "So. What's brought this on?"

To her surprise, Tal told her everything.

"I've always thought he was older than he looked," he said. Csorwe realised she had never thought about it, as if he had come into existence fully formed at the House of Silence eight years ago.

"He lied to us," said Tal. "About the Reliquary. Bunch of bullshit."

"I don't know," said Csorwe.

"Unless he really just *forgot*," said Tal. "Do you think that's possible? Imagine being immortal."

Csorwe tried. All she could think was that if she were she could throw herself at the doors of the prison and howl for the Quincuriate to come down and fight her. They could cut her down and she would rise up again and go back, and even then she could never kill enough of them to stop what they were going to do to Shuthmili.

"No wonder he's like that," Tal went on, dismally. "No wonder he wanted the Reliquary so badly." He shrugged. "I always thought I was just doing something wrong, but—"

"Yeah," said Csorwe. "Guess we're both traitors now." She looked down at the Reliquary for a second longer.

"What's new?" said Tal. He shifted his weight restlessly, and when Csorwe made no reply, he went on. "We should go, or we're never going to leave. I ought to visit my mother or something. Apologise for being such a piece of shit. You can do whatever you like. Go and buy as many newspapers as you want. Kidnap yourself a whole harem of Qarsazhi babes."

"Shut up, Tal," said Csorwe, beginning to have an idea, suddenly transfixed by her own audacity. It had occurred to her that, after all, even very large machines could be stopped if you knew where to throw the spanner.

She didn't want to hope. She couldn't bear it. It was a breathtakingly dangerous idea. She could try and hope and fail and die, or she could stay here, alone, and live.

The only real question was whether it would be hard to get Tal on board.

"Why have you done this?" she said. "The Reliquary, I mean. What are you going to do with it?"

"I don't know, I just thought it would be funny," said Tal, clearly certain that it would, eventually, be funny. "Serve him right."

"Oh, sure, I should've remembered you're a fucking joke," said Csorwe.

"*You're* a joke," said Tal, for form's sake.

"More and more every day. Want to do something stupid?" she said. Realising she could rely on him for this was like falling out of a window and landing on something soft: you felt more ridiculous than ever but god, it was a relief.

"If you can think of something stupider than this, sure."

She told him the plan. It was loud and dumb and very likely to hurt, so, of course, he agreed.

27

Leverage

O N THE DAY THAT Qanwa Shuthmili was condemned to die, Inquisitor Tsaldu Grichalya came to the Grand Arena to observe the spectacle from the Inquisitorate box.

He would have preferred to sit with the Qanwa, a few boxes away. In a just world he would have been owed an invitation. He had caught Qanwa Zhiyouri's murderer. It seemed unfair that they had invited Chancellor Sethennai and left him out.

Tsaldu took his seat among his fellow Inquisitors, regretting the immense noise, the stink, and the heat of the day. Down below, the lower tiers overbrimmed with groundlings. Beneath them, in the arena itself, an oval of combed white sand glowed like a mirror.

"Oh, the violence is rather undignifying," one of Tsaldu's colleagues was saying. "But I understand it is a wonderful deterrent of crime."

"And the people love an execution," said a High Warden.

"Oh," said a young Inquisitor from the Bureau of Censorship, fanning herself with a programme. "First of all, we are to be enlivened with a pageant."

"Oh, yes," said the High Warden. "'The Combat of Linarya Atqalindri and the Dragon Zinandour.' Marvellous."

The pageant began with a deafening noise of horns and a flood of dancers, all costumed head to toe: black for the Dragon and her attendants, and red for the dancer playing Linarya, who wore a crown of roses and lilies.

"How warm they must be in those cloaks," said the young censor, yawning hugely.

In addition to the cloaks, every dancer wore a mask of paper pulp, gaudily painted in accordance with the role. The Dragon's mask had an articulated jaw and required two dancers to operate the hinge. Tsaldu watched the dance from a sense of obligation rather than enjoyment. The High Warden was paying close attention to the drama, leaning forward over the barrier with the enthusiasm of a much younger man.

At last the dancers retreated to a bench near the edge of the arena, just behind the lower barrier. The executioner came out, with suitable fanfare, and the Emperor blessed his blade.

Tsaldu listened attentively as the Most High Immaculacy gave the sermon. Then they brought in the first lot of condemned criminals, a group of arsonists who had killed twelve people. He did his best to pay attention to this too. This was why he did his job, after all. To ensure that goodness was protected and wickedness was punished.

The arsonists came up one by one and were destroyed. Tsaldu thought of the murals in the Inquisitors' private chapel, where—among other things—tiny sinners were painted at every stage of their judgment and torment. The artist had used a hair-thin brush to mark down the features of each sinner in individual detail, though none was larger than Tsaldu's thumb. Art was an improvement on life. The sun was so bright that he would have had to squint if he had cared to see any of the arsonists' individual features.

Other criminals faced the penalties for their various sins. The announcer gave a detailed description of the murders, the abductions, the dark heresies. Noon approached, and one of Tsaldu's colleagues elbowed him.

"It's your one next, isn't it?" he said. Tsaldu bridled at the unwanted contact, but nodded.

They brought Qanwa Shuthmili in alone. Her hands were bound in silver bracelets to keep her from channelling.

Shuthmili didn't struggle as she was brought in, nor did she laugh and kiss her hands to the crowd as some did. The crowds quieted a little, perhaps surprised by how young she looked, how small and harmless. Tsaldu had seen the dead at the Traitor's Grave, and knew better.

Shuthmili stumbled along in her chains as though her thoughts were elsewhere. They had not yet sprinkled fresh sand, and the ground was wet and dark with spilled blood.

The announcer seemed delighted to reach the main attraction. He rolled out the charges like barrels down a ramp. "Condemned for traffic with the powers of evil and for disgracing the office of Adept, for *basest* corruption, for the destruction of Quincuriate personnel, and the premeditated *murder* of a High Inquisitor of the Church!"

"That seems like rather a lot," said the young censor.

They made her chains fast to one of the posts in the middle of the arena, and retreated.

There was now a pause in the proceedings. It took a few minutes for the Mouth of Radiance to be prepared. The Inquisitors shivered with satisfaction as the Mouth shuffled into the arena.

In the harsh sunlight all that could be seen of the Mouth,

at first, was a tall manlike figure, wrapped in a bulky tar-black shroud. The shroud was belted in with chains of iron and silver, and six handlers in formal Inquisitorate livery held the ends of these chains, moving in a cautious halo around the Mouth as it hobbled across the bloody sand.

Everyone else—guards, priests, announcer, executioner—slipped quietly back behind a spelled barrier. Qanwa Shuthmili did not even look up.

An uneasy silence crept up through the arena. Nobody wanted to cheer the Mouth of Radiance. It did not feel like a good idea to attract its attention.

Unlike most people, Tsaldu knew how the Mouth had been created. Spinel Quincury had devised the monster as a parody of its own existence: many fragmented minds tethered into a single indestructible body. The chaff of a half-dozen failed Quincury coadunates, swept up and compressed into a single miserable hunger.

The handlers released the fastenings of the chains and stepped hastily back. Slowly, as though awakening from sleep, the Mouth struggled out of its shroud and advanced on the condemned woman.

It walked awkwardly, slowly, like a wounded spider. Its ankles were chained together, and its wrists were shackled behind its back. It should have been tall, but it was bent over into the shape of a fishhook. Braces of leather and steel were strapped to its neck and waist to support its frail body.

What most people saw, though, was the face. Tsaldu did not know what Spinel had done to a mortal body to create the Mouth, and he was glad of it. The Mouth of Radiance wore a mask and hood that covered its eyes and brow. The nose was nothing more than a shattered smear of cartilage. The jaw had been wrenched open, beyond what bone and sinew should be able to withstand, dragged down to hang open on the breastbone, like a locket with a broken clasp. Both lips were cut and peeled back, revealing two distant crescents of clean white teeth.

It did not speak. It had no visible tongue. Its throat was an empty well of ichor. As it moved across the sand it left a heat haze in the air, and its bound hands twitched.

Tsaldu was not certain whether the Mouth could understand orders, whether it had been instructed to immolate Qanwa Shuthmili in particular, or whether it simply destroyed any living thing that it perceived. He had seen it before and he knew what to expect. The cloud of dust that smelled like molten metal. The terrible jaw unhinging. And the screaming, of course.

The rumour was that the Mouth took a fragment from every mage it killed, that it drank up the dregs of their agony and grew stronger. Tsaldu thought that was probably just a ghost story.

Shuthmili, who had not moved until now, stood up straight and watched as the thing limped toward her.

A small commotion broke out a few levels below them. At first, Tsaldu assumed it was the crowd. A little rowdiness was to be expected. Usually, if the family of the condemned started making a fuss, the guard would come along to settle them, but it couldn't possibly be the Qanwa making trouble. Their box was only a little way from the Inquisitorate box, and, after all, Qanwa Zhiyouri had been one of their own, far more so than Qanwa Shuthmili. No, they were all sitting solemnly, with the exception of Chancellor Sethennai, who had sat up very straight in his seat.

It wasn't the crowd. The disturbance was among the dancers, gathered behind the barrier at the lowest level. One of the servants of the Dragon Zinandour, dressed in black, had broken away from the rest. She dropped over the barrier, landing lightly on the border of the sand, and darted toward the condemned woman, swift and sharp as a hunting-hawk taking its prey.

As she moved she tore off the paper-pulp head. It rolled away, and somehow, as the Wardens rose hastily and drew their weapons, Tsaldu found himself watching its dizzy arc, turning and turning on the bloody sand.

"Get down, Inquisitor!" said one of the Wardens, tightening an arm around Tsaldu's middle and dragging him down behind the rail.

As he went down, he caught sight of the Qanwa box. Chancellor Sethennai leapt up from his seat and ran toward the barrier. He seemed to be pulling on a pair of gloves.

"*Csorwe,*" said Sethennai. His voice was not loud, but Tsaldu heard it as clearly as if Sethennai had been standing beside him.

Sethennai raised his hands, and time stopped.

Csorwe's boots hit the sand. She ignored the stink of drying blood, the scream of metal on metal as the Mouth's handlers released its chains. The crowds faded, burnt out by the glare of the sun. There was only her own speed, her own fury, and Shuthmili standing there bound to a post, hanging her head. Csorwe sped across the arena like a stone skimming a pond, and called Shuthmili's name. She looked up and seemed to see her.

"Csorwe, no," she said, as if she couldn't believe what she was seeing. "Please, no. Leave."

"It's all right," said Csorwe. She put out a hand and touched her shoulder. Under the rags they had put her in, Shuthmili was trembling. Csorwe was shaking too, for that matter, out of fear and battle-readiness and the sheer relief of seeing Shuthmili alive. If she had got it wrong, if it turned out this was the end, then so be it. There had been many opportunities to die in Csorwe's short life, to break on the rocks of ignorance or loyalty or recklessness. But this was the end that she had chosen.

"Go," said Shuthmili, licking dry lips. "I can't watch you die." The Mouth loped toward them, starved and implacable. It was close, now—ten feet—eight feet—Shuthmili's wrists shook, bound to the post, each locked within a silver bracelet.

Csorwe took her other shoulder and grinned. "We're not going to die today," she said. She pulled the Reliquary of Pentravesse from under her robe and looped the chain around Shuthmili's neck. Shuthmili looked down at it, too numb even to be puzzled.

"Trust me," said Csorwe, then turned to face the Qanwa box and waved. "You want it back, Sethennai?" she called, although there was surely no way he could hear her. "Then come and take it back!"

Many things happened at once, or perhaps only one thing. A man-shaped shadow came down from the Qanwa box as if all the tiers of the Grand Arena were only a flight of steps.

The Mouth of Radiance froze in mid-stride. It turned its long neck toward the shadow, and lifted its jaw as though trying to speak. Then, with a cry that could have been relief, it disintegrated into a column of grey sand. The column became a cloud, and blew away, as Belthandros Sethennai stepped down into the arena.

There was a flash of light and heat—the sand of the Arena melted and froze to a single pane of volcanic glass—and then the glass illuminated chrysoprase-green, and they fell through.

They hit the ground. Csorwe struggled upright, catching her breath, and hauled Shuthmili after her. They stood on the shore of a gleaming sea. The light of a poisonous sun sparked on the waters. Up ahead, above them, was a monstrous tower, a mountainous spike of black rock and glass.

Csorwe didn't know what she had anticipated. Not this.

"I know this place," said Shuthmili, faintly, clinging to Csorwe's arm as though she trusted nothing else in this world. "I'm certain I know this place—"

Csorwe knew it too. They had been here before, chasing Oranna. This was the Lignite Spire, the throne and earthly mansion of Iriskavaal, as it had once been, as it always was and always would be. Even a sleeping divinity lives always in the present moment.

Here is the Spire in earnest. It is built from petrified wood. The light and rain of ancient days are imprisoned in rings within rings.

A broad flight of steps leads up to the door, flanked on each side by paired statues.

At the foot of the steps the first pair of statues show two mortal figures obscured by undulating leechlike forms. These figures are supported in midair by the seething parasite life around them, so that they seem to bend in agony or ecstasy.

Then follow others, all troubling: angels erupting with flowers, robed and skeletal things, warriors armoured like insects, whose stone mouthparts seem to thresh the air.

All else fails, and only the Spire is inalterable.

*

"Keep hold of the Reliquary and nothing here can harm you," said Csorwe, walking toward the steps. "He won't hurt you."

She took Shuthmili's hand in hers, wrapping Shuthmili's thin fingers round the box, hoping fervently that she was right.

"You think this impresses me?" said Csorwe, shouting into the wind that whipped around the spiny turrets. "You think I'm afraid of this? Come out and talk to me!"

You will return to me what is mine. It was his voice, clear enough, but amplified many times, as though it was part of the wind and the corrupted sea.

"Come out and take it back!" she called, though her voice sounded pitifully small and piping.

The doors of the castle were dark wood, carved all over with knotted snakes and polished to a shine. They did not open.

I am here. You will return to me what is mine.

"I'll destroy it," she said, clasping Shuthmili's hand and the Reliquary in hers. Shuthmili didn't move; her eyes were squeezed shut.

Then you will die here. Both of you. The Lady of the Thousand Eyes will crush you in her coils.

"But you'll be dead," she said. This was the gamble. Belthandros Sethennai was the lever that could shift the world, and the Reliquary was his fulcrum. "You've lived a long time, but if I destroy your Reliquary you won't live to see it happen. Isn't that true, Pentravesse?"

The doors opened. Beyond them was a formless darkness, and on the threshold was the wizard, in his robe of green brocade.

"I should have known," he said. "You were never one to be taken in by dramatics."

He looked just as he always had, but he was lying. The castle was not a disguise. It was closer to the truth than this living body with its sad smile and its sympathetic eyes.

"I am now as I have always been," he said. "I see you must be upset, but I had my reasons for hiding my true name. I had forgotten it myself, you know. There were long ages of searching in the dark, and occasional sparks of light. I never misled you about anything of importance."

"I don't care. Whoever you are, you can die," said Csorwe. "You're more afraid to die than we are."

"Yes, I can die," he said. "I know betrayal. But I never expected this. Not from you, Csorwe." For a moment the only thing she wanted was to return to the palace of Tlaanthothe, to the way things had been, to her work and her routine and Sethennai's regard. "I took you in. I have never treated you unkindly."

She tightened her grasp on the Reliquary. "Sure. That seems about right," she said. "Call me ungrateful."

"I made you what you are." He came no closer. The doors of the castle had closed behind him, and he did not take his eyes off her and the Reliquary.

"You made me your sword-hand, you mean. Your instrument."

There was more to say. She had learned to kill for him. She had learned cruelty on his account from every angle, in theory and in practice. Every part of her that did not serve his purpose had been cut away. A great wave builds over hundreds of miles, gaining force and speed as it rushes toward the coast, and Csorwe's anger was something close to this. Still, if there was anything to gain from becoming such an instrument, it was the power to channel and divert such a feeling. She restrained herself.

"Csorwe," he said. "If I had known you disliked it . . . Do you believe I never cared for you? I gave you your life."

"It wasn't yours to give!" she said, and bit her tongue, reining in her anger again. She had nothing to gain from convincing him. She only needed him to do what she told him.

"You know this is unfair of you," he said.

Csorwe laughed. It was almost funny. "Is it?" She took the Reliquary from Shuthmili and pulled at the chain, which broke, hundreds of links scattering like sand. "It's unfair that you need me to give you back your life."

"This is all very clever—" he said, and saw that Csorwe was about to open the Reliquary, and winced.

Here was the throne, just as Tal had told her. Here was the earthly mansion. She cracked open the lid of the Reliquary. Inside, carefully laid among its wrappings, like a gigantic jewel, was a living, beating heart, as fresh as the day it was cut out. She still had her sword, but if she needed to she could just as easily crush the heart in her hands.

"Guess it was all a lie, then," said Csorwe. "All that arcane knowledge." She wasn't surprised. Pentravesse had never intended to leave a legacy. It was not in his nature to give anything away for free.

"I believed it myself," he said. "When you live so long it's so easy to forget."

"The thing is," she said. "The thing is, I could ask you for anything. If I wanted to be Chancellor of Tlaanthothe. If I wanted your palace. If I wanted your ship. You'd give me anything you have. There's nothing you care for more than this. There's nothing you wouldn't do."

Perhaps that had been the real lesson she had learned in Psamag's fortress. Beyond fear, beyond pain, she had cared for Sethennai more than life. Despite all his pride and power, there was nothing the wizard loved more than his own immortality, and that was a weakness.

He moved toward her as though to seize the box, then thought better of it. "What is it you want?"

The last trace of warmth had faded from his voice and from his face. This was a business transaction, and it was better that he understood that.

"I want you to take us out of here," said Csorwe. "I want you to take us somewhere safe."

"How sensible," said Belthandros, almost managing to sound bored. "Will that be all?"

"No," said Csorwe. "Then I want your gauntlets."

"You want—" He laughed, incredulous. "Why? You can't possibly have any use for them."

"You wear them and you stay in control," she said. "They protect you. The power doesn't hurt you. Tal told me everything."

"Ah," he said. "You're looking to live forever, are you?"

"No," she said. "I don't care about that. I bet you can make yourself some more, but I don't want you coming after me for a good long while."

"Other than that, what do you think they can possibly do for you?"

"With the greatest respect, sir, that's none of your fucking business," said Csorwe.

"And then? As you've so eloquently expressed, you have me on quite a leash. Do you have it in mind to keep me on your staff?" Every word as sharp and clear as a shard of ice.

"No," said Csorwe, with undisguised disgust. "When we're far away from here, when we're safe, when I've got your gauntlets and I know you're not going to turn me into a statue or send me to hell—*then* you can have it back." She shut the box with a snap, and he winced. "That's all. It's done. Come on."

They turned, the three of them, an awkward group clustered around a single point, and walked down toward the door that had appeared in the sand.

For a moment Csorwe worried that he might take them straight back to the arena and the aim of the Emperor's archers. Instead, the door opened into a back alley in lower Qaradoun, so narrow that it was in shadow despite the heat and brightness of the day. Several yards away, a man was pissing against the wall. At the sight of the three of them he took a step back in dismay. His eyes widened, and he ran for it, fastening his breeches as he went. They must have presented quite a picture. The wizard in all his magnificence. Shuthmili, in the rags of the condemned. Csorwe still dressed as an attendant demon.

Shuthmili opened her eyes, blinking against the sun, and said, "Enter stage left."

The journey from there to the docks passed in a kind of fever dream. As long as Csorwe held on to the Reliquary, she was certain he wouldn't do anything now to harm or resist her. Nothing—not even offended pride—could come between him and his own immortality.

Still, he wouldn't speak, or look at her, and whatever she knew about him now, it was painful to walk at his side and know him as her enemy. She wasn't proud of what she had done. She just wanted the day to be over.

The streets began to fill with people, all talking rapidly about the terrible scene at the Grand Arena and the sorcerer who had threatened the Emperor. Yet somehow nobody noticed that the sorcerer himself was walking through the crowd, towering over the Qarsazhi like a cat among songbirds. Still less did anybody notice Csorwe or Shuthmili. They made it to the maze-docks with no trouble, even when a troop of Wardens marched down the street toward them. The soldiers simply did not see them.

Up and down the waterfront were seaships at anchor. Dozens of mazeships were docked in cradles, and more were moored in midair. Somehow Csorwe had imagined that Sethennai could simply transport them wherever they wanted to go with a snap of his fingers, but of course, things were never so easy.

"From here, you may go wherever you wish," he said. "Up to a point, of course. I see you've bound yourself to Oranna. I'm sure she's very gratified to have taken you from me."

"That's not what happened," said Csorwe, repulsed.

"Of course not," he said. "At least *I* never made you carve anything into your skin."

Csorwe raised a hand and, without breaking his gaze, traced the scar that curved all the way down the side of her face.

"I see," he said. "I must say I think you're making a mistake. The world is changing, Csorwe. Thanks largely to you, I am now fully aware of certain realities. The Lady of the Thousand Eyes is a generous patron, and the chances to come are beyond anything I have ever offered you. You could face them at my side."

Csorwe wanted nothing more to do with that kind of power, and it hurt that Sethennai knew her no better than this, after all these years. But then, it was good to know that he could be wrong. His idea of her was a flat shadow that she could step away from.

"Give me the gauntlets," she said.

"But of course." He gave a half smile that was not remotely pleasant, and reached into the inside pocket of his surcoat.

He held out the gauntlets and she took them. They were very soft, warm, unassumingly bulky, like a pair of recently killed rabbits.

"Tell me, then," said the man she had known as Belthandros Sethennai. "How much longer do you plan to hold me to ransom?"

Csorwe felt as though she had been awake for a hundred years. There was nothing she wanted to do less than threaten someone, but she didn't see any other way to get it done.

"You know, obviously, that if I hear you're looking for me, I can do this again," she said. "You trained me too well, Belthandros. I don't want to deal with you, or make trouble for you, or really ever see you again. I want to go away. But if you come after me or anyone I know then I can do this again, and I will. Do you understand that?"

"Perfectly," said the wizard. "I understand the desire for a quiet life as well as anyone. But I feel I should warn you that you won't find one. You already carry the mark of one divinity. That tends to draw attention."

Csorwe shrugged. She didn't trust him to tell the truth even if he wanted to, but after a certain point there was no use clinging to doubt.

"You will need to be careful," he said. "Things cannot be put back the way they were. I am not the only one who has awoken."

Lucky for Csorwe that she had no intention of putting things back the way they were. It wasn't the first time she had left a whole life behind her. She knew how it was done, and how it hurt. This time she could set her own course.

She dropped the Reliquary into his waiting hands, and nodded goodbye. She did not wait to watch him leave. It was done.

At the time of the disturbance at the Grand Arena of Qaradoun, Talasseres Charossa was already gone. He left the *Thousand Eyes* and went down to the city to look for the next ship back to Tlaanthothe. The idea of returning had already begun to feel like a shoe that pinched. More painful the longer you lived with it, but arguably better than no shoe at all.

There was a clipper to Tlaanthothe that would leave that afternoon. Tal watched them loading up, hoisting aboard all the rolls of paper and the cans of olive oil and the crates of sugar and sacks of coffee and barrels of wine, and almost without thinking about it he turned away and boarded the next ship he saw. It turned out to be a small passenger shuttle—not even Gate-worthy—taking day-trippers out to the coast. There was a single large Qarsazhi family on board, with half a dozen little children climbing up on the seats to peer over the edge.

Tal didn't have it in him to be annoyed by them, even when they started singing a song about the beach. He couldn't even remember what it was that would have annoyed him. He sank back in his seat and shut his eyes. Nobody at home knew where he was, and nobody here knew who he was. He felt as if his strings had been cut.

It couldn't last, of course. He had to go back. Tlaanthothe was where he belonged. Sethennai would want some kind of explanation. He would have one day to himself. Then he would go back to the capital that evening and catch the mailship home.

The shuttle landed and he followed the other passengers along a green headland. The top of the cliff was bright with gorse, and a sweet-smelling breeze blew in from the sea. Tal wandered along at a distance, betting with himself on which child was most likely to fling itself into the ocean.

What was he going to say to Sethennai? There was no way to avoid seeing him. All of Tal's things were still at the Chancellor's Palace.

Of course there was the fantasy of telling Sethennai exactly what he thought of him. He tried it out in his head a few times, wondering what kind of reaction he would hope for. It was impossible to imagine Sethennai apologising. The only thing he could really picture vividly was the prospect that Sethennai wouldn't ask why he had left because he wouldn't even have noticed Tal was gone.

The idea was enough to make him surly again. He turned around, intending to go straight back to the shuttle, but it had already taken off. Up ahead, though, a flight of steps was carved into the side of the cliff, and at the bottom was a beach of silver sand like a drift of pure salt.

The bay was sheltered on both sides from the wind and from the open sea by the cliffs, like two enclosing arms. Within their span the water was the blue-green of stained glass, clear enough that you could see the beds of kelp, washing back and forth as the sea rose and fell.

Tal made his way cautiously down the steps. After all he had been through at the Lignite Spire and afterward, he didn't entirely trust his balance, and dying at the bottom of a cliff was not yet his idea of a good time.

At the foot of the stairs was a stall with a white awning, where a woman who looked like a dried apricot was selling cones of nuts and cups of some kind of horrible wine punch. Tal bought a cup and was disappointed to learn that it wasn't terrible at all, but sweet, cold, and soothing.

The Qarsazhi family set up their encampment along with a few other groups, farther down the beach. Tal went in the opposite direction, spread out his jacket on the sand, and sat down on it to sip his drink and watch the sea.

He shifted his weight, feeling the warm sand pressing back against him. There were no wizards here, no divinities, nobody for him to chase or catch or kill, nobody to hate him.

He could just stay here for a while. The idea came to him as if someone else had whispered it in his ear, if anyone had been in the habit of whispering nice things to him.

For a moment he felt as if he were floating, adrift, and approaching disaster. He couldn't just do what he wanted. You had to stick somewhere. Otherwise you were nothing more than this, a failed son of the Charossai, a man with no friends, no loyalty, and no calling.

A man who could lie on the beach in the sun, perhaps. A man who could rest for as long as he needed.

He tried to remember the things he had left at the Palace, and concluded that he had no use for them. Sethennai deserved no more of an explanation than he had ever offered Tal for anything he had done. Let him keep Tal's shitty knife collection and see if that helped him figure it out.

From the docks of Qaradoun, you could see the sails and canopies of hundreds of mazeships rising to the Gate, white crests one above another, like so many waves. Shuthmili stood beneath them, looking as if she had lately been pulled from a burning house, whole and unconsumed.

"Well. These are for you," said Csorwe. She held out the gauntlets. "I don't know if they'll help, but they might."

Shuthmili took them, turned them over. They were far too big for her, of course—each one was like a much larger hand encompassing her own. Csorwe wondered whether she should have bargained with Sethennai for something else, perhaps a ship of her own, or an enormous pile of cash.

"Where are you going to go?" said Shuthmili, still looking dazed. Csorwe wondered whether she regretted what had happened on the roof of the Traitor's Grave. It was easy to say and do things when you didn't think you were going to live to face the consequences.

"I don't know, yet," said Csorwe. "There are lots of places I've never been."

All she knew was that she wanted to go far enough that Oranna would really have to make an effort to enforce the blood-pledge. It would catch up with her inevitably—these things did—but Csorwe had no intention of getting hooked back in any sooner than fate mandated.

She would have to make a decision eventually. That was something she was going to have to get used to. There was no home to crawl back to, nobody's judgment to fall back on, nobody to keep her safe except her own ingenuity, nothing to live for except what she picked for herself. She couldn't fool herself into thinking it would be easy.

"Well," said Shuthmili. "There's always the mealworm tour of the Echo Maze. I hope you don't think I've forgotten about it."

Or maybe it *would* be that easy. There were all the vast worlds of the Maze, endless and intricate and alien, and there were familiar station canteens, where she could sit and eat reheated vat food with Shuthmili, and they could keep each other safe. Maybe she could have both.

Or maybe it was too much to expect. She couldn't make that kind of assumption, and she didn't want to be followed out of gratitude. "Look," she said, "you don't have to come with me. You can go wherever you want. I have some money left—I can take you anywhere you like—if you have friends anywhere—I don't want you to owe me. You don't owe me anything."

"Only my life," said Shuthmili.

"Not even that," said Csorwe.

"I think, traditionally, I have to follow you, now, until I can save *your* life and thereby redeem my debt."

"You have saved my life," said Csorwe. "Twice. Maybe more than twice. We have to call it quits eventually. And look, you deserve a better chance. I know we said a lot of things back when we thought we were going to die but you're not—you're not bound to me, or anything. A normal life, whatever you want—"

"Csorwe. Do you think—does anything you've seen—have I ever done anything to suggest that I've been pining for a normal life? Have you ever heard me utter the words, *When this is all over I hope to settle down as a prosperous greengrocer* or, *If only I could achieve my ambition of modest success in the civil service?*"

"But what *do* you want?"

"You said you wanted to take me to places. I want to go away from here. I want to go with you. And I'm a tremendously powerful magician, so I'd like to see you try to stop me."

"Oh," said Csorwe.

"Yes. And if I get to save your life again, I will regard it as a privilege."

They went aboard a ship. They sailed through the Gate. And it seems certain they were seen again, in some place far from here.

Acknowledgments

With enormous thanks to:

Mum, Dad, Katie, Toby, Daphne, and Rowena, for years of forbearance with how much I like wizards.

My agent, Kurestin Armada, a being of pure wisdom who still encouraged me to write about Talasseres.

My editor, Lindsey Hall, without whose efforts this book might make a modest paving stone but would not be much good for reading.

Emily Tesh, for telling me to make things worse. She was right.

Tamsyn Muir and Matt Hosty, for keeping me company in this ancient sacrificial pyramid.

Rachel Alday, Jennifer Giesbrecht, Arkady Martine, Everina Maxwell, Alice Sharp, Waverly SM, Heather Watson, and Livali Wyle, for their fellowship, good counsel, and extreme flattery of various early drafts.

Everyone in the Armada Slack, for their endless and sensible kindness.

And to Maz, who actually *is* the greatest genius who has ever lived.